I0583047

All for Love:
on the charity dating show

Written by Cecelia Hopkins

ISBN: 978-0-6481160-2-8
Published by CGH Literacy Institute,
Adelaide, South Australia, 2018

ISBN-13: 978-0-6481160-2-8 (6x9 paperback)

ASIN: B079C6HZPV (e-book)

Dewey Decimal Classification suggestion:

Australian Literature 823.3 HOP

Acknowledgements:

Cover image for Kindle Scout from Kindle stock images

Cover Image for print edition by Allan Schultz

Fashion design by Genista Drewer

Inspired by watching television dating shows, including:
"Perfect Match" with Tony Barbour & the American "Bachelor".

Fictional disclaimer:

CONTENTS

PART I: THE EARLY EPISODES

PART II: THE TOP FIVE

All For Love

All for Love on the Charity Dating Show I:

The Early Episodes

PROLOGUE: PRODUCTION ISSUES

Leticia Anderson had once harboured serious ambitions to be an investigative journalist. She earned degrees from the best university journalism programs, and after leaving university completed additional certificates from the media schools; even donating months of her time to labouring away in unpaid internships with the most respected television stations, magazines and newspapers.

However, the brilliant young woman remained undiscovered and unemployed, until to her great embarrassment, she was offered the contract for *The Charity Dating Show,* which the producers thought would be most successful with a female compere. Although she had hoped for better, and believed that *The Charity Dating Show* was a terribly unliberated production, Leticia accepted the job.

The Charity Dating Show followed the premise in which twenty beautiful young females vied for the attention of one more-or-less desirable male. The inequality was obvious, because the male was perceived as the prize for which all the girls had to compete. The young man also handed out pink carnations at the end of selected segments, implying that the fate of the girls on the show, and ultimate decision regarding a relationship were all within his power.

The Sydney based production appealed to public tastes, despite being an imitation of similar American dating shows. There was one main difference - all the contestants in *The Charity Dating Show* dedicated a percentage of their expense allowance to worthy community causes.

However, the glitz, the hope of romance, the parade of glamourous dresses, and the tourist attractions visited on dates, all enticed viewers who were jaded by a society where few people found lasting love. Leticia comforted herself that as hostess-director she had a respectable role amongst the production team, and steady employment as *The Charity Dating Show* was filmed year after year.

This year, as Leticia surveyed the selection of girls, she felt some misgivings. First there was the socialite whose father owned part of the television station, and then the super-model, who although still beautiful, was nearing the end of her career in an industry that

1

prioritised youth. Neither of those women were likely to follow the rules of the show and take a back-seat to the choices of the 'Charity Eligible'!

Other contestants included established career women, a ballet dancer who had appeared in enough productions to be moderately well-known, and a member of a state symphony orchestra.

To top it all off, there was the editor of an activist magazine, whom Leticia had been told she absolutely must involve - at least for the first episode! Even the younger girls appeared less pliable than usual, and Leticia shuddered to think what might happen when the women were all locked up together in one mansion, with nothing to focus upon but one male nominee.

"What do you think?" Leticia inquired of key members of her trusted team, Simon Steeple who headed camera crew one, and George who led camera crew two.

The contestants' photographs were all pinned to a giant cork board in Leticia's office, along with a few pertinent biographical details. The men bent over the display to give their opinions.

"If he is anything of a man, he will notice those dark eyed beauties," Simon Steeple said, pointing to Constance and Nadine.

"Mm," Leticia murmured thoughtfully. "What about her?" She pointed to model girl Alison.

Simon shook his head: "Too skinny," he remarked critically.

"According to my fashion magazines, her career is suffering because she hasn't been able to stay thin enough," Leticia said. "Some people say that is her motivation for volunteering to go on *The Charity Dating Show*."

"Whatever her motivation, she is going to look spectacular on camera and we are lucky to have her," George remarked. He pointed to another contestant who was naturally thin, clad in a designer label suit and wearing designer glasses. "I predict very few of the contestants will get along with that one. A snobbish background and preppy looks as well. The Charity Eligible will probably eliminate her early."

"These two blondes look a bit pale," Simon said, pointing to Janny and Vonda. "We will have to make sure they are well made-up."

"Which girls do you think are most suited to our Charity Eligible?" Leticia asked.

"Anthony is educated," Simon said, "So he might like Heddy." He pointed to an African Australian beauty who was also a vet. "Or find something in common with Constance, who works in hospitals."

"Nadine seems very traditional if he is old fashioned," George remarked. "Or the Monroe look alike, Betty is very beautiful."

"Thank you for your opinion guys," Leticia said. "If our Charity Eligible fails to notice those girls or eliminates them too soon, we may consider putting them in his way once again..."

"This show is not rigged by any chance is it?" Simon joked.

Leticia laughed. "Of course not," she said. "But we have to make ratings, and not everything that happens on the set makes it into the episodes; but on the other hand, not everything that happens on the screen is random! You boys know your job."

CHAPTER ONE: THE CANDIDATE HOUSE

Leaving her camera crew to finalise their preparations, Leticia hurried to meet the contestants. There were twenty of them, carefully chosen from the various states of Australia. The main thing they had in common was they all were willing to give up some of their time to raise funds for charity on the slim chance of finding love.

"Hello everyone and welcome to the set of the *Charity Dating Show*," Leticia said, greeting the girls assembled before her. "My name is Leticia, and I will be living with you for the next few weeks. The television station has booked an entire resort villa for our use, complete with swimming pool, games room, private digital video library and landscaped garden area."

The girls looked impressed.

The hostess-director continued her opening spiel, "This villa will be affectionately known to us as the 'Candidate House', which can be shortened to the 'Candi-house'."

Several girls giggled and Leticia acknowledged their amusement.

"I know that unfortunately sounds a bit like 'candy' house," the hostess admitted, "However the nick-name tends to stick! In spite of that, it is my fond hope that everyone here will have a great time!" The hostess viewed the contestants expectantly.

The girls giggled and whispered amongst themselves, as was only natural for a bevy of young ladies gathered together for a festive purpose. The majority sounded happy and excited. A few eyed each other speculatively, as if assessing their competition. Simon pointed his camera towards the assertive ones, because he expected they would be the source of dramatic interest for the very first episode.

"I assure you that there will be no need to be bored waiting for dates," Leticia announced. "You will have every opportunity to make friends amongst the girls as well as meet the current Charity Eligible. There are laundry and cooking facilities in the villa should you wish to avail yourself of them, but we have engaged a maid service and all the meals will be fully catered for you. Please let me know if there is anything special you require, it would be my pleasure to oblige, as I always have a good time hosting these events. Any questions?"

"What is the Charity Eligible like?" asked a tall African Australia girl called Heddy. She carried herself with an air of assurance which was very attractive.

"Yes, what can you tell us?" cried a lively dark haired girl whose name was Rozanne. According to her biographic notes, she was often 'the life of the party'.

Leticia smiled. "All I am allowed to say at this stage is that his name is Anthony, and that he is a doctor by profession."

A buzz of conversation broke out on all sides as the girls reacted to the news. A medical doctor was clearly perceived as a quality suitor and the ladies all appeared pleased.

"He sounds wonderful," gushed a dark eyed girl called Constance. "I think I love him already." She clasped her hands together and the look in her eyes became dreamy.

"The fellow could have some potential," the socialite called Deborah observed coolly. Several girls gave her quizzical looks. Keeping a level head was obviously an unpopular game tactic.

"How can you be so cynical?" asked a thin girl called Saidee. She wore her light brown hair pulled tightly back into a top-knot. "You could at least go into this with an open mind!" Saidee glared at Deborah severely.

"My mind is plenty open," Deborah retorted sturdily. "I can envision several scenarios, either he is the right guy for one of us, he breaks several of our hearts, or he is not the right guy for any of us!"

Saidee snorted derisively.

"I like to be realistic," Deborah added. "Not like some of you, half in love already, and you haven't even met the guy!"

"A doctor does sound nice," murmured a temperate girl called Kendra. "You have to admit that Deborah."

Deborah shrugged. "I thought I did that," she said. "Just not as effusively as some."

Kendra laughed, and some of the other girls sniggered. Rozanne looked like she wanted to say something more, but could not find the right words. Constance still appeared to be lost in her dream world.

Leticia called the group back to order. "Are there any other questions less related to the Charity Eligible?"

"I am looking forward to the pampering and the beauty treatments," said Mirage, an attractive ash-blonde with glasses.

"When does that all begin?"

"What happens to those of us who get sent home after the first episode?" Ilese inquired. "It would be awfully disappointing to turn around and go straight back home."

"You will get your chance to enjoy yourselves here for at least a day," Leticia replied. "In acknowledgement of the fact that some of you have had to travel some distance to attend, we will be having a relaxing time this evening."

"The beautician and hair-stylist will arrive in the morning, and you will be prepared to look your best for the debut party with the Charity Eligible tomorrow evening," Leticia continued. "If Anthony sends you home after the carnation ceremony, transport will have been arranged for you."

Some girls looked relieved, while others looked intensely excited.

"I expect we will have a lot of fun however it works out," said Ilese. She was a friendly girl who displayed a love of layering and fringe work on her clothing. "Twenty-four hours and one television episode are better than none."

"Yeah!" agreed Phaera, a plump brunette with shoulder-length hair. "Even if we only get to stay one night, being on the show will be an adventure."

"I am not here for any of the usual reasons," announced a brunette with a blunt haircut and heavy make-up. According to her name-tag, she was Orb. "I am here to prove that the Charity Eligible would never pick an activist."

The other girls turned in surprise and surveyed Orb from head to toe. Several of the more fashionable ladies were inclined to turn up their noses at her outfit, which was also on the chunky side.

"I don't know about that," a lovely girl called Nadine ventured. "I support a lot of good causes and still get dates."

"Are you saying the rest of us are not liberated?" cried a red haired called Becca. According to her biography she worked in retail. " I have a great career and I work forty hours a week. I think that fulfils the feminist charter!"

"You may all work, but you are still willing to put yourself on parade in a dating show," Orb retorted. "And one in which the male calls all the shots!"

"Um – so are you," murmured Kendra.

Orb shrugged. "A necessary strategy."

"The Charity Eligible won't be calling all the shots around me," Deborah muttered, and Heddy nodded in accord.

"There are a number of ways of managing a man," Janny added, with a giggle and a flutter of her eyelashes.

"I can drink any fellow under the table, " Gabby announced, "And I play darts and pool against the best. If a liberated woman is a girl who can beat a man at his own games - I sure can! "

"My definition of an activist is a woman who continues to fight for women's rights, " Orb explained.

"But which rights?" Even shy blonde Vonda appeared to have something to say.

"Exactly," model girl Alison spoke up. "We now have the vote, careers and our independence; what we don't have are safe loving relationships!"

"The situation is almost the exact opposite to the 1950s, where the women were all housewives and dependent on their husbands." Deborah remarked practically. "Most of us are now liberated and educated."

"As if you have to work," Gabby snorted looking at Deborah's immaculate suit, hair and shoes. Deborah shrugged. She could have said a lot, she was a librarian, a good one who worked for the sheer joy of having an occupation, but she was used to other people's perception of her wealth.

"My grandmother campaigns against domestic violence," inserted the peaceable Kendra. "I've always looked to her as the most enlightened woman I know!"

"The Charity Eligible's choice would be a matter of personal taste wouldn't it?" added Betty. "Not necessarily anything to do with activist philosophy or lack thereof."

Leticia chose that moment to re-enter the conversation. She privately agreed that the structure of the show was highly patriarchal, but viewer ratings were high, and women were always keen to enrol to strut their stuff on television.

"I would like your attention for a few more minutes while I show you to your rooms," the Hostess-director said. "There are six spacious bedrooms in this villa. One is occupied by myself and a mountain of television station equipment, while the second has been assigned to Vonda, Kendra, Janny and Rozanne. It has a lovely view of the shrubbery and direct access to the patio. The en-suite bathroom should be sufficient to your needs. I do hope you girls like it."

The group followed Leticia along the corridor and peered into the allocated bedroom. Kendra, Janny, Vonda, and Rozanne squealed as they recognised their luggage.

"The next bedroom has been assigned to Heddy, Racquel, Becca and Orb," Leticia continued. "This room is also very nice, being on the shrubbery side of the house. Moreover, it has its own luxury spa bathroom suite. You girls should be very happy there."

Leticia opened the door to reveal the suitcases belonging to Racquel, Becca, Heddy and Orb. Then the group moved along once again.

"The third bedroom faces the morning sun, and also has direct access to the patio," Leticia announced. "This room has been reserved for Constance, Nadine, Deborah and Alison. I hope that you are early risers because the mornings are very pleasant beside the pool. And once again, you do have your own en-suite."

Moving along quickly, Leticia led the way to the next room: "The fourth bedroom has handy access to the hedgerow, and also features a luxury bathroom. It has been arranged to accommodate Ilese, Phaera, Mirage and Saidee. I think you will love it."

Leticia opened the door to the last room: "My personal favourite is the last bedroom. It has a balcony overlooking the native herbarium. The bathroom is quite generously proportioned, and although it doesn't have a spa like the other two, it does have the most fantastic mirrors. The room has been allocated to Gabby, Ebony, Betty and Yana."

Leticia paused, and then said: "Well, that was the grand tour ladies! I suggest you take an hour to settle into your rooms and freshen up. Then we will have lunch together in the communal dining room, before playing some games designed to determine your positioning in the debut line-up tomorrow evening."

An hour later, all showered and freed from the grime of travel, the young ladies returned to the communal area looking relaxed and casual in a selection of jeans, slacks and track pants. Lunch was a light hearted affair with meat and cheese platters, gourmet sandwiches, and a selection of salads that were both mouth-watering and friendly towards those contestants who preferred to maintain a low calorie diet.

At the end of the meal, Deborah and Alison volunteered to clear the table. Leticia looked at the pair in surprise, and then murmured her thanks.

"Just take everything to the kitchen dears," the Hostess said. "Then they will be out of the way and the maid can get straight to the washing-up. I will see you in the large lounge in a few minutes."

Deborah and Alison began to stack the plates, while Leticia led the other girls into the sunny room next door.

"We have plenty of room to do everything we want here," Leticia said. "Please make yourselves comfortable, I don't want to start without Deborah and Alison."

The hostess settled herself down on one of the cushioned wicker lounges and allowed the girls to socialise at will. She noticed that Saidee talked the most to Phaera and Ilese, while Heddy chatted with Racquel, Becca and Gabby. Nadine, Constance, Vonda and Janny formed another group. Rozanne was speaking in an animated fashion to Ebony and Kendra, but the conversation did appear to be a bit one-sided.

"Aha," Leticia said, jumping to her feet when Deborah and Gabby arrived. "We can get started now. May I have your attention everyone?"

The girls giggled and turned their faces towards the hostess's couch. An expression of expectancy out-lined most of their faces.

"Thank you," Leticia said, producing a sheaf of paper and a bundle of pens from her briefcase. "Would you hand the sheets out for me please Janny?"

Janny obediently took the stationary and began to circulate around the room. The girls accepted a sheet of paper and a pen each. They held the material poised on their laps.

"Tomorrow afternoon, we will have a debut ceremony where the individual contestants are presented to Anthony," Leticia began. "After your presentation, you will go and join a line-up along the back wall. These formalities will take us through to the intermission, where you will all go to a special buffet supper."

Checking that she had their full attention, Leticia continued: "Anthony and I have an interview to perform for the camera, and then we will join you in the ballroom for a period of unstructured socialising. These two events will give you a chance to make an impression on Anthony. I suggest that you enjoy yourselves and make the most of them."

Several girls laughed.

"We'll sure try," Racquel said.

"What sort of impressions we'll make, I don't know," Deborah muttered.

The tom-boyish Gabby eyed Deborah suspiciously. "Speak for yourself," she said.

"Oh, I am," Deborah's laugh was a little snort.

Gabby quietly clenched and unclenched her fists. She didn't like high society types with their privileges and pretensions, but everyone was different. In the long run, what mattered was that the girls were all there for the Charity Eligible.

"At the end of the evening," Leticia announced, "Anthony will be required to offer pink carnations to twelve young ladies. This unfortunately spells the end of the contest for the other eight young ladies! However, you must try not to be too disappointed. Our sponsor has put together a bundle of pamper packs and gift vouchers for everyone who has to go home after the first carnation ceremony."

"It sounds lovely," Ilese said, "Everyone is a winner!"

"That depends what you are looking for," Orb said dryly.

"Oh don't be a spoil sport," Deborah remarked sternly. Orb choked, but she did not say anything in return. Enough girls had been vocal about their reasons for being on the show to subdue the activist somewhat.

"Back to the game please everyone," Leticia called. "As many of you will only be present for the first round, I would like to make sure you have as much fun as possible. To facilitate that, I want to work out a specific order in which you will be presented to the Charity Eligible. Your first task is to write down two reasons why you would like to be the first to be presented to the Charity Eligible tomorrow. I will collect them up and draw three out of a hat. These will be our first three ladies."

There was much "Umm-ing" and "Ah-ing" and scratching of pens, and then Leticia circulated around with the Stetson hat to collect the folded sheets. She performed this task herself to make sure everything was strictly fair. When she had collected all the sheets, Leticia shook the hat and placed it on the table before her.

"Becca," she said, "Would you please draw a sheet out of the hat?"

Becca stepped forward, selected a folded note and handed it to Leticia. Leticia unfolded the paper. "It is Heddy's!" She said: "I hope you don't mind you don't mind me reading it out loud Heddy?"

"That's okay," Heddy murmured.

"Heddy wants to be the first to meet the Charity Eligible because that will give her the longest to observe him," Leticia continued. "She also wants to show him that she is confident and can be an ice breaker. Well done Heddy! You will get your wish."

Becca selected a second note from the hat, and Leticia opened it. "This belongs to Janny," the hostess said. "Janny wants to be one of the first to meet Anthony because it saves her from waiting nervously. She also wants to make a good early impression upon him. Good luck Janny!"

Becca selected the third and last folded note from the hat. Leticia straightened the sheet and read its contents aloud: "Constance wants to be amongst the first to meet Anthony because she is eager to see what he looks like. She also wants to stand out from the crowd. Go for it Constance!"

Leticia put the last note down on the table and looked around. "Now we are going to vie for the final position," she said. "Some people believe that going last can be very advantageous. For example, the Charity Eligible will be more relaxed; you get to make a dramatic delayed entrance, and there will be fewer people coming after you to distract his attention."

The maid appeared carrying a box of bingo sheets and counters. Heddy, Janny and Constance, who already had positions, assisted Leticia in administering the game, while the remaining seventeen girls observed their sheets keenly. The first to call "bingo" was Deborah.

"That is the final position decided," said Leticia. "Good luck Deborah!"

"Last but not least," Deborah remarked with a grin. The socialite knew she offended everyone around her on a regular basis, and yet she still managed to be popular amongst people who knew her well. It was part of her extreme honesty policy.

The maid removed the bingo implements and Leticia addressed

the ladies once again: "We are going to ask girl number ten to pin a carnation on Anthony's lapel. This is symbolic of the carnations he will be giving out later in the evening. The person who does this job needs to be handy with a corsage pin. Our camera operator Simon Steeple will pretend to be the Charity Eligible for this exercise. I want each of the ladies who are currently unplaced to go up to Simon and practice pinning a corsage onto his jacket."

Simon, who was normally attached to the video camera, finished setting it onto a tripod. He beckoned to Constance. "Here pretty one," he said. "I have focussed on the centre of the room. Just keep looking at the screen and make sure I am getting a picture. Thanks so much!"

Vastly flattered, Constance positioned herself behind the camera. The remaining contestants all walked up to Simon and attempted to pin the corsage onto his tweed jacket. Several girls fumbled with the corsage, and one girl actually dropped it. Everyone had a good laugh.

"It needs a better pin," Yana remarked when it was her turn. She succeeded in hanging the corsage precariously from a few threads of Simon's jacket. Phaera fastened the corsage more firmly, but everyone agreed she had the arrangement upside down. Betty, who occasionally handled flowers at her work, made a passable job of attaching the corsage to the jacket.

In the end, however, it was Orb who surprised everyone. She marched up to Simon, unceremoniously lifted the corsage up to his lapel, and forced the pin neatly through the material. It hung there elegantly and securely.

"I think we have a winner," Leticia observed.

Several girls clapped, but Becca was heard to mutter, "Now he will have to notice Orb for sure..."

"Some people are clever," Nadine whispered. "But don't you worry, we will have our chances."

"Now the rest of you are to draw straws to see who will enter before and after the central position," Leticia said. "This mug on the coffee table contains a selection of red straws and blue straws. Those who draw a red straw will join the first ten, and those who draw a blue straw will form the second wave."

The fifteen un-ranked girls gathered around the stone mug, and each selected a straw. Leticia noted the colour each one drew.

"That leaves us with an entrance order something like this:

Heddy, Janny and Constance; Rozanne, Gabby, Nadine, Yana, Ebony and Ilese. The central girl is Orb, who will offer the corsage. Then will come Saidee, Vonda, Phaera, and Racquel; followed by Becca, Mirage and Betty. The final three are Alison, Kendra, and Deborah," the Hostess announced.

"It seems fair enough," Deborah remarked.

"Chance is completely unbiased," Alison concurred. "The rest is up to us!"

"What happens now Leticia?" the ever-restless Gabby asked.

"You might want to relax and use the pool area until dinner," Leticia suggested. "After dinner, I have an advance screening of a new release movie to show you all. However, those of you who are especially tired are free to retire to your rooms early."

The next morning dawned bright and pleasant. Some girls were up and swimming in the pool before breakfast, while others slept in until elevenses. All were bright with anticipation. A beautician and hair-stylist arrived around one pm, and the young ladies were rostered to take advantage of their services.

The contestants had brought their own evening wear, so advice from the wardrobe department was kept to a minimum. The only contestant who gave any trouble was Orb, who insisted on maintaining her heavy make-up style, despite advice from the beautician. Moreover, she had brought an evening blouse and skirt that everyone agreed clashed. The long sleeved blouse was purple, while the skirt was a reddish brown.

"A black skirt would be lovely," the Stylist said and offered to lend Orb a satin skirt from stock.

Orb however refused stubbornly. "I have the right to wear my own things," she said. "Don't I?"

Simon Steeple, who had been called in to adjudicate, nodded. "Of course you do," he said. "We just wondered if you would like something special for the camera."

"Nah I'm happy enough," Orb said. "If the guy can't take me as I am, that is his problem."

"Let her do what she wants," said Deborah, who was waiting next in line for the stylist.

"What concerns me," whispered Leticia to Simon under cover of the contestants chatter: "Is that prophecy Orb made at the beginning - that the Charity Eligible would never choose an activist! She seems determined to make it self-fulfilling."

"If the guy is half-way decent," remarked Kendra who was also waiting for the stylist, "He won't say anything rude. And if he simply doesn't pick her, she will have fairly harmless material for that column she writes."

"I say let her wear what she likes. Good looks aren't everything," added Alison.

"Such generosity from the truly beautiful," Deborah said dryly. "Weren't you up on a billboard beside the freeway once? Advertising something like a fizzy drink?"

"You got me!" Alison retorted good naturedly. "Thanks for the sarcasm."

Deborah laughed. "You're welcome," she said. "It seems you are learning how to take me."

"In short doses seems best at this stage," Kendra interjected with unexpected spirit.

Deborah chortled: "Priceless!" the socialite agreed.

As the afternoon drew to a close, the ladies were all beautified and prepared for their presentations. They talked amongst themselves during this process, swapping details such as town and state of origin, age and occupation. A common topic of discussion was the Charity Eligible. Leticia had refused to say anything more about him, but there was much speculation regarding whether he was tall or short, heavy-set or fit, blonde or dark haired. Each girl clearly had their own dream guy in mind, but all were open to getting to know the man once they were introduced.

Leticia appeared and asked the ladies to confine themselves to the lounge, as the Charity Eligible was ushered through the front door and into the small reception room. His entrance was shielded from the girls, but if they had caught a glance they would merely have seen a slim outline in a dark evening suit. His hair was light coloured and neatly combed either side of a parting. His step was confident and his posture was upright.

Once Anthony was safely installed in the reception room, Leticia assembled the girls in their assigned order and led them through the corridors. The group stopped in single file formation just outside the double doors.

"When I give my word, the doors will be opened and you may enter one by one," Leticia said. "Please remember to give me enough time to announce each of you, and be polite enough to allow your fellow contestants a few words with Anthony."

"Yes Leticia," everyone chorused.

Leticia knocked gently on the doors and they were opened wide. Leticia stepped inside, and a handsome male model called Tim, who had been hired to escort the ladies, appeared. He offered his arm to Heddy, who was first in line. Heddy and Tim waited at the head of the line, while Leticia went ahead into the reception room.

CHAPTER TWO: THE FIRST CARNATIONS

The figure in the neat black suit, white shirt and stylish navy waistcoat blinked in the glare of the television cameras. The latest Charity Eligible, Dr. Anthony Jones, was overwhelmed by his first appearance on the show.

"Normally Anthony would rate himself as an average kind of guy," the voice-over said. "About six feet tall, with short blonde hair and in his early thirties, his medical career makes Anthony extremely eligible, but also exceedingly reclusive on the relationship front."

Leticia stepped up onto the red carpet beside the new Eligible and patted him on the shoulder. "A typical Cancer according to the astrological charts, Anthony is inclined to be neat and precise. After work, he prefers to go home and relax, while his friends usually seek him out, and not the other way around. Isn't that right Anthony?"

"Yes, Leticia," Anthony replied meekly. "I have been lucky enough to retain some good friends from school and university."

"And it was your friends that nominated you for the role of Eligible on our *Charity Dating Show*, wasn't it Anthony?" Leticia inquired theatrically.

"Actually it was my sister who nominated me, but my mates did help her complete the audition material with anecdotes from my private life," Anthony grinned. "Even so, I was totally confounded when I found out I had been selected for the show."

"At first we didn't think you would accept the role," Leticia said. "Would you like to tell us how it came about that you did?"

"My first thought was of my work, and that I had always been unlucky in love," Anthony said. "Regarding work, I found I had just enough leave accumulated to cover the duration of the show; and on the love front - I decided to take a few risks."

"I guess you feel that is enough about you and your private life at this point," Leticia said kindly. "But you did have a special reason for coming on the show. Would you like to tell us what it was?"

"Ah Leticia," Anthony sighed. "Thank you so much for letting me out of any more personal revelations - at least for the next five seconds! As everyone knows, this is a charity dating spectacle. The television station has already donated two hundred thousand to the emergency ward of my hospital in return for three months of my time. Viewers who agree that this is a worthy cause are welcome to send a donation to the special post office box that will be displayed on the screen during the advertisement break. Our city is certainly in need of more emergency and children's services!"

"Are you looking forward to meeting our contestants?" Leticia asked specifically for the cameras, which were all focused upon them by this time.

"Oh yes, very much," Anthony said. "I love to meet young ladies. Unfortunately, in my line of work, they are usually sick." He laughed self-consciously at his own joke.

"Well then, let me introduce you to some ladies who are not only very well, but quite lovely," Leticia said. "The first lady through the door will be Heddy."

Heddy appeared on cue. She was wearing a bright green dress that fitted perfectly and set off her dark hair and skin. Her smile was brilliant. Tim gave her a little push towards the Charity Eligible and returned to the waiting area to collect the next girl.

Anthony viewed Heddy appreciatively as she approached. "I am very pleased to meet you," he said.

"I am happy to be here too," Heddy said with conviction. The pair exchanged a few other pleasantries and Heddy told Anthony she was a veterinarian. Then she moved to take her place at the beginning of the line-up.

"I will remember you," Anthony murmured as she left.

Heddy grinned. "That's what I like to hear!"

"The next lady is Janny," Leticia announced.

Janny appeared through the doorway and walked towards Anthony with a bounce in her step.

"Wow!" Anthony said. "I am impressed. Are you a gymnast?"

"Close," Janny said. "I'm a dancer."

"I love the theatre when I get the chance to go," Anthony said. "Sadly it is not very often."

"You must be a busy man," Janny responded. They talked briefly and then Janny declared she must move along.

"I would like you to meet Constance next," Leticia intoned.

Constance entered the room and walked across to Anthony. He thought that she was very attractive.

"Hello," Constance said. "You must be Anthony!"

"Yes I am," Anthony said.

"I am not ashamed to admit I am on a quest for love," Constance said. "I work in a busy hospital and I never have any personal life."

"We can form a club," Anthony exclaimed. "I am in exactly the same situation!"

A bright eyed girl called Rozanne was introduced to Anthony next. She was remarkable for her quick movements and choice of red leather outfit.

"I bet there is never a dull moment around you," Anthony observed.

"I am usually in the middle of the action," Rozanne replied. "Sometimes even controversy! You will find out." Her neat bottom swayed cheekily in its red leather casing as she stepped towards her place in the line-up.

"Here is Gabby," Leticia said, and Anthony found himself looking at a girl with an athletic figure. Her choice of evening attire was also boyish, as she was clad in tailored slacks and a silken shirt. Her tanned skin spoke of the outdoors.

"You look like a sports woman," Anthony observed.

"You look like a doctor," Gabby replied.

"What exactly does a doctor look like?" Anthony asked curiously. He saw a lot of doctors at the hospital and didn't think they were limited to one 'type'.

"Elegant, but a bit bookish," Gabby said.

"You will have to get me out jogging," Anthony joked.

"Can do!" Gabby replied. "Fishing too if that is something you would like."

Nadine had tender brown eyes and lovely dark brown hair. She definitely made an impression with her looks and her sweet smile.

"I hope to see you later in the evening," Nadine said.

"I will make a point of seeking you out," Anthony promised.

Yana passed Anthony by very quickly and he barely caught her name. She gave the impression she was not very comfortable being on the show.

Ebony seemed very composed. "Hello," she said.

"Hello," Anthony replied. "How are you?"

"I am well thank you," Ebony said. She said very little, but her posture conveyed intelligence and a little mystery. Ebony represented an enigma, and Anthony made a note to pursue her later.

Ilese's clothing was original and unusual, representing a combination of classical and bohemian styling. Perhaps she enjoyed fashion design, Anthony mused. He couldn't tell what she was like as a person though as she seemed far too nervous.

An odd-looking girl called Orb fastened a corsage upon his lapel. She also gave him a forward and not too gentle pat on the bottom. Anthony murmured, "Thank you," politely, but he was mostly embarrassed.

A neat girl in black velvet followed. Once again Anthony said, "Pleased to meet you." He thought her name was Saidee, but his head was whirling from all the introductions.

Vonda was a sweet girl who could barely raise her eyes to Anthony's at first. She was so shy that she instantly touched his heart.

"I hope you are enjoying being on the show," Anthony said.

"Yes, I am really," Vonda whispered. "Just let me have a little time to get used to these cameras and everything."

"I used to be shy myself," Anthony said.

"I think I can tell," Vonda murmured. "You are doing a great job tonight though." She raised her eyes to his face, and Anthony could tell they were a beautiful blue.

Phaera, Racquel and Mirage passed him in quick succession. Anthony was beginning to get confused by all the new faces. These particular girls were all that bit too eager to please, and he found himself shutting off his emotions.

However, his eyes re-focussed immediately a curvaceous blonde with something of the starry appeal of Marilyn Monroe swung into view. She was called Betty, and Anthony promised himself the opportunity to get to know her later.

A tall red-head called Alison was beautiful in a cool classical way. She appeared older than some of the others and walked like a model. Anthony drew out the small talk as long as he could, and extracted a commitment from her to chat again after supper.

The second to last girl was called Kendra. She seemed sensible, and was clearly very good natured. Anthony got the impression she would always be a very pleasant person to have around.

Anthony's final exchange was a short conversation with a society type called Deborah. She refused to fawn over him like some of the less memorable girls, and her presence on the show made him very curious. Anthony promised himself the opportunity to explore the anomaly later.

Then the debut ceremony was over, and the ladies moved on to the ballroom for the buffet. Leticia told Anthony that he would be free to join them all after he had answered a few more questions for the audience.

There was a short break, and when Anthony was allowed to re-join the ladies, he began wending his way through the room. Each of the women had been introduced to him briefly before, but now were confusing in their sheer number.

"Twenty women have come here to meet me," Anthony confided to the lapel microphone, hoping that the viewers were sympathetic. "I can hardly believe it! Indeed, I would be very embarrassed about the little matter of names, if they weren't wearing gold name tags. I thought earlier I knew who I wanted to talk to, but now I am challenged to put first impressions back with the faces."

Anthony stopped beside a friendly looking lady in a light grey evening dress. He couldn't tell whether her hair was dark blonde or light brown, but he thought it looked very neat swept back from her face. She also looked approachable and he vaguely remembered her name.

"Hello Kendra," Anthony said. "I am looking around to see if I can find the ladies who impressed me the earlier. However this is becoming much more difficult as I was so nervous I barely registered anything beyond a swirl of colour and the shine of your dresses."

The Blondette laughed. "Was I one of the ones you wanted to talk to?" she asked.

"To be honest I can't remember," Anthony replied bashfully.

"It gets a bit like that," Kendra said. "I am only just sorting the girls one from another and I have been in a dormitory with them for twenty-four hours."

"What did you do all day?" Anthony asked curiously.

"Raided the refrigerator and swapped home stories," Kendra replied. "Some of us slept and others swam. We all spent a while on our hair and make-up. The rest depended on the personality involved."

"Thanks for making the girls sound human to me," Anthony said. "I had better circulate now."

"Good luck!" Kendra called as he left. "I hope you find the others you are looking for."

Anthony quickly located one lady who had made a distinctive impression upon him earlier. She wore a pastel dress with pink, blue and purple swirls on the delicate fabric. The sleeves were long, but also transparent. She had seemed quite modest, and at the same time, very intelligent.

"Ah Constance!" Anthony exclaimed, and a slim brunette with a blunt shoulder length hair-cut parted the crowd to reach his side. "I was hoping for a chance to speak to you again."

Constance smiled. "I am happy to see you too," she said. "I was really hoping we could talk some more."

"I am normally quite shy with the ladies," Anthony said, "But I need to know more about you to make my decision tonight. I hope you won't mind answering a few questions."

"I will tell you anything you want to know," Constance replied assuring.

"Well for instance," Anthony said, "What was it you did for a living again? I know it was something that rang a bell with me."

Constance's face lit up. "I am a medical administrator," she said. "I understand that you are a doctor. It really does give us something in common."

"We could talk about our work for ages," Anthony said. "However, it might not be appropriate for a show like this. What are your hobbies?"

"I can cook," Constance said, "And I enjoy organising my unit. Are they what you mean by hobbies?"

"It's a start," Anthony said. "I know myself how little spare time you get while working in a hospital." A flash of red to the right caught his eye. "Please excuse me, there is someone else I must speak to."

Rozanne was a tall girl with short cropped hair-style. In contrast to the others, who mostly wore skirts, she was wearing a red bustier and red leather trousers. Her figure was pleasantly curvy in such an outfit.

"How are you tonight?" Anthony asked.

"Very well thank you," Rozanne replied. "And yourself?"

"A bit overwhelmed, I must admit," Anthony said. "I have to get to know everyone, but it is inevitable that I let some ladies go home by the end of the evening. It is an impossible task!"

"You will be relying a lot on your first impressions then," Rozanne said.

"I guess so," Anthony said. "It will be all I can do to take in their looks and one or two things about their personality. What do you do for a living for instance?"

"I am a counsellor," Rozanne said challengingly. "I spend most of my time helping young people through the last couple of years of high school."

"That is a worthwhile activity," Anthony said. "I will have to talk to you about that some more later. For now, would you mind telling me what you do for fun?"

"I like the movies," Rozanne said, "And I take photos. I have a huge collection of landscapes."

"You are outgoing and confident," Anthony said. "I noticed that earlier." To tell the truth, he was feeling a bit intimidated by her vivacity.

Rozanne nodded: "I guess you could say that, but I have my faults too. I can be very intense."

"It is very honest of you to admit it," Anthony said. He judged the girl to be very different from him, but perhaps he should get to know her better. "It's nice talking to you, although I should speak to someone else now."

Nadine was wearing a pink satin dress and had her dark brown hair piled high on her head. A matching pink hairband kept the style in place. She was pert and pretty, which inspired Anthony to like her instinctively.

"Hey there," he said.

"Hey there yourself," Nadine said. "How does it feel to be king for an evening?"

"Great!" Anthony said. "Although I do stand to lose almost half of my subjects by the end of the evening."

"Make sure you don't lose me," Nadine said playfully.

"I will do that," Anthony said. "And what do you do with yourself?"

"I am a paediatric nurse," Nadine said. "I just love kids!"

"That is great," Anthony said. "What else do you do?"

"I like to cook, and I enjoy fixing things," Nadine said. "I know that is not part of the feminine stereotype..."

"But it makes you all the more interesting!" Anthony said. "I will be sure to talk to you more later."

The next lady was wearing a creamy Grecian style gown. She was unusually tall, and piled her auburn hair high upon her head to heighten the effect. "I am glad I found you again," Anthony laughed. "I remember thinking that you must be a model."

Alison looked flattered. "I have been modelling for some years," she said. "Mostly commercials for television, a few catalogues and the occasional catwalk. I'm not at all sure whether it gives me an advantage at a thing like this, or not."

"Whatever do you mean?" Anthony exclaimed, "Surely any man would be thrilled to be going out with you?"

"They usually are quite keen," Alison said, "But I am looking for someone who can see past the surface looks and take me seriously."

Anthony privately reflected that this was a bit too much like an ultimatum delivered up-front, and it contained something of a negative judgement of the male gender. However, he was willing to explore the issue and contest her on it later. "I will have to talk to you more sometime," he said.

Alison nodded. "I would like that," she murmured.

Deborah, the haughty lady in canary yellow, looked Anthony up and down carefully through her tinted glasses. "You will make quite a presentable Eligible," she said. "That is, if you choose to behave like a gentleman."

"I am glad to meet your approval," Anthony said briskly. "I could be offended, but I choose to accept your challenge."

"Better and better," Deborah replied. "We are going to need all the honesty we can get around here before the show is half over."

"I suspect you can dish it out to the point of being brutal," Anthony said. "What do you do every day?"

"I am a librarian," Deborah said. "Although my family are quite well off, and I don't really need to work."

"I could tell you were somewhat upper-crust," Anthony said. "Whatever are you doing here then?"

"I like to try something new at times," Deborah replied. "Besides, it is for charity. My father's generous donation has already been forwarded to the hospital."

Anthony was secretly very pleased to hear additional money had gone to the hospital, but he did not dare ask the socialite for more information. "I'll be seeing you around," he said. "It could be fun."

Anthony had secretly been avoiding eye contact with the funny girl who had pinned the corsage on his lapel and publically patted him on the bottom. However, she was clearly not going to allow him to omit her from his itinerary.

As he turned around from speaking to the socialite, she placed herself in his way and they almost collided. Anthony put out a hand to steady the girl and peered into the face which had slowly come into focus before his eyes. She would not be bad looking if she used a little less starting make-up.

"Orb isn't it?" he stammered.

"Yes," Orb replied.

"The one who patted me on the bottom," Anthony blushed. He decided to be straight with her. "Why ever did you do that?"

"To show you how hundreds of women feel when they are subjected to unwanted advances from men," Orb replied.

"Aha," Anthony said. In his work as an emergency doctor he had treated the victims of many forms of abuse. He had a fair idea what some of the women must have felt – but he wasn't going to subject this young lady to such brutal descriptions. "And what do you do?"

"I am writing a thesis on feminism in society," Orb replied.

"I wish you all the best with your research," Anthony responded diplomatically.

"Thanks," Orb said. "Don't you think this show is horribly patriarchal? With twenty women and one man?"

"I am thrilled so many women want to meet me," Anthony said. "And I am not responsible for setting up the premise of the show - but I do wonder what chance I would have of meeting the right person if I had no choice of partner?"

"Market research has shown that shows featuring multiple women and a single man attract higher ratings than shows with an even number of participants from each category," Orb announced.

"There you are in your own field of expertise, not mine," Anthony hedged. "Tell me honestly, do you see me as a person or just as a man – and enemy?"

"You tell me," Orb retorted. "Do these other girls see you as a person or as a fantasy?"

"I've never thought about that," Anthony said. "Some elements of fantasy must come into love, surely."

The Charity Eligible's head was reeling, and his confidence had just taken a new knock. It was already confusing to be the object of the women's attention without trying to psychoanalyse them all.

"I will talk to you again later," he said and moved along determinedly.

The next girl was in his sights was the ballet dancer. Anthony had noticed her much earlier and made a mental note to make her acquaintance. Her ash blonde hair was tied back into a pony tail behind her head, and her clingy outfit outlined her athletic body. The bodice and skirt were cut in two pieces and bared her mid-rift.

"That is an interesting outfit," Anthony commented. "I have been dying to ask whether it is a costume."

Janny grinned. "I am glad you like it," she said. "No, it is not an actual costume, but I am used to wearing a lot of lycra. I had my seamstress transfer the designs into my everyday wardrobe as well."

"I suppose you are very energetic?" Anthony said. "I am afraid I could never keep up with you."

"On the contrary," Janny said. "I like to catch up with my sleep on weekends."

"That leaves a chance for me then," Anthony said. "I will be sure to talk to you more later."

The last girl who had really caught Anthony's eye in the line-up had been a short-haired blonde dressed in pale blue. She was the quiet type, and he had to search around for her, finally locating her sitting alone on a couch.

"What are you doing back here?" Anthony asked.

"Just taking a moment," Vonda said. "I can never feel part of a large group."

"Will you be all-right in the Candidate House?" Anthony asked in sudden concern. He knew a little of what it was like to be retiring.

Vonda laughed. "Of course," she said. "People are nice enough taken one by one."

"What do you do outside of here?" Anthony asked.

"I am a violinist," Vonda replied. "I compose a bit, although my real income comes from playing with the symphony orchestra."

Anthony looked surprised.

"The music is very inspiring," Vonda said. "I am fine whenever I get past my performance nerves."

"It is exactly the same for me at work!" Anthony exclaimed. "My role and training give me confidence, but I have never heard any one explain it quite like that before."

Soon after that, Anthony found himself talking to Gabby, the boyish brunette who explained that him she was a swimming instructor; and Ebony, the short-haired blonde who turned out to be a research assistant in the science department of the local university. Gabby was inclined to inquire nosily about his fitness routine (or lack thereof as so happened due to his hospital schedule), and Ebony's conversation was intellectually demanding, but he somewhat liked them both.

The last girl Anthony spoke to in any depth was Betty. She was a curvy blonde with long wavy hair, whom he was sure any man would adore. Her figure made his pulse race, and he judged she knew that fact as she laid a gentle hand upon his arm.

"I am so pleased to be talking to you again," she said.

"I am glad to chat to you," Anthony replied. "What do you do for a living?"

"I manage the perfume counters at a major store," Betty said. "It took quite a while to work my way up to that level, but a clever man like yourself would know that. There are levels in any work place."

"Of course there are," Anthony replied. "I am afraid I don't know much about the perfume industry though."

"I would love to explain it to you some time," Betty said. "But I would like to hear about your work first. Have you always worked at the same hospital? Do they value your services very much? They would if they were smart."

Anthony was barely half way through the most gratifying conversation he had in a long time, when the presenter interrupted him.

"I am sorry Anthony," Leticia said, "But it is time to go now."

"Oh no," Anthony said, "Give me a few more minutes, do!"

"You know how this game works," Leticia said.

Anthony sobered up. "I guess you are right," he said. He waved to the girls in the room. "I will see you again soon," he said. "And I will have the privilege of giving twelve of you a pink carnation. For those of you I won't be able to give a flower, I want you to know right away how much I have appreciated meeting you."

All of the girls waved and some of them blew kisses, as Leticia led Anthony away into the deliberation room.

Once in the deliberation room, Anthony settled down on the sofa to wait. As he understood the rules, he had half an hour in which to think uninterrupted. He regretted not talking longer to some of the girls, but otherwise, his decision seemed fairly straight forward. A number of girls had caught his eye for various reasons, and it would be a fairly simple matter to give out twelve pink carnations.

Rising to his feet after an interval, Anthony crossed the room to where a row of portraits were arranged artistically along a low table. Brushing past those faces he had barely noticed, and whom he believed he could safely dismiss, Anthony focused upon the pictures that intrigued him.

It was pointless regretting not speaking more to Heddy at this stage, and there was no evidence that any of the others would have interested him any further. He had met them twice, and for some reason they had failed to leave him with a clear impression of either their person or personality. It was safest to leave it at that.

"They are all lovely girls, but they may not all be the most compatible girls for me," Anthony remarked to the overhead camera, conscious that the audience required an explanation of his behaviour at this point in the game. "It is not about making judgements at this stage, it is just about who has established a rapport with me."

"I am thinking," Anthony continued, "Of choosing Constance, Rozanne, Nadine, Alison, Deborah, Janny, Vonda, Gabby, Ebony, Heddy, Kendra and Betty. I am selecting Constance because she is clever and we have so much in common, Rozanne because she is interesting for her energy and individuality, and Nadine for her dark good looks and warm heart. Alison makes it onto my list because of her outstanding beauty, Deborah for her refreshing bluntness, Janny because she is so amazingly fit and glamorous, and Vonda because she is sweet and shy and reminds me of myself. Gabby is very refreshing, and I do believe in exercising whenever I can find the time, Kendra is nice and calm, and Ebony is as specialised in the sciences as I am in medicine. Last, but not least, I am choosing Betty because she is so outright sexy. She is a modern Marilyn Monroe, and every guy's dream."

Leticia entered the room on cue. "Are you ready?" she asked.

"Yes," Anthony replied. "I am happy with my decisions."

"No doubts, no regrets?" Leticia asked in surprise. "The Charity Eligibles are usually pretty torn about letting such a huge number go at this early stage."

"Not really," Anthony said. "I can't let myself worry about what-might-have-beens."

Leticia's eyebrows rose. "I can see what has got you this far in life," she said.

Anthony wasn't sure whether to take that as a compliment or not. Decision making was essential in the emergency room and moments of doubt could cost lives. The Charity Eligible vaguely suspected that a brusque attitude was less appropriate in his personal life, but being moderately secure in his own world view, he decided to accept the comment at face value.

"Thanks," he said. "Do lead the way."

They arrived in the small reception room to find the twenty girls all waiting eagerly. The ladies were standing in a semi-circle facing a small end-table covered with a white lace cloth. A pile of long stemmed pink carnations lay upon the end-table, and it was obvious that Anthony was required to position himself behind it.

Leticia moved to one side, and Anthony's comfort level dropped as all twenty pairs of eyes fastened eagerly upon him. What was most disconcerting, was that girls whom Anthony had not spoken to at all were eyeing him just as keenly and apprehensively as those with whom he believed he had developed some acquaintance.

"Oh no," the Charity Eligible exclaimed, "This is going to be much harder than I expected."

A nervous titter ran around the room.

"Well here goes," Anthony said. He reached for the first carnation and stepped around the desk. "Constance, will you accept this pink carnation and the next round of the game that comes with it?"

Constance blushed as she detached herself from the crowd. "I surely will," she said, coming up to Anthony. She reached for the carnation and their fingers touched briefly. "Thank you ever so much."

Anthony watched in bemusement as Constance made her way back to the girls, then he reached for the second flower.

"Rozanne," Anthony said glancing around the group, "I would like to get to know you better. Will you accept this carnation?"

Rozanne strode her way out of the circle. "I would be happy to spend more time with you," she said, throwing her arms around him in a big hug.

"I will do what I can to make it happen," Anthony murmured.

Rozanne returned to her place in the circle and Anthony picked up another carnation. He held it out in front of him.

"Nadine," Anthony said, "I would like to spend some more time with you. Will you accept this pink carnation?"

Nadine smiled as she approached. "I would be delighted to continue this dating process," she said. "Of course I will accept the carnation."

After Nadine had returned to her seat, Anthony selected an especially fresh looking bloom. He was a bit nervous about this one, because its intended recipient was the most composed looking of the girls upon the Persian carpet.

"Alison," Anthony said, "Would you please accept this carnation from me?"

Alison smiled serenely. She walked forward and came to a halt neatly in front of Anthony. "Yes, I will accept the carnation," she said. Anthony placed the carnation in her hand and she held it delicately.

"Thank you," Anthony said as the model girl walked back to her place.

The Charity Eligible glanced around the group, taking in the fact that some of the girls were beginning to shift around apprehensively. Almost half of the carnations had been assigned and some girls were beginning to suspect they would not be amongst the recipients.

"Have patience with me please," he begged.

Anthony picked up another long-stemmed carnation and looked firmly towards the left of the group. "Deborah," he said, "I think I will enjoy crossing words with you. How about sticking around for a while?"

Deborah stalked her way to the front. "Thank you Anthony," she said, "I think I will accept the carnation."

"Well that's settled then," Anthony muttered as Deborah moved back to her place. There would never be a dull moment with Deborah around. He seized another carnation.

"Janny," Anthony called. "I am hoping to get a dance with you. Would you accept a carnation?"

Janny stepped forward gracefully. "I would love a carnation," she said. Anthony handed her the carnation and she bobbed a theatrical little curtsy.

Anthony clapped. Then he reached for another flower.

"Vonda," Anthony said in the warmest of voices, "I think it is really great that you have come on the show. Would you accept a carnation tonight?"

"Yes I would," Vonda said with surprising conviction as she stepped forward. "I am here to make friends, and I will say this to the girls as well as Anthony: don't judge me because I am quiet. I really do want to get to know you."

Everyone clapped, and for a moment the tension was broken. Leticia was overheard to say, "Good for you," and the girls milled around giving Vonda hugs. Eventually Leticia called them back into formation.

"There are five more pink carnations," the Hostess said.

"Thank you so much," Anthony said, as the ladies turned their attention towards him once again. "And I am sorry there are only five carnations."

Anthony picked up one of the remaining floristry items and glanced around the group. "Gabby," he said, "Where did you go? I was hoping you would accept a flower."

Gabby emerged from the back row and gave Anthony a peck on the cheek. "I will have that flower," she said. "Thank you very much."

Anthony picked up the fourth-to-last pink carnation. "Ebony," he said. "I enjoyed hearing about your research. Please accept this carnation."

Ebony stepped forward. "Thank you," she said in a tone that revealed little, and walked back to her seat holding the flower. Anthony was a little taken aback. He wondered whether she had really wanted the carnation, but it was too late to ask now.

Anthony picked the third-to-last carnation up and looked over towards Betty, who gave him a huge smile. His heart leapt, and then Kendra put her arm around Betty, ready to congratulate her. Anthony had a sudden memory of Kendra soothing his feelings at the beginning of the social. Kendra was nice and calm and stable, whereas Betty was the sort of bubbly beauty he had always envied his more outgoing friends dating. His head whirled, and his mouth stammered something of its own accord.

"Kendra," Anthony stuttered, "Will you accept this carnation?"

Kendra stepped forward and graciously accepted the latest carnation. "Thank you Anthony", she said. "I really appreciate the gesture."

Betty was looking disappointed because she had been sure Anthony had made eye contact with her a moment ago. It had really looked like he was going to call her for the next blossom.

Anthony smiled to assure the beautiful blonde. "Betty," he called.

Betty stepped forward, her doubts forgotten and face all smiles. "Yes Anthony?"

"Will you accept this carnation?" Anthony proffered the second-to-last flower.

"Gladly," Betty murmured. She took the long stemmed bloom and joined the girls who had been selected.

Leticia interrupted Anthony's thoughts to remind everyone that they had now reached the final carnation. Anthony picked the final carnation up, pondering the power the little flower carried. Any name he called now would be included, and any girl he did not give this flower would leave the show.

"Orb," Anthony said.

Orb looked shocked. The unthinkable had happened – the Charity Eligible had really picked the activinist! Anthony was a little shocked too, as he had really meant to say Heddy, but got the names mixed up! However, the look of stupefaction on Orb's face was worth it, and he dismissed his doubts so they did not show on his face.

"Please step forward," Anthony said.

Orb mechanically covered the paces between her position and that of the Charity Eligible. She held her hand out woodenly. The article she had already written in her head about having joined *The Charity Dating Show* and proved its patriarchal bias would have to be severely edited.

Orb wondered briefly whether she had somehow reformed the Charity Eligible. Such an article would not have the same ring to it, and would not fit her thesis. She would also be bound by the television station contract not to criticise the show for at least another episode, because she was still a participant.

"Will you accept this carnation?" Anthony said, extending the flower towards her.

Orb briefly considered saying, "No," to make a point, but she had no real reason to refuse the flower. The Charity Eligible seemed a nice enough guy, and he had listened to her point of view.

"Thank you," she muttered and returned to the other girls clutching the bloom. Her cheeks were blushing an unaccustomed pink.

Leticia made an announcement that ran something like: "The final carnation has been assigned for tonight. We wish the remaining girls the best of luck as they prepare to leave the show."

Several girls shifted restlessly, and the hostess hastened to continue: "I have a surprise package containing a special sterling silver channel logo bracelet and some pamper products to give to each of you before you leave. There are also gift vouchers from our many sponsors. Stop and say goodbye to your fellow participants; and then the service personnel will assist you with your travel arrangements."

Anthony found himself surrounded by the unsuccessful contestants. "I am so sorry," he said to each and every one, "I wish I had more carnations."

He met with a variety of reactions from the ladies. Some girls assured him that they had enjoyed the evening and that the hour of fame on the television would promote their popularity at home. One or two girls upbraided Anthony for not taking the time to circulate around the group more thoroughly.

Anthony was surprised to discover that he agreed with them. Moreover, he felt a sense of genuine regret at parting from these lovely ladies who had all been prepared to travel to Sydney to meet him.

"I would have really liked a chance to get to know you," said pretty little Mirage, and Anthony found himself noticing her for the first time.

"I am so sorry," he said. "Please don't hold my ineptness against me."

"Just don't spend the rest of your life going around with your eyes shut," Mirage said.

Anthony nodded dumbly: "I will try not to," he agreed.

The Charity Eligible's most awkward moment was facing Heddy, whom he had actually meant to keep.

"I am sorry Heddy," he said. "I just ran out of flowers."

The African beauty laughed and assured him that although she had enjoyed their meeting, she was prepared to be philosophical about the limitations of the programme.

"I'll see you around, bro," she said.

"That's just it," Anthony said. "I won't see you again."

"Need to take more care counting your flowers next time then," Heddy chortled. "It's a small world too bro, you never know what might happen."

Leticia listened to this exchange in amusement. In the structured world of television dating, you never did know what management might get up to! Moreover, she had almost certainly selected Heddy as an intruder for further down the track.

Finally the hostess decided to rescue the Charity Eligible.

"Goodbye Mirage, goodbye Heddy," Leticia said, handing the two girls their respective gifts.

The girls focused on the baskets full of tempting looking shapes and packages. They thanked the hostess and made their way out of the room together.

Leticia turned to Anthony: "It hits you doesn't it?" she remarked sympathetically.

Anthony nodded. "Is it always like this?" he inquired.

Leticia nodded. "More or less. But there is also a sense of achievement that you are one step towards enjoying the exclusive company of your chosen partner, providing you have used your dates wisely."

Anthony nodded and pondered her statement briefly. Then he went off to try and enjoy the company of the ten women whom he had selected.

CHAPTER THREE: THE PRIMARY DATES

Leticia's alarm went off at six o'clock the next morning. She opened a sleepy eye and stumbled out of bed. Deciding that she was in desperate need of a hot drink, the hostess wended her way through the common area and towards the kitchen. She stopped in amazement at the entrance to the large lounge, because Constance, Nadine, Vonda and Deborah were all watching television in their pyjamas.

"When did you girls get up?" Leticia asked in surprise.

"Actually we never went to bed," Constance replied.

"We were too excited to sleep after meeting the Charity Eligible," Nadine added.

"I am glad he doesn't have that effect on me!" Leticia said. "I have work to do! Deborah, I am surprised at you! You didn't strike me as the impressionable type."

"Nah!" Deborah said. "These two kept moving around, and I didn't want them to wake Alison, who somehow did fall asleep... Vonda got up at one stage and started creeping around like a mouse, so I invited her to join us."

"Well what are you finding to watch at this hour?" Leticia asked. "Cartoons?"

"That's right," Constance said.

"And there was an old police show before that," Nadine commented.

"The late night mystery was actually quite good," Vonda said.

"It sounds like you made a party of it," Leticia remarked. "However, I suggest you go to bed now and catch a bit of sleep while the house is still relatively quiet. Things will liven up when the camera crew arrives."

"We were actually all wondering what will happen today," Deborah announced.

"There will be two group dates," Leticia replied. "Half of you will be going out to lunch, while the other half will be going out to dinner. Now go get some sleep in case you are part of the lunch group!"

Breakfast was served over a leisurely two hour time period, and around mid-morning, Leticia called the girls to her.

"Constance, Janny, Vonda, Betty, Alison and Gabby," she said. "Anthony will be here in an hour to pick you up for your date. I suggest that you dress in clothing that is both elegant and casual. You will want to be comfortable, but you may also want to look nice."

"Where are we going?" Janny asked.

Leticia shook her head. "I cannot give any more clues," she said. "Anthony will tell you when he arrives."

The young ladies in question ran off to their rooms, asking each other what to wear.

"What exactly is both comfortable and elegant?" Vonda said to Alison. "That sounds like a contradiction."

"A trouser suit maybe," Alison said. "Say, why don't you and Janny bring your selected outfits to the room I am sharing with Constance, and we can all get dressed together. You are welcome too Gabby!"

"I'll be okay on my own," Gabby said. "I will see you later."

"I will take you up on your offer though," Vonda said. "Thank you Alison."

"Me too," Janny said. "The more the merrier! We can joke around and take the edge off our nerves."

"Are you nervous too?" Vonda asked in surprise. "I thought it was just me."

"I think every girl here ought to be nervous," Janny said as they hurried towards their room. "We are all dating a good looking guy, and we don't know what he will think of us yet. Knowing guys, he probably won't tell us much either. Hearts could be broken all over the place!"

"Anthony seems like a nice guy, but I will be guarding my heart," Vonda said wisely, "Especially as I know he is dating all you other girls!" She opened her wardrobe door and looked inside: "What do you think of a short navy skirt and jacket? I can jazz it up with a cream silk blouse."

"Sounds okay to me," Janny said. "So long as you have some low heels that will match."

"I do too," Vonda exclaimed. "I think I will ask Alison if they coordinate though."

"Fine," Janny said. "I think I will wear a halter neck top and brown slacks." She picked up her clothing items.

"Yes do!" Vonda exclaimed. "They are lovely."

Garments in hand, Vonda and Janny hurried to the room assigned to Alison and Constance. Alison was elegantly attired in a khaki trouser suit with a tailored short sleeve jacket that the other girls admired very much, while Constance was changing into a ruffled skirt and stretchy top. Being a professional model, fashionable clothes were part of Alison's job. She was proud of her appearance and always happy to give other girls style hints.

Betty of course, looked absolutely stunning in a full skirted sunfrock and light crochet cardigan. The other girls were surprised to learn the Grace Kelly - Marilyn Monroe look alike was not at all vain about her looks.

"I work in retail," Betty explained. "I have to look good to sell the products. It's just a part of the job!" The shop-girl had brought along a selection of cosmetic and perfume samples which she generously distributed amongst the other girls, greatly enhancing her popularity in the Candidate House.

"We are ready to go out on the town," Alison exclaimed when they were all fully attired, made-up and styled. "Let us go down stairs."

"I wonder why Gabby wouldn't get dressed with us," Constance said.

"I don't know," Alison said. "Either she likes to be on her own, or she just felt like her room was too far way."

Betty shrugged. "I share with Gabby, so my room was just as far," she reported amiably. "Look, there she is down in the hall waiting to go on the date."

Anthony arrived in a stretch limousine. "Hello ladies," he said to the bevy of girls clustered around the door. "It is my privilege to escort Janny, Alison, Gabby, Constance, Betty and Vonda this afternoon. Are they ready?"

"Yes," Alison said, stepping out from the crowd.

"You look lovely," Anthony said. His eyes were resting mainly upon Alison and Betty, but he glanced across at the others as well. It was obvious who he meant, but no one felt completely left out.

"Where are we going?" Gabby asked.

"A visit to the observatory and lunch at the top of the tower," Anthony said. "Followed by a tour of the shops below."

"Wonderful!" Constance exclaimed. "It is ages since I did anything like that."

"It is every girl's dream," remarked Alison.

Anthony looked pleased. "It was the television stations' idea," he admitted, "But I am very happy to be the person who delivers it to you. Here, let me help you into the car."

Anthony opened the front passenger door for Constance, Gabby and Vonda; and the back door for Janny and Alison. Then he took his own place on the back seat. Betty had to ride in the front beside the chauffeur, but she did not appear to mind.

"I think it is so cool that we all fit into one car!" Janny exclaimed.

"I like the way we can sit facing each other," Vonda concurred.

"It is very convenient," Alison agreed. "Although to be fair, Anthony needs to be in the middle."

"I thought about that," Anthony said. "But then how would I have been a gentleman and held the door for you all?"

"So you weren't arranging things so that you would be next to Alison?" Constance asked coyly.

"No," Anthony said. "I promise that you will be next to me on the way home, Constance."

"I will look forward to it," Constance said.

The car drew up a mere block away from the tower.

"It looks like we get out here," Gabby commented.

They all piled out, and linking arms, posed for the camera with the thin stem and round bowl of Sydney Tower in the background behind them. Then Anthony led the way into the base of the tower and straight toward the lift.

"The observatory first," Anthony said, pushing the button.

"I don't really like heights," Vonda murmured, and Janny offered to hold her hand. The two blonde girls stuck together defensively, and Anthony found himself talking to Constance and Betty. Alison and Gabby brought up the rear.

When they reached the top, they all stepped out into a glass-sided room. Vonda and Janny stuck to the centre near the lift column, but the others circled around the edge taking in the view of the city.

"You can see the roof-tops!" Constance exclaimed.

"The cars look just like toys," observed Gabby.

"We are almost as high as the clouds," commented Alison.

Anthony drew near and casually draped an arm over Constance's shoulder. "Let me show you how the telescope works," he said. The couple drew away from the others and became exceedingly occupied with the viewer. Anthony was behind Constance and she leant into him.

"Those two look intimate," Alison said.

"I don't mind," Gabby remarked. "I don't really think he is my type."

"When did you make that decision?" Alison asked.

"I don't know," Gabby said. "I had an inkling last night, but I became sure in the car today."

"And yet you accepted a carnation," Alison marvelled.

"And I would again if he offered," Gabby said. "These outings are fun."

"It doesn't seem really fair," Alison said cautiously.

"Fair to whom?" Gabby inquired. "The girls who missed out or Anthony? Face it, nothing is fair when there are too many parties involved. What about you? Are you truly interested in Anthony?"

"I don't know," Alison conceded defeat graciously. "I am still getting to know him.

"I tell you one thing," Janny said approaching cautiously. "I wouldn't be rushing things the way Constance is."

"That's her choice," Gabby said shortly. "Where is Vonda?"

"She found a chair in the centre where she can't see any great heights and Betty offered to keep her company," Janny said. "So now I am taking the chance to look around."

Anthony and Constance re-joined the group some time later. The other girls had finished looking around, and wandered over to the lounge to sit beside Vonda. They looked up at their escort quizzically.

"It is time to go in to lunch," Anthony said. "I will ask the waiter to seat us well away from a window for your sake Vonda."

"Thank you Anthony," Vonda said gratefully. "I hope you don't think the worse of me for this."

"On the contrary Vonda," Anthony said, "I think you are a good sport for coming up here anyway."

"I do hope you are alright," Constance said, displaying polite concern. She and Anthony were still holding hands. "And I hope we weren't away too long."

"You pushed the boundaries of politeness," Alison observed bluntly. "However, it was no big deal."

The party entered the lift and travelled to the restaurant level. Anthony made his request at the reception desk for a sheltered table, and the waiter led them to a position where they would be surrounded by other diners.

"I hope mademoiselle is very comfortable," the Waiter said to Vonda. "Do let me know if there is anything else you require."

Everyone selected an entree and main course, while Anthony put in an order for a selection of juices and soft drinks for the table. When he had finished, he noticed that Gabby was frowning.

"Aren't you going to order any wine?" the Swimming Instructor asked.

Anthony looked surprised. "I thought you were really into your health," he said.

Gabby shrugged. "I am," she said, "But I am on holiday at the moment. Besides I can exercise it all off later."

Anthony turned to the waiter: "A glass of the lady's favourite wine please," he said. He turned to the other girls: "Do any of you want to order alcohol?"

Janny shrugged, "It is early in afternoon," she said. "I am quite happy without."

The other girls agreed, and indeed Vonda thought it might increase her giddiness.

"That is settled then," Anthony said. He looked pleased. "Perhaps I should explain! I don't drink very often. Being a surgeon, I am usually on call for emergencies, and I can't risk having alcohol in my system. It is usually simpler to avoid it altogether – so I'm out of the habit."

Gabby sniffed. "Do you ever have any fun?" she said. "I love to unwind in the pub of an evening."

Anthony shrugged. "Maybe by your standards, I don't have much fun," he said. "To be honest, I don't get much free time. However, I can enjoy a good conversation or concert better sober."

"Extremely high-brow," Gabby muttered under her breath. It was not a compliment.

"I think it's sweet," Betty breathed, her film star eyes meeting Anthony's gaze. For the first time during the date, Anthony regretted paying such close attention to Constance. While he was enjoying the company of one girl, he was missing out on spending time with the others.

"What about when you were at university?" Janny asked. "Don't all medical students get wasted?"

"I tried it once or twice and it didn't help my grades," Anthony said. "So I decided to eschew the pub scene and study for my exams."

"Some models drink and some don't," Alison commented. "Alcohol contains hundreds of calories and is said to be bad for the skin."

"Do you?" Janny asked.

"I like a little white wine," Alison replied. "What about yourself?"

"Not when I am dancing," Janny said. "I need heaps of water then."

"I think you are a bunch of spoil-sports," Gabby said. Her wine had arrived and she was sipping it defiantly. "Next thing, you will say you are a vegetarian."

Anthony laughed. "No I am not," he said. "Indeed you are about to see me eat a huge steak."

"I think Ilese was a vegetarian," Vonda said. "I never quite worked it out."

"Can we talk about something else?" Alison said. "Everyone is different and it is such a lovely day."

"It is, isn't it?" said Constance. "And isn't this place magnificent?"

"It's great!" Janny said. "I have never been to the restaurant here before."

"I've heard that you can book it for weddings," Constance murmured dreamily.

The conversation progressed steadily towards lighter topics, and the laughter level at the table rose. In the end, everyone (with the possible exception of Gabby, who had become sullen after finishing her solitary wine) agreed that it was a lovely lunch.

After the meal was complete, the party descended toward the base of the tower and entered into the shopping precinct, which featured an exclusive department store, a number of designer fashion boutiques and several jewellery stores.

The girls were delighted and stopped frequently to try on hats, gloves and dresses. Vonda looked delightful in a pale pink evening dress embroidered with beads and sequins, although she swore she would never buy anything like it. Alison looked sophisticated in a black organza number with pleats, and Constance looked startlingly different in a red jumpsuit with a plunging neckline. Janny tried on a pair of impossibly high heels she would not dare wear as a dancer, and even Gabby unbent and joined in the fun, trying on a pair of designer jeans.

At one stage Anthony remarked that although he was enjoying the fashion parade, the activity represented a test of the limit of his male tolerance for shopping. Nevertheless, the ladies assured the Charity Eligible that he was doing very well.

"It is fun pointing out things we like," Alison said, "And we are all relieved to find you are the sort of guy who will wait while we try them on."

"We do understand you won't want to stand around forever," Constance added.

"And that the car will be back for us around four," Janny said.

"Well I would like to thank you," Vonda said. "Thank you for freeing us momentarily from the feeling that we need to compete for your attention."

"Ah!" Anthony said. "I don't perceive myself as a prize. Just a nice boy-friend for the right girl, should she be here!"

"That sounds wonderful," Constance murmured, her eyes shining.

"I work in a store," Betty said. "Shopping isn't really a novelty to me. I will keep you company if you like."

"Thank you Betty," Anthony said, secretly relieved the beautiful blonde was making it easy to spend some time with her. "Shall we go somewhere for a coffee?"

"Of course," Betty said. "Girls, we won't be very far away. Come and find us when you are ready."

Constance looked mildly disconcerted, and then her expression became coquettish. "That is very nice," she said, and linked her hand through the crook of Anthony's arm. "Enjoy having coffee with Betty, but don't forget that you promised to sit with me on the way back."

"I am looking forward to it," Anthony said gallantly. He

extended his spare hand to Betty, "Come along and help me find a coffee stall."

When the lunch date girls arrived home, they were greeted eagerly by the rest of the occupants of the Candidate House.

"Where did you go?" Nadine cried impatiently.

"How was it?" Rozanne added curiously.

"We went to the Sydney Tower," Constance replied. "And then we went shopping."

"Anthony waited patiently while we tried things on," Alison remarked. "He is a genuinely nice guy."

"He doesn't expect everything to be about him!" Vonda added.

"Although he does like some things done his way," Gabby commented, referring to the low-alcohol lunch. "He is not the ultimate party boy."

"What do you mean?" Kendra inquired curiously.

"She means that he doesn't drink much," Janny replied. "It didn't bother us particularly."

"Speak for yourself," Gabby retorted. "I felt lonely with my sole glass of wine. He could have joined me."

"At least he let you order it," Vonda said. "Some non-drinkers can be really critical of anyone who does order a drink. He just treated it as your choice."

"You girls could have had some too," Gabby remarked somewhat resentfully, "To keep me company."

"We didn't really want any alcohol," Alison said. "It seems you have an issue with all of us and not just Anthony."

"I wouldn't like to feel left out either," commented Deborah equitably. "Come on Gabby, you can talk to me as I prepare for the evening date."

Gabby and Deborah were not a natural pairing, but it appeared they had found something in common. Gabby relaxed and followed Deborah to her room.

The Candidate House was a hive of activity for the next hour, as one group of girls gossiped and unwound from their lunch date, while another group prepared for their evening date. The majority were wearing jeans and stretch tops, for they had been warned the venue would be casual and even a little chilly. A selection of jumpers and coats had been laid out to go along with their owners.

Leticia, observing the excitement in the air, spent a moment feeling sympathetic towards the Charity Eligible, who had a mere two hours in which to rest and change, before he was due to pick up the second lot of girls.

"We scheduled it pretty tight!" she thought. "But I bet he is loving every minute of it."

Anthony arrived back at the Candidate House around seven in the evening. He had been expected at six-thirty, but a phone call had warned the girls that the Charity Eligible was running behind time. Nadine, Kendra, Rozanne, Deborah, Orb and Ebony were all on the porch waiting eagerly.

"We are so glad to see you," Nadine exclaimed candidly. "We thought our turn would never come!"

"I am sorry I am late," Anthony said. "I had such a good time this morning, I wasn't nearly ready to go out again!"

"I hope you have some energy left for the second shift," Rozanne remarked teasingly. "We want to have every bit as much fun as the morning group."

Anthony threw his arms wide in mock exasperation: "Ladies, Ladies," he said, "I am afraid I can't live up to such great expectations!"

"Calm down everyone," Deborah ordered. "I am sure there is something lovely planned."

Kendra nodded. "I have every confidence in you Anthony," she said. "Would you like to tell us what are we doing?"

"Yes," Ebony added. "Everyone is dying to know."

"Leticia tells me that the television station has hired one of the smaller Sea Catamarans for our use," Anthony said. "We are having our very own cruise of the harbour and private boat party."

"Cool!" Rozanne exclaimed.

"We'll get into the limo and be on our way," Anthony said.

The Charity Eligible held the door open for the girls as he had that morning. Rozanne scrambled in immediately, and Ebony followed her quietly. Deborah and Kendra said, "Thank you," as they clambered past, and Nadine commented on his lovely manners. This time it was Orb who sat in the front with the Chauffeur.

When they were all seated, the limousine drove through the dusky streets towards Darling Harbour. The street lights came on just as they approached, and everyone gasped in delight.

"Look at the reflection on the water," Nadine cried.

"It is beautiful," Kendra agreed. "Which one do you think is our boat, Anthony?"

"I don't know," Anthony said. "Perhaps we should look for around for a sign."

"I reckon it is that boat over there with all the bright lights," Deborah said.

"Let's go over there and see if we recognise our camera crew," Rozanne said. The short haired girl jumped out of her side of the car and ran ahead while the others disembarked in a more leisurely fashion. She returned grinning: "It's okay," she said. "I have seen Simon Steeple. He is setting up the cameras to film us walking onto the boat."

The party walked across the dock towards the railing. A sloping plank led up onto the boat, and Anthony ceremoniously assisted Nadine and Ebony in their climb onto the deck. Then he turned and walked back down the ramp to lend an arm to Deborah and Kendra. Orb refused to accept his assistance.

Rozanne was the last to be ushered on board, and she grinned at Anthony cheekily. "Just so as you know," the short haired girl remarked, "I only play the helpless female for the camera. Other than that, I am perfectly capable of being independent."

"I thought it was an extremely romantic gesture!" Nadine exclaimed. "It reminded me of the olden days, when gentlemen lifted ladies out of horse-drawn carriages." The brunette patted Anthony's hand, and he flushed slightly.

"I am not used to being the centre of everyone's attention," Anthony said. "I thought that I ought to be a gentleman while on the show. However, I got the impression the morning girls didn't know what to think when I opened the limousine door for them."

"The other girls might have been surprised," Deborah commented. "So few guys behave in a courtly manner today."

"A gentleman is honourable all the time and not just when he is opening doors," Kendra said. "But it was a nice way to start, Anthony."

Orb refused to comment. She knew the other girls had been impressed by Anthony's chivalry, and expected several of the more assertive ones would take her to task if she criticised the Charity

Eligible for being old fashioned.

The engines shuddered as the boat got under way, and the few sea-gulls who had roosted on the railing squawked and flew off in alarm. Presumably the birds would find somewhere else to settle.

"Let's explore the boat," Ebony said. "Debating our social customs doesn't really matter to me."

Anthony agreed and surged ahead with Ebony by his side. He had noticed that the fair girl steadfastly refused to be drawn into small talk, and while he admired what Ebony had told him about her work, he was eager to find out more about her as a person.

"I was interested in the things you were telling me yesterday," Anthony said.

Ebony shrugged modestly. "I might have gone on a bit," she said. "I can get like that about my research. However, no one really understands what I am saying."

"You are right," Anthony said. "I didn't understand everything. What I did understand was your dedication. I have thought of specialising in a specific type of surgery myself."

"I see," Ebony said. "There is no real connection to my field though."

"No," Anthony admitted. "The parallel is an ideological one. I honour your ability to focus on one area of endeavour."

"Oh...," Ebony murmured, "Thank you." The girl seemed embarrassed by the compliment. "It is nothing really."

"I think it is a big deal," Anthony said. "It put you into the group of girls I wanted to know more about."

"Mm," Ebony barely responded. "What else could you want to know?"

"How old are you?" Anthony inquired.

Ebony looked embarrassed. "Twenty-five," she said.

"I am thirty," Anthony said.

"Oh, really," Ebony replied. She was obviously uncomfortable with this line of questioning.

Anthony concentrated on talking to Ebony for a few more minutes, but no matter how hard he tried, it was impossible to get past the polite facade with which the girl had surrounded herself. He fell silent in frustration, and glanced around to see what the other girls were doing.

The spirited Rozanne darted back and forth, looking at things that caught her attention; while Deborah and Kendra were talking to each other. Nadine and Orb brought up the rear. They had circled once around the deck and then descended into the body of the boat. Anthony hastened to catch up with the group.

The interior of the catamaran consisted of a cleared area, which could be used as a dance floor, a state of the art stereo and light system, and a cafe bar. The walls were lined with a long bench seat, and windows looked straight out over the water.

"The boat is superb!" Nadine gasped in delight. She crossed over to the port-side and sat down to enjoy the view. Kendra and Ebony went to join the pretty brunette beside the window.

Rozanne spun around the dance floor in an inelegant funk routine. "We can have ourselves a real party tonight!" she exclaimed.

Deborah threw Anthony a challenging look. "You don't mind if I go and get myself a beer from the bar do you?" she said.

"Go ahead," Anthony said. "Be my guest. I wouldn't have picked that as your drink though."

"Sometimes the simple things in life are the best," the Socialite retorted. "And I wanted to see the expression on your face!"

"I thought as much," Anthony said. "You always make your point, Deborah!"

"Makes life interesting doesn't it Anthony?" Deborah said.

"Yeah sure," Anthony said. He was a bit surprised at himself. Sparkling repartee was not usually his forte, but Deborah did have a knack for drawing those around her out of their comfort zone.

Anthony crossed the boat and approached Nadine and Kendra, who parted to allow him to sit between them. Orb also shuffled along to make room for them. Ebony avoided his eye, and Anthony reflected it was almost as if he had frightened her with his attempt at meaningful conversation before. "Are you having a good time girls?" he asked.

"Yes thank you Anthony," Kendra said.

"It is wonderful," Nadine gushed. She had stars in her eyes as the lights reflected back from the water.

"Can I get you a drink?" Anthony asked.

"Oh yes," Nadine said. "A coke for me!"

"Lemon squash," Kendra said.

"What about you Ebony?" Anthony asked.

"I don't know," Ebony said. "Maybe a coke."

"I can get my own drink," Orb added stiffly.

"Two cokes and a lemon squash coming up," Anthony said and made his way across to the bar. "Are you coming Orb?"

"Yeah sure," Orb said. She stood up and accompanied Anthony to the bar.

"Thanks for helping me carry the drinks," Anthony said after they had placed their orders. "I'm sorry if this is not your sort of evening."

"The boat is fine," Orb admitted grudgingly. "It is just that if I were out on a normal date with a man, we would be good friends and behave like equals."

"I would honestly prefer that too," Anthony said. "But I've got to start somewhere getting to know the girls." He picked up several of the glasses. "How is your thesis coming along?"

Orb flushed. "I, err can't get a lot done here."

"So being on the show is a bit of an inconvenience?" Anthony sounded amused. "Why did you say yes then?"

"You do seem like a nice guy," Orb said. "The show isn't my style, but the company is actually all right."

"I'm glad to hear it," Anthony said.

The Charity Eligible and Orb passed Deborah and Rozanne at the stereo as they returned to the main group of girls.

"What sort of music do you like?" Deborah called.

"Rock and roll," Anthony replied.

Rozanne pulled a face, but Deborah dialed up a fifties classic. She grabbed Rozanne by the hand and pulled her into a couples dance. Anthony laughed as the girls both did a spin.

"You don't see that too often," he said. "Which one of you is the man?"

"You are," Deborah said. "We fully expect you to join us later!"

"I can barely waltz," Anthony said. He collected the drinks and returned to the seated group of girls. "Did you see that?" he asked.

"It looked like fun," Nadine said wistfully.

"I might manage to shuffle with you later," Anthony said.

Rozanne changed the music and some techno rhythm filled the room. She started into a jerky routine and attempted to induce Deborah to mirror her. After a couple of steps the socialite gave up and a friendly scuffle broke out between the two girls.

"Should we break that up?" Nadine asked in concern.

"I think they are okay," Kendra said. "It looks good natured."

"I expect a hot meal will be served to us soon anyway," Anthony said. "Would you believe they are actually cooking at that little bar?"

In due time they were all called across to a little table set into the ship wall and served a simple meal of fish, with a choice of chips or salad. Luckily no one had any allergies and all were able to enjoy the food.

After dinner was finished, Anthony invited Rozanne out onto the upper deck for a stroll.

"You've obviously been having fun," he said as they emerged into the open air.

"Yes!" Rozanne said.

"You must be the youngest girl here," Anthony said.

"I am older than I look," Rozanne said. "I am actually twenty-four!"

"I would have guessed something like twenty-two," Anthony said. "Except for your line of work."

"Ah!" Rozanne said. "I have been working in schools since around then. As long as you are qualified, being young helps you relate to the students."

"And you are planning to stay young at heart, I guess," Anthony said.

"As long as the fire burns in me," Rozanne said. "You are not planning to get old in a hurry are you?" she teased.

"I am not in a special hurry," Anthony said. "Although, being a doctor, I often have to take a serious approach to life."

"You need someone to shake that out of you after hours," Rozanne said flirtatiously. She leant up against him, and Anthony thought she might be expecting a kiss. However, he did not know how to read her cues and could not be sure. He froze in embarrassment and confusion.

"I think we should get back to the others," he stammered awkwardly.

"Okay," Rozanne said amiably.

Anthony was relieved and puzzled. He thought he might have mistaken Rozanne's stance the moment before. Most girls wouldn't be thinking of kissing a guy on a group date with a lot of other girls present anyway.

When Rozanne and Anthony arrived in the hold, they found Nadine, Deborah and Kendra gently stepping around to some popular music. Ebony was curled up on the bench and Anthony suspected she might be asleep.

True to his promise, Anthony slow danced with Nadine and Kendra. Nadine was very pleasant to hold as she relaxed against him, and Kendra was surprisingly light and confident on her feet. Anthony attempted one or two waltzes with Deborah, but she challenged him too much with her competition steps.

The night passed away in a whirl, and rays of light began to colour the water long before the party expected.

"I am sincerely glad I am not driving!" Anthony exclaimed, glancing at his watch. "Limousines do have their uses."

"I will have to sleep all day!" Nadine exclaimed.

"I'm sorry I stayed up all the other night," Deborah admitted wryly.

Rozanne giggled and Orb clucked reproachfully. She didn't really approve of the socialite, but did not have the temerity to take her on.

"Let's wake Ebony," Kendra said in a caring tone. "We are pulling into dock."

CHAPTER FOUR: A CASUAL DAY BY THE POOL

Janny, Alison, Vonda, Betty, Gabby and Constance were puzzled to find themselves alone with Leticia at breakfast the next morning.

"The other girls went straight to bed," the Hostess said. "They didn't return until early this morning."

Eyebrows were raised all around the table, and a wave of discontent ran through the group.

"They stayed out all night with the Charity Eligible?" Constance exclaimed jealously.

"They were booked onto a boat cruise," Leticia said. "I am sure that nothing untoward happened with the camera crew around and everything."

"Still, they got a much longer date than us," Gabby remarked, displaying only mild dissatisfaction. She appeared to have recovered her equilibrium since her talk to Deborah the previous day.

"They had to go second, and then their date lasted longer," Leticia said. "Those sorts of things happen. It is all part of the game."

"What do we do today?" Alison asked curiously.

"Anthony won't be over for the carnation ceremony until this evening," Leticia said. "And the other ladies will be asleep. Therefore your time is your own. I will be around if you need anything, but I will be working on the arrangements for the next segments of the show."

Leticia retired to her office, where they could hear the sound of muffled telephone conversations; and the girls looked at each other.

"I am going for a swim," Janny said. "My exercise routine is a bit lacking since I've been shut up in this house."

"That sounds good for starters," Alison said. "I think I will join you."

"I vote for spending the whole day in the pool area as we are stuck together," Gabby said. "I will see the housekeeper about drinks and all the necessary items for a barbeque."

Vonda asked to be excused, as she said she would prefer to read a book. "I will join you lunch time," she said. "In fact, if you can arrange it with the housekeeper, I would be happy to cook."

Janny and Alison swam firm laps up and down the pool, while Constance circled around more casually. Betty's hourglass figure was flattered by her underwire bather top as she floated lazily. Gabby returned with a large cooler box packed with beer and soft drink and placed it on the side of the patio. The she dived in and began to overtake the other two on their laps.

Alison stopped and began to tread water. "Hey you are good!" she said.

"Of course!" Gabby replied. "I do this all day, every day for a living. Would you like some pointers on your stroke?"

Alison and Constance allowed Gabby to coach them on their freestyle, but Janny determinedly continued her lap programme. When she had finished, she swam across to the others.

"I just do it for the exercise," she said. "I don't really care what I look like."

"Actually you are quite competent," Gabby said generously. "Have you ever thought of getting your scuba ticket?"

"No," Janny said. "I assume my fair skin would be a problem, and I do prefer an indoor pool setting."

"You would wear a wet-suit and heaps of other protection," Gabby said. "I think you would be okay."

"I will think about it," Janny said. "But I'm mostly too busy performing on stage or teaching dance."

"Speaking of fair skin," Alison said, "I am a red head and Betty is a natural blonde, even if she does admit to adding a few highlights with her wonderful cosmetics. We had better get back under the veranda."

Constance, Betty and Alison climbed out of the pool and settled themselves down on lounges in the shade. They donned their sarongs and wraps, and reapplied sunscreen just to be safe. Janny and Gabby continued to swim, lapping the pool until they were exhausted.

"Even I can get out of practice," the dark haired Gabby announced, clambering out of the pool and grabbing a towel. She cracked open the cooler and selected a beer. "Let's get this party under way. Where is Vonda?"

"I will go and get her," Constance volunteered, and departed into the villa.

Constance re-appeared a few minutes later with Vonda, followed by the housekeeper and a trolley. Vonda and the housekeeper lit the barbeque and started the food preparation.

"We have sausages, onions and buns," Vonda announced. "There is sauce too."

"I will leave you to it," the Housekeeper said. "I hope you have fun with your cooking!"

"Oh I will," Vonda said. "I love cooking, even simple things like this."

"Very good miss," the Housekeeper said.

Vonda called Alison over to set out the plates, and soon the smell of sizzling sausages filled the pool area.

"How perfectly Australian," Gabby exclaimed, helping herself to another beer. "All we need now is a man or two."

"There is only one of those on the show," Janny said, "And we are not allowed to do what we want with him!"

"What a pity," Constance said. "I have been dreaming about Anthony ever since yesterday." She sighed and settled back onto her banana lounge in a romantic languor.

"I bet none of us have been dreaming about that one," Alison said, as the blonde-bearded figure of Simon Steeple hove into view with a camera carrier under one arm, and swimming trunks in the other. He was of average height, had an athletic figure and hair that almost reached his shoulders. "Yet he ain't bad looking."

"He isn't the object of the game," Janny said. "Talking of which, from what I saw yesterday, Constance has the prize in the bag!"

"Either that, or she is riding for a fall," Alison said cautiously.

"Don't say that to Constance," Janny said sharply, looking around to see whether the dark haired girl had over-heard.

"Oh, I wouldn't," Alison said. "Not unless I thought it would be of some help."

"Well," Gabby said challengingly, "Which one of us is going to pull Simon Steeple into our net?"

"I don't know," Janny said. "Why don't you use your model girl charm Alison?"

The impasse was broken by Vonda, who in complete ignorance of the other girls' intentions, bounded up to Simon and offered him a plate of sausages. The long-haired fellow put his camera aside on a ledge in the shelter and accepted the food.

"Oh wow!" Gabby exclaimed. "It's the shy ones you have to watch after all!" She led the girls toward the barbeque. "Serve us too, Vonda."

Soon the candidates and single cameraman were all seated around the outdoor table, feasting themselves to repletion. Even Alison ate two plate's full of bread and meat. Then the housekeeper appeared with a stunning serve of pavlova and ice-cream for each of them.

"Oh my diet," Alison moaned as she sunk a spoon into the delicious desert.

Simon swiveled around to face the model. "Surely you girls don't need to diet," he said.

"I need to be a size ten for some jobs," Alison said. "And at my height, that is quite a challenge."

"Photographically speaking, you would look lovely with a little more weight on," Simon said. "I suggest you forget those impossible jobs."

"You may be right," Alison said. "What do you think Janny?"

"I agree," Janny said. "I've always found exercise a good substitute for extreme dieting, and if your employers don't want a naturally fit figure - tell them to go off and photograph someone else."

"That's exactly what I'm afraid of," admitted Alison. "I'm twenty-nine this year. I will be dropped sooner rather than later."

"You shouldn't have to kill yourself for work," Vonda said.

"I have natural curves," Betty said, "I maintain my optimum weight and the guys love it."

Gabby hooted in delight. "Like I keep telling you girls, you've got to have a bit of fun," she said. "Where is another beer?"

"I think you have had enough," Janny said valiantly. "I hope you weren't thinking of going for another swim in that condition."

"Nah," Gabby said. "I was going to get some cards. I know just what game to play while Simon is here."

"I'm not really meant to be playing with you girls," Simon began to object conscientiously, but Alison laid a slim hand on his knee.

"Come on," Alison wheedled in her best modelling tone. "We are all bored. Surely you would only be doing your bit for the show by entertaining us?"

"If you put it like that I can hardly refuse," Simon said.

"Although I don't know what Leticia will say if she catches me! "

Gabby raced into the bedroom and returned carrying a pack of playing cards. "Who knows how to play poker?"

Vonda went red. "I think I know what is coming," the musician said. "And I can't play because I really don't know the rules."

"Simplify it for the beginners," Alison said. "We will each draw one card, and the lowest score loses an item of clothing."

"Stop at our bikinis for goodness sake!" Constance exclaimed.

"Set some ground rules," Simon said. "Anyone who doesn't want to lose another item of clothing has to jump into the pool and stay there for the rest of the game."

"That sounds fair enough," Constance said. "Although I've never done anything this naughty in my life."

"Then it is about time you started," Gabby remarked sharply, and Constance flinched.

"Don't worry," Janny said, "It is really only the thought that is naughty."

"Ah...but what a delicious thought," Simon said. He leered at Alison, who responded by pulling a face at him; and winked at Constance, but she was so wrapped in thoughts of the Charity Eligible that she barely noticed. The cameraman looked mildly disappointed.

The game provoked many hoots of laughter as one and then another of the girls lost their outer wrap. Then Simon lost his watch and shirt in quick succession, and jokingly accused Gabby, who was the dealer, of cheating.

"You will never know, will you?" the Athlete replied, pressing another card upon him.

Simon turned the cardboard over and groaned. "Tell me girls - does the ace represent one or eleven in this game?"

"It's a one if you are holding it!" Alison replied.

Simon groaned and unbuckled his belt. "This game is getting dangerous," he said. "And I notice you have me in the centre of the circle."

"Yeah," Gabby said. "We are a bunch of wild women, and you are loving it!"

Janny was the next one to lose, and she kicked off a sandal.

Then Simon lost both of his shoes, and a sock.

"This game is definitely rigged," he said, looking at Gabby. "You must be a regular card shark!"

"No, I will prove it to you," Gabby said, and passed all the cards to Alison.

"I don't trust you either," Simon said, as he found himself divested of his other sock. Now he was stripped down to his jeans.

Vonda lost her earrings, and then Simon found himself holding a losing card once more.

"That does it girls," he shouted, and picked Constance up bodily. He trotted over to the side of the pool and walked out onto the spring-board. "I am going into the pool Constance and all!"

There was a splash and everyone cheered. They gathered around the edge of the pool and waited for the struggling pair to re-emerge.

"What is going on here?" Leticia exclaimed, appearing out of the large lounge. "I can hear your voices from my office."

"We were just playing a game," Vonda said.

Simon's bedraggled head bobbed to the edge of the pool, and he clambered onto the siding. "I am sorry Leticia," he said.

"Simon Steeple!" Leticia said sternly. "Have you been molesting my girls?"

"No miss," Simon said. "You could more likely say they have been molesting me."

"Well just remember, while they are on the show, they belong to the Charity Eligible," Leticia said.

"Yes boss," Simon said. "I hope he evicts them all real soon, I do! They are a bunch of horrors."

"Well that may be," Leticia said. "But you have to get yourself dry and ready for work by this evening. How come you are awake anyway, I thought you were on the boat with the others?"

"I was that miss," Simon said, "But I can't rarely sleep during the day."

"So long as you can stay alert tonight," Leticia said. "We should have a classic of a carnation ceremony."

The girls looked around at each other. "We had almost forgotten the carnation ceremony!" Janny said.

"I wonder who will leave?" Alison said.

"I have to go to get changed and make sure it isn't me," said the dripping Constance.

"I think I'll take a short nap," Gabby said. "I've swum, and I've drunk and I've laughed until I'm tired."

"I'm going to have a shower," said Vonda. "See you later!"

Tea was served in the communal dining room, which had been decked out with balloons. Leticia had invited Simon to attend, although it was an hour before he was due to start filming.

"Your behaviour this afternoon was vaguely unprofessional," the Hostess said. "However, it is my judgement that you had better get out amongst the girls and break the ice; or else we will have some of them snickering whenever you point a camera in their direction. That would show up on screen most oddly."

"Your wish is my command boss," Simon replied.

Leticia gave him a sharp look: "You aren't after any girl in particular, are you Simon? I have warned you before that could ruin the show."

"I assure you I know my place," Simon responded. "It was the girls that started the fun and games."

"Six bored girls sitting around in one place," Leticia said. "I can see how that could happen."

Simon handed his camera equipment to his apprentice George. He then approached Constance, who was just entering through the door. She looked lovely as ever in a blue shift-dress.

"How are you?" the Cameraman asked.

"I am sort of okay," Constance said. "It isn't every day that some clown throws me into the pool."

"I'm sorry," Simon said. "I was in a tight spot!"

"I know it was in fun though," Constance added. "I am not going to hold it against you."

"That's good," Simon said. "I would hate to have offended you. Leticia has set up a refreshment bar over there, can I get you something to drink?"

"Not just now thank you," Constance said. "I want to talk to Kendra and Ebony. I haven't heard how the evening date went last night."

"It looked okay to me," Simon said. "There were no great dramas."

"That is not what I am wondering about," Constance said. "And I think it would be best to get a female's point of view."

The neat brunette turned and crossed the room, leaving Simon standing alone a few meters from the door.

Deborah, who had come up behind the Cameraman, coughed: "Don't worry about Constance," she said. "She only has eyes for the Charity Eligible at the moment."

"That is understandable," Simon said, looking Deborah up and down. She looked particularly cool in a cream shirt-waist dress, checked with light brown. "I hope you don't mind my saying you look lovely tonight."

"Compliments are always welcome," Deborah said. "How come you aren't burdened with your camera tonight?"

"I gave my camera to George," Simon said.

"Ah, the assistant," Deborah said. "I must say, he looks like a cheerful fellow."

"He is pretty good," Simon said. He looked at Deborah conspiratorially. "Actually, I am meant to be doing some damage control."

"I heard some was needed," Deborah said dryly. "Do you dance at all?"

"Actually I do," Simon said. "How about we go across to the stereo."

Anthony arrived a few minutes later, and Simon was forced to say goodbye to Deborah. "Thank you so much," he said. "Duty calls now."

"Get lots of lovely film," Deborah said. A minute later she was deep in conversation with Alison.

Rozanne approached the Eligible. "Did you have a good time last night?" she inquired.

"As a matter of fact I did," Anthony said. "It is not every day a guy gets to spend the night on a boat with five lovely girls."

"Did anyone in particular stand out?" Rozanne asked. She was stunning as usual, encased tightly in a black mini skirt and pink off the shoulder tee-top.

"It is too soon to say," Anthony said diplomatically. "Although your conversation is always very stimulating."

Rozanne looked flattered. "I enjoy talking to you too," she said. "And I enjoyed our walk on the deck."

"Hmm," Anthony said. It was the deck incident that puzzled and concerned him. However, he had too reserved a personality to ask for clarification. "Well, it was all very pleasant. Shall we get something to eat?"

There was a group of girls congregated around the table, and Anthony found himself talking to Janny. She looked beautiful in an amber sheath dress.

"Did you hear what Gabby got us all up to this afternoon?" she asked.

"No," Anthony replied. "Do you want to tell me, or is it secret women's business?"

"I am happy to tell you," Janny said, and recounted a short version of the story.

Anthony laughed. "It is funny," he said, "Although I am glad it was Simon and not me."

"Yeah that's what we thought," Vonda said. She was wearing a light floral print that complemented her delicate features. Its styling was loose and modern.

"Actually, I have been wondering about something," Anthony said. "I have danced with a lot of the girls, but not with you Janny."

"That would be because I am not really a social dancer," Janny said. "I do ballet."

"I only shuffle," Anthony said.

"That I can do," Janny said. "And a little bit of waltz. I will catch you sometime later."

"That would be fun," Anthony said. "I don't care what it looks like, I am losing some of my inhibitions on this show."

"That's a good thing," Vonda said. "And I think it is happening to me too!"

"I am glad to hear it," Anthony said.

Constance claimed his attention then. "I have been waiting for you," she said. "Although I did get into one or two other pretty deep conversations."

"That's okay," Anthony said. "I was happy to see you talking to Alison."

"I guess you have heard about my little misadventure," Constance said, blushing fiercely. "I assure you I don't behave like that all the time."

"I didn't think you did," Anthony said. "Everything I know about you so far points to you being my type of girl."

"I am so glad to hear that!" Constance said, sliding a hand

through the loop of Anthony's arm.

Nadine across the other side of the room, tensed. "Oh no!" she said to Deborah. "It looks like they are an item already."

"You are such a romantic," Deborah exclaimed. "This is only a game."

"I believe it would be possible to meet the right person on a show," Nadine said. "Indeed you could meet them anywhere."

"Indeed," Deborah said. "And I think we all have about the same chance with Anthony at this stage."

"Oh no!" Nadine murmured. "I am sure I felt something special last night."

"Last night was pretty cool," Deborah said. "I think Anthony liked a few of the girls."

"Well I am going to go and say hello now," Nadine said. "I am sure Anthony would like to speak to me in particular. Come on Kendra, help me join the group around him without looking too pushy."

The two girls crossed the room, Nadine confident in her purple pant-suit, and Kendra casual in a green halter-neck frock with a full skirt. As Nadine had predicted, Anthony was pleased to see them, and the three singles talked for a few minutes.

Everyone's attention was caught by a series of popping sounds as Leticia began circling the room symbolically bursting balloons. "It's time for Anthony to go into the deliberation room now," the hostess said. "We will see him again in the small reception room in about half an hour."

Everyone sighed, and little bits of coloured elastic scattered across the room like confetti. "You have a sick sense of humour Leticia," Deborah remarked.

"Yes!" Leticia agreed. "It goes along with the job!"

Having learnt from the previous carnation ceremony that he would regret any lack of attention to detail, Anthony spent his half hour deep in thought. He reviewed his interactions with all the girls, and while he concluded at the end that he was still of the same mind about which girls to keep and which two girls to let go, he was able to congratulate himself on the thoroughness of his decision making process.

When Leticia came to collect him, Anthony was doing a final check of the portraits laid out before him. "They are all very attractive," Leticia remarked, following his gaze.

"Yes," Anthony said. "Therefore I cannot choose on their looks."

"I am curious," Leticia said. "How are you choosing the girls this time?"

"At this stage, it is about how open and pleasant they have been to me," Anthony said. "I haven't known them very long, so I have to take their word on their interests, and the degree of compatibility they feel for me."

"That is an interesting idea," Leticia said. "I take it you are satisfied?"

"Yes," Anthony said. "I think this carnation ceremony will be fairly painless, it is the later ceremonies that will be complicated."

"Well, let us go and see if you are right," Leticia said.

When Anthony and Leticia arrived in the small reception room, the girls were milling around nervously. At a signal from Leticia, the girls arranged themselves in a line along the back wall, and Anthony walked to his place beside the end table.

"Hello again everybody," the Charity Eligible said. "The good news is that I have ten carnations to give out, so ten of the twelve of you ladies will continue dating me."

Anthony coughed nervously because of the cameras. "I am hoping that each of you ladies will accept the carnation I offer you. Two ladies will not receive a carnation, but I trust that you will see this as an opportunity to get on with your lives outside the show."

Leticia handed Anthony the first carnation.

"Here goes," The Charity Eligible said. "Rozanne, you are a bright and interesting young woman. Will you please accept this carnation?"

Rozanne bounced up and took the carnation in her hand. "Of course I will accept the flower Anthony," she said. The short-haired girl threw her arms around Anthony and gave him a hug. "I hope to have many more great dates with you."

"Thank you," Anthony said. He allowed Rozanne a minute or two to return to her place in the line, and then selected a carnation from off the table.

"Alison," he said. "You are as clever as you are beautiful. I want you to remember that, and wish you will accept this carnation."

Alison glided up to Anthony and gave him a kiss on the cheek. "When you put it that way my dear," she said. "I just have to accept the carnation."

Anthony blushed and fumbled for another carnation. "Kendra," he said, "You always have a kind thought for another. Please accept a flower from one who has kind thoughts for you."

Kendra walked forward and accepted the carnation. "Thank you Anthony," she said. "That was very poetic!"

"Yes," Anthony said. "I am amazed at myself. Being surrounded by all you ladies is turning me into a regular greeting card."

"You don't look white and rectangular to me," Kendra said, and everyone laughed. Kendra returned to her place, and Anthony collected another posy.

"Constance," Anthony said. "I want to offer you a flower with all my heart."

Constance beamed as she stepped forward. "Am I to take that literally?" she said.

Anthony looked confused. "I meant I was sincere," he said. "Anything else must have been a slip of the tongue."

"A Freudian slip," Constance said, giving him a hug. She looked entirely satisfied.

Leticia pressed another flower into Anthony's hand and he looked around the group.

"Nadine," he said. "You are sweet and lovely. Please accept this perfumed offering from me."

A couple of girls clapped, and Nadine walked forward to accept the carnation. "You are very sweet yourself Anthony," she said.

Leticia whistled: "Compliments are flying fast and free," she said. "Try to keep your minds on the job!"

Anthony selected another carnation and held it out. "Deborah," he said, "I don't know what we would do without you."

"I do," Deborah said, coming forward and giving Anthony a firm peck on the cheek. "You would get lost in a romantic maze."

"Most likely," Anthony said. "So I am asking you to stick around and guide us for as long as possible."

"I'll see what I can do," Deborah said. She took the carnation and continued back to her spot.

"Betty," Anthony called and the blonde beauty stepped forward. "I have been pleased to discover you are as good natured as you are beautiful. Please accept this carnation and grant me the pleasure of your continued acquaintance."

"When you put it like that Anthony, " Betty laughed, "I cannot resist."

"Vonda," Anthony said, "I am so glad that you are still with us, and I am thrilled to see you coming out of your shell! Please accept this carnation."

Vonda blushed as she walked up to Anthony. "I am having fun," she said, "So I think I will stay around a little longer."

Anthony handed the carnation to Vonda and gave her a little hug. Then he picked up the second to last carnation. "Two to go," he said. "I would like to give this flower to an especially good natured lady. Janny, will you stay here with me?"

"Why certainly!" Janny said with energy and optimism. She collected her carnation and returned to the group.

"Gabby," Anthony called. "This is my last carnation, please say that you will accept it despite our few differences?"

"Sure," Gabby said. "I am having a lot of fun on the show, so why wouldn't I stay?" The lively girl collected her carnation and joined the other girls in the group.

As Gabby stepped back into position she tipped the camera a generous wink. Simon Steeple suppressed a chuckle, and shifted the focus of the camera to pan across the candidates' faces coming to rest upon the sweet face of Constance for a few frames.

"Ebony," Anthony said, "I guess you have worked out you are not getting a carnation by now. I have really tried to get to know you, but I can't seem to get you to open up. Hence, I am letting you go back to your job, and all the things that seem to matter most to you."

"You have put me on the spot," Ebony said looking a bit white. "But I have to say that you are right and there are no hard feelings."

Ebony said her farewells to the girls sedately, and then left the room.

"Orb," Anthony said. "I wish you all the best with your studies. I have enjoyed getting to know you, but expect you can use your time out of here more fruitfully than on the show."

"I must admit you are right, Anthony," Orb agreed. "You are a nice guy and you have proved you can see beyond the surface; but this show is still designed on a premise of inequality."

Leticia signalled to George to film Orb making her final activist statement. Letting that go to air would reduce the number of legitimate complaints the girl could make against the production. The women's rights activist then waved goodbye to the other girls and stalked out of the room.

The girls who had been selected clustered around Anthony thanking him for giving them a carnation. "It was my pleasure," he said, and smiled happily.

CHAPTER FIVE: A ROSE HAS THORNS

There was a certain amount of nervous twitter amongst the girls the next morning because they had heard that Anthony was going to begin selecting the girls he found most compatible for individual dates. Up to this time, interactions between the Charity Eligible and the ladies had been limited to large cocktail parties and relatively impersonal group dates.

Constance, Nadine and Rozanne were all visibly crossing their fingers and hoping they would be picked, with Rozanne in particular expressing the belief that as she had received the first carnation last ceremony, she ought to be the forerunner in the dating stakes. Janny and Kendra were nursing their secret yearnings; while Betty, Deborah and Alison were quietly confident, and expressing much less concern.

Vonda said she would be happy whatever the outcome, as she was having a lot of fun and getting to know people. Gabby also said that she would be happy to continue hanging around beside the pool, so long as there were hunky cameramen to harass and sufficient beer to drink.

The girls were all chatting and speculating regarding who would receive the single dates when the phone began to ring. Constance was the first to move, leaping up and racing across the tiled floor.

"Hello," she said, lifting the receiver, "Constance speaking."

"Hi Constance," Anthony said. "Is everyone there?"

"Yes," Constance said. "Everyone is here. Shall I put you on speaker?"

"Not yet," Anthony said. "I want to speak to you first. I know it sounds corny, but would you come to the movies with me?"

"I would be delighted," Constance said.

"It is not just any old movie," Anthony said. "We are going to the Fox Australia Studio complex where they have all the production sets and memorabilia."

"I can't wait," Constance said. "It sounds great, and the main thing is - I will be with you!"

"That's good," Anthony said. "You had better go and change, because the limousine will be picking you up in an hour."

"Okay," Constance said.

"Put Kendra on the line now," Anthony said. "I want to speak to her next."

Constance handed the phone to Kendra: "I have the first date," she said. "It sounds like you have the second." The neat brunette trotted off into her bedroom to prepare for the outing. She looked pleased and excited.

Kendra accepted the phone. "Hello Anthony," she said. "It's Kendra."

"I was wondering if you could help me with something," Anthony said. "I am trying to work out something that will suit Vonda. She didn't have such a good time up the tower. Would you like to ask her if a drive to the Rose Farm up on the coast would be to her taste?"

"Just a minute," Kendra said. "Vonda do you like the sound of a Rose Farm?"

"Oh yes!" Vonda said. Her eyes were shining. "Tell Anthony it was nice of him to think of it."

"Vonda likes the idea," Kendra said into the phone.

"Do you think it would suit the rest of the girls?" Anthony asked. "I mean to ask Deborah, Alison, Betty and Rozanne."

"It sounds pretty good to me," Kendra said, "but I will ask the others to be sure." She pushed the speaker phone button and turned around. "Deborah, Alison, Betty and Rozanne, is a Rose Farm of any interest to you?"

"Just dandy," Deborah said. "I'm putting in an order for shortbread with my tea."

"Fine by me," Alison agreed. "I'll wear a wide brimmed hat."

"It sounds novel," Betty said. "I don't mind going gardening for once."

"I was hoping for something more exotic," Rozanne said sulkily. "But I guess it would be okay." Truth to tell, the girl was bitterly disappointed not to have been selected for the single intimate date.

"Almost everyone is happy Anthony," Kendra said.

"I heard," Anthony said. "Thank you Kendra. I will see you all early tomorrow, and we will make a day of it."

"Goodbye Anthony," Kendra said. "We will see you later then."

The limousine arrived for Constance around eleven that morning, and drove her around to the Charity Eligible Residence, where Anthony was waiting out on the front step. He leant into the car and greeted her warmly.

"Hi there Constance," Anthony said. "You look very pretty in that silky blouse and full skirt. I do like you in pink and other pastel colours."

Constance laughed. "Actually, my top is mauve," she said. "However, I am impressed by the compliment. You look pretty smart yourself."

It was Anthony's turn to look flattered. "I hope you didn't mind coming around here this morning," he said. "I thought you might like a peek at the place they have got me for lodging."

"It looks lovely," Constance said, observing the façade and beautifully landscaped front garden. "And I am the first girl to see it!"

"I am sorry we don't have enough time to go inside," Anthony said, "But we are due at Fox Studios Australia by twelve. So we had better get under way."

"I agree," Constance said easily. "I always like to be punctual."

"We do so match!" Anthony exclaimed, sliding into the seat beside her.

Anthony and Constance arrived at the studio complex a little before twelve, and were able to take a casual stroll around before their formal tour commenced. The studio complex had been built on the site of the former Sydney Show Grounds at Moore Park and occupied around 32 acres.

The site was about 15 minutes by car from the Sydney Central Business District, given light traffic of course, and featured eight sound stages, several production offices and workshops. There were also almost 60 independent entertainment industry businesses co-located at the site.

The studio had been involved in the production of a number of blockbusters, including The *Matrix* films, *Moulin Rouge!*, *Mission: Impossible II*, *Star Wars* (Episodes II and III), and *Superman Returns*. The reception area featured several large rooms, all floored with a bright plush pile carpet. The walls were attractively painted, as well as being hung with a variety of prints and posters.

Anthony studied the posters intently. "I don't get to the movies a lot," he said, "But I do like to know what is coming out, and what would be worth seeing."

Constance giggled. "I think some of these films have already been released," she said. "In fact, some are very famous."

Anthony shrugged. "Shows how out of touch I get," he murmured.

"It's fascinating," Constance said. "There is such a variety of genre. I can see everything from blockbuster thrillers, to science fiction and romance."

Anthony stopped beside a model of a sailing ship. It had been set up on a display table with a number of figurines, some artificial water and grass. "I wonder what movie that is from?" he murmured.

"I could hazard a guess it is something literary or historical," Constance said. "And it sure is cute!"

"I love the detail," Anthony said. "If I had the time, I would learn to sail an old style ship."

"Oh you should, if you want to," Constance exclaimed.

"I might get around to it someday," Anthony said. "Ah, I see someone official looking. It seems our tour is starting."

The studio guide, who was a young man called Tobias, took them through the studio, chatting all the way. The special guests were shown the cinemas, the projection rooms, and several displays of costumes and props on loan from America. Constance viewed the garments with delight, and asked which actress had originally worn them.

Anthony asked to be allowed to hold a wooden sword used in filming fencing matches. He was surprised to find it was quite heavy. "I would have to work out to use this," he commented.

"Yes," Tobias said. "Some of the actors have been weight lifters and martial arts champs. On occasions when the actors themselves are not able to wield these implements, a stunt double is required to do the muscle work. However, some of the famous action heroes take especial pride in doing their own fight scenes."

"I can imagine," Anthony said. He ran a finger along the edge of the sword. "It is almost sharp!"

"It has to look convincing without actually killing anybody," Tobias said.

Tobias then led Constance and Anthony into a darkened, secluded room. He handed them both a set of glasses and activated a switch. "This is our three dimensional, or virtual reality set-up," he said.

"It is fascinating," Constance said, reaching her hand out before her. The display altered as her appendage intruded into the projection space, and she jumped: "It's almost scary!"

"Let me try," Anthony said. He walked forward a couple of steps and laughed. "I am surrounded by the picture!"

When the visitors had finished experimenting with the three dimensional set-up, Tobias led them into computer room. "You are especially lucky today," he said. "We have installed a programme which allows the user to generate their own special effects for a short movie clip."

"Wow!" Anthony said. "Do show me how this works."

"Well," Tobias said. "A short disaster sequence has already been programmed into the computer. You use this menu to choose whether you want the background to be light or dark. This changes the flood scene from night to day."

"I see," Anthony said, "I want night please."

Constance hit the correct button, and the screen darkened. The sky was now a dark blue and the water almost inky black, with lighter patches and wrinkles to indicate movement. "That's cool," she said.

"Now," Tobias said, "You get to choose whether you will have lights in the houses along the bank, and whether there is a fire in the background."

"Turn everything on Constance," Anthony said. "I want to see what happens."

Constance pushed another couple of buttons and stood back to survey the effect. "It's a right proper catastrophe," she said.

"Most of the work is already done for us," Anthony commented. "Someone has already programmed the images."

"Yes," Tobias said. "The CGI artwork can be very complex and time consuming."

"I see how it works now," Constance said. "It is so clever. I never expected to learn such things at the cinema."

"Movie making is a complex art," Tobias said. "It utilises the imagination of writers and artists, and the skills of craftsmen and technicians."

"I am impressed," Anthony said. He put an arm around Constance and she snuggled closer. "Do you have anything else to show us?"

"That is the grand and deluxe tour completed," Tobias said. "I understand that you two are scheduled to have lunch at the nearby cafe before attending a private screening of a black-and-white classic."

Constance and the Charity Eligible spent the lunch hour discussing their respective workplaces and other medical related issues. The time passed quickly and it was obvious they did have a lot in common, at least in a career-wise sense.

At the end of the lunch, Anthony said: "Interesting though this conversation has been, it shows me that we are both very serious people. I believe that if we had met in the course of our natural lives, we would not have taken the time to get to know each other."

"I think I would have always fancied you, Anthony," Constance said. "But like you say, you might not have asked me out in a workplace environment. I think that it is wonderful we have gotten to know each other socially!"

"Oh so do I," Anthony said. He reached across the table and took her hand. "Let's go to see our movie."

The dating couple were led towards an exclusive side cinema, with cushiony seats and a modest sized screen. An organ had been moved into the room, and a musician played an accompaniment to the film, for it was an old black and white comedy-romance with no sound-track. The live music filled the room and made the movie viewing a unique and interactive experience. During the movie, Constance and Anthony were able to snuggle together without much being picked up by the television cameras.

They were comfortably quiet on the drive back to the Candidate House, and after Anthony dropped Constance off, he got out of the car and led her around into the shrubbery, intending to give her a passionate kiss. To his surprise, the neat dark-haired girl pushed him away.

"I just can't," Constance said. "Not without something more from you."

Anthony frowned. He was perplexed. "I thought you had been giving me romantic signals ever since we met," he said.

"I admit that I have been dreaming about us commencing a

relationship," Constance said. "But I need to feel secure before I kiss someone. Can you promise me that I'm likely to be the one you pick at the end of the show?"

"I'm sorry Constance," Anthony said in resignation. "I just cannot give you that assurance under the circumstances. I am due to date other girls over the next week or so, and I can't make promises to anyone yet."

"I think I might really be falling for you," Constance whispered, "But I still need more of a relationship before I can kiss you."

"I'll discuss it with you another time," Anthony said. "I think I had better go now though." He appeared uncomfortable and was clearly keen to exit what had become an embarrassing situation.

"I guess so," Constance said. She appeared truly conflicted, but unable to think of anything more to say, she turned and walked into the Candidate House.

Anthony was preparing to climb back into the car and leave, when he heard the slight creak of the front door. He spun around expecting to see Constance had returned, and found himself greeting Janny and Vonda who were hovering in the hallway: "How are you girls?"

"We are fine," Janny responded.

"We had an enjoyable afternoon," Vonda said. "Swimming and watching some television."

Kendra appeared briefly at the top of the stairs, and Anthony gave her a wave. "Come down here," he said. "I have a moment or two before I have to leave."

"It is nice to see you again Anthony," Kendra said soberly as she descended the stairs.

"You look like you have something on your mind," Anthony said.

"There was something," Kendra murmured. "I don't know whether I should say exactly." She glanced around at Janny and Vonda, who both nodded encouragingly. "We are all concerned about Rozanne," Kendra continued. "The girl won't join our games, and she seems a bit depressed."

"We think she might have been expecting an individual date today," Vonda said. "She may have been frustrated about having to stay home."

Anthony frowned. "Nine girls missed out on an individual date today, and the majority of them are dealing with it well," he said. "From what I hear you girls have a pretty good time while you are waiting. I sometimes wish I could come over and hang around with you myself."

Kendra looked amused. "Maybe you will be able to get away with that sort of thing later in the show," she said. "However, everything seems very structured at the moment."

"Thank you for telling me anyway," Anthony said. "I just don't know what I can do about it - Rozanne is a resolute and active girl with a definite mind of her own."

"Perhaps you could talk to her," Kendra said.

"She has been invited on tomorrow's group date," Anthony said. He was eager to avoid another awkward tete-a-tete with one of the girls. "She should feel better then."

"Yeah that's true," Kendra said. She smiled: "I am sure things will work out the way they are meant to in the end."

The next day, Vonda, Deborah, Kendra, Betty, Alison and Rozanne busied themselves getting ready for their trip to the Rose Farm. The majority of the girls chose to wear attractive stretch tops, or cool cotton blouses over casual skirts or shorts. Several girls packed a hat, sunglasses and sunscreen.

Anthony was due to arrive around nine in the morning. Six ladies and one gentleman made for an unwieldly group, so the television studio had hired a mini-bus to transport them all in some sort of comfort. The bus was also packed with a picnic hamper and an ice chest full of drinks.

The Charity Eligible jumped to the ground and greeted all the participants. Then he welcomed them onto the bus. A sort of hierarchy formed immediately, with Anthony on the back seat together with the quieter girls, Kendra and Vonda.

Deborah, Rozanne and Alison, who were all more outgoing, chose seats toward the front of the bus, and at first they got on very well together, talking and laughing throughout the trip. Betty sat somewhere in the middle, linking the two groups.

The Rose Farm was situated on the Central Coast, which was over an hours' drive from Sydney, depending on traffic conditions

along the freeway. When they arrived, everyone was very impressed
by its beauty and tranquility. There were rows upon rows of roses
being cultivated on an open acreage.

Towards the side, a greenhouse had been set up to nurse young
cuttings and delicate new bushes. A small fountain decorated the
nearby visitor's area, and several wooden love seats hung from metal
frame-work beneath the branches of some large trees.

Vonda and Anthony immediately headed towards one of the
swings, and squeezed onto it. The seat had adequate room for two,
although it may have been designed to hold teenage lovers rather
than full grown adults. They sat there for some time, swinging and
talking.

"It is charming out here isn't it?" Anthony said.

"Oh yes," Vonda responded. "It reminds me of a symphony."

"Tell me more about your music," Anthony said. "How long
have you been playing?"

"I have been playing since I was about six," Vonda said. "I think
it was hard at first, but then it became second nature." Her face
became dreamy. "I can paint pictures with the sound, and dream my
dreams."

"Did you bring your violin on the show?" Anthony inquired.

Vonda looked shy. "Why yes, I did," she said.

"Would you play for us one night?" Anthony said.

"I don't know," Vonda said considering. "I may need an
accompaniment."

"Think about it," Anthony said. "No pressure, mind you."

The pair fell into a dreamy silence, enjoying sitting together and
drinking in the rural surroundings, while the slight breeze was gentle
and soothing.

Betty and Kendra walked through the garden. They were thrilled
by the variety and scent of the roses. Kendra located one of the
horticulturalists, who told her that new varieties of rose were being
propagated all the time. Kendra asked when she could acquire some
blue roses for her garden at home, and she was told that the new
species would be released onto the market as soon as the plants were
commercially viable.

Deborah, Rozanne and Alison were joking together as they
walked the perimeter of the garden. To all intents, they appeared to
have become each other's new best friends. Snippets of conversation

blew across the garden, and it was evident they all liked an active life. Ignoring their surroundings, Deborah grabbed Alison and demonstrated a few marching manoeuvres. Alison laughed and showed off her own style as a former cheerleader for a football club.

When the girls had wearied themselves, they returned to where Anthony and Vonda sat. A few minutes later, Betty and Kendra, who had completed their information gathering, joined them and everyone decided to open the picnic hamper and break out the drinks. It was a bit early for lunch, but everyone agreed that the country air had given them an appetite.

Kendra adopted the role of hostess, distributing sandwiches, cold chicken and salad onto paper plates. Deborah turned bar-tender, pulling out a can of beer each for Rozanne and herself, and pouring soft drink for the rest.

Anthony relaxed and allowed the group activity to flow around him. It was pleasant to be able to allow the girls to do their own thing, and not try to impress them all the time. He had found Vonda a very restful companion, and assumed that he would enjoy the company of the other girls at various times throughout the day.

After lunch, Kendra invited Anthony to accompany her in taking a closer look at a sundial she had seen located in a space between the beds of roses. It was obvious that Kendra anticipated a few minutes intimate conversation with the Charity Eligible, but Alison also volunteered to join them.

The model girl was plainly accustomed to being the centre of attention, and was confident that she would be welcome with the other two. Neither Kendra nor Anthony wanted to hurt the red-head's feelings, so they politely included her in their jaunt.

When they returned, Deborah was settled on one of the tree swings. The socialite invited Anthony to join her, but Alison rushed ahead of him and took the seat. Alison quickly fell into an animated conversation with Deborah, who shrugged and waved apologetically at Anthony.

The Charity Eligible was startled, and looked around for an alternative position. Observing Rozanne seated alone on the other swing, Anthony chose to join her. Here he was in for another surprise. The short-haired girl, who had been animated that morning, was going through some sort of mood variation. She barely acknowledged his presence and refused to enter into conversation.

"What is wrong?" Anthony asked at last.

"I don't know exactly," Rozanne said. "I think it's that there are too many girls on this date. None of us will get to talk to you much. Besides Vonda, that is."

"I am talking to you right now," Anthony said.

"Nah," said Rozanne. "If you had wanted to talk to me, you would have picked me out a long time ago."

"Is this about the individual dates?" Anthony said. "I could only assign one, even though there were several ladies I wanted to spend time with."

"Yeah I know," Rozanne said noncommittally. She continued to swing in silence.

"No one else is upset," Anthony said. "Look at Kendra, she even had to share her potential alone-time with me. Alison joined us and it was very pleasant, but not the same."

"Kendra is a saint," Rozanne said. "I am not like her - I have more intense feelings."

"Ah feelings," Anthony sighed. The Charity Eligible was a somewhat stereotypical reserved male. He did not like to discuss a lady's inner feelings, unless she expressed herself in the most unthreatening way possible. He guessed it was a hang-up he would need to overcome to develop a relationship. "I am trying to be fair and respect everyone's feelings."

"I am not everyone," Rozanne said.

" I can see you feel that," Anthony said. "You are special.... However, I do think you need to calm down and let this process play itself out. You never know, it might be fun."

Rozanne looked doubtful. "I like to take hold of life with both hands," she said.

"I admire that," Anthony said. "But there is a time and place, and what puzzles me is that you work as a counsellor and should therefore be able to manage your feelings!"

"You are assuming that repression is a good thing," Rozanne retorted. "I am all about self-expression."

"Self-control isn't all about suppression," Anthony began, but he stopped. He knew he had a point, but was the first to admit his arguments might be weak. As an undergraduate, he had studied a little psychology, but his focus had been mainly upon the mechanics of the human body and disease.

The pair fell into an uncomfortable silence. Eventually, Anthony stood up and left the sulky girl to her thoughts. He walked across to the greenhouse, where Deborah and Vonda were admiring the roses.

The other girls welcomed him in the nursery area. Anthony walked up and down beside the worktables exclaiming at the delicacy of the new bushes, and Vonda pointed out a hydroponic tank in which cuttings were being germinated. Betty crossed over from the far side of the greenhouse to join the group.

One of the gardeners, obviously charmed by her film star looks had presented Betty with a basket of cut flowers. Vonda admired Betty's basket of flowers and began to cast eyes around for a friendly gardener who might cut a few blooms for her.

The party had been in the greenhouse for about a quarter of an hour, when Rozanne raced inside. Ignoring the others, she went straight up to Deborah and eyed her challengingly.

"You bitch!" Rozanne cried.

Deborah looked mildly amused. "I am often a bitch," she said. "Which particular piece of bitchery is bothering you now?"

"I thought you were my friend!" Rozanne stormed.

"I will be your friend as long as you want me," Deborah responded. "It is a bit difficult at the moment though."

"How come you didn't ask me to come in here with you?" Rozanne cried.

"Do you really want me to answer that?" Deborah inquired. "I didn't know you wanted to come. Besides, the rest of us go wherever we want. I'm sorry, but this isn't primary school you know."

Rozanne glowered: "You stopped HIM asking me," she declared.

"I assure you I have no control over Anthony," Deborah said. "He makes his own decisions."

"You are always interfering," Rozanne cried.

"I regret that is my personality," Deborah said. "You will just have to deal with having me around."

Rozanne hissed in exasperation. "You don't get it do you?"

"No I don't!" Deborah declared. "I'm sorry, but I think you are making me the scapegoat for your myriad of frustrations."

Rozanne glared at her and stomped off.

Alison wandered inside. "What was all that about?" she asked.

"I don't know," Anthony said. He looked embarrassed: "Rozeanne is either lonely or jealous, although I can't for the life of me see that she has reason to be either."

"I think that she is used to coming first with people," Vonda said carefully. "At home that might be natural. Either that, or she is deeply in love with Anthony already."

Anthony looked seriously perturbed. "No," he said, "If Rozeanne thinks she is in love, it is too sudden to be real."

"It would be total fantasy," Alison said, "But she might very well think it was real."

"Do you think we should go after her?" Vonda said timidly.

Anthony looked alarmed. "No," he said firmly. "Let her cool off. I have already tried cheering her up once this afternoon. You saw how ineffective that was."

"Kendra has it under control anyway," said Alison, and looking out into the garden, they could see the empathetic girl speaking calmly to Rozanne.

Around three o'clock the Bus Driver approached and suggested the party board the vehicle in preparation for a return to the Candidate House. This time Deborah and Vonda sat up the back, while Betty and Kendra chose seats in the centre.

Anthony went to sit beside Rozanne, but she still appeared sulky, so he crossed over to the other side of the aisle to sit beside Alison. Alison welcomed his presence and chatted cheerily all the time they were driving along.

The group left the Rose Garden around three o'clock in the afternoon, and arrived back at the Candidate House around four-thirty. Anthony said goodbye to the girls and hopped back onto the bus to ride back to the Eligible Residence.

The girls retreated to their respective rooms to unwind. The majority of them were laughing and talking. Constance, who had been home all day along with Janny, Nadine and Gabby, waylaid the girls in the hallway.

"You were away a long time," Constance observed nervously.

"We did a lot of things," Kendra said. "There was a drive, a rose farm, and a picnic lunch."

"It sounds lovely," Constance sighed wistfully.

Rozanne looked at Constance sharply. "Don't worry," she said. "It really wasn't that good."

"You did get to talk to Anthony for a while Rozeanne," Deborah murmured reasonably.

"Just you shut up!" Rozanne snapped. "I can do without your sarcasm."

"Oh dear," Deborah said. "I had forgotten you were mad with me."

"You have nothing to fret about Constance - at least you got the individual date," Rozanne turned, and stamped her way towards her room.

"What is wrong with her?" Constance asked.

Vonda shrugged: "None of us know for sure. Why were you being so inquisitive anyway?"

"I don't know," Constance said. "My date went well yesterday, and then afterwards...I had so many doubts...I don't think I am cut out for this sort of thing either."

"So you spent the whole day worrying?" Kendra hazarded a guess.

"Something like that," Constance admitted. "I did watch some good movies though."

"Cheer up," Vonda said. "You can talk to Anthony later this evening. I am sure he will re-assure you."

CHAPTER SIX: TOUGH DECISIONS

A sea-food buffet had been set out in the communal dining room that evening, as Leticia had decided that would best fulfil the varied needs of her guests. Constance, Janny, Gabby and Nadine were both well rested, while the other six were fatigued after the day-trip.

Anthony arrived at eight and went straight inside to join the girls. He picked up a plate and began to pile it up with food. Being an active male, he was always ready to eat another meal.

"How are you this evening?" he said to Nadine, who was hovering nearby.

"I'm good I suppose," Nadine said. "It was quiet at the house today and even Gabby did not start anything much!"

"I think all the noise and activity came along with me," Anthony said. "With six girls involved in the one date!"

"How did the group date go?" Nadine asked curiously.

"It was interesting," Anthony said. "There were so many different personalities involved, I fear I may have neglected a girl or two. There is also someone I need to clarify a few things with."

"Good luck with that," Nadine said. The pretty brunette patted Anthony on the arm, and then headed across the room to sit on a chair. She moved with an elegance that showed she was conscious of her ability to attract the eye.

Anthony turned from watching Nadine and gravitated left to where Deborah stood. "I trust you and Rozanne are all sorted now," he said.

Deborah shrugged. "It doesn't seem possible," she remarked. "Rozanne doesn't share a bedroom with me, she is actually supposed to be rooming with Vonda and Kendra. However, she followed me into my assigned room to continue this afternoon's argument."

"Oh really?" Anthony said. "I find it hard to imagine any girl going that far."

"She seems truly miserable," Deborah said. "I went into the shower to escape, and she waited outside the bathroom door until I was finished to start in again. I told her that I wanted to be friends, but nothing seemed to help."

"I am sorry if she is bothering you," Anthony said, somehow feeling vaguely responsible. "I'm not very happy with her myself. I genuinely tried to spend time with all of the girls who did not get an individual date, but every time I try to speak to Rozanne, she spurns my overtures."

"Don't worry about me," Deborah said. "I've survived disagreements before. It's not surprising as I seem to attract them! Work out what you want to do for yourself."

"Yeah," Anthony said. "Thank you." He turned to Alison who was standing alongside Deborah: "Did you have a good time today?"

"Oh yes," Alison said. "The Rose Farm was pleasant and it was a long date - therefore pretty good value, even with six of us along!"

"I am glad to hear it," Anthony said.

Alison extended an arm, which was showing slightly pink. "I got a touch of the sun," she said, "But I've put some moisturiser on. It should be okay."

Anthony continued his circuit of the room, and found himself talking to Janny and Vonda. The girls greeted him warmly.

"It's a nice evening isn't it?" Janny said.

Anthony agreed.

"I do so like the cool of dusk," Vonda said. "With the lights around the pool here, it would be ideal for a pajama party."

"You must suggest it to Leticia some time," Anthony said. "I would be happy to attend - I can't have that Simon Steeple having all the fun again!"

Vonda laughed. "That won't happen," she said, "Simon does work hard behind that camera."

"Except he seems to be having a spot of bother over there," Anthony said. They glanced across at the cameraman, who was busy replacing a light bulb in the spot-lamp.

"I guess those can go anytime," Vonda said.

"It has put a halt to filming," Janny said. She sidled up to Anthony and eyed him conspiratorially. "Anything we say for the moment will be off the record."

"Oh wow Janny," Anthony said. "Such freedom! I haven't gotten to speak to a girl without it being recorded for at least a week."

"Make the most of it while it lasts," Janny said. "Simon is pretty much finished. Filming will now resume."

"No there is another problem," Vonda said. "Rozanne is blocking George off from the camera equipment. She seems to be arguing with him."

"Whatever would she find to complain about?" Janny said. "The camera crew are all so very well behaved."

"Well whatever it is, George looks considerably frazzled," Anthony said.

"Leticia has taken it in hand," Vonda said. "She is talking to Rozanne."

Kendra joined them then just then. "Did any of you see the sunset?" she asked. "It was absolutely beautiful. I watched it from the herb garden. In fact, it gave me an idea for an album cover design."

"That sounds nice," Anthony said vaguely. He was looking around for Constance, whom he had barely seen since their individual date. She appeared to be keeping a low profile. At last he spied the neat brunette around the other side of the pool.

Anthony hurried across to speak to her: "Hello Constance".

"Hello Anthony," Constance returned. "Did you have a good day?"

"Pretty good," Anthony answered. "What did you do?"

"I went to the video room to view some of my favourite movies on the television," Constance said calmly. "All the movies seem so much cleverer now than they did before yesterday."

Constance did not say anything personal, or refer to their single date in any other way. Anthony assumed that she was not ready to discuss their relationship. He was not sure whether to be relieved at being spared the recital of her emotions, or disappointed at the lack of feedback.

"Let's go inside for tea," he suggested kindly, and Constance agreed.

As they entered the dining room, however, Anthony found himself face to face with Rozanne. It was the opportunity for which he had been looking. Constance discretely joined the other girls, and Rozanne and Anthony were left facing one another.

"Rozanne," Anthony said. "I would like to speak to you privately."

Rozeanne looked apprehensive, but she nodded. "The others are all on the other side of the room," she acknowledged.

"I am concerned about you," Anthony continued. "You started this process bright and happy, and now you are at odds with everyone."

"Yes," Rozanne admitted. "I haven't been very comfortable today."

"You obviously don't appreciate the company of the other girls," Anthony said. "And that is a problem. There is only one of me, and I cannot be with everyone at once."

"I know," Rozanne said. "I have found this situation much more stressful than I expected....I am used to a very full lifestyle, and the men I went out with always gave me their undivided attention."

"I am sorry I can't make favourites at this stage," Anthony said. "And if it is upsetting you this much, I think I ought to send you home."

"Oh no!" Rozanne exclaimed. "Let me stay. I will try to hang on until we are all having individual dates."

"There will always be a lot of waiting around," Anthony said. "If you can't play the game, you would be better off out of here. I hate to see you unhappy."

"Please, please, please don't send me home," Rozanne cried. She caught hold of Anthony and clung to his jacket. "Give me another chance, do!"

Anthony disengaged himself slowly. "I have thought this through very seriously," he said.

It was clear to the Charity Eligible that it would be best for everyone if Rozanne were to go home, but he was unable to think of a way in which he could reconcile the girl to the idea.

"Rozanne," he said. "I am so sorry. I need to ask you to leave even though there is no carnation ceremony tonight."

"Oh no," Rozanne said. She spoke through her teeth, and a tear or two slid down her cheek.

"I want you to be happy," Anthony said. "And that so obviously isn't happening here. Please try to see things that way."

Rozanne buried her face in her hands, and began to sob. Kendra and Vonda appeared from the double doors and raced to her side. They threw their arms around the girl and supported her out of the range of the cameras.

Janny and Nadine also rushed to give their support to Anthony, who looked almost as devastated as Rozanne. Rejecting someone was hard work, especially in such a public situation. Deborah, Constance and Alison stood quietly, attempting to look neutral.

When Kendra and Vonda returned from escorting Rozanne out, Leticia made an attempt to rally everyone's spirits.

"I am sure Rozanne will be all right when she gets back with her family and friends," the Hostess said. "I don't usually give an opinion, but I think Anthony did a wise thing in Rozanne's case."

After breakfast the next morning, the girls lay down on banana lounges beside the pool to await further instructions from Leticia. It was a lovely sunny morning, and Gabby and Janny had been swimming until they were exhausted. A few of the other girls had been splashing around in the pool for fun and when they got out, everyone settled down to sunbake.

The mood was somewhat somber due to Rozeanne having been asked to leave the previous evening. Some of the girls had not slept well that night and consequently dozed off to sleep on the sun lounges. They were lost in a dream world when the shrill peals of a telephone sounded across the patio.

Vonda and Janny woke suddenly, and stretched and blinked. Alison and Kendra jumped up, and looked around in disoriented amazement, while Gabby broke off from a snore and rubbed her eyes sleepily.

"Where are we?" Alison exclaimed.

"Out by the pool," Kendra said. "But I didn't know I had fallen asleep."

"We all must have," Vonda said languidly. "Wow that phone is loud!"

"I am glad we didn't miss it altogether," Constance said.

It was Janny who was first to lift the receiver that morning. "Hello," she said. "Oh Anthony! We weren't expecting you. Yes – I know Gabby and I missed out on the group date yesterday – oh how nice."

Janny turned to Nadine: "Anthony wants to speak to you now."

Nadine took the phone. "Hello Anthony," she said. "It's Nadine speaking."

"Hello Nadine," Anthony said. "How are you this morning?"

"I am very well," Nadine said. "And I have been looking forward to hearing from you."

"I am happy to hear that," Anthony said. "I was wondering whether you would like to have dinner tonight with me in Chinatown? We can eat and then look around."

"It sounds lovely," Nadine said. "Thank you for asking me Anthony."

"I will collect you this evening then," Anthony said. "Could I speak to Janny again?"

Nadine turned to Janny: "Anthony is taking me to a Chinese restaurant tonight," she said. "He wants to talk to you now."

Janny spoke to Anthony a few more minutes and then hung up the receiver and turned to the other girls.

"An unexpected group date!" she exclaimed. "Anthony will be here to pick up Kendra, Betty, Gabby and me soon."

"Do you know where we are going?" the girls cried.

"Some Art studio," Janny said. "And we have the mini-bus you girls used yesterday."

Gabby frowned: "It's only a small complaint," she said, "But Kendra and Betty went on the group date yesterday."

"I get what you are saying," Deborah acknowledged. "But yesterday's group date was very hectic. I guess Anthony figured he did not get to talk much to them."

Gabby and Deborah were usually friends, but Gabby remained unconvinced and refused to allow Deborah to console her. "It's not fair," she wailed.

"Unless it is something else altogether," Alison suggested. "The Charity Dating Show has been known to throw the occasional spanner in the works!"

"What do you mean?" Janny asked curiously.

"She means it could be an elimination date," Gabby exclaimed glumly. "Just my luck. And the type of date – an Art studio – it sounds like it was especially designed for Kendra - so she won't be the one leaving."

"I'm sure it won't be an elimination date," Kendra remarked confidently. "Not with Rozeanne having left last night!"

"Come on, let's make the best of it," Janny said. "Perhaps Anthony thought that two girls and one guy might be too awkward."

"In comparison to four girls and one guy do you mean?" Gabby scoffed, but she joined the general race to the bedrooms to change out of their bathers into casual clothes.

It was not long before Anthony arrived, and the quartet all piled onto the bus. The automobile traversed a couple of winding roads, and emerged at a point where the freeway and the local roadways were connected. The tea-shop combined gallery showed up as a delightfully rustic cottage set back on a spacious block.

Two rooms had been transformed into a display centre for pottery and paintings, and the third was in use as a workshop. The business was managed by a mature lady who introduced herself to the group as Frances, and her daughter, Megan. Frances described herself as a great cook and keen potter, and Megan as an Artist and business-woman.

Kendra, who loved all things creative, began to browse the paintings along the wall. "Are these all yours?" she asked Megan.

"Most of them," Megan said. "I have one or two friends who paint as well."

"I love your style," Kendra said. "You are quite lavish with the use of colour, and it makes a rich canvas."

"You sound as though you know a bit about oil colours," Megan said.

Kendra looked pleased. "Actually, I am a graphic artist," she said. "Most of my work is done on a computer. However, I did learn to sketch by hand, and have done one or two oil paintings."

Kendra and Megan fell into a technical conversation in which they compared the use of several different artistic medium. Anthony, who was hovering nearby, was secretly very impressed. Their conversation opened up a new world to him, and he thought it would be wonderful to know more about the creative Arts.

Betty and Janny, who were intrigued by the row of home-style pottery, asked Frances to demonstrate the use of the potters' wheel for their benefit. Frances waited until Gabby was ready to join them, and then led the way into the back room. She started the wheel rotating, and selected some moist clay from out of a sealed container. Anthony and the girls all exclaimed in delight as a symmetrically shaped bowl took form under the potter's hands.

Janny and Betty both begged to be allowed to have a try, and Frances lent them smocks.

"I keep a few spares here for when I run classes," the Potter said.

Janny eagerly kneaded the clay into a ball, and placed it onto the spinning part of the wheel. It slid across to the side, and she moaned in shock. "It looked so easy when you did it!" she said.

The others all had a turn, and one by one, they gave up in despair. Betty surprised everyone by proving to be the most skillful. Her clay did not turn into a pot, but it did at least stay upon the wheel.

"You have an excellent hand for a beginner," Frances remarked.

Betty blushed. "I usually sell pretty things, not make them," she remarked.

Kendra entered the room, and seeing that she had missed the demonstration, commented that she would like to paint a pot that had already been moulded. Frances obligingly produced a few pots that had previously undergone one firing.

"You can paint one each," the Potter said. "I will put them into the kiln and dispatch them to you care of the television station later."

"Cool," Janny exclaimed, "Our own personalised pot."

The girls and Anthony set to, and worked steadily for about half an hour. Between them, the group produced an array of pots, ranging from those with a plain coloured stain, to those with simple geometric patterns.

Everybody but Gabby seemed very happy with the results.

"I'm having a bad day," the dark haired girl said dully, surveying the pot she had just painted.

"It is fine," Kendra said. "The base coat is good, and the only fault lies in that line of paint which smudged when you tried to add the second colour."

"I don't know," Gabby said. "I like to do everything well."

"Some things are new," Betty said soothingly. "They take practice."

"Look at my pot," Janny added. "It looks like a crazy person put all those spots onto it."

"Well it was made by you!" Gabby returned a little more pointedly than was warranted.

Janny laughed and pretended that Gabby had made a joke. The other girls exchanged glances warily. They hoped Gabby was not going to begin stressing out the way Rozeanne had the previous day.

"Could we have that tea now?" Kendra asked. She hoped that liquid refreshment would soothe Gabby.

"An excellent idea," Anthony said. He looked at their hostess. "Would you be ready to serve us Frances?"

"Of course," Frances said. "Do come into the tea room."

The Devonshire tea included scones and jam, with a generous helping of cream. There were short-bread biscuits on the table, and a pot of tea. Frances offered to percolate coffee for those who preferred the stronger drink. Gabby looked up at that and inquired hopefully whether the café was licensed, but Frances shook her head regretfully.

"We looked into it once," Frances said, "But there is too much paperwork and red-tape involved in maintaining a licensed venue, and our main focus is the artwork."

"That's a pity," Gabby muttered, but she subsided and allowed herself to be served coffee.

The girls had barely begun to eat however, when Leticia appeared.

"I heard a rumour that this might be a surprise elimination," the Hostess said.

"Oh no!" Janny exclaimed. "That Alison!"

"I think you might have heard wrong, Leticia," Kendra joked. "None of us are due to go home yet."

"I'm afraid someone does have to go," Leticia said. The hostess turned to Anthony. "You must choose one woman to leave with me now, and the other three will ride home with you."

It did not take Anthony long to decide who he would jettison from the group. According to the other girls, Gabby was an instigator of fun at the Candidate House, but she had little in common with the serious Doctor. The boisterous girl had also displayed her impatience with his temperate way of life several times. Therefore she was the obvious target for this elimination.

"Gabby," Anthony said. "I think that you and I both know that you were looking for a different type of guy. I wish you luck in your search."

"That's cool," Gabby said, rising to her feet and slapping her hands against her legs nervously.

Gabby was disappointed, because she had been enjoying her time on the show, but she had already dismissed any idea of a relationship with Anthony.

"You win some and you lose some," the Swimming Instructor pronounced. "It was good while it lasted."

The brunette said goodbye to Kendra and Janny and stalked out of the tea room alongside Leticia. Anthony found that he was mildly relieved to have her gone. Her disappointment with his personality had hung over him like a cloud.

Climbing into the bus on the way home, Anthony looked for a chance to sit beside Betty and congratulate her on her talent with the pottery wheel, but the beautiful blonde did not glance in his direction.

Anthony hovered indecisively in the bus aisle for a few seconds, waiting for some sign of interest on the Monroe-look-alike's part. Completely oblivious, Betty slid into the seat beside Janny and they began gossiping good naturedly about the surprise elimination.

If Anthony had been more assertive he could have asked to sit beside Betty, but she appeared comfortable socializing with the other girl. After a moment, Anthony's insecurities overcame him and he decided to sit beside the calming and comforting Kendra instead.

When they reached the Candidate House the girls and the Charity Eligible shared a brief goodbye; then Anthony left Kendra, Betty and Janny to explain Gabby's absence to the other four because he had a date with Nadine that evening.

CHAPTER SEVEN: NADINE SCORES THE FIRST KISS

Anthony arrived back at the Candidate House to pick Nadine up around six o'clock. He looked around for Constance, but she was nowhere to be seen, and he concluded that she was still keeping a low profile. In any case, the only polite thing the Charity Eligible could do was concentrate upon Nadine, who was his current date. She was looking truly stunning in a fluorescent melon coloured evening gown with a body hugging silhouette.

"Hello," Anthony said. "I love your outfit!"

"Thank you," Nadine said. She executed a tiny pirouette: "It's not too showy for a simple dinner is it?"

"I don't know these feminine technicalities," Anthony said. "But you do look absolutely delicious. I trust you are ready to go now?"

"Oh yes," Nadine said. "I am very hungry, as well as quite excited! Goodbye Kendra, goodbye Vonda and Janny."

"Goodbye Nadine," the girls chorused. "Have a good time!"

Anthony opened the car door, and the couple climbed inside. They made themselves at home on the rear passenger seat.

"There is plenty of room here," Nadine said, stretching out her legs.

"Yes," Anthony said, "It is almost wasted on the two of us."

"It means we can lounge around," Nadine commented. "I feel sort of comfortable with you."

"I know what you mean!" Anthony exclaimed. "It seems really easy for the two of us to relax together. That is one reason why I picked you for this date."

"Only the one reason?" Nadine asked coyly.

"Your looks counted too," Anthony said. "I do find you attractive." The Charity Eligible put an arm loosely around his date's shoulder, and she accepted the gesture in good faith. They made no attempt to become more intimate.

The limousine drove through the city centre and promptly entered the colourfully lit precinct of Chinatown. Here the character of the architecture altered dramatically. While some of the buildings were tall, they adopted a narrow-fronted east-Asian structure. Other buildings were relatively short for the inner-city. Electric lanterns hung from the front verandas of these slant roof buildings, and bright cross-hatch script glowed upon prominent signs.

"It is truly exotic," Nadine whispered.

"I know," Anthony said. "It is fun!"

The limousine came to a halt in front of a radiantly lit Chinese restaurant. Although it was clearly solid brick, it had an exterior facade of bamboo screening, and a small flight of steps led up to a recessed doorway. The interior consisted of one huge room, and the white walls were papered with pictures of finches, parrots and other more eastern species of bird, while the floor was a mosaic of cool grey slate.

A man in traditional Chinese attire hurried forward to meet them: "Welcome, welcome honoured guests," He said. "I am Mr. Lim. Happy to offer you special evening."

"We are happy to be here," Anthony responded truthfully. He was warming to the place already.

"I must take you to meet chef," Mr. Lim, the restaurateur said. "Then you cook own meal."

"I say!" Anthony exclaimed. "I didn't expect anything like that...and I am starving already."

"Oh our staff chop," Mr. Lim said, "But you learn to fry."

Nadine tugged Anthony by the arm: "Let us do what he says," she begged. "It could be a lot of fun."

Nadine and Anthony followed the restaurateur into the kitchen area. Here a number of benches were occupied by workers preparing ingredients, and throwing the various stir fry selections onto a huge row of sizzling flat-plates. A gleaming set of sinks along the far wall testified to the hygiene standard of the establishment.

"This is our cooking area," Mr. Lim said proudly. "And this is our head chef, Wong."

Chef Wong ceased his work momentarily to acknowledge the visitors. "You are from the television show," he said. "I will make sure you have nice meal. What is your favourite Chinese dish?"

"Satay beef," Anthony said.

"Honey chicken," Nadine said.

"Good choices both," Chef Wong said. "I will also show you ginger vegetables. They are sweet with a little bit of spice. And fried rice, lots of fried rice."

He gave a clipped order and the workers began assembling the ingredients for the dishes named. Chef Wong showed them how to fry the beef and the chicken, getting just the right texture and flavour for each distinct dish.

"There you are," Chef Wong said. "I reckon you don't know how to do that at home. I keep cooking a little longer while you fry rice and vegetables."

"Thank you," Anthony said. "It smells delicious."

"I have made enough for two," Chef Wong said. "So you can try each other's favourite dishes."

The rice was prepared by the staff and sprinkled with small pieces of meat and bean sprouts. Chef Wong placed it on a hot-plate in front of Nadine. "You stir that now," he said. "Keep it moving and make it nice all over."

Nadine set to with a will, and Anthony was assigned the ginger vegetables to sauté. The dishes were ready within minutes, and the couple were allowed to scoop them onto oval. The plates were placed upon two trays, so that they were easy to carry.

"You are good cooks," Chef Wong said. "Go and sit at your table now. The waiter will bring you drinks and anything more you require."

Anthony and Nadine enjoyed their meal, for they were all the more hungry after the effort of frying it themselves. Anthony attempted a few bites using chop sticks, and then gracefully accepted the offer of western cutlery from the Waiter, Nadine persisted for a little while longer, and then gave up in frustration.

"I am getting left behind," the lovely Brunette said.

"I was too hungry to persist in learning to manipulate the chop-sticks," Anthony said. "I suggest you change over to a fork too."

They washed the meal down with soft drink and espresso coffee, before finishing up with fried ice-cream.

"I am so full," Nadine said, laying her spoon aside at last.

"So am I," said Anthony. "But it was really good to eat!"

"I want to take a walk," Nadine said. "I think I saw a little garden out the back door. Do you think we are allowed to go there?"

"I'll ask," Anthony said.

The Charity Eligible waved to Mr. Lim and made his inquiry. The answer was a swift and confident, "Yes."

Apparently the small 'friendship' garden was designed for the pleasure of the guests. It boasted some lights, the statues of some lucky cranes and ibis, and a planetarium which had been especially designed to feature the signs of the Chinese zodiac.

"It sounds fascinating," Nadine said. "I do want to go out there."

Anthony took Nadine by the hand and guided her through the array of tables and out into the garden. It was pleasantly cool and starry outside, and a small fountain bubbled into the night.

Anthony, who was always fascinated by things scientific, looked the planetarium over. It was designed to educate the viewer on the animals of the various Chinese years, and guide the eye toward the appropriate star-formation.

Anthony squinted at the sky through the device, and gave up in resignation. "Either I don't have the knack," he said, "Or it is set for the northern hemisphere."

Nadine squinted through the eyepiece. "I can't make it out either," she said. "And the city lights don't help any. However, what I can see is really interesting."

Anthony hovered over the device in an attempt to reduce the ambient light leaking into the viewer, and they took turns in surveying the sky.

"What a romantic classic!" Nadine murmured. "Here we are, star gazing on our date."

"It is romantic, isn't it?" Anthony said. He straightened up and pulled Nadine towards him. Things had been going very well on this date, but the incident earlier that week with Constance had made him more circumspect. "I don't want to misread any signals, but would it be okay if I kissed you?"

"A closed mouth kiss would be okay," Nadine said and raised her face towards him.

Anthony kissed Nadine lingeringly on the lips, and she kissed him warmly in return. It was a kiss of pure affection, with no tongue passion. Both parties were mindful of the fact that Anthony was dating a number of women on the show.

This was the first kiss on the current season of the show however, so the camera crew zoomed in capturing the kiss from several angles ready to exaggerate its importance when the episode was screened.

"That is a nice start for our relationship," Anthony observed gently.

"Relationship or friendship?" Nadine asked cautiously.

"Please don't ask me to predict the outcome at this stage," Anthony said. "I would like to respectfully continue getting to know you."

"I think I understand," Nadine said. "And I feel safe expressing a certain amount of affection towards you on that basis."

"That is good," Anthony said. "Do you want to go inside again now? I think I saw a little lounge where we could sit and talk."

Nadine was pleased to agree, and the pair settled down onto the plump cushions of a cane-work sofa. They talked for half an hour or so about their jobs, their individual likes and dis-likes.

Then they exited into the street and strolled through the section of city that was Chinatown, exclaiming over the unique buildings and businesses. It was two o'clock in the morning before the limousine caught up with them, and whisked them home to their respective abodes.

The girls greeted Anthony warmly upon his arrival at the Candidate house the next morning. Anthony curiously asked Vonda and Janny what the remaining candidates had done while he and Nadine had been out on their single date.

"We actually had a lovely evening," Vonda said. "Leticia had an eight-ball table installed in the large lounge to amuse us girls who had to stay home."

Anthony smiled. "That sounds like a great idea!"

"It was," Janny said. "We all played a few games, and Deborah, who knew the rules for pool and snooker taught us others."

"That sounds nice," Anthony said.
The Charity Eligible turned to Kendra who had joined them. "I am fascinated by what I hear about your work, Kendra. To be able to create beauty and soothe the mind is almost as important as being able to heal."

Vonda who was also artistic, nodded. "I believe music and art have been incorporated into certain forms of therapy," she said.

"I have seen art used as a form of rehabilitation after a stroke," Kendra said. "And to overcome trauma and work through depression. It isn't really my field though. Most of my work is commercial."

"What if you were to team up with a Doctor?" Anthony asked intently.

Kendra gave him a probing glance. "It could be interesting," she said. "I will think about that sort of thing when I am under no form of financial pressure."

"Commercial art also has its uses," Janny said. "Take furnishings for instance. How many women keep themselves happy by decorating their houses?"

"And recreational art," Vonda said. "How many working people de-stress at a movie or concert?"

"Or the ballet?" Janny added.

"The Arts are certainly an important part of our culture," Anthony said. "I am pleased to have met you ladies. I feel like I have been given the chance to explore a new concept or two."

"That is absolutely right," Constance said politely, appearing beside Anthony's elbow. "Anthony dear, could I speak to you alone for a few minutes?"

"Certainly Constance," Anthony said. He took her by the arm and led her out of the communal dining room and across into the lounge. "I had been thinking about you."

Constance looked pleased. "You were?" she asked.

"Yes," Anthony said. "I wondered how you were going, and I wanted to speak to you more the other evening, but you were sort of shy." He sighed. "Perhaps it was for the best though. Sometimes dwelling on things only makes them worse."

"I don't know," Constance said. "I felt like I made a fool of myself at the end of our individual date. It has taken me a little while to recover my balance."

"Things did become awkward," Anthony said. "I will tell you what I saw."

"Go on," Constance said. She looked slightly apprehensive.

"You and I had a good early connection," Anthony said. "I wanted to explore it, but you were more cautious then me."

"That is correct," Constance said. "It was caution, not lack of feeling, Anthony. I would like to make that clear."

"I understand that now," Anthony said. "The air is cleared between us, do you want to go back into the dining room?"

"I guess so," Constance said. She and Anthony turned and made their way back towards the others.

Anthony noticed Nadine standing by a pot plant and hastened to greet her as well. "How are you today?"

Nadine glanced around to make sure they had a little privacy before she answered. "Last night I was floating on a cloud, we had such a lovely meal, and a great conversation. Then we had our little kiss."

"I had a good time too," Anthony assured her. "And only time and more dates can tell what else could happen between us."

"For sure," Nadine agreed. "I'm glad you see it that way too."

"I expect it is time for me to go to the deliberation room now," Anthony said. "Leticia doesn't usually allow me long to socialise."

That afternoon, however, Leticia required more of Anthony than a simple trip to the deliberation room, as she wanted to do an update interview on his romantic progress on the show.

Anthony cleared his throat uncomfortably as he stood in front of the camera crew waiting patiently for Letitia to continue interviewing him. The hostess patted the Charity Eligible on the shoulder and assured him that he had done very well while greeting the girls and participating in the early dates.

"Thank you," Anthony said. His head was reeling from having his love-life placed under the microscope like this, but he was determined to appear calm.

"I would like to ask you about something you said in an earlier interview," Leticia began. "What did you mean, when you said you were unlucky in love? A handsome guy like you must always have had women interested in him."

Anthony shrugged. "If I did, I didn't know anything about it prior to coming on this show, Leticia," he said. "As a youth I was always buried in my books, and since then, it has been my patients. Indeed, my one and only girlfriend - my college sweetheart, described me as stuffy."

"Ouch!" Leticia gasped.

"It was during my final exams," Anthony admitted. "She was full of hope for the future, and I could only see an internship at the hospital looming. We were going in vastly different directions."

"How do you feel about love nowadays?" Leticia queried.

"I am trying to be hopeful, but I find I am a bit reluctant to place myself in a position whereby I am vulnerable to criticism and demands," Anthony said.

Leticia nodded. "That is understandable."

"I don't like being judged by someone else's standards," Anthony continued. "I can only hope that it would be better if the two people involved were in accordance with their goals and values."

"Could you describe your ideal woman to me?" Leticia asked gently.

"My dream lady would be someone who was well balanced and confident by nature," Anthony said thoughtfully. "Someone who could give a lot of support to a hard-working and sometimes stressed-out man, because she was happy within herself!"

Leticia nodded encouragingly: "Tell me more."

Anthony blushed: "I know it sounds like I am asking a for lot…and maybe even looking for perfection, but I am willing to be completely faithful and supportive towards the lady in return."

"Do any of the girls on the show fit your ideal woman?" Leticia inquired leadingly.

"I would have to date them some more to find out," Anthony said carefully. "However several girls do seem quite lovely…and there is a good chance one could well fulfil my ideal!"

Anthony spent the majority of his half-hour in the deliberation room feeling anxious, because the focus and pressure had been placed upon his decisions once again. He was also puzzled by his relationship with Betty, which reminded him of his past rejections by glamorous women.

The friendship with the blonde beauty had started so well, however the girl had hardly approached him during recent dates, and now appeared happy to allow things to fizzle out between them. If Betty was interested, she was not showing it, and Anthony feared she was not interested in him at all.

In the last five minutes, the Charity Eligible gave up focusing on the negative, and spent a few minutes anticipating the positive. Anthony reflected that Nadine and Constance had already indicated they had strong positive feelings towards him; and he also hoped to spark a warm response in Kendra, Vonda and Janny.

Only the model Alison seemed difficult to read, and Anthony concluded that it would be best to assign her an individual date as quickly as possible and try to quantify their association. These things in mind, the Charity Eligible rose to meet Leticia as she entered the room.

"Are you ready to go?" asked the Hostess.

"As ready as I will ever be," Anthony said. He grimaced, and Leticia looked sympathetic.

"Well let's get out there," she said.

Anthony and Leticia arrived in the small reception room to find the girls lined up against the wall and waiting for them. As their numbers dwindled, the space along the wall increased, and the nine remaining girls could now stand in one straight line.

"Hello ladies," Anthony said. "I have seven carnations to give out tonight." He positioned himself in front of the cloth covered end-table and selected a pink carnation.

"Nadine," Anthony said. "I very much enjoyed our evening in Chinatown. You were warm and open towards me, and that made it all the more special. Please accept this carnation so we can go out again."

Nadine coloured fiercely and walked forward. "I would love to go out with you again Anthony," she said. The pretty brunette gave him a hug, and he gave her a kiss on the cheek. They were obviously very comfortable together.

"Constance," Anthony said next. "I had a good time out with you at the Fox Australia Studios. I am hoping you will want to stick around and further explore our friendship."

Constance stepped forward and gave Anthony a hug. She suddenly seemed determined to out-do Nadine in her level of demonstrativeness. "I am so glad you have asked me to stay," she said.

Anthony tensed under her touch. "It's okay Constance," he said. He levered her away from him gently. "It really is okay," Anthony said. "I am sorry if you had even a moment's worry."

Constance accepted the carnation and went back to her position in the line.

"Deborah," Anthony said. "I know the last couple of days have had their dramas. However, I am the Charity Eligible, and I enjoy having you around. How about staying a little longer just for me?"

"I will think about it Anthony," Deborah said, stepping forward. She gave him a theatrical peck on the cheek and snatched the flower. "Yeah okay. So long as you make it worth my while!"

"Janny," Anthony said. "I still haven't spent the time I would have liked to have with you. Please spend some more time on the show and give me another chance."

Janny laughed. "That's cool," she said. "I like you Anthony, but I must be the only lady who is not counting their minutes with you! What happens - happens, I am here to enjoy the dates." The ballerina accepted the carnation and gave Anthony a friendly hug.

"Kendra," Anthony said. "I value your soothing presence in the group, and enlivening conversation whenever we have a moment together. I hope you will stay a little longer."

"It would be a pleasure Anthony," Kendra said. "Thank you for asking." She stepped forward and accepted the carnation. Anthony reached forward to give Kendra a loose hug, and she patted him on the shoulder.

Kendra returned to her place beside the wall, and Anthony smiled.

The Charity Eligible looked around. "Vonda," he said. "I am glad that you enjoyed the Rose Farm more than the Sydney Tower. If you stay around, I promise to make sure you always have a good time!"

Vonda laughed. "That offer sounds grand," she said. "I accept." She walked up to Anthony with a shy bounce in her step, and he gave her a kiss on the cheek.

"There you go," Anthony said.

Leticia stepped forward. "I probably don't need to remind you," she said, "This is the last carnation."

"Why so it is," Anthony exclaimed. He turned towards Alison. "Alison, I am hoping to learn a lot more about you in the next day or so. Please, please accept this carnation."

Alison hesitated for a moment, then she smiled her cool smile and stepped slowly forward. "I will accept the flower," she said. "I would like to find out more about you too."

That left only Betty who had not received a carnation, and would have to leave The Charity Dating Show that evening. Betty began to cry and Anthony rushed over to placate her.

"You are a really lovely person," he said. "I just thought nothing was happening between us lately. Some other man will be really, really lucky to meet you."

"Do you truly think so?" Betty asked, her tears beginning to abate.

"Yes I do," Anthony said fervently. "If only I had more carnations! I wanted to give you one, but I have less to distribute each round."

He placed a brotherly arm around the blonde's shoulders and prayed for her to regain her composure. Leticia finally took over the comforting duty, and Betty was led away to receive her basket of consolation prizes.

"I was afraid I ought to refuse the last carnation," Alison said. "I felt so guilty accepting it when I knew Betty would miss out. However, it is Anthony's choice who he offers a carnation, and I hoped she would accept that."

"It would have been wrong to refuse the carnation if you really wanted to accept it," Constance said.

"You would have confused the issue for me properly," Anthony said. "I am glad that you chose to follow the protocol."

"Anthony do you want to tell Alison why you are so glad?" Leticia asked. "I think we all need something to look forward to."

"Yes Leticia," Anthony said. "That is a fine idea! Alison, you are coming out with me tomorrow. We are going to visit the Sydney Aquarium."

Gasps of envy fluttered around the room. "You are a lucky girl Alison," Vonda said. "I love looking at aquariums."

"I have heard there are some great gift shops along the foreshore as well," Alison said. "Thank you Anthony. I understand now that I was really meant to accept the carnation."

"In the evening," Anthony said. "I would like to take Kendra out to dinner. We are going to the Egyptian Club Restaurant."

"Oh wow Kendra," said Janny. "I love the spices."

"I have never been to an Egyptian restaurant before," Kendra said. "It will be a new experience for me."

"Now Anthony," Deborah said assertively. "Just tell the rest of us what the group date is going to be."

"Deborah, Nadine, Janny, Vonda and Constance will be going out somewhere with me," Anthony said. "I can tell you it is a really great date, but I don't want to spoil the surprise."

Nadine and Constance clapped. "We love the idea of a surprise," they said. "Knowing would just make the waiting all that much harder."

"I guess I can wait too," Deborah said. "It is all part of the game."

"Right you are," Janny said.

Betty was last seen being tucked safely into the prestige car by Tim, the male model who was employed to occasionally escort the girls onto the set. Tim appeared very attentive and Betty was no longer crying. Someone saw her borrow a pen and scribble something, possibly her phone number on a small card and give to Tim.

"It looks like Betty has made a start on dating other guys already," Janny giggled.

"Tim and Betty are both beautiful people," Deborah laughed. "I can't think of a better match!"

CHAPTER EIGHT: A DATE WITH A DIFFERENCE.

It was around ten o'clock the next day when Anthony arrived at the Candidate House to pick up Alison. The red-head girl looked stunning in a tan dress which daringly featured a collar, but had no sleeves, thus leaving an expanse of shoulder and arm bare. The skirt was full and reached down to mid-calf length. Her casual leather sandals were flat soled, making her just slightly shorter than the Charity Eligible himself.

"You look fantastic," Anthony said.

"Thank you," Alison said. She allowed Anthony to open the car door, and climbed inside gracefully.

Anthony climbed into the car and sat down beside Alison. "Do you like marine life?" he asked.

"I don't know," Alison said. "I have always been too busy with drama, elocution and deportment lessons to learn about animals."

"Didn't you ever have a pet fish?" Anthony asked.

Alison shook her head. "No, my mother wasn't into that sort of thing, and she knew what she wanted for us kids. You could say she planned my early career. No teenager gets far in modelling without a push from their parent."

"It sounds as though you didn't get to play much," Anthony said sympathetically.

"I guess not, by your terms," Alison said. "I got to do dress-ups and make-up and I had some dolls. No muddy games though." She shrugged: "It wasn't bad. Girls like the sort of thing I was doing most of the time."

Every instinct told Anthony that his reasons for asking Alison out on an individual date were astute. The girl was very beautiful, and he was sure that he could fall for her in the physical sense, however, she had made it clear from the outset that she wanted to be appreciated for more than her looks. Therefore, he planned to spend some time alone with her in an interesting setting, and find out whether their particular personalities clicked.

The limousine arrived at the harbour, and the couple disembarked. Anthony led Alison towards the entrance of the Sydney Aquarium. The aquarium was a sizeable structure full of tunnels and rows of individual tanks. The base was covered with industrial floor covering, and the neutral looking walls were lined with panels.

They were surrounded by tourists, and Anthony pushed his way through to the information panel located next to the nearest aquarium. He eagerly read through the species information and studied the habitat map. Then he spent a couple of minutes gazing at the creature in the tank.

After a while, Anthony realised that Alison was holding herself aloof from the displays. He beckoned to the girl and tried to explain the distinctive features of each marine animal for her benefit. They continued in this manner until they reached a tank full of sting-ray. Alison exclaimed how ugly the creature was, and shuddered.

"Yes," Anthony said. "I always hope I will not personally step on one of them. Although, they do have a savage beauty don't they?"

Alison nodded, but she appeared unconvinced. She admired the star-fish and the ganglier sea-star, but she flinched at the sight of the sea-urchin.

"It looks prickly," Alison said, pointing at the spines through the glass.

"I don't think they bite," Anthony said. "Although I suspect you would be ill advised to be rough with them."

"I want to look at something else," Alison said, and moved on to a tank of coral. "These are okay," she said. "Unless a lot of the funny things live with them."

"Fish and everything live around a reef," Anthony said. "It forms a complete habitat."

"In that case some reefs would be nicer than others," Alison said.

The sea-horses were more to her liking, and Alison exclaimed how cute they looked. However, when Anthony began to explain what he understood of their unique biology, the model shushed him.

"No don't," Alison said. "Let me stick with how exotic they look, and how many fairy tales have been written about them."

After that, Anthony concentrated on interesting trivia and descriptions of the species' distinctive appearance, but he could tell that his companion was bored on more than one occasion.

When they came to the shark aquarium, Alison shuddered. "Are you sure they cannot break through the glass?" she asked.

Anthony admitted that the sharks did have an uncanny savagery and put his arm around Alison to protect her. They walked quickly through the tunnel underneath the shark enclosure and emerged safely on the other side. Alison was shaking, and Anthony looked at her in concern.

"Would you like to go outside and have coffee?" the Charity Eligible asked.

Alison looked relieved. "Oh yes please!" she said.

Anthony led Alison out of the Sydney Aquarium and into the surrounding tourist precinct. A paved area had been constructed around that particular section of the waterfront, forming a promenade with a selection of cafes and curio-shops around the perimeter. They selected a pleasant looking coffee shop and ordered a cappuccino each.

Alison brightened and became her usual vivacious self. Then she began to talk about the lovely weather they were experiencing. Apparently it was just sunny enough for her taste without being too hot. Anthony agreed it was a lovely day, and then he asked Alison whether she would like to return to the aquarium to view the rest of the display.

Alison shook her head. "I would rather not," she said firmly. "I get a slight touch of claustrophobia in enclosed spaces like that." She looked at Anthony. "You would like to go back though, wouldn't you?"

"Well yes," Anthony said.

"Why don't you go inside without me?" Alison said. "I would be perfectly happy looking at some of the stalls in the market area."

"I don't want to leave you," Anthony said. "After all, we are on a date."

Alison shrugged. "We could synchronise our watches," she said. "I will meet you over there by the outdoor fountain in half an hour."

"Okay," Anthony said. "If you are sure. It would let me check some of the scientific things that interested me."

Anthony returned to the Sydney Aquarium and browsed through the latter half of the marine displays in a more leisurely fashion. He conscientiously checked his watch and emerged on the mall area exactly when the half-hour was up. Crossing the paving, he located a bench along-side the fountain and sat down to wait for Alison, who emerged from the shopping precinct soon thereafter.

Alison had a small package which she showed him contained

mementoes for her friends back at home. "They have some great stuff in there," she said.

"I am sure they do," Anthony said.

Alison then pointed to a nearby bakery: "I would like to try that place, if you don't mind."

"Of course," Anthony said. He led the way into the bakery and encouraged Alison to choose the wickedest desert her heart desired. Alison laughed and reminded Anthony that he was a doctor, and ought to be promoting healthy food, but she allowed him to buy her a creamy cake.

The couple collected their pastries and took them to a seat in front of some play equipment. They ate in companionable silence, although Anthony was pondering their diverse reactions to the aquarium.

"I loved the different aquatic tanks," Anthony said. "I guess I have this insatiable curiosity about living beings. However, doctors have to study so much about the human body that they don't have much time for comparative biology."

"I understand that," Alison said. "However, there were just too many fish for me. I got to the point where I couldn't tell one tank from the other, and the sharks were really scary!"

Anthony was going to offer to escort Alison on a further shopping expedition when the antics of some children on the play equipment caught his eye.

"Look at that," he exclaimed.

"What?" Alison said. "Oh, you mean the kids. They are cute."

"Do you like children?" Anthony asked.

"Yes," Alison said. "I have worked with one or two on photo shoots. They were sweet, until they got tired out, which was only natural."

"I love the children in paediatrics," Anthony said. "Except I try not to get too involved. The good cases go home with their parents, and the others...it is too sad for words."

Alison gazed out across the play area and squinted. "I am glad all those children out there look well."

"I asked you out for a reason," Anthony said. "You threw out quite a challenge when we first met, telling me that you wanted to be appreciated for your mind as well as your body. Therefore, I thought we should talk things through before we went any further into a relationship."

"Yes," Alison said. "I guess it could have come across as a challenge. It wasn't anything personal though. I reckon I had better be more careful how I express that priority in future."

"I took it on board," Anthony said. "I have been trying to be considerate towards you ever since."

"I appreciate your efforts," Alison said. "That comment resulted from my experience of men. Some photographers can be quite inhumane towards their models, while drunken guys in bars only see the basic shape of a woman."

"Still," Anthony said. "I am wondering whether you are really ready to open up and show me your whole personality."

"I don't know," Alison said. "The girls have been saying challenging things to me about my dieting and my career. It has occurred to me that I may have some work to do to become truly comfortable with myself."

"You have some self-discovery to do then," Anthony surmised.

"Yes," Alison said. "I am beautiful - I accept that now. And most of what I have done has involved modelling or acting, so to a certain extent, what you see is what you get."

The model stopped and laid a hand on Anthony's arm.

"Up till today, I was fighting that concept. Something clicked for me when you showed me all those fish though," Alison continued. "I felt weird trying to match your preoccupation with them. It was more comfortable to follow my own interests, and I am really glad you let me."

"Hence the difference between someone treating you as an object and treating you as a person might be whether they care about your feelings," Anthony said. "Not whether they talk to you about all the diverse subjects in the universe."

"Some things obviously don't interest me," Alison said. "However, aptitude tests have shown I am very intelligent. I should be able to plan and organise a fashion show, not just feature in one."

"That sounds interesting," Anthony said. "You should talk to Leticia about it."

Anthony concluded that the girl had a way to go to find her niche in life, and the best he could do was to wish her well. He sighed. Alison was really beautiful, and he would have loved to find there was some viable interest they could share, unfortunately the beauty appeared to be moving on and away from him.

The couple strolled through the shopping precinct before making rendezvous with the limousine. As Alison had said, the place had some remarkable curios and bric-a-brac. Anthony found himself stopping and purchasing a delicate shell necklace for his mother, and a bracelet for his sister. He thought about getting a tiny token for Alison, as she was with him, but also worried about the six ladies left at home.

Alison solved the problem by stopping and pointing at an array of rings carved out of shell and died various colours. "Those are only a few dollars each," she said. "It would be such fun to take them home to the girls."

"I could buy them," Anthony said. "I have some of the date spending money left."

"I will give the rings out for you," Alison offered. "Then no one will think they are engaged to you."

"That is a good idea," Anthony said. "I can trust you with that can't I?"

Alison laughed. "Yes sure," she said. "We have sorted something out today, but it sure ain't an engagement."

They selected seven rings in pearly colours and smaller sizing, and one large brown speckled ring for Anthony himself. Then it was pretty much time to go back to their accommodation. Anthony left Alison with instructions to give the rings out at afternoon tea, because then every girl would be there.

"I hope you enjoyed your date after all that," the Charity Eligible said to Alison. He was clasping both her hands in his as he bid the model farewell.

"Sure," Alison said. "I had a great time Anthony."

"Despite all the fish?" Anthony said.

"Despite the sharks even," Alison said. "We are very different people, but the important thing is, we didn't try to push each other around."

"Yay to that!" Anthony exclaimed. He left the Candidate House in good spirits. The beautiful girl appeared to be gravitating towards self-development and career changes, rather than a relationship with him. The outcome was mildly disappointing, but left him free to concentrate on the other girls.

While Anthony was at the Sydney Aquarium with Alison, the other girls had settled around the pool. After a while, Deborah who was perennially restless, decided to wander off by herself. Being of a curious nature, she walked out around the house, past the landscaped garden and the herb area, and circled around to the rear of the kitchen.

The socialite concluded there was nothing of interest behind the service area and continued her circumnavigation of the house. However, her progress was stalled by the discovery of a large pit of sand in a recess beside the laundry.

A small boy was playing in the sand pit, and he had actually constructed a fairly impressive sand castle. Ever analytical, Deborah paused to inspect the creation.

"Hello," she said, "I'm Deborah. What is your name?"

"I'm Parker," the little boy responded.

"Your castle is pretty good," Deborah said. "But I think it needs another tower over here."

Parker looked up in surprise. "It's my castle, lady," he said. "Who made you the sand castle expert?"

"No one," Deborah said. "I just know what I like."

"You may be right," Parker said, surveying his creation from several angles. "Help me make it."

"Oh no!" Deborah exclaimed. "You had better do it. I would not be able to square off the edges the way you do."

"Okay," Parker retorted. "But you are to try and make a castle of your own over there, I dare you!"

Deborah was never one to back off from a legitimate challenge, even from a small child, so she dropped onto her knees in the sand, regardless of her designer sundress. She picked up a small bucket and filled it with sand.

Selecting a flat portion of the pit, Deborah upended the bucket, fully expecting a neat cylinder of sand to appear. Instead, an avalanche of dry dust slid across the area, forming an unwieldly and unsteady pyramid.

"You should try dampening it a bit lady," Parker said from deep within his side of the sandpit.

"Oh thank you," Deborah said, and trotted across to the outdoor tap.

"Don't make mud mind," the boy warned.

"Okay," Deborah said. She carefully mixed the sand and water into a firm dough like consistency. "Will that do?" she said.

"Almost there," Parker said. "Pack in a bit more sand, and you will be able to tip out a good bucket shape."

"Okay," Deborah said working hard. When she was finished, she upended the bucket and carefully lowered the moulded sand to the ground. She clapped her hands and surveyed the result.

"You learn fast for an adult," Parker said. "If you tie something to a stick, you can put a flag on the top.

"Good idea," Deborah said. She selected a straight twig from under a nearby tree and pulled out her handkerchief.

"Hey lady," Parker said. "I hope your handkerchief is clean!"

"Of course it is," Deborah said indignantly. "I have lots of handkerchiefs, and I take a new one out of the drawer every day."

"You must be very rich," Parker said. "I only have three handkerchiefs, and my dad washes them all the time."

"I guess I am rich," Deborah said. "But people don't usually talk to me about it."

"Why ever not?" Parker demanded.

"Because they are adults," Deborah said. "And adults have funny rules."

"I am going to fill the moat now," Parker said, getting up and fetching the hose.

Deborah sat and watched the child calmly. "I like the way you have finished your castle," she remarked.

"Here comes the water," Parker said. "Aren't you going to move?"

"Why?" Deborah asked.

"You are sitting in the moat, that's why," Parker explained in a matter of fact tone.

"Oh!" Deborah said, surveying her surroundings, "I must be in the lake."

"Yes you are," the child agreed. "And your castle will soon be an island."

Deborah scrambled backwards toward safety, but the heel of her stiletto sandal caught on the board-work at the edge of the sand pit and she sat down hard. "Look what you have done," she said accusingly.

"I didn't do anything lady," Parker said. "You fell over yourself. Besides, my dad says you shouldn't play in your best clothes."

"Turn that hose off," Deborah shouted. She grabbed the offending implement and accidentally pointed it at the boy, who shouted in delight.

"Water fight!" he said. "You are one cool lady."

Deborah was vaguely pleased. She hadn't done anything this silly for so long she could hardly remember. She allowed Parker to wrestle with her for the hose. Soon they were both soaked and covered in mud.

A masculine voice eventually interrupted the proceedings.

"Deborah," It exclaimed. "Whatever are you doing with my son?"

Deborah stopped wriggling and looked up blinking. The speaker turned out to be the camera assistant, George.

The socialite smiled: "I think I am playing," she said.

"I think she is too," the boy concurred.

"I will talk to you later Parker," George said. "Go and ask Maidie for a snack." Parker ran into the house through the laundry door and George extended a hand to Deborah: "Would you like some help getting up?"

"Oh thanks," Deborah said. She allowed George to lever her to her feet, and surveyed the damage to her person. "I think I got a bit carried away!"

"I think you did too," George said. He was beginning to smile.

"You have a great little boy," Deborah commented. "He is so energetic, and not at all shy."

"He has his moments," George said. "He shouldn't really be here on the set, but I have to bring him along when there is no other baby-sitting available."

"Funny thing," Deborah said. "It didn't occur to me that you were married."

George looked slightly sombre. "I am not," he said. "My wife was killed by a hit-and-run driver soon after Parker was born."

"I am so sorry," Deborah said. Her eyes filled with unaccustomed tears. "I can only imagine what that was like."

"I got over it," George said. "I was very grateful that the pram was not hit at the same time."

"So am I," Deborah said. "That would have been too horrible for words."

George hesitated. "I don't want to lay anything tragic on you," he said. "I don't know why I am telling you at all, except that I haven't seen anyone play with Parker the way you just did."

"It is okay," Deborah said. "I am cynical, not shallow. Tell me how it was that Parker survived."

"My mother was out shopping with Parker and Adelie, and managed to knock the pram out of harms' way," George said. "Mum couldn't do anything to save Adelie though. The car was coming along far too fast."

"I am very sorry," Deborah said. "I guess you have been a single father ever since."

"Yes," George said. "I have a little help from my parents, but I mostly do everything myself."

Deborah shivered despite the warm day. "I must get changed," she said. "I am so wet and muddy. Whatever must you think of me?"

"You look fine for someone who has been playing with a child," George said. "You should see me in my old gear."

"I think that is a bit different," Deborah said. "Thank you for confiding in me. You are welcome to come around to the large lounge later and have a coffee with me."

George looked worried. "I don't know," he said. "I don't want to lose my job - for obvious reasons."

"You won't be in any trouble," Deborah said. "I promise! I will speak to Leticia on your behalf."

CHAPTER NINE: KENDRA SCORES A KISS

When Alison arrived home from her date to the aquarium, she was greeted by a number of the girls. Vonda, Janny and Nadine had been waiting around in the pool area and the large lounge. The candidates had completed their swim, eaten a nice lunch, and played a few games of billiards. Then they had begun to watch for Alison to return.

"How did it go?" Janny exclaimed, bouncing up to Alison in the hall soon after the model arrived back at the mansion.

"Pretty good," Alison said. "I wasn't so into the Biology lesson, but then Anthony and I had a lovely chat and a look around the gift shops."

"Lucky you," Nadine said. "Anthony is the best company!"

Alison laughed. "He can be super-smart one minute, and super-sweet another," she said vivaciously. "We bought surprises for you all, and I am supposed to give them out at afternoon tea."

"Oh wow," Janny said. "It is almost tea time, so I will get the others."

Alison went to her room to wash off her make-up and comb her hair. She checked herself for sun-burn and applied some moisturiser. Then she walked into the communal dining room where Vonda and Nadine were already waiting. Kendra came in rubbing her eyes, because she had attempted an afternoon nap.

Constance came in carrying the lifestyle magazine, behind which she had retreated for most of the day. Although Constance had resolved things with Anthony regarding her single date, she remained somewhat reclusive in the Candidate House. The girls feared the dark haired girl might be brooding because her initial connection with Anthony was not the only connection he had made.

Janny came into the room puffing slightly from having run around looking for the others, and Deborah was the last to arrive, her hair still damp from an unexplained shower. Leticia and the housekeeper served biscuits and dip, along with salad sandwiches designed to carry the girls through to their real dinner. Fruit salad was available for anyone with a sweet tooth, and could be consumed without whipped cream for the figure conscious.

"What is this surprise?" Deborah said when they were finished.

Alison produced a patterned paper bag, and opening the folded top, peeled away several layers of tissue. "I was looking at curios with Anthony, and we thought these would be nice for everyone. They were cheap, but they are real natural shell."

"Oh how sweet," Vonda said looking at the closest ring. "You got us something while you were out on your date!"

"They are all slightly different," exclaimed Nadine, observing the variegated combinations of pink, cream, brown and mother of pearl.

The ladies began to try the different rings on their fingers. Janny and Constance chose delicate rings that fitted their ring fingers and slipped them onto the right hand. Alison delicately followed suit, and Deborah chose a slightly larger ring and slipped it onto the index finger of her left hand.

Vonda chose the smallest ring of all and slipped it onto her pinkie finger, where it was slightly loose because Alison had not expected anyone to have a finger that thin.

Kendra chose the ring Alison was beginning to fear would not be selected by any of the girls, and slipped it onto her thumb. "I've never had a thumb ring before," she joked, and everyone laughed. The blondette had slim artistic fingers, so the hoop actually fitted her thumb quite well.

Nadine took the last ring and slipped it onto the ring finger of her right hand. It was slightly too tight, so she removed it and tried the ring finger of her left hand, where it fitted perfectly well.

"An omen," exclaimed Vonda, and Constance frowned.

Alison noticed Constance's clouded face and shook her head. "No omens," she said. "It just shows I am a good judge of jewellery."

"Thank you for the ring," Kendra said. She hugged Alison and turned to go. "I have to get ready for my date now."

The six other contestants remained in the dining room, Laughing and admiring their rings. It was amazing how much joy could be created by so little financial outlay.

Leticia pulled Alison aside: "That was very well done," the hostess said.

"Thank you Leticia," Alison said. "I have been thinking..."

Leticia looked at Alison astutely. "You aren't in love with Anthony, are you?" she said.

"I don't think so," Alison said.

"And you do have acting and modelling experience," Leticia said. "I think I know what is coming next."

"I would like to know how to get a job like yours," Alison said.

Leticia drew her breath in through her teeth as she considered the request. "You put in a resume and portfolio, something like you did before the audition for the show. However, hostesses also need to know how to organise, plan and write. You need to demonstrate those abilities somehow."

"I will think about that", Alison said. "Thank you very much."

"I actually think you would be good," Leticia said. "However, I would strongly advise you to enjoy your time on *The Charity Dating Show*. Don't make a premature exit simply because you have a new goal in mind. I feel that I have to warn you it took forever for me to get this gig."

"I understand," Alison said. "I guess the others have also put their careers on hold to participate in the show."

"Exactly," Leticia said. "Even the Charity Eligible, who is an extremely busy surgeon in real life, has taken holidays."

"I will wait and see what happens then," Alison said. "It might be best to let Anthony make the decision as to whether he wants me around at the next carnation ceremony."

"Don't tell me you have discussed this with him!" Leticia exclaimed.

"Not in so many words," Alison said. "However he did ask some very searching questions when we were at the Sydney Aquarium."

"He was probably just trying to get to know you," Leticia said. "The outcome will depend upon his perception of your compatibility."

"Then I am gone," Alison said. "I am sure he concluded we were just friends."

"I don't know," Leticia said. "It is really hard to predict what the Charity Eligible will do. I try to avoid being sexist, but male reactions can be enigmatic."

Kendra was waiting in the hall when Anthony arrived to escort her out for the evening. She was wearing a long satin dress in a flattering dark blue. It featured a fitted bodice and full flowing skirt.

Anthony was impressed. "You look gorgeous," he said.

"Thank you," Kendra said demurely.

Anthony opened the car door and Kendra slid onto the back seat. The Charity Eligible climbed in beside his date, and settled himself comfortably. The car began to drive and there was a moment of silence which threatened to become awkward.

"I don't know what to say," Anthony said. "And I am surprised because I am usually so much at ease around you."

"We are alone for the first time," Kendra said. "Being on an individual date is somehow different, and it increases the pressure."

"Do you feel pressured?" Anthony asked.

"Yes and no," Kendra said. "I don't feel any pressure from you - you are a nice guy. However, I am aware that while this happening during a game-show, it is also quite real. Any feelings I commit will be sincere."

"I appreciate your honesty," Anthony said. He reached out and took Kendra by the hand. "Please try to relax and enjoy my company. If we have fun tonight, it means it will be worth our having other dates."

The car drew up outside the restaurant that had been selected for the date. It was distinctive looking in the light from the street lamps, which had just begun to trigger for the evening. The outer walls had been covered with plaster and painted light blue, while the lower section was tiled with turquoise wall tiles.

"It is different," Kendra said and laughed.

"Oh yes," said Anthony. "Let us see what it is like inside."

The couple entered the restaurant, and stood still for a moment absorbing the atmosphere. They were in a large dining room with low-pile brown carpet and palm patterned wall paper. The potted plants along the walls were prickly cacti, and a faint scent of incense pervaded the place. Traditional desert-style music based on the maqam played faintly in the background, and a painting of a glamourous Arabic woman adorned the most prominent wall.

"It is very exotic," Kendra said.

"The decor certainly transports you into a different culture," Anthony said.

They were approached by a waiter wearing a turban and loose robes. The waiter was impressive because he carried himself in a natural fashion, and there was absolutely no sense of costuming about his attire.

"Hello," Anthony said.

"Hello Sir and Madam," the waiter said. "I am Mahmood. I believe that you have been told this is an Egyptian restaurant. I am here to explain this is true. The food is mainly Egyptian, with a few extra spicy dishes borrowed from our Arab cousins."

"It sounds lovely," Kendra said. "Where should we sit?"

"I have reserved a table in the centre," Mahmood said. "There you will have the company of other diners, and a good view of the entertainment."

"There is entertainment?" Anthony exclaimed.

"Oh yes," Mahmood said. "We have the best belly dancer in the state here to perform tonight. She is known as 'Farrah' which means happiness."

"How exciting," Kendra said.

"Perhaps madam will get up to join the dancers," Mahmood suggested.

Kendra flushed. "Oh no," she said. "I never could...I am shy about that sort of thing."

"You wait and see," Mahmood said. "The music, it gets into your blood - even western blood; and the movements - they are made for every woman."

"I'll see," Kendra said.

Anthony drew her attention to the menu. "What would you like?" he asked.

"I don't know," Kendra said. "The names are written in Arabic. This one says it is chicken fried up in a salted garlic sauce. I think I would like to try it."

"I am going to have the grilled fish," Anthony said. "I expect it will be spiced differently than Australian fish, but it should be very nice."

"And of course I will have flat bread with the chef's special sauce or soup," Kendra said. "I can't quite work out which it means."

"I will have the bread and the stuff that sounds like a dip or chutney," Anthony said.

Mahmood took their order and departed. Anthony turned his full attention upon Kendra. "Have you ever been overseas?" he asked.

"Unfortunately no," Kendra replied. "It is every artist's dream to tour Europe, if not Asia, but it isn't so easy to arrange."

"Some of my mates went while they were young," Anthony said.

"They were working and living with their parents, so they raised the money quickly enough."

"Ah!" Kendra said. "Unfortunately I was at university then. I had to study the arts, and computer aided design to qualify for the field in which I work. I paid my own fees, and I had no time or money for travel."

"I was pretty broke too," Anthony said. "As a medical intern, I was invited to go to the north of Australia and give free injections at the clinics, but that was the furthest I got."

"Would you like to travel one day?" Kendra asked.

"Sure," Anthony said. "I dream of being asked to give a paper at an overseas conference. If all else fails, I could tour the world in my retirement years."

"I think I will do it sometime too," Kendra said. "Perhaps I will get an overseas commission, or I will book a tour during my long service leave if I stay at this design company long enough."

"That is something to look forward to," Anthony said. "What else do you like?"

"I love animals," Kendra said. Her face lit up. "I love all things natural. Sometimes I drive out of the city and go for a walk in the bush amongst the native birds, butterflies and kangaroos."

"I like to be surrounded by plants," Anthony said. "I would like to have a little land around my house someday, even if have to I move out of the city to do it."

"I don't mind being caught in the rain," Kendra said. "It sounds weird, but I think that is very romantic."

"It is in an eighteenth century, Wordsworthian sort of way," Anthony said.

"I was thinking more 1950's musical like *Singing in the Rain*," Kendra said.

"I personally prefer standing out amongst the fields on a sunny day though," Anthony concluded. "It is much more comfortable."

"Well, we agree on the essentials, if not the details," Kendra said. "It wouldn't do to be too much alike."

"I suppose not," Anthony said. "Do you like kids?"

"I do like children," Kendra said. "I see myself having at least two, but maybe not just yet."

"Two children would be sweet," Anthony said. "I can almost see us with two girls. Bright, funny, smart girls with light red hair."

Kendra almost choked on her chicken. "Wherever did you get that idea?" she cried.

"Nowhere," Anthony said. "My mind was wandering."

"My hair was reddish when I was young," Kendra said. "It darkened into this colour as I neared my teens."

"I am still on the sandy side of blonde," Anthony said. "You can only see it in bright sun-light though."

Their attention was caught by a sudden change in the background music, which was switched from pleasant surround-sound to a stronger volume. The chords and strings of a rhythmic ballad echoed through the restaurant, and a veiled figure glided onto the bare space in the forward portion of the floor. Several strong pulses of sound accompanied a circular movement of hands and hips, and the veil was unwound to reveal a curvaceous and highly bejewelled woman.

Anthony watched in delight, but paradoxically, it was Kendra who was the most fascinated. Moreover, as the dancer launched into a series of swan-like movements of the head and chest, Kendra found herself identifying with the fascinating figure.

The dancer, Farrah, wore a two piece outfit comprised of a brassiere and separate skirt slung low on the hips. The bra top was embroidered with an elaborate selection of beads, and supported a series of tassels which swung across her lower ribs.

The skirt featured a solid panel around the hips and then divided into a series of scarf-like sections which overlapped each other and revealed even as they concealed. The beading was obviously hand sewn, possibly by the belly-dancer herself.

Farrah was fit, but not impossibly thin, and was obviously proud of her feminine form. The gyrations she performed were obviously practiced and skillful, but they were also instinctive, and highly connected to the music. The song and routine completed, Farrah paused to allow the audience to applaud. A satisfied smile curled her mouth and she waved gracefully.

Farrah beckoned to several women who were obviously regular patrons of the establishment, and they too stood, looping scarves and shawls loosely around their hips. The transformation from sedate house-wife or controlled career-woman to eastern handmaiden was instantaneous as the women launched themselves into simple forms of the hip and shoulder shimmy.

The watching men began to stamp, and the stereo music was turned up another notch.

The dancer circled towards the table occupied by Kendra and Anthony and extended a hand to Kendra. Although she had only sipped one glass of wine, Kendra found her inhibitions overcome by the combination of music, incense and general good spirits. She stood and allowed Farrah to lead her onto the forward of the floor. Lifting her hands above her head, she attempted a rudimentary wriggle.

"Like this," one of the women said, and demonstrated the bent knee stance, which enabled her to perform a larger circle with her hips.

Kendra copied her and laughed.

"Very good," Farrah said as she glided past.

"Try this," said another woman and dipped one shoulder before the other.

Kendra tried and laughed as her movement became a clumsy shrug.

"That is a difficult move," Farrah said, observing Kendra's attempt. "Try keeping your shoulders level and aiming your bosom forward."

Kendra managed a stiff wriggle, and several women cheered.

"It takes months of practice," Farrah said. "Relax and simply enjoy yourself tonight."

Kendra found herself swept up in a moving line of women and copied their mincing gait as they circled around the floor. Eventually she noticed women were dropping out of the line and returning to their seats. Energised and exhilarated, she slid to her table and sat down beside Anthony. She looked up into his eyes and found their blue had darkened.

"You were really sexy out there," Anthony whispered.

"No," Kendra said. "I was just having fun."

"Well I had a glimpse of what you could be like if you let go," Anthony said. "It was mighty powerful stuff!"

"Thank you," Kendra replied. "I think."

Anthony reached across the table and took Kendra by the hand. "I am so glad I asked you on this particular date," he said.

"It has been liberating," Kendra said. "I went from not knowing what to talk about, to frolicking in front of the whole restaurant."

"Don't be embarrassed," Anthony said. "It was very tastefully done. Farrah obviously knows her art, and the other ladies must be taking classes somewhere."

Kendra looked pleased. "Do you think it is something I could learn?" she said.

"I expect so," Anthony said. He beckoned to Mahmood and questioned him about the night's performance. Mahmood then left their table, and returned sometime later with a coloured brochure.

"This is a list of professional belly dance schools," Mahmood said to Kendra. "Very good exercise, and nothing like western club dancing. You will like."

"Thank you," Kendra said. "I might just learn."

Anthony looked smug. "It would be worth your while," he said. "Trust me. Every man of your acquaintance will suddenly come running."

Kendra pulled a face at the Charity Eligible. "Then you will have competition," she said.

"Ah, but I have the advantage of an exclusive contract," Anthony said. "At least for the next few weeks."

"That's what you think," Kendra said spiritedly. "Don't forget all the other women that are after your tail!"

"Duh!" Anthony said. "I almost had forgotten...I almost thought this was a normal date."

"As we said earlier," Kendra said, "We are having fun and seeing whether it is worth our while having more dates, on or off the show."

"I'm feeling warm and I imagine you are worse, having been up to dance," Anthony said. "I think I saw a balcony over to the side - do you want to get some air?"

"Is that a metaphor for something?" Kendra inquired.

"Only if you want it to be," Anthony replied. "I am not normally that devious."

"Okay," Kendra said.

The couple strolled past the tables and the dancing area and turned to the right where an open door led onto a sheltered veranda. A bench stood against the far wall, looking inviting, and a hard wearing wool Persian mat softened the concrete floor. Blue lights were attached to the walls and a romantic glow pervaded the whole enclosure.

Kendra trembled as Anthony pulled her against him. "Here goes," he said. "I am going to kiss you after all."

"Not yet," Kendra said, but her hands slid up around his neck. "You haven't told me why."

"Because I want to, and I need to gauge our level of chemistry," Anthony said.

"I'm curious too," admitted Kendra, "But there has to be a limit while you are dating other women."

"Agreed," Anthony said. He leant towards Kendra and kissed her gently. The kiss lengthened and Anthony began to apply some mouth pressure, which Kendra returned momentarily. Then she pulled back.

"Limit reached," Kendra said.

"I'll say," Anthony said. He was flushed. "Thanks for stopping me."

"Weird thing to thank me for," Kendra observed. She remained close to the Charity Eligible.

"I didn't come on the show to take advantage," Anthony said. "So I do need to know the extent of your comfort zone."

"I think I may have reached it," Kendra said. She disentangled herself gently. "Please take me back to the Candidate House."

"That is a good sort of 'take me home' request, isn't it?" Anthony asked anxiously.

"Oh yes," Kendra said. "I have had a very happy evening."

CHAPTER TEN: PLAYING THE GAME

Deborah, Nadine, Janny, Vonda and Constance were all very excited when the essential call came through from Anthony the next morning. The big news was that they were going to attend a training with one of the major basketball teams from the women's league. Despite their varied personalities, every girl in the group had played the sport to some degree.

Deborah had been an A grade player at her all-girl high school, and Nadine had been a team captain at the local public school. Janny had been an excellent all-rounder and sometime vice-captain at her school, and Vonda had played the game as a recreational outlet during her years as a student.

Constance was perhaps the least keen, her experience being limited to the occasional "friendly" game hosted by the hospital social club. However, she too was excited at the thought of meeting with the professional players and touring a well-equipped sporting facility.

Each girl retreated to her assigned room to change into suitable sports clothes. Their outfits ranged from smart shorts to lycra tops and dapper track-pants, but one and all, they looked ready for action when Anthony arrived.

Anthony greeted each girl warmly, and ushered them into the waiting limousine. Deborah offered to hang back, and allowed Anthony to climb into the centre of the back seat. She then jumped into the car and pulled the door shut behind her. This placed Anthony snugly between Nadine and Deborah.

"The State Sports Centre is a top idea for a group date," Deborah said. "It has the advantage of being prestigious, and it is easy to involve everyone."

"Thank you," Anthony said. "I cannot take all the credit, but I did select it promptly when I saw the idea amongst the list of possibilities Leticia had compiled."

"I am excited," Nadine said. "This takes me right back to school." The pretty brunette laid a casual hand on Anthony's knee. Anthony casually lifted Nadine's hand and cradled it in his own. The gesture was cosy and affectionate.

Constance, who was sitting directly opposite, observed this and frowned. "I hope we get there soon," she said.

The limousine pulled up in the reserved parking area for the Olympic Park, and the contestants all piled out. Deborah climbed out of the car first, and then Anthony followed. The Charity Eligible held the door open for Constance, Vonda, Janny and Nadine to exit the vehicle. Once everyone was assembled on the pavement, Anthony slung a casual arm around Janny, and linked arms with Nadine.

The group set off to cross the car park with Deborah in the lead. While it was evident that Anthony was attempting to spread his attention around amongst the girls, Nadine was the most frequent recipient of his gestures of affection, and Constance was once again frowning.

They were met half way across the paved area by a sporty looking woman in a red track suit, who introduced herself as "Jackie" the coach of the league team.

"Welcome to the home complex," Jackie said. "It is my job to show you around the facilities."

The basketball club itself was a brick building with a light linoleum floor. There was one large indoor court and stadium with ample seating for spectators, and a small gymnasium. The indoor area also included a kitchen facility with a generous amount of bench space; a toilet block and locker room with showers. The grounds included a flower garden and some outdoor training courts.

"This is a really cool set up!" Janny exclaimed. "I can see myself now, practicing every day on the court, and playing home matches in the stadium."

"That is the idea!" proclaimed Jackie, the coach of the league team. "It is important to have happy players and a consistent practice routine. The game does require a high level of fitness, good ball skills and a healthy amount of motivation."

"Some of us played at school," Deborah said with a surprising degree of modesty. "So we are thrilled to be here at this centre."

"Would you like to meet some of the players, and maybe participate in a mock match?" Jackie inquired.

"Oh yes," Nadine said. Her eyes were shining. "You may need to go a little easy on us though, we are not professionals."

"I won't insult you by going too easy," the Coach said. "You all look like fit young ladies, so I will start you on some warm-ups and we will soon find your level."

Jackie led the way into the main court, where a handful of the players were waiting. Some were standing talking casually, while others were stretching their leg muscles. They all snapped to attention when the party entered.

"I would like you to meet Susan, our captain," Coach Jackie said. "And this is Angela, our vice-captain. Melita, Tania and Whilemina regularly play in the forward positions, with Jacque, Carina and Olivia as our best defence. We have several substitutes and rotate our positions on a fairly regular basis."

"I see," Vonda said. The quiet girl was looking very comfortable in the team situation. "I guess you would like us to introduce ourselves."

"I will do the honours," Anthony said. "You would have heard we are from a television production, *The Charity Dating Show*. I am Anthony, and these are my dates. The first lady is Deborah, while the lady on my other side is Nadine, the ladies over there are Vonda, Constance and Janny. We are all very pleased to meet you."

"We are happy to meet you too," Susan said. "We play for the cameras all the time, but for trophies instead of love!"

"Today is fun and novel, almost like a day off," Angela said, and the others nodded.

"Well let's get to work," Coach Jackie said. "I want everyone lined up in two straight lines for warm-ups." She then took them through a series of wrist and leg warm-ups, shuttle runs and side shuffles across the court. This exercise was followed by some dribbling and ball passing practice.

When the visiting party were pleasantly energised and slightly sweaty, Coach Jackie called them to a halt. She then divided the television contestants into two groups and distributed them evenly amongst the competition basketball players, forming two mixed teams.

One team was headed by Susan and included Deborah, Constance and Janny. The other team was headed by Angela, and included Vonda, Nadine and Anthony. The two teams were launched into an informal match, where the pace was brisk and challenging for all of the amateur participants.

Deborah was pleased to find that she bonded to her team well. The old skills were returning, and she managed a number of credible catches and passes. Her game was complicated by the immense skill of the defence upon the other team, but she even managed to shoot one basket.

Janny was light upon her feet, and maintained a good level of fitness in the duration of her dance work. She was able to dodge between players and managed to capture the ball. She dribbled it and passed it adroitly to one of the professional players.

Anthony joined into the game with the sheer strength and energy of the male player. He was intrigued to find that the ladies of the league could out-pass and out-run him. He increased his effort, and with the exception of a few clumsy fouls which the coach identified immediately, comported himself very well.

Vonda played with the quiet confidence of someone whose experience of the game was up-to-date. Her strength was in team work, and she made no attempt to rival the professional players. However, she managed to place herself well to make catches and pass the ball to the other team members.

Nadine found her skills were somewhat rusty, but she had retained her sheer enjoyment of the game, and threw herself into the forward position to which she had been assigned. Unfortunately, she found herself in direct competition with Constance, who was attempting to play a defence position in the opposite team. Nadine attempted to circumnavigate the other girl discretely, but Constance responded with an unexpected display of aggression, pursuing the player instead of the ball.

It soon became evident that Constance's annoyance was personal rather than sporting. The blunt-haired brunette looked uncomfortable and miserable amongst the more confident players; while Nadine was someone with whom she could almost keep pace, and with whom she was evidently aggrieved.

When one of the professional players made a strategic pass, Nadine found herself in possession of the ball. Constance, ever hovering close, attempted to snatch the ball out of Nadine's hands. Nadine resisted, and Constance closed in, hovering over Nadine in a shepherding posture. Nadine bounced the ball and attempted to pass it on, but Constance blocked her. Nadine bounced the ball again, and Constance slapped at her hands.

The coach blew her whistle, and the girls stopped. They stood panting and shaking. "Play the ball and not the person," Jackie said, and Constance grimaced.

The ball was given to Nadine for a free shot at the goals, and play resumed. It was a while before the ball returned to the central part of the court, but when it did, Constance made a dash and a desperate grab at it. Nadine, being the more skilled player, made a neat tackle, and easily obtained the ball from Constance. However, as she began to dribble the ball and move away, Constance reached out with fingers splayed and curved, to claw Nadine from elbow to wrist.

The coach blew the whistle again. "What's wrong with you girl?" Jackie said to Constance. "Any more of that and you will be sent off the court."

Nadine rubbed her arm. The scratches were not very deep, and while there was a mark upon the skin, it was not bleeding. "Perhaps it was an accident," she said generously.

Play resumed, and the rest of the game proceeded smoothly, with the team incorporating Nadine, Vonda and Anthony finishing four baskets ahead. Everyone shook hands and congratulated each other, even Constance and Nadine.

"It is time for lunch," Coach Jackie said, "That was an excellent game. If we had more time, I would give you a few pointers, but for now, all I can say is that you responded to the challenge of joining in with highly trained professional players in a very positive manner. You did not allow yourselves to be intimidated, and you managed to apply the basic skills to contribute to the team work!"

Everybody cheered and clapped. Then they made their way into the Olympic Park Canteen, which would cater for the visitors and players alike. Anthony and Constance were the first to collect their plates. They made their way to a table next to the wall and sat down. Soon they were deep in conversation.

"Are you okay?" Anthony said. "I thought I detected something wrong out there on the court."

"I don't know rightly," Constance said. "I guess I thought things were better between us than they seem to be."

"Do you mean you and me?" Anthony said. "I think we are okay. I am finding that things develop different ways with different people. It isn't all under my control."

"Things seem a bit too cosy between you and Nadine,"

Constance said. "There, I've said now, and I sound all jealous and everything." She hung her head in mild shame.

"Come on, cheer up," Anthony said. "Nadine and I have come to an understanding. We are very comfortable, but it doesn't mean that I like her any better than I like you."

Constance looked unconvinced. "The public affection has to mean something," she said.

"Of course it means something," Anthony said. "I won't know quite what for a while, and here's what makes Nadine so cool - she can risk her feelings a bit, and still wait until things work out one way or another."

"Is that all?" Constance said. She looked relieved but not convinced. "Are the rest of us girls still in the running for your affection?"

"Of course," Anthony said. "I am busy getting to know you all. For instance, I have noticed that basketball is not your game. What do you prefer?"

"I don't know," Constance said. "I never was that sporty, but I did once fancy learning to play tennis."

Deborah, Janny and Vonda had sat down at another table with the Captain and Vice-Captain of the league team. They were evidently enjoying the social interaction with the professional players.

Nadine approached Anthony and Constance. "May I sit down?" she asked.

"Sure," Anthony said. "Constance and I were just talking about tennis. Do you like to play?"

"I enjoy the occasional game," Nadine said. "I have even been known to win at doubles."

"You would," Constance said huffily. Her stance indicated a degree of over-reaction as she picked up her plate and moved away from the table. "You could leave me and Anthony alone for five minutes, but no, you always have to have him." Constance turned on her heel and stalked away.

"What was that about?" Nadine exclaimed ingeniously.

"She is getting a bit over-sensitive," Anthony said.

"I noticed it out on the court," Nadine said. "However, it is not the first time I have experienced heightened aggression from a defence player. Something about the game brings that sort of thing out."

"Do you think that is true of the dating game too?" Anthony inquired thoughtfully.

"I guess dating heightens feelings too," Nadine said. "It would depend how one was used to dealing with things."

Lunch over, the professional players bid the visitors goodbye and moved on to another part of their training regimen. Anthony invited Vonda and Janny to oppose him and Nadine in a half-court game on one of the out-door quadrangles.

Deborah remained inside talking to Constance. She had noticed that the young brunette was looking mournful, and was making a conscious effort to cheer her up. At first Constance resisted the process and teased Deborah about behaving in an uncharacteristic manner.

"You were the first to comment on my fantasies about the Charity Eligible," Constance complained. "I can't believe you understand how I feel now!"

Deborah merely laughed. "I admit have no sympathy for unrealistic romanticism," she said. "However, I don't like to see someone I have come to think of as a friend get so down-in-the-dumps."

"I am sorry," Constance said. She sniffed: "I am surprised to hear you think of me as a friend."

"It is true we don't have a lot in common in practical terms," Deborah said. "However, I don't actually require that to consider someone a friend. You are a fellow female and participant in the show, and that is good enough for me."

"Really?" Constance asked. She began to look a bit more cheerful. "What is your life like normally?"

"I work in a library even though I don't need my wage," Deborah said. "I do it because I love books and facts, and the structured atmosphere. Once or twice a year, I take a little flight or cruise somewhere and rub shoulders with those of my own so-called class."

"What is that like?" Constance asked. She was fascinated.

"Sometimes it is stimulating to be amongst those who are successful in big business," Deborah said. "However, other times I am impatient with those who focus on cars, material possessions and other status symbols. The trappings aren't always part and parcel of the real thing."

"It sounds like fun," Constance said.

"It can be," Deborah said. "How long is it since you have taken a holiday?"

"Other than coming on this show," Constance said, "I haven't had a holiday for a long time."

"I bet you work hard," Deborah said.

"I do," Constance said. "And so does Anthony. I expected him to recognise that and admire me for it."

"I believe he does," Deborah said. "From what I have seen, you were one of his early favourites."

"Then why did the relationship fall apart?" Constance said in bewilderment.

"Only you can answer that," Deborah said. "I am guessing it could be because you haven't learnt to relax and go with the flow."

"Anthony said something similar earlier," Constance said. "Only he was complimenting Nadine on her calm attitude."

"There you go," Deborah said. "I wouldn't let myself take it personally."

"I have to be myself," Constance said.

"Of course you do!" Deborah exclaimed. "I am all for that. Except, are you sure Anthony is the right guy for you?"

"I don't know," Constance said. "He is the only man on my mind at the moment."

"I have to respect that," Deborah said. "In fact, I wish it were that easy for me." She glanced up, and looked across at George who had remained to film them while the majority of the television employees had followed the Charity Eligible outside with the large camera. "I think I may have met someone else."

Constance widened her eyes in surprise. "Really?" she exclaimed. "You met someone around here? What are you going to do about it?"

"Tell Anthony the truth I suppose," Deborah said. "And hope he allows me to remain on the show."

"He just might," Constance said. "You two do seem to be good friends."

The two girls brewed coffee using the club expresso machine, and drank it together. Then Deborah went out-side to join in the half-court basketball, and Constance sat down on a rustic bench to watch the game. She looked thoughtful, but very alone. Half an hour later, the limousine arrived to transport the ladies back to the Candidate House and the Charity Eligible back to his residence.

Tea was served out beside the pool that evening. The overhead lights had been switched on to combat the encroaching dusk, while the elegant dining table and chairs had been set up on the tiled patio. Bowls of roses had been arranged all down the centre of the table, and the flowers lent their scented perfume to the evening air.

Deborah and Kendra arrived early and surveyed the area. Deborah was vibrant in a red mini-dress, which co-ordinated uncannily with the red tips in her light brown hair, while Kendra was looking exceedingly feminine in a pale mauve chiffon dress which flowed down to her ankles.

"The outdoor area is very nicely set out," Kendra said. "A formal dinner beside the pool is a novel idea."

"I think I have seen everything at least once," Deborah said cynically. "Still, I must say, this crowd do their best." The socialite crossed over to where George and Simon were setting up their camera equipment. "How are you tonight boys?" she inquired.

"Good, thanks Deborah," Simon said.

"We are working hard as usual," George said.

"I can see that," Deborah agreed. "How do you intend to get a picture once the evening falls?"

"I am counting on the flood-lights being strong enough to give a normal picture," Simon said. "I do have some infra-red equipment, but it doesn't look quite the same."

"Interesting," Deborah said. "I wish you luck with that." She turned to the assistant, "And how is Parker, George?"

George smiled: "Parker is fine," he said. "He has been asking what the feisty lady has been doing."

Kendra, who had followed Deborah across the patio looked inquiring.

"George has a seven year old son," Deborah explained. "I met the boy out in the garden yesterday afternoon." The socialite winked at George: "I spoke to Leticia. She says it is all right for you to bring Parker up to the house as long as it does not interrupt any filming."

"You must have pulled a few strings to arrange that one!" George exclaimed.

"I merely approached the subject the right way," Deborah said. "There is no reason to believe any of the girls will mind."

"This is the first I have heard of it," Kendra said. "But all I can say is that it would break the monotony to have a few visitors."

"Excuse me please ladies," Simon said. "I like to socialise as much as the next guy, but more people are arriving, and I am going to set the camera rolling. Back to work with you too now George."

Kendra and Deborah wandered across to the dining table, where Janny and Vonda were already seated. Janny was wearing a slinky brown crushed satin two piece outfit, and Vonda was wearing a pale green sheath. They were joined by Alison and Constance. Alison looked classical and beautiful as ever in a silver-lame skirt and kami-top, and Constance was looking smart in a black satin skirt and silk top.

Alison asked Janny whether the group date had gone well.

"Pretty good," Janny replied, and Vonda nodded.

Nadine was hovering around the door that led from the house interior, obviously awaiting the arrival of the Charity Eligible. A few minutes later Anthony arrived and the neat brunette ran straight into his arms. The couple kissed openly and spontaneously. When they had finished kissing once, they did it all over again.

Deborah whistled. "Nadine and Anthony are getting a bit full-on there," she exclaimed.

"I'll say," Janny observed.

"Not everyone who has had an individual date is carrying on like that!" Alison shrugged: "I guess it would depend on the outcome of the date."

Kendra blushed: "Speak for yourself Alison," she said. "I am not giving away any secrets!"

"I expect Anthony will come over here in a minute and say 'hello' to the rest of us," Deborah said. "If he doesn't I will go and get him."

Constance stared stonily at the ground. "I don't think I can compete," she said.

"Of course you can," Vonda said. "Look at me...I started off so shy, and now I am really enjoying myself."

"It has sort of gone the other way for Constance though," Janny said. "She started off confident, and then got unsettled."

"I'm not really self-assured," Constance said slowly, "Especially about matters of the heart."

"It's only a competition if you think of it that way," Vonda said. "Otherwise, it is an experience."

"We are all your friends," said Janny.

"Thanks girls," Constance said.

"The trouble is," said Janny, "There is only one Anthony, and he can't possibly end up with all of us!"

"I wouldn't expect him to," said Vonda. "That would be too weird for words. There are plenty of other guys in the world."

"There must be someone nice out there for all of us," Kendra remarked. "And we won't always be stuck on *The Charity Dating Show*."

Constance groaned. "Don't remind me of the elimination," she said.

"I'm sorry," Vonda said. "I didn't mean to."

"Here comes Anthony now," exclaimed Alison.

Anthony drew level with the table and approached Kendra.

"You ladies seem preoccupied tonight," he said. He laid his hands upon Kendra's shoulders. "Aren't you glad to see me?"

"Of course we are," Kendra said. "We were just talking."

"Clear me a seat then," Anthony said. "Somewhere in the middle, so that I can see all of my favourite ladies."

Everyone shuffled around, and Anthony ended up being seated between Kendra and Vonda, and opposite Alison and Nadine. The meal was delicious, as sizzling steak in pepper sauce was served straight from the kitchen. The side vegetables consisted of baked potatoes and boiled spinach. Desert consisted of apricot cheesecake and vanilla ice-cream, and a selection of sparkling ciders and wines were available to drink.

Soon after the meal was over, the table was cleared and the party moved over onto the lounge chairs arranged under the veranda. Constance remained behind, admiring the roses and allowing their beauty to soothe her wayward thoughts. She leant forward and buried her face in an especially large bloom and sniffed in the scent. When she raised her head, she was surprised to see the smaller video camera focused upon her.

"I'm sorry," Constance stammered. "That was an extremely private moment."

Simon Steeple lowered the lens and switched off the camera. "The footage doesn't have to go to air," he said. "However, you looked very beautiful."

"Thank you," Constance said. "I think...." She was very hesitant.

"I tell you what," Simon said. "I will put together a private tape, just for you. It will be full of scenes involving you, that were not necessarily shown on air. A lot of our film does end up in the editing room archive."

"That sounds lovely," Constance said. "But why would you bother?"

"Because I love to fiddle with the equipment," Simon said. "And because I am a nice person.....a very nice person, but sometimes people don't see me at all when I am behind the camera."

"I hadn't really thought about it," Constance said. "But a personalised tape would be interesting. Will you do one for the others too?"

"I don't know," Simon said. "If I get some inspiring footage, I suppose."

"It is nice to know my image is inspiring," Constance said. She eyed Simon curiously for a moment, taking in his shoulder length hair and alternative style charm. "I don't know when I have received a nicer compliment."

Constance hoped Simon was not the man Deborah was interested in, because, next to the Charity Eligible, he did seem like the most interesting man around. Constance reigned her mind in from wandering into new romantic fantasies. How Deborah would chide her for constructing an entire new delusion based on a kind word or two. "Excuse me, I had better go and join the others now."

Constance walked over to the outdoor lounges to merge with the group assembled in the glare of the main spotlight, and lens of the large camera, which was being operated by George. The neat brunette spent a few minutes talking, and then she put a hand to her forehead.

"I have a headache," Constance said. "If Anthony will excuse me, I will lie down on my bed. Please send someone to call me if I am needed for the carnation ceremony."

Kendra looked at Constance in concern: "I will accompany you and see that you are all right," she said.

The two girls spoke briefly to Leticia, and then headed into the house.

A few minutes later, Kendra returned alone and settled into the group, who were consuming sweets and caffeinated drinks on the patio. They were also developing increasingly high spirits, with a great deal of laughing and talking, and the occasional spatter of teasing banter. Soon Alison suggested changing into their bathing suits for a late night swim.

"That is a great idea," Deborah said. She looked across at Leticia. "Do we have to stay in our formal wear for the carnation ceremony?"

Leticia glanced at her watch. "At this rate, and with Constance sick, we won't get to the carnation ceremony until morning," she said. "Go ahead, have some fun!"

The girls retired briefly to their bedrooms, to wash off their make-up and change into their bikinis. Anthony, who had not brought his bathers across to the Candidate House, was supplied with a pair of board shorts from the change room; and they all began splashing around in the main pool.

Leticia powered up the spa mechanism and the smaller pool began to bubble and heat-up. Nadine, Kendra and Vonda moved across to the smaller pool and invited Anthony to join them. The Charity Eligible agreed, and placed himself strategically between Nadine and Kendra.

The foursome began to lounge around in a relaxed fashion, talking about music and dance. The conversation drifted from subject to subject in a casual manner and Vonda remarked how much she admired dolphins.

"They are so peaceful and graceful," she said, and Anthony and Kendra agreed.

Janny remained in the main pool doing laps, and Alison and Deborah splashed around the side, chasing and ducking each other. After a while, the two outgoing girls approached the rim of the spa.

"Squash over and let us in," Alison said.

"It is comfortable for four," Deborah said. "Let's see what it is with two more." She and Alison climbed in between Anthony and Nadine, while everybody else shuffled around.

"I'm coming in too," an amused voice remarked as Janny appeared along-side the spa. "Don't think you can block me out!" The blonde inserted her slender body between Vonda and Kendra, wriggling down into the water. "Here we are, all packed like sardines."

The Charity Eligible allowed his arms to encircle the shoulders of the girls on either side of him, and his legs reached out to contact the limbs of those opposite him. "Six beautiful ladies in the spa with me," he said. "This is a luxury I never expected."

"Don't get too carried away," Deborah remarked. "It is a party, not an orgy."

"I would be presumptuous to expect anything more than this," Anthony said. "I do believe I am the luckiest guy on earth at the moment!"

CHAPTER ELEVEN: A TIME TO SHINE

Anthony arrived at the Candidate House around nine o'clock the next morning and was greeted by Leticia, who led him directly into the deliberation room. The Charity Eligible stood facing the row of portraits and assembled his thoughts. He was pretty sure that he was getting unusual vibes from several ladies.

Nadine was a pleasing beauty with whom Anthony could feel supremely confident, and Kendra was a complex package of stimulating intellect and soothing empathy, with a dash of sexuality thrown into the equation. There were also Janny and Vonda, whom Anthony was keen to date in the future.

Constance, however, was no longer happy, and would need a great deal of attention and reassurance if she was to remain on the show. Given the strength of their initial connection, Anthony thought that it might be worth giving her another carnation on the chance things would improve.

This left Deborah and Alison with whom Anthony had less romantic potential. Deborah was quickly turning from impending challenge, to platonic friend. However, she was a good sort of friend, and it might be useful to have at least one person around who was not in love with him. On the other hand, when they had been at the aquarium date Alison, had seemed completely happy to finalise her time on the show, and move on with her career. All-in-all this was one of his more difficult decision points.

By the end of the half hour, Anthony had made his decision. There was an element of uncertainty, but he assured himself it was not only the wisest, but most practical of the moves possible for him to make. He greeted Leticia with relief, and followed her into the small reception room, where the bevy of beauties awaited him.

"Hello ladies," Anthony said, "I had a lot of fun at the pool last night, and was very glad Leticia postponed the carnation ceremony until this morning. It was almost like having a night off - and in the best company of course!"

The women crowded around the Charity Eligible, giving him their best wishes and greetings for the day. He returned their felicitations and was in the process of shaking hands all around when Leticia interrupted.

"Would you ladies please go and stand in a line against the far wall?" The Hostess instructed: "Anthony you are to stand beside the flower table."

There was a general re-shuffle, and Anthony faced the women. "We have come to the difficult part of the show once again," he said. "I am happy to be able to give carnations to six of you, and I believe we will all miss the seventh lady, who of necessity will have to go home."

The row of faces ranged against the wall nodded. Some of the women were smiling, while some looked serious, and there was a general acknowledgement that degrees of relationship had developed.

"Nadine," Anthony called. "I would like to give you this carnation, and I hope you are as happy as I am to continue our interaction."

Nadine smiled and flushed with enthusiasm. She stepped forward and gave Anthony a big hug. "I would love to go out with you again," she said. "I don't mind whether it is on a group or individual date, as long as we have a good time."

"Good," Anthony said. He returned her hug and gave her a peck on the cheek.

Nadine returned to her seat caressing the carnation, and Constance gave her a hard look. The Charity Eligible observed this and sighed.

"Constance," Anthony said, changing his intended order slightly: "I would like to offer you a carnation too, but I charge you to consider whether you can be happy dating me on this show."

"I feel a bit strange saying this in front of everybody," Constance said. "But I think every girl here will agree with me when I say that it feels strange to see the guy you are going out with hugging and kissing another woman."

Several girls looked pointedly at Nadine, who attempted to appear nonchalant.

"I am sure that is true," Anthony said, and a murmur of agreement arose from the ladies along the wall. "However, this is a television show, and you know all about the other ladies. I am not practicing any form of deception on you, and I am being as open and honest as possible."

"I appreciate that," Constance said. "And it is because of your honesty that I am able to accept the carnation. I hope everyone else accepts me and the way I feel."

Most girls nodded their support, and Nadine alone remained aloof. "Different people are comfortable with different levels of intimacy," she was heard to mutter rebelliously.

"Game, set and match to Constance," Deborah whispered to Vonda. "On this round at least."

"Oh, I hope they don't keep it going," Vonda said. "The last thing we need is a feud amongst the girls."

"It won't get out of hand if the rest of us refuse to join in," Kendra observed calmly.

"Ladies, ladies," Leticia said, calling them back to attention. "We are in the middle of a carnation ceremony right now."

"Sorry Leticia," Deborah said. She winked at Simon Steeple: "I'm sure it was an interesting piece of drama though. I trust you are not going to edit it out."

"That comment I WILL censor," Leticia said firmly. "I am so glad we don't have you on a live show Deborah. It would have to be packaged as a satirical comedy! Let's get on with it Anthony. I would like to finish filming before midday."

"Thank you everyone," Anthony said. He picked up the next carnation: "Kendra," he said. "I really enjoyed our time at the Egyptian restaurant, and I hope we will have many more happy dates together."

"I hope so too," Kendra said coming forward slowly. She accepted the carnation and gave Anthony a kiss on the cheek. "I think you know how special it was to me."

"Me too," Anthony murmured.

Kendra re-joined the other girls, and Anthony turned his attention back to the group.

"Deborah," the Charity Eligible said. "I never know where I stand with you, and I think things have changed again recently. However, I do consider you a friend, and I would like you to stay on a bit longer."

"I will make things clear as soon as we have a chance for a heart to heart," Deborah said stepping forward. "I am very happy to accept the carnation though, you may be assured of that."

Anthony patted the socialite on the shoulder. "Okay," he said. "As long as you are certain."

Deborah returned to the group, where Janny, Kendra and Vonda looked at her inquiringly. She shrugged and whispered: "Later".

"Janny," Anthony said. "Thank you for being patient while the other girls went on their individual dates. I hope to have the chance to get to know you better very, very soon."

"That is cool Anthony," Janny said, as she accepted the carnation. "I always knew my turn would come." The ash-blonde patted Anthony affectionately on the arm before returning to her place amongst the women.

"Vonda," Anthony said carefully, picking up the last carnation. "I want to say something similar to you. I am pleased that you have participated in the group dates, and I hope to take you out on an individual date soon."

"Thank you Anthony," Vonda said. She blushed: "I have been happy on the group dates. It has been a low pressure way of getting to know you, and of course, the other girls."

"I am glad to hear you say that," Anthony said.

Vonda accepted the carnation and returned to her place in the line-up.

"Alison," Anthony said. His hands were empty of a flower and everyone knew this was a farewell speech: "I really like you as a friend, and I am sorry to have to say goodbye to you."

"I am sorry to go too," Alison said. "I was enjoying the experience." She reached out and gave Anthony a hug. "The walls I keep around myself were crashing down, and of course, there was the television exposure."

Anthony looked concerned. "I hope I have done the right thing," he said. "Sometimes I thought you wanted to go, and other times I thought you wanted to stay."

"Someone has to go," Alison said, "And I guess I have a career to proceed towards." She glanced across at Leticia, who nodded reassuringly.

"I wish you all the luck in the world with your career Alison," Anthony said. "I expect the offers will pour in as soon as this show goes on air."

"Ah," Alison said, "But I am looking for something where I can be a bit creative and not just look beautiful. Selling based on my looks generates so much pressure, and looks don't last forever."

"I am sure you will find it," Anthony said. He gave Alison one last squeeze, and she turned and walked over to hug each of the girls.

"Goodbye everyone," Alison said. "You have all impressed me in different ways."

"We enjoyed living with you," Deborah said, and Nadine nodded.

Constance gave her a hug. "You have been an excellent room-mate," she said. "And we all loved your style-tips."

"Have a good time out there in the work-a-day world," Kendra said, and Janny and Vonda added their best wishes.

Alison waved goodbye to the girls and walked out of the small reception room. Knowing that the cameras were following her every move, she proceeded to the waiting limousine, and allowed Tim to help her onto the seat.

"I am disappointed that I was not the right girl for Anthony," the model girl announced for the cameras. She brushed a theatrical tear from the side of her eye. "However, I must make the best of things after all. The girls left in the house are all lovely!"

There was a package of papers on the passenger seat next to her. Alison waited until the cameramen had turned away from her and then picked the papers up and read them through.

"Application forms for television station work," Alison mused. "Thank you Leticia. It's up to me from now on, but at least I know I have some good friends in the industry!"

Back at the Candidate House, Anthony turned to Janny.

"Get changed into something warm this afternoon," he said. "I will be back soon after lunch to take you out on the next date."

The Charity Eligible and the remaining candidates took luncheon in their separate residences, and Anthony arrived back at the Candidate House soon after one o'clock. He was dressed in a white t-shirt and quality denim jeans, while a thick wind-cheater was tied casually around his waist.

Janny was waiting for him in a blue shirt and quilted black ski-pants. She was carrying a knitted sweater.

"I am ready," Janny said, "And I'm dressed warmly as you asked."

"Excellent," Anthony said greeting her with a hug. "I can see you are well dressed."

"I am curious as to where we are going," Janny said. "It is the beginning of summer, and I am quite warm here even in the air-conditioned hall."

"Keep your jumper handy until we get there then," Anthony said practically. "I assure you, it will be pretty cold at the ice arena."

Janny began to laugh: "The ice arena," she said. "How classic! You have assumed that because I am a ballerina, I can figure skate!"

Anthony looked perplexed. "Can't you skate?" he asked.

"Not very well," Janny replied, although a wicked twinkle began to sparkle in her eye. "You could say that I am positively hopeless in that direction."

"Really?' Anthony exclaimed. "I will have to help you then."

"Ah yes," Janny sighed. "You can be my teacher." A little smile played around her lips. "I will enjoy that."

"Oh why?" Anthony was intrigued.

"Because I like to have a strong man put his arm around me and help me along," Janny murmured provocatively.

Anthony looked flattered. "I thought you would have your pick of partners at work," he said. "They all get to put their arms around you."

"It's exactly what you said," Janny retorted. "Work! The contact is choreographed, and there isn't a scrap of romance in it."

"So I don't have a muscular dancer as my rival then?" Anthony asked.

"No rival," Janny said, laughing as she patted Anthony on the knee. "Around here, I am the one with all the rivals."

"Do you mind having rivals?" Anthony asked anxiously. He had noticed that the ladies all had different perspectives *on The Charity Dating Show*s' structure.

Janny shook her head. "I've had to compete to get where I am in my career," she said. "It is all good clean fun if you can keep your head."

"You are different this afternoon," Anthony said, observing the ash-blonde minutely.

"I have you to myself," Janny said comfortably. "I always knew my time would come, and now you get the full Janny treatment."

"I see," Anthony said. "What else do you have in mind?" he asked curiously.

"I don't know for sure," Janny laughed. "It depends how much you play up to me."

Just then, the limousine arrived at the ice arena. The skating complex was a large blue-grey looking building and surrounding constructions. Anthony took Janny by the hand and they stepped through the main entrance of the ice-arena. The staff at the ticket desk waved the dating couple through, and they found themselves standing in an attractively decorated lounge area. The lounge was lined on all sides with comfortable seating, and a variety of arcade game machines were set against the wall.

To the right, the building opened out into a snack bar with a selection of small tables along the front wall. The carpet was industrial low-pile, but still managed to look luxurious because of the bright pattern. The area was heated in case participants leaving the ice rink were chilled and wanted to get warm.

Two ice rinks opened to the rear of the carpeted area. One rink was smaller and obviously designed for children and beginners. The children's area was brightly lit, and the atmosphere was relaxed and playful.

The larger arena was dappled with disco lights, and the ice gleamed white and smooth. The rink was surrounded by a safety rail and variety of popular and jazzy music blared out of a fifties style jukebox set into the back wall. Industrial matting covered the area outside the ice rink and a row of trophies were mounted in pride of place upon a pedestal.

"It's pretty cool in there," Janny said, admiring the large arena.

"No kidding," Anthony said. "You had better put on your sweater."

"Ha, ha," Janny said, poking Anthony in the ribs. "You know that wasn't what I meant."

Anthony twitched. "That tickled," he said.

"What you going to do about it?" Janny inquired teasingly.

The ballerina's stance invited the Charity Eligible to tease her in return, but Anthony held back because he was embarrassed to lay hands on her so familiarly.

Janny shrugged and settled for ordering Anthony around instead. "Go and get me some skates. I am a six-and-a-half in a street shoe."

Janny remained standing by the door while Anthony crossed over to the skate hire area. He talked and gestured to the attendant at the counter for a few minutes, and then returned carrying several pairs of skates. The pair leant against the rail at the edge of the ice and fastened their skates.

"You promised that you would help me skate," Janny reminded Anthony as the ominous twinkle returned to her eye.

"When I'm ready and get my own balance," Anthony said.

Janny smiled placidly. "Take as long as you need," she said.

Anthony stood up and braced himself. He took a couple of experimental steps and reached his hand out to Janny. "I think I've got the hang of it," he said. "It's been a while since I skated myself."

Janny placed her hand in his. "What do you want me to do now?" she asked sweetly.

"Try to balance as I pull you along for a couple of steps," Anthony said. "There, that went well. You must be a natural. Are you ready to take a step the next time I do?"

Janny nodded.

"Here goes," Anthony said. "Right...left...right, that's it! We will circle around the outside slowly."

"I think I'm getting the hang of it," Janny said as she meekly followed all his instructions.

"You do have good instinctive balance," Anthony said. "It is hard to believe you are a beginner!"

Janny grinned and threw away the pretence. "I might have been once or twice before," she said letting his hand go.

"I don't think you are ready for that!" Anthony exclaimed in concern.

"I insist," Janny said, taking off with an awkward lope.

Anthony followed her in concern. "Hey slow down," he said. "You will fall."

"Bad luck if I do," Janny replied. She sped up and soon lapped past her companion, who was too busy trying to stay on his feet to admire the way her gait had smoothed out.

"You are not a beginner after all," Anthony gasped.

"I didn't say I was," Janny called as she over-took him. "I said I was not a figure skater." She laughed. Then spun around and circled back to the Charity Eligible. "Too many people expect me to perform tricks, and I can't risk injury."

"Pretending to be a beginner was a pretty good trick in itself," Anthony said. "You sure had me fooled."

"I like to have fun sometimes," Janny said. "Otherwise life lacks a certain something."

"Fun is important," Anthony said. "All work and no play makes a dull day. But you nearly gave me a heart attack." He was beginning to get warmed up and access his aerobic energy. "Do you want to have a nice straight skate around the arena now?"

"A straight skate," Janny said. "No triple jumps."

"I couldn't do a triple jump to save my life," Anthony said. "Give me your hand, and don't try to pull me along."

"Would I do that? Janny asked slyly.

"I don't know," Anthony said. "It is obvious you could though."

The two linked hands and skated smoothly around the arena several times. It was poetry in motion to skate alongside Janny, and Anthony was enjoying himself. He had always thought that the ash-blonde would make good company, and here she was, proving to be a regular surprise package. At last they slid to a halt near the exit rails.

"What is that I can see over there?" Janny said, pointing to a shadowy door over to the right. The door obviously led into a large area situated between the junior and senior skating rinks.

"It is the ice slope," the Rink Supervisor informed her.

"What do you do there?" Anthony asked.

"You can toboggan if you like," the Supervisor said. "The youth absolutely love it!"

"Would you like to do that?" Anthony asked Janny. "It would be new to me, my local arena wasn't large enough to have a slope!"

"Sure," Janny said. "Tobogganing sounds like fun."

The couple unstrapped their skates and handed them to the attendant, who promised to look after the boots. Crossing to the shadowy door, they looked onto the ice slope.

"It looks like a children's wonderland," Janny said.

"I've found out I am a big kid at heart," Anthony said, looking over her shoulder onto the snowy field.

"Yeah," Janny said, turning and pinching one of his biceps, "You are a really big kid."

Anthony flushed. "I'm actually not used to anyone doing that," he said.

Janny laughed: "I guess you wouldn't be, over at the hospital, with everyone so sick and serious," she agreed.

"Your work as a dancer has made you unusually comfortable with physical contact," Anthony said. "I could tell immediately by the way you held my hand going around the arena. The question is, are you interested in me romantically when you link up, or not?"

"Yes - no, I don't know," Janny said. She threw her arms around Anthony and kissed him quickly on the mouth. "It is early days yet. I think I'll keep us both guessing."

Anthony disengaged himself in confusion. "I reckon I'll go and get us a toboggan," he said.

The Charity Eligible returned in a few minutes with a sled just large enough to fit the two of them, and motioned to Janny to climb the slope with him. At the top, he rested the toboggan on the ground and climbed on the front. Janny climbed on behind him and linked her arms around Anthony's chest. There was barely enough room for two adults on the toboggan.

"This feels a bit unsteady," Janny said. "I think we are too old to play doubles."

"You don't have to ride the toboggan if you don't want," Anthony said, stalling the board with his foot.

"I didn't come on the date to go solo," Janny retorted.

"Hold on then," Anthony said. "I warn you, I don't know how to drive one of these things!"

Janny tightened her arms around Anthony, and they began to careen down the slope. "Slow it down somehow," she gasped.

Anthony tugged squarely on the steering rope, but had little effect. The couple sped down to the bottom of the slope and fell off in an inglorious heap; while the toboggan shot past them and stopped against the wall.

Anthony picked himself up and hauled Janny out of the snow. The pair looked at each other and burst out laughing. Their hysteria lasted quite a few minutes.

"I'm sorry about that," Anthony said at last.

"I'm wet all over," Janny said shaking herself, "But I guess I won't actually die of cold. I think you are meant to steer from side to side, using little curves to slow the toboggan."

"That might work," Anthony said. "Are you game to have another go?"

They pulled the sled back up to the top of the slope and climbed on again. Anthony took a strategically wide hold upon the ropes, and gave the sled a push off with his foot. As the toboggan gained in speed, he tugged the rope in his right hand harder than that in his left and the sled veered slightly. A bit more steering and they performed a turn towards the level ground on the right. By this time they had neared the bottom of the slope, and Anthony allowed the toboggan to plough itself to a halt.

"I think I am getting the hang of it," he said.

"At least we are both still on the toboggan this time," Janny remarked, and the pair began to laugh once again at the memory of their previous descent.

"Are you game to have another go?" Anthony said.

"Yes sure," Janny replied. "However, I warn you, if we come a cropper again, you are buying me hot chocolate - and lots of it!"

"It's a deal," Anthony said.

They managed to navigate the slope several more times with increasing skill. At last Anthony called a halt.

"My arms are getting tired," he said. "How about I buy you that chocolate now?"

"Okay," Janny said. "I won't absolutely insist that you tip us off again before I drink hot chocolate."

Compared to the ice slopes and the two rinks, the lounge area was heavenly warm. Janny sat down on a sofa and Anthony crossed over into the cafeteria to order two cups of steaming chocolate. He returned carrying the drinks carefully and handed one to Janny.

"There you go," he said. "I hope you wouldn't have preferred coffee." He stood facing Janny and hovered uncertainly over her.

"The chocolate is great," Janny said. "Why don't you sit down next to me?"

"I don't know," Anthony said. "I almost feel as if, once I sit down and relax, my legs will be too stiff to stand up again."

"Come on," Janny said. "Sit down and I will give you a shoulder rub, then you can return the favour."

"Out here where everyone can see?" Anthony said, looking mildly surprised.

"Of course," Janny said. "No one is taking any notice."

"There are the television cameras filming us," Anthony whispered.

"We won't be doing anything obscene," Janny said. "It will just turn our date into good drama."

Anthony gave in and sat down beside Janny, who ran her surprisingly strong little hands across his shoulders and up and down his back. The effect was very soothing. After a few minutes Janny stopped, and Anthony started to massage her shoulders in return. Janny's sweater flattened itself to her form, and Anthony found himself enjoying touching the slight but shapely body of the dancer.

Janny relaxed and leant back against him. "You are good at that," she said with a sigh.

Anthony slowed his hand movements, and finally allowed himself to simply sit holding the blonde girl. He noticed her head droop towards his shoulder and allowed her to snuggle into him. Janny's feisty attitude fascinated and titillated Anthony, and he opened his mouth to ask whether she had any romantic feelings towards him. Then he closed it again.

If Anthony knew Janny at all by now, it was his guess that she would give him a nonsensical answer, and maybe she didn't even know her own mind yet. As a gentleman, all he could do was wait. It also seemed slightly unfair of him to put her to question when the rules of the show prohibited him answering with complete transparency.

CHAPTER TWELVE: A SYMPHONY OF DISCORD

When Anthony went to collect Vonda that evening, he found her looking elegant in a black satin evening dress with a silken wrap. Her short blonde hair was brushed glamorously tight against her head, and curled upwards just below her ears.

"You look lovely," Anthony exclaimed, and remarked how well they matched, as he was also formally dressed in a dark double breasted suit.

Vonda blushed both pink and white, prompting Anthony to put a protective arm around her shoulders.

"Relax," he said. "We are going to have a great time."

"I am sure we are," Vonda replied demurely. "I am so glad you sent word ahead to say that we were going to the opera."

"I thought you might like it," Anthony said. "Although I was half afraid it wouldn't be a proper holiday activity for someone who works in an orchestra."

"Oh no," the petite blonde Musician exclaimed. "I rarely get to see a performance from the audience's point of view. The excursion will be a real treat."

"I am happy to hear that," Anthony said. "I hope you don't mind our attending the late performance, I had an active day and needed a bit of rest before going out again."

"It all adds to the adventure," Vonda said, her great blue eyes glowing in the half-light.

Anthony found himself gazing at Vonda and admiring the tip of her cute little nose. He had an almost irresistible urge to say something flirtatious, but restrained himself in case it frightened her. Vonda was obviously the gentle type of girl a man had to treat courteously.

The car drew up in front of the Sydney Opera House and the distinctive sail-shaped architecture of its roof reflected white from the lights of the city. Anthony climbed out of the limousine and assisted Vonda to alight on the paved forecourt. They walked up the steps towards the glass doors and mingled with the late night crowd.

Anthony showed their special VIP passes to the official at the ticket desk, and they were led through the carpeted public area and into the main theatre. Vonda whispered that they had been seated at an optimal position amongst the rows of seats.

"Thank you," Anthony said politely to the usher, and glanced around. The white walls were ornately plastered, and the lighting was pleasantly low key. Despite the fact that they were attending a general performance of the operetta, Vonda and the Charity Eligible appeared to be amongst the first to be seated. Over the next few minutes the other seats began to fill and the lights were dimmed, however, the curtains did not open.

"The production must be running a bit late," Anthony said to Vonda, and the blonde nodded.

"It happens," Vonda said. "I don't mind. We can observe the proceedings all the better."

"Would you like to talk while we are waiting?" Anthony asked, aiming to keep his companion at her ease.

Vonda smiled. "Let's talk about music," she said. "It's a great subject - even though it isn't your field."

"I assume you prefer the classical style," Anthony said.

Vonda wriggled that cute nose. "I've mostly had to play classical with the orchestra," she admitted. "I guess you could say I do know it the best."

"Do you like any other styles?" Anthony asked curiously.

"Actually, I have a secret passion for world music," Vonda said. "Those insistent drums and genuine African and Brazilian rhythms."

"Fancy that," Anthony said. "I should have thought that ethnic music would take a bit of appreciating."

Vonda laughed. "It does take a true music lover to partake in all the styles," she said. "I have noticed it is easy to get settled with the familiar."

"You told me once that you composed," Anthony remarked. "I guess it is your creative streak that leaves you open to all forms of music."

"Maybe," Vonda mused. "I also like to believe that I have an adventurous streak." She looked at Anthony a little defensively: "I know that most people see me as terribly timid, but I am not always like that. I back-packed around Europe one summer when I was an Arts student."

"Really?" Anthony was impressed. "I haven't been to Europe yet myself!"

"Yes," Vonda continued. "I had a scholarship to study in Germany for six months, and when I had finished - I went off on my own. My family were absolutely livid!"

"Do you come from a strict family?" Anthony asked. He was curious as to what had gone into making this girl so reserved, and yet so bravely determined to overcome her diffidence.

"I guess you could say my father was strict," Vonda replied stoically. "It was safest to keep quiet most of the time."

"Surely now you are a grown woman, you can do what you like," Anthony suggested.

Vonda caught on quickly. "Yes," she said. "My family do trust me now I have proven I can conduct my career successfully."

"Your reasons may be different than mine," Anthony said, "But it sounds as though being quiet has become a habit."

"Yes," Vonda said. "I don't always know what to say. And then, I wonder how people will react if I do speak my mind."

"Some people found me too serious," Anthony said. "All work and worry, so I learned to keep it to myself."

"I haven't found you that way in the least," Vonda said, looking at Anthony in surprise.

"This television experience has been very broadening for me," Anthony said.

"Me too," Vonda said.

"You did notice that the first ladies I went out with were nurses though..." Anthony trailed off, but Vonda understood perfectly.

"You had a lot in common with them career-wise," she said.

"I've found it takes more than sharing a career path to create a successful relationship," Anthony remarked.

"Ah yes," Vonda said wisely. "I bet the lady you end up with will not be a nurse."

"What makes you say that?" Anthony asked curiously.

"I haven't had much relationship experience myself," Vonda said. "But of those I've seen around me, it is better if people are not too similar."

"You may be right," Anthony said.

He was silent for a moment, reflecting on the fact that Vonda intrigued him by the very fact that she appeared to be a person of many layers. Whenever she was quiet, he wanted to know what she was thinking and why she was thinking that particular thing.

He considered dropping a hint that the blonde was one of the ladies that he would be happy to have standing next to him at the end of *The Charity Dating Show*, but he restrained himself from comment.

"The curtain is rising at last," Vonda remarked.

"Oh good," Anthony exclaimed, and the pair settled down to enjoy the musical drama.

The operetta had all the classic elements, enabling Anthony and Vonda to enjoy it very much. At one point they found themselves almost crying, another laughing. There was elaborate costuming; farce, confusion and mistaken identity. There was affliction caused by the machinations of a villain, and the prejudices of proud families. The whole story was backed and overlaid with a selection of the finest music from the world's greatest composers.

"That was incredible," Vonda exclaimed, when the curtain fell at the end. Traces of tears still lingered upon her face, but it was impossible for Anthony to tell whether they were tears of laughter or empathy.

Anthony's arm had crept around Vonda during the performance, and upon seeing the tears, he tightened his hold. "It sure was an emotional roller coaster," he said.

"All the best works of musical Art are," Vonda said. "If they don't stir or soothe the feelings, they have failed somehow."

"That one really succeeded," Anthony said. "And you really look wrung out now."

"I respond a bit too well," Vonda said. "When I am playing, I am protected by my concentration upon technique, however, when I listen and watch, emotion overcomes me."

"I felt privileged to share the experience," Anthony said. "Without you showing me where to respond to the story, I would have understood far less of it myself."

"I don't remember saying anything," Vonda was puzzled.

"You didn't have to say anything," Anthony said. "Your body language told me what you were thinking and feeling."

Vonda suddenly seemed to notice the arm Anthony had placed around her, and she shrugged somewhat self-consciously. Anthony gently removed his arm and pretended to stretch.

"You are safe with me," he said reassuringly.

"I know," Vonda murmured.

"What would you like to do now?" Anthony asked.

"I think I would like a quiet coffee," Vonda said. "Although I do need to go to the ladies' room first."

Anthony walked along with Vonda towards the foyer, and stood aside discretely as she veered into the ladies' convenience. He waited patiently for about ten minutes, and then began to look worried.

"Vonda is taking a long time," Anthony said to the camera crew, who had gathered around, their cameras slung inoperative at their sides.

"Stay calm," Simon Steeple advised. "There can be unbelievably long queues in these public ladies' rooms - or so I have been told!"

George nodded. "It's impossible to hurry a line of women," he said.

Anthony waited for ten more minutes, chatting jovially with the camera crew. Then he glanced at his watch: "That does it," he said. "Vonda has been gone almost half an hour."

"That does seem like a long time," George said. He turned to Simon: "Do you think half an hour is too long for someone to queue in the ladies' room?"

Simon frowned. "It's stretching it a bit," he said. "She might be sick."

"We are all men," Anthony said glancing around the crew, "How are we going to find out?"

"I will call one of the female ushers," Simon said. He waved a hand and a member of the staff looked their way inquiringly.

Anthony stepped forward, as it was his date that had gone missing.

"I'm sorry to bother you," he said apologetically, "But my lady friend went into the rest room half an hour ago..."

The Usherette nodded understandingly. "I will go and see whether she is all right," she said. The neatly uniformed woman crossed to the ladies' room, opened the door and passed inside. It was a couple of minutes before she returned, and there was a puzzled look on her face.

"There is no one inside," the Usherette said.

"What?" Anthony, Simon and George exclaimed simultaneously.

The Usherette viewed them quizzically. "Could she have come out without you noticing?" she asked.

"I guess it is possible," Anthony said. "The crowd did block our view at times."

"Would she have gone home without you?" The Usherette inquired.

Simon shook his head. "No," he said. "We have a limousine and a hire car. She wouldn't have had any reason to leave without us - even if she got angry with handsome here!"

"Is there anywhere else the lady might have gone?" The Usherette asked carefully.

George looked thoughtful. "It is possible that Vonda thought you were meeting her down in the cafe area, or even out by the car," he said to Anthony.

The Usherette looked relieved. "Then I suggest you look for her in those places," she said.

Anthony and the camera crew made their way out to the roadside to check on the waiting limousine, where the driver assured them that he had not seen Vonda.

"Vonda must still be inside then," Anthony surmised. He turned to George: "Can you take us to this coffee shop?"

George and Simon both frowned. "The theatre coffee shop might actually be closed at this hour," Simon said. "There is only really the cabaret bar still open."

"Well let's go there then," Anthony said impatiently. "I don't know why Vonda would have gone ahead without me, but it must be where she is."

The men climbed back up the front steps, crossed the foyer and passed down a corridor into another area altogether. Here the lighting was dim, and a live band was playing blues guitar music. A bar counter was tucked off to one side, and a number of small tables dotted the periphery. A small carpeted area in front of the band was being used as a dance floor by some rock enthusiasts.

"It is a sort of after opera party," Simon said, showing their VIP passes at the entrance. "It doesn't run every night, but when it does, it goes really late."

"I don't see Vonda," George began, but Anthony caught him by the arm.

"Mightn't that be her over there?" he asked, pointing to a girl at a table with a rough looking man. The man in question had a shaven head and short beard, and was wearing a brown fringed cowboy shirt.

"It could be Vonda," George said doubtfully, "But what is she doing with someone other than Anthony?"

"Ex-boyfriend maybe," Simon said sceptically. He activated the power button on his camera and lifted the viewfinder to his eye.

"Whatever are you doing?" George exclaimed.

"My job," Simon said imperturbably. "This could be good! George, you can go along with Anthony in case this boy turns nasty and our Eligible needs back-up."

George pulled a wry face that was barely visible in the dim room, and turned to Anthony. "Come on then," he said, "Let's see what is going on here."

As the men approached the table, they were able to ascertain that it was indeed Vonda sitting there. The blonde appeared to be held under restraint by a strong hand, and the fellow with her was talking loudly.

"If you were a classy chick," the Cowboy pronounced, "You would be thrilled to get to know Roy. I have my own motor cycle and I work out twice daily."

"That sounds very impressive," Vonda was saying in an appeasing tone. "However, I keep telling you that I came here with someone."

Roy was obviously very drunk, because he snorted loudly. "Nonsense," he said. "You were alone when I saw you."

"I was just coming out of the ladies' toilet," Vonda said reasonably.

"Why did you speak to me then?" Roy asked. "You must have liked the look of me a bit."

"You asked me for the time," Vonda replied, "And I had no idea you were going to grab me by the arm and drag me down here."

Roy looked illogically pleased. "I've got good muscles then?" He reflected her statement as if accepting a compliment, and tugged harder at Vonda's hand.

Vonda looked sincerely frightened. "Please let me go," she cried.

George and Anthony had heard enough to feel justified interrupting this little scenario. Anthony stepped forward and laid a protective hand upon Vonda's shoulder. "Please do as the lady asks," he said firmly. "As you can see, she really is here with me."

"Bags of garbage," Roy exclaimed with an expletive, but he did loosen his hold upon Vonda's hand.

Vonda pulled herself clear of her harasser and shrunk against Anthony. "I am glad you came," she said trembling.

"You didn't think I would leave you?" Anthony asked, and Vonda squirmed.

"I wasn't sure you would actually find me," the slim Blonde admitted.

Roy rose to his feet and approached Anthony belligerently. "What are you doing interfering between me and the lady?" he growled.

"Like I said before," Anthony repeated non-defensively, "The lady was with me."

"Stinking garbage," Cowboy Roy said again, with more colourful expletives added.

The ruffian reached across and tugged at Vonda, who resisted his touch. Anthony inserted himself between Roy and his victim, with the result that a scuffle ensued. It looked ugly for a minute, and then George stepped in from behind the Cowboy Roy and immobilised his shoulders.

"Take it easy mate," George said diplomatically.

Roy struggled, but George was joined by one of the security guards. Together the two men pulled the drunken ruffian away from Anthony and Vonda, heading him out towards the back exit.

Vonda looked up at Anthony. "Don't worry about a coffee," she said. "I would like to go back to the house now."

"I'll take you back to the limousine," Anthony said, and Vonda nodded gratefully.

Once in the privacy of the car, the Blonde collapsed into Anthony's arms. "I've never been able to deal with that sort of thing," she whispered.

Anthony looked down at her pale face. He felt a rush of tenderness and lifted a hand to smooth her mussed hair. "You are too gentle for your own good," he whispered.

Vonda began to cry softly and Anthony cradled her to him. She had all the appeal of a damsel in distress, and his heart lurched. "You need someone to look after you," he said.

Vonda stifled a little sob: "I would sort of prefer to be able to take care of myself," she said.

"Okay," Anthony said reasonably, "The next date we go on, we will be learning self-defence."

"You would really organise that for me?" Vonda asked incredulously.

"Yes," Anthony said into her blonde hair. "Your safety is very important to me."

"Thank you," Vonda breathed. She cuddled into his side as if he were her knight-in-shining-armour, and Anthony basked in the blonde girl's gratitude. It wasn't every day that he got to be a hero.

Anthony arrived at the Candidate House around mid-morning the next day to pick up Deborah, Nadine, Constance and Kendra. The group was planning to attend a 'Ladies' Day' at the Royal Randwick Race course and the girls had spent the previous day designing their costumes.

Nadine was wearing a peasant style off-the-shoulder blouse in white cotton and a flowing green skirt in a muslin fabric. Some braiding had been appliqued around the hem to add weight and interest. Her shoes were flat leather sandals, and she wore a row of large plastic beads around her neck, and huge studs in her ears. Nadine's hair, which was usually piled elaborately on her head, was caught back in a traditional pony tail, with two curly wisps escaping towards the front. Her make-up was heavier than usual to provide glamour and sun protection.

Deborah was wearing a burgundy shirt with a horsey motif on the pocket, and reddish-brown leather pants. She had sturdy leather boots upon her feet, and a Stetson hat on her head. All in all, it was a sporty combination for the socialite.

Constance was looking modern in dark blue denim jeans, a checked cotton shirt which buttoned down the front, sneakers and a baseball cap decorated with the number five. A denim jacket was slung casually over her shoulder.

Kendra was wearing tight grey leggings, black boots and a long navy jacket. Her hair, which was usually pulled straight back from her face, was brushed slightly forward and caught up in blue a hippy-style band.

"You all look great," Anthony said, surveying the girls.

"Thank you," Constance and Nadine each said coyly. They both pirouetted around as if inviting more attention, and Anthony reflected upon the awkwardness of having them both on the same date.

"You look smart yourself," Kendra remarked, as Anthony was wearing a brown striped polo shirt with blue jeans and black boots. He had a leather Stetson on his head as well.

"Let's get going," Deborah said. "I enjoy the occasional visit to the races."

They all climbed into the limousine, Nadine making sure that she was on one side of Anthony, and Constance pushing herself forward to sit on the other side. The two girls gave each other hard looks across his broad shoulders. Kendra and Deborah shrugged and settled themselves down on the opposite seat.

"I like show jumping," Kendra said, "But I've only seen it at the Royal Show."

"I have heard they can be cruel to the horses that race," Constance ventured somewhat timorously.

"I should hope that doesn't happen very often," Deborah said. "The race horses are considered very valuable, and most of the trainers go out of their way to ensure they are in good condition."

"There must be accidents," Nadine said, sounding slightly surprised to find herself siding with Constance.

"Yes, racing accidents are very unfortunate," Deborah said. "A good owner would be upset if something happened to his horse."

"Does your family own any horses Deborah?" Kendra asked.

"My father had one or two when I was younger," Deborah said. "Then he lost interest for a while. I believe he might have a mare again now."

After about three quarters of an hour's drive through the city, they came to the racecourse. The limousine pulled up, and the girls jumped out onto the dusty edge of the road; where the grass was obviously worn down by the passage of many feet, both human and equine.

The race track was situated behind The Australian Turf Club, which offered stadium seating and function rooms. The betting office was situated at the back of the club rooms, and then there was the great green oval of the racecourse, with the dusty brown track around the perimeter. The stables which provided temporary accommodation for the horses had been built out behind the longest stretch of seating.

Anthony led the group to a comfortable looking area beneath a shady roof.

"We will sit here," he said.

Nadine and Constance began eyeing each other jealously and making meaningless small talk. Both girls seemed determined to keep the other occupied and well away from Anthony. Kendra settled herself comfortably and sat looking perfectly contented. Deborah opened the race guide and consulted it earnestly.

"Leticia gave me some spending money for the lot of us," Anthony announced. "I suggest we keep our wagers small, because none of us want to develop a gambling problem!"

"I expected you wouldn't approve of gambling," Kendra murmured lazily.

"Not normally," Anthony said. "However, betting is part of the fun of the day. I will put a small amount on one horse for each of you ladies. Which do you fancy?"

"I can never pick horses," Kendra said. "Put ten dollars on something from a good stable for me."

"*Bright Boy* in the third sounds right according to your criteria," Deborah suggested, "Bet to place, it's safer than betting to win".

"Okay," Kendra said. "Go for it!"

Anthony pulled out a notepad and a pen. "Ten dollars on Bright Boy in the third race, to place only for Kendra," he wrote. "What about you Constance," he asked, "Do you fancy any of the horses?"

Constance glanced briefly at the race guide. "I like *Lucky in Love* in the fifth, she said.

"Ah - you're a name girl," Deborah remarked cynically.

"To place or win?" Anthony asked.

"Oh to win, definitely," Constance said glaring at Nadine. "There is no point in coming second."

Anthony ignored the by-play and wrote down: "Ten dollars on Lucky in Love to win in the fifth." He then glanced up at Nadine. "Do you have a choice?" he queried.

"I like the odds on *Globe Derby* in the fifth," Nadine said.

Deborah laughed. "Actually those numbers mean it is unlikely to win," she said.

"I like to take a small risk and have it pay off big," Nadine said.

"Watch it - you could turn into a real gambler!" Deborah said. "Are you aiming to win or place?"

"I mean to win," Nadine said firmly, and Constance scowled.

"*Globe Derby* in the fourth - to win," Anthony noted seriously.

"What about you Deborah?"

"I will have *Scrawny Bird*, *Yellow Brick Road* and *Tilly Trotter* to make the trifecta in the sixth thanks," Deborah said.

Anthony whistled. "Very confidently called," he said. He wrote Deborah's choice down and then hesitated. "What horse should I have?" he said.

"Do you have any preference?" Deborah asked thoughtfully.

"Not really," Anthony said.

"Well if you are quick, you can get good odds on *Super Stud* in the second," Deborah said. "It's from a good stable, as well being an amusing choice. I would recommend betting on it to place, however."

"Okay, I'll try that," Anthony said. He wrote the horse's name down and hurried across to the bookie's office. When he returned, the Charity Eligible settled himself down between Deborah and Kendra. "You promised to tell me what had changed for you," he said to Deborah.

Deborah glanced cautiously across at the camera crew. "Do you have to ask right now?" she asked.

"I don't know when else we might get to talk," Anthony said.

"I think Deb means this is not private enough," Kendra added helpfully. She purposely kept her voice low.

"I know," Anthony said, "But the camera crew are always around."

Deborah took a deep breath and placed her mouth close to Anthony's ear. "I know I am not in love with you," she whispered. "But I might be in love with someone else around here!"

"Ah," Anthony murmured. "I should have guessed."

"It hit me like a ton of bricks," Deborah whispered again. "He is friendly, but I don't know how he feels."

Anthony shielded the lower half of his face with the race guide. "I can't imagine any man you genuinely like not responding to you," he muttered under the cover.

"Thank you," Deborah said. She dropped her voice to a whisper once again: "I reckon we could be exact opposites and there could be some difficulties."

"I still wish you all the best," Anthony said. He turned to Kendra on his other side. "I hope you are not thinking of deserting me too," he said jovially.

Kendra patted his arm affectionately. "Of course not," she said. "Although my level of commitment does depend on how your other dates are progressing."

"Should I be telling you about them?" Anthony asked cautiously.

"I don't really know," Kendra said.

Anthony pursed his mouth thoughtfully. "I would like to be honest with you," he said. "I don't see how things could possibly work out if I am not."

"Give me the briefest of summaries then," Kendra suggested.

"Well," Anthony said, "You know I had first dates with Janny and Vonda this round."

"Oh yes," Kendra said, "And I've got a fair idea how your earlier dates with Nadine and Constance must have gone." She glanced meaningfully at the bickering brunettes.

"Okay then," Anthony said, keeping his voice low because of the nearby cameras. "You could say that Janny and I had fun, but she is keeping me on my toes, and Vonda is a real live sweetie. I can't help wishing Vonda happiness, whatever happens."

"I am glad to hear that," Kendra said thoughtfully.

Deborah poked Anthony in the side. "Race two was just run," she said. "Your horse *Super Stud* did manage to place."

"Really?" Anthony exclaimed in excitement. "That is the first time I have won anything on the horses."

"Watch you don't get hooked," Deborah said cynically.

"I may not bet again," Anthony said. "But it was great to have won just this once."

"Shush," Deborah said. "They are running the third, and I have to listen for Kendra's horse."

"How's it going?" Kendra asked, displaying some excitement of her own.

"Good," Deborah said. "See that is him down there."

Kendra leant forward and watched eagerly as *Bright Boy* ran around the track. He was a good strong horse and kept well to the front all of the race. Unfortunately, he was overtaken by a nose at the finish.

"He lost!" Kendra wailed.

"Actually," Deborah said, "You are okay. You betted to place, not to win."

"You did that for me," Kendra said. "Thank you Deborah, you are so clever."

"You are welcome," Deborah murmured lazily.

Anthony turned to Kendra: "I believe we have drinks and a lunch hamper to collect from the Grandview Restaurant," he said. "Do you want to help me go and get them?"

Kendra agreed and the couple began walking back to the club room. A few minutes later they returned to the group talking companionably and carrying a large cooler box.

Kendra announced that she was hot and unbuttoned her jacket. The bandeau top she wore underneath proved to be brief and clingy.

"I like your shirt," Anthony said. "You also have a very good figure."

"Thank you," Kendra said.

She leant over with a complete lack of self-consciousness and began to serve the picnic food, while Anthony continued to eye her chest appreciatively. The Charity Eligible couldn't help noticing that Kendra was full busted, whereas the other girls were predominantly fashionably thin.

Constance and Nadine, despite their mutual enmity, exchanged loaded glances. Kendra's firm bosoms represented good reason for Anthony's decision to move on from both of them. Moreover for all they knew, back at the Candidate House, Vonda and Janny might each pose just as strong a threat.

Anthony, who was only vaguely aware of the competitive by-play, thoroughly enjoyed his lunch. He washed the last sandwhich down with soft drink and glanced across to where the other bench, where Nadine and Constance had retreated to indulge their sulky moods.

"I am going to sit with Nadine and Constance for a while till their races are run," he announced.

"Wish them luck for us," Kendra said.

"Yeah, I will do that," Anthony said. "Goodbye for now."

Deborah and Kendra chorused goodbye in turn and then sat chatting in friendly fashion.

"You know," Deborah said, "If men were as straight forward as horses, I would be able to make a good guess who Anthony would pick at the end of all this."

Kendra blushed. "I can't pretend I don't have some interest in the outcome," she said. "Who do you think it will be?"

"I'm not saying," Deborah said coyly. She opened the race guide and started studying it again. "Unfortunately, men are not as straight forward as horses."

"Well, do you think you have a winning bet on the trifecta then?" Kendra asked.

"I don't know," Deborah said. "Trifectas are hard to pick. I just had to have a try."

"Like love," Kendra mused.

"Yes, a bit like love," Deborah said. "I can't believe I am beginning to talk this way!"

Anthony approached the bleacher that Nadine and Constance were perched upon. "May I join you girls?" he asked.

"Oh yes sure," Nadine said, wriggling across to make an appropriate amount of space between herself and Constance.

"We thought you were never coming," Constance murmured. "Whatever did you have to say to Deborah and Kendra all that time?"

"This and that," Anthony said defensively. "Deborah helped me work out the bets earlier."

"Talking about bets," Constance said, "My horse, *Lucky in Love*, is about to run."

The trio watched intently as the third race was run. Lucky in Love failed to win, but did achieve third place in the finishing line-up.

"Oh no," Constance wailed. "So near and yet so far. It happens to me every time."

"Perhaps it is an omen," Nadine said somewhat smugly, and Constance gave her an offended look.

"It is a pity you didn't bet to place," Anthony said. He reached out and put a comforting arm around Constance's shoulders, but she remained incredibly tense.

"What would be the good of placing?" Constance demanded fretfully.

"The chances are better," Anthony explained, "And you do get something out of the experience."

"It doesn't sound very exciting," Constance said.

Nadine snorted. That's the trouble with being a perfectionist," she said. "You are never satisfied."

"Hush," Anthony said as he felt the tension mounting around him. "It's time for Nadine's horse to run."

Nadine's horse failed to either win or place, in fact it trotted happily across the finish line last. "I thought that might happen," Nadine said resignedly.

"If you thought that, why did you bet on the horse?" Constance asked irritatingly.

"Because someday I will have the luck, and the reward will be that much better," Nadine returned imperturbably.

"I don't know whether you have a lot of confidence, or are just incredibly stupid Nadine," Constance said darkly.

"Now that is enough ladies," Anthony declared uncomfortably. He was aware that the girls were metaphorically clashing swords over him, but he was unsure what he, the mere male in the equation, could do about the situation. "I am sorry that neither of your horses won, you might do better another time."

"We don't really mind about the horses Anthony," Nadine began, but Constance cut her off with a howl.

"Speak for yourself," Constance said, leaping to her feet. "I did care about the horse, and about my date, and the basketball too, although I seem not to have your advantages."

"I don't know what you mean," Nadine said petulantly.

"I was the first person to feel close to Anthony," Constance cried, "And then you set out to move in and spoil everything."

"Be fair," Nadine said. "I wasn't to know what happened on your date, and I had just as much right to get close to Anthony as you did."

Constance was incensed. She raised her right hand and delivered an open palm slap across the cheek of the shorter girl.

Nadine said, "Ouch," and rubbed her cheek. She appeared to be considering some form of retaliation when Anthony broke in on the drama.

"I don't understand this, and I am really shocked," he said. "You girls appear to have both forgotten you are not the only ones involved here. I went out with you on those dates, and I do have an opinion about what happened too."

Nadine stared at the Charity Eligible in consternation, but Constance seemed to barely register his words. The fire continued to burn in Constance's eyes, and she looked incredibly sulky.

"It is all her fault," Constance muttered stubbornly.

"I don't see how," Anthony said, "And I resent you fighting over me as if I didn't have a say in who I end up with. If those are your attitudes, I will be forced to choose neither of you."

"I am sorry Anthony," Nadine said appealingly. "You must understand that I didn't mean to hurt anyone, and it certainly wasn't me who did the slapping."

"That is true," Anthony said. "However, I did hear you doing some goading."

"There were two of us in the fight," Constance said bitterly. The tears were streaming down her face, as she turned and walked across to where Deborah was sitting on her own, because Kendra had gone to the conveniences.

"Did you hear that Deborah?" Constance said.

"I sort of couldn't help it dear," Deborah said. "You do take things so seriously."

"What happened to your horses?" Constance said, leaning on the other girl's shoulder.

"Two of them placed, but the wrong horse won," Deborah said. "It is really hard to pick the trifecta."

"Why do you try then?" Constance asked.

"For the challenge," Deborah said. "Once or twice, I have actually gotten it right."

"Let me have a go then," Constance said and the two girls bent over the race guide speculating regarding the horses abilities. The race guide appeared blurred through her tears, but at least it was a distraction.

Anthony invited Nadine to go for a walk in a bid to rescue their friendship, but brunette declined his invitation.

"No thanks," she sniffed. "I'm normally easy going, but I've had a bit of a shock. I think I will sit down for a bit."

Anthony looked concerned. "Let me know if you need a headache tablet or anything," he said.

Nadine nodded: "I appreciate your concern, although it does come a bit late."

"I have my limitations," Anthony said. He sighed and remained seated beside Nadine.

The last horse race was run about four o'clock in the afternoon, and then the party returned to the limousine. The return journey was quiet, with Deborah and Kendra talking together casually, Constance looking forlorn, and Nadine remaining defiant.

Anthony attempted to console Constance as he bid her goodbye, but she turned away to hide her face and marched straight into the Candidate House. Nadine also gave Anthony a cool hand-shake instead of her customary kiss and hug, and he steeled himself to match the change in level of fondness. Luckily, Deborah was as friendly as ever in her farewell, and Kendra was also cordially affectionate.

CHAPTER THIRTEEN: THE TABLES ARE TURNED

Anthony had been invited to dinner at the Candidate House that evening. The majority of the girls having been out all day, it was a slightly hum-drum affair, despite Leticia having made an effort with the decorations. The theme was the African jungle, and the floor was covered with imitation leopard pelts and rugs.

Several ecstatically primitive prints adorned the walls, and a number of rubber tree plants and potted ferns had been placed around the room. The most exotic touch was the little fountain which had been set up indoors.

The girls all filed in, collected their food and sat around talking quietly. Deborah and Kendra appeared perfectly content to relax after their outing, and Nadine was compensating by displaying a feverish form of vivaciousness that did not reach all the way to her eyes. Only Janny and Vonda, who had spent the day at the house swimming and watching movies on the big screen television, appeared to have any natural energy.

As Anthony dipped his fingers into the water of the little fountain, he noticed Constance slink into the room, attempting to look as unobtrusive as possible. He crossed the floor and approached the slim brunette.

"Please believe me," Anthony said earnestly. "I never intended for you to get your feelings hurt - I was merely following the procedure and getting to know everyone."

Constance shrugged: "We had a talk once before Anthony," she said. "And we agreed that there was an early connection. I am sad that it dwindled into nothing – but that is the way things are."

Anthony frowned. "I can't quite fathom what happened," he said. "And how our disappointment turned into a battle with Nadine."

"I am afraid you cannot be best friends with everyone," Constance said. "It just doesn't work somehow. Please excuse me now Anthony, I would like some time to myself."

"Are you sure there is nothing I can do?" Anthony asked anxiously.

"I am sure," Constance said. "Over is over, and I need to move on right away." She glanced around the room, and her gaze lit upon Janny and Vonda who were negotiating their way into a cosy corner behind some palms. The tall brunette turned and walked purposefully towards the two blondes.

"Hello girls," she said.

Vonda and Janny greeted Constance with warm hugs. "We heard there was some drama," Janny said.

"I know," Constance said. "I lost my cool today. I have been losing it for some time to be honest."

"We have seen it happen, and we are sorry," Vonda said. "We would have helped if we could, but we all have been set up by the show as rivals."

"I need to get my mind onto something or someone else," Constance said, "And I need to do it quickly!"

"That's the spirit," Janny said. "Find a hobby or get really involved in some group."

"I am thinking about something like that," Constance said.

"Talk to Kendra," Vonda suggested. "She has heaps of creative ideas."

"Kendra is nice," Constance said. "And Anthony is very attentive to her. I don't know why it is Nadine I am so angry with!"

Janny and Vonda exchanged cautious glances. "It was probably just something in the interaction between you and Nadine," Janny said. "She does like to be provocative."

Part way through the African evening, George brushed up against Deborah, and she looked at him in surprise. George coloured and gave the socialite an appealing look.

"Hey Deb," he said. "We are losing sound on one of the microphones. Come and help me check the electrical cords."

Deborah obligingly followed George over to the sound board, which was cleverly tucked behind a screen. "What is wrong?" she asked, looking at the tangle of cords.

"Nothing I couldn't have gotten one of the technical support to look at," George said. "But I wanted to talk to you without being sprung."

"Oh sure," Deborah said, "What should we do about the sound then - I take it there is a real issue?"

"I reckon something must be coming unplugged behind those palms," George said. "Go and look for a loose connection, and I will manage the board so that it doesn't make an almighty squeal when the power comes back on."

"Yes sir!" Deborah said smartly. "If you think I can manage that sir."

George grinned: "From what I've seen you are pretty capable," he said. "Especially for a rich bitch."

Deborah jumped sharply. "Just let me go find that loose cord, and then I will come back here and rich bitch you," she said.

"I'm looking forward to it," George remarked cheekily.

Deborah traced her way along the wall, peering behind the large potted palms. At one point, she did come to a join in which two cord ends seemed quite loose, and she plugged them tighter together.

"All done," she said, returning to George behind the screen.

"Excellent!" George said, "And with minimum of back feed too."

"Glad to be of help," Deborah said. "Now what else did you want to talk to me about?"

George flushed once again. He had fair skin and seemed to make a habit of blushing, especially around the boisterous socialite.

"I really appreciated you and Kendra playing monopoly with Parker yesterday afternoon," he said.

"It was our pleasure," Deborah said. "We had finished our shopping and had no dates to go on that day. Constance was pacing and moping, and Nadine was getting her hair conditioned. Parker was actually the best company we had."

"He gets bored and lonely hanging around the kitchen staff," George said. "It is better for him on a school day than on the weekend."

"I can imagine," Deborah said. "In fact, I can almost identify! My Dad was too busy with his business to take much notice of us kids, and my Mum had lots of social lunches."

George looked alarmed. "I hope you don't think I neglect Parker," he exclaimed.

"Oh no!" Deborah said. "I think that you are an excellent father. It is just that there is only one of you."

"Very true," George said. "I am sorry that I was only able to drop by for a few minutes for coffee between shifts. We had a very big day filming a carnation ceremony and two dates."

"I can imagine," Deborah murmured. "In fact, you are at it almost twenty-four-hours a day, seven days a week."

"Yes," George said. "Luckily, the races started mid-morning and I was able to catch a couple hours of sleep."

"Luckily you can sleep," Deborah said. "I would tend towards insomnia on such a variable schedule."

"I think I am well suited to my job," George said. He looked flustered. "This is a bit awkward with you being a contestant and all, so theoretically I shouldn't be asking, but I have been wondering how you feel about me."

"I like you a lot," Deborah said. She had never been one for beating about the bush, and now that she was in love, she didn't see any reason to play coy.

"I was beginning to get that impression," George said.

"Something about me kissing you in the corner of the lounge room perhaps," Deborah suggested slyly.

"It was only on the cheek," George said, "But it did make me wonder."

"I'm fairly effusive by nature," Deborah said, "However it does usually mean something."

"I am glad to hear that," George said all in a rush. "I happen to know tomorrow is a big picnic, but there is no filming scheduled for the evening. How about sneaking out for a rendezvous with me?"

"I would love to," Deborah said. She looked ecstatic.

"Eight o'clock by the shrubbery," George said. "That's settled then. You need to go and get yourself filmed talking to Anthony now. The show must go on as usual."

"Your word is my command," Deborah said with military emphasis.

The socialite slid out from behind the screen and sidled her way into the communal scene once again. Anthony was deep in discussion with Kendra, and Nadine was hanging around trying to pretend she was a part of their conversation. It seemed no one had noticed Deborah's temporary absence.

Anthony was called into the deliberation room soon after dinner. He settled himself down to think, and found that his mind was dwelling upon the question of Nadine and Constance.

Both girls seemed charming and easy-going while alone with him, however, this relaxed quality appeared to diminish in the presence of the other ladies; when their competitive streaks emerged. Moreover, Anthony feared their attitudes might eventually irritate the equality-valuing Kendra, sensitive Vonda or spirited Janny.

Anthony drummed his finger-nails upon the table, and then he did an unprecedented thing. Leaving the deliberation room, he sneaked into the hall and picked up the receiver of the phone situated on the stand. He dialed a number and waited patiently.

The receiver on the other end was lifted and a familiar voice said: "Hello." The voice was that of Anthony's best friend Abraham, whom he had invited onto the show to meet the girls and make a friendly assessment.

"Ah - mate," Anthony said. "I was hoping you could do me a favour. I really do need your opinion on these girls."

"Keep them around and I will check them out tomorrow," Abraham replied cheerfully.

"I think I need some advice tonight," Anthony said. "I have an elimination and I don't know what to do."

"How can I advise you without seeing the girls mate?" Abraham objected. "You better let whatever is meant to happen go down tonight, and I will be there very soon."

"That sounds a little fatalistic," Anthony said.

"Que Sera, Sera – what will be, will be," Abraham said. "It is the only way to manage the ladies sometimes!"

"I'm really looking forward to your visit," Anthony said. "It will be great to have some back-up amongst all these women."

"Tomorrow then," Abraham said. "Hang in there mate."

Anthony hung up the phone and sneaked back into the deliberation room. He was sitting there demurely when Leticia came to collect him for the carnation ceremony. If the hostess suspected anything out of the ordinary, she did not comment.

Once in the reception room, Anthony crossed to the small table and picked up the first carnation. The six remaining girls stood along the far wall looking at him. Constance and Nadine both looked very intense, Janny looked relaxed, and Vonda had a shy smile on her lips. Kendra appeared serene, while Deborah was attempting to exchange a sly glance with George.

"Come closer please ladies," Anthony said.

The girls obediently advanced their line a couple of steps forward, and stopped at the edge of the mat. Anthony fumbled towards the first carnation, although he was still undecided as to whose name he would be calling first.

Constance, however, stepped out of the line and continued to advance until she was facing Anthony squarely.

"This has been an interesting experience for me," Constance began politely. "However, I do not feel that a viable relationship can develop for me while on this show."

"I am very sorry to hear that Constance," Anthony acknowledged.

"Under these circumstances," Constance continued. "I think it would be best if I left and started pursuing something of my own."

"I wish you all the best Constance," Anthony said lamely. "I hope you find someone to make you happy."

The Charity Eligible put the carnation he had been holding back down on the table and considered what else to say. Constance was not waiting until she was eliminated - instead she had chosen to take control and depart on her own terms - and had taken the power completely out of his hands. Constance nodded in the briefest acknowledgement of Anthony's statement and then turned to hug the women.

"I have enjoyed meeting you," she said to Janny, who hugged her back warmly. "You have my address, please keep in contact," Constance urged Deborah. "I hope things turn out well for you," she said to Kendra, who was blinking tears of sympathy out of her eyes; and finally "Keep on coming out of your shell, I can see this show has done good things for you," was her advice to Vonda.

The only girl Constance did not hug was Nadine. The two brunettes faced each other truculently, and in the end, Nadine was the first to look down.

"Whatever my faults, and whatever mistakes I made," Constance said, "I always tried to be fair. I haven't see the same quality in you."

"I don't care what you see," Nadine said. "I have my own way of doing things, and I have to stick to it."

"I think we had better leave it at that too," Constance said firmly. She hugged the other girls once again.

"I will miss you," she said. "You have been there for me the last few days. Some more than others - you know who you are!"

The tears began to gather in her eyes, and Constance ducked towards the door-way. Reaching out in front of her blindly, Constance pushed the door open and exited into the hall. Once in the hall, she walked towards her room and flung herself down on her bed. The brunette was shaking from the enormity of the stance she had taken, but she did not regret a word of what she had said.

A few minutes later, she stood up and stumbled right into the arms of Simon Steeple. The pretty brunette looked up at the camera man in surprise. He was normally very respectful and had never approached the girl's bedroom area before.

"Whatever are you doing here Simon?" Constance asked.

"I handed the main camera to George," Simon said. "Darling, I noticed you from the very first day of the show, and I have been waiting for you to give up on that Anthony dude and go out with me."

"I am sorry," Constance said. "I never figured. Even when you dropped a hint or two – I didn't realise."

"You were just doing what you came here to do," Simon said, "And you have finished doing it now."

"I have haven't I?" Constance said with some satisfaction.

She noticed that Simon still had his arms around her. He smelled like cologne and his long hair was silky against his collar.

"You are holding me very tight," she whispered.

"That's not a problem is it?" Simon said. "I made sure the door was shut."

"I don't know," Constance said. "I can be a bit cautious-like at first. That is what went wrong with Anthony."

"The Charity Eligible has other women on his mind," Simon Steeple observed. "You need someone who has eyes only for you."

"Isn't that what all women need?" Constance shrugged.

"I assure you that I will treat you well," Simon said. "I have seen many beauties come and beauties go, and I promise that I am serious about you!"

"Oh, in that case," Constance said, relenting: "You can give me a little kiss."

Constance knew that Simon was a hard worker and that despite his bohemian appearance, he was an extremely gentle man. He would never force himself on a woman who did not want him, but was in her room to offer her the whole-hearted commitment that Anthony had been unable to give.

In the light of Simon's sincere regard, Constance's romantic fantasies could safely flower into a relationship. She relaxed and returned his kisses with shy enthusiasm. It was much more fulfilling than kissing a man she was sharing with six other girls.

"Please stay a little while and help me pack," she whispered, " "That is, unless you need to get back to the camera work."

"It's cool," Simon said. "George can finish this particular shoot by himself."

The couple talked while Constance bundled her things into her suitcase and hatched a cunning plan for keeping in contact for the next few weeks. Once the current season of *The Charity Dating Show* went to air and they would be free to reveal their relationship to the world without risking Simon's career.

An hour later, a limousine arrived to carry Constance out of the Candidate House and into the future. She was in high spirits and looking forward to the future, although she toned her final speech down for Simon to film as the car drove away.

"Please don't think of me as the villain of the season," Constance appealed to audience through the camera lens. "I don't believe that fighting with the other women is the right thing to do. I felt like I lost myself over time, and I am very sorry I slapped Nadine. I am leaving the *Charity Dating Show* of my own accord to regain my sense of independence and dignity."

"Bravo, it's a wrap," Simon cried.

Constance settled back into her seat and fondled the precious card Simon had given her with his contact details. "I cannot believe I found love on *The Charity Dating Show* anyway," she whispered to herself.

Meanwhile, back in the small reception room, Anthony faced the remaining girls, who now represented his top five choices. They were all atwitter, discussing Constance's assertive decision to leave the show. Nadine looked pleased that Constance had left, although she had not come through the encounter in the very best of lights herself. Deborah and Kendra were primarily admiring Constance's resolve and initiative, while Janny and Vonda were wondering what Constance would do once she got home.

"Can I have your attention please?" Anthony said. "Anyone would think that Constance had been the star of the show!"

"She has certainly turned the tables on you," Deborah remarked.

"I have five carnations to give out, and there are five ladies here," Anthony said. "I get to keep you all, which is almost the ideal scenario. Why don't you come forward and collect your carnations?"

"Come on Anthony," Janny remarked cheekily, "We expect you to do better than that... you have to grovel and ask us to stay."

"Yeah, some more of us might want to leave!" Vonda observed, almost choking on her own audacity.

"At least you will know that we are all thoroughly empowered," Kendra announced. "Good for Constance!"

"Ladies!" Anthony exclaimed. "It's not the easiest for me to stand here, without thinking you are all going to stage a mutiny."

"No mutiny here," Nadine said. She stepped forward and extended her hand to Anthony. "Let bygones be bygones, I want to stay."

"Do you believe you can work in with the others Nadine?" Anthony asked. "I don't want any more scenes like yesterday."

"I think so," Nadine said in a more subdued tone. She did not look thrilled to receive a caution, but she accepted her flower and returned to the edge of the carpet.

Janny stepped forward: "I am waiting Anthony," she said provocatively. "Make me your best offer!"

"Okay," Anthony said. "Janny dear, I enjoyed ice skating with you. I even enjoyed falling off the toboggan. Will you come out on a boating picnic with me tomorrow?"

"Yes I guess," Janny said airily. She collected her flower and bounced back to the other girls. "Go on ladies," the ballerina said.

"This is a lot of fun."

Kendra stepped forward next: "I am putting my heart on the line by staying here Anthony," she said. "What are you risking?"

Anthony looked serious. "Contrary to popular belief, I am every bit as vulnerable," he said. "My heart is right on the line next to yours Kendra."

"That is good enough for me," Kendra said.

The graphic artist accepted the carnation and walked back to join the other females.

Vonda stepped to the fore: "You promised me some martial arts training," she said, blushing at being in the limelight. "What has happened to that?"

"I always keep my promises," Anthony said. "I will organise a self-defence date very soon Vonda."

The Charity Eligible handed Vonda her carnation, and gave her a kiss upon the cheek for good measure.

Deborah stepped forward last. She looked amused: "As it seems to be ladies choice today, I will tell you that I am enjoying being on the show. I do believe you and I are becoming good friends Anthony."

"I would be honoured to have formed a lasting friendship with you Deborah," Anthony said. "*The Charity Dating Show* might ultimately be about love, but let us not undervalue friendship!"

Deborah laughed. "Thank you," she said.

Anthony handed Deborah the last carnation and looked around the group. They were five different girls with five different hopes and dreams, and he had to negotiate the murky waters of dating them all, before he was allowed to declare his heart to the woman of his dreams. It would be a pleasure and a responsibility.

"You all heard me invite Janny on an outing for tomorrow," he said. "I am pleased to be able to tell you that everyone is included, and there will even be a surprise guest!"

"Male or female?" Kendra exclaimed in sudden concern.

"Male," Anthony explained. "I have asked one of my best mates to meet you all and he will give me the benefit of his advice."

"How exciting!" Janny exclaimed, and even shy Vonda looked delighted.

The girls exclaimed in pleasure and milled around, talking amongst themselves and to the Charity Eligible. Nadine and Vonda were anxious about making a good impression on Anthony's friend; while Kendra was eager to learn more about Anthony through his friend.

Deborah allowed herself a brief glance towards George when the camera was pointed in another direction. The socialite was glad that her private romance was safe for another round, and was looking forward to her secret rendezvous with the camera man. Soon after that, Leticia broke the party up by sending everyone to their respective residences.

EPILOGUE: A HAPPY ENDING

Some weeks later, a guest column mysteriously appeared in the activist magazine edited by early episode eliminee and social activist, Orb. It was an interview with Constance, regarding her more recent, and much more extensive experience on the Australian reality production called, *The Charity Dating Show.*

The article commenced with Orb thanking Constance for agreeing to be interviewed exclusively by the small press magazine, and praising her for being the first contestant on that particular season of *The Charity Dating Show* to take an assertive stance against the inherent inequality of a reality show that featured one 'Charity Eligible' and a dozen or more female contestants.

"Thank you for asking me to comment on my stint on *The Charity Dating Show,* Orb," Constance responded. "It is true, as you say, that the premise of the show, which involves one man and multiple women, may not be conducive to healthy relationship formation."

"Would you say the show was damaging to your self-concept?" Orb inquired.

"As a former contestant," Constance continued, "I can testify that if one focuses solely upon the Charity Eligible and the competition with the other women, things can go pear-shaped very quickly."

"Tell me more," Orb demanded.

"There were a few moments that I found highly perplexing and even occasionally, traumatic. However, if one remains open to other possibilities, the uneven, patriarchal premise fades somewhat and becomes, what it is, a form of window dressing."

"Isn't that patriarchal window dressing still harmful?" Orb probed intently.

Constance laughed. "Let's face it, reality television is popular entertainment - a bit of fun! It isn't meant to be taken seriously. And over time, I think that the messages that it sends are changing. In the end, a contestant is only as powerless or powerful as they perceive themselves. And the prize may be whatever they choose."

"Tell me more about this concept of 'alternate prizes'," Orb demanded.

Constance hedged mysteriously. "Well, television offers several things, including fame and a possible boost to your career - if you are in the right industry."

"Do those things particularly interest you?" Orb asked practically.

"No," Constance said. "I went on the show purely for LOVE, and my career field is not particularly enhanced by media notoriety."

"So what happened?" Orb demanded. "Did you find love on *The Charity Dating Show?*"

"Due to the continuing terms of my contract," Constance replied carefully. "I am not allowed to answer that question directly. I can however, tell you that I HAVE found love since. I cannot specifically say whether I found it ON the show, but I can say that if I had not participated in the show, I might not have met an incredibly talented and loving man.

"That sounds nice, if a bit mysterious," Orb conceded. "Are you sure it is the 'real thing'?

"Well only time will tell," Constance admitted. "But I can say that my boyfriend has been wonderfully true to his word. He is also faithful, honest and a good communicator. I am very happy! And in the meantime, I am back at work, pursuing my career fully."

"What more can you hope for?" Orb reflected. "Do you have any advice for other young women, Constance?"

"Yes!" Constance exclaimed. "Liberation is a state of mind. Do not wait for the situation to be perfect - get in touch with your inner power and make the change yourself. Then good things - like love coming into your life - can follow...."

Constance trailed off dreamily, a happy smile on her lips.

All for Love on The Charity Dating Show II:

The Top Five

Prologue: Early Episodes revisited

Leticia Anderson, who once hoped to become an investigative journalist, has settled for the job of hostess-director of The Charity Dating Show. This glamour reality show is filmed in Sydney, Australia, and despite its formulaic premise, has a huge audience following.

This season, Dr. Anthony Jones has been persuaded to appear on the show as the 'Charity Eligible' to raise funds for the hospital in which he works. In the early episodes, Anthony was introduced to twenty young women. He was obliged to immediately reduce the number to twelve.

This resulted in eight girls being sent home on limited first impressions. At least one of the number was a girl Anthony had fancied, but by some mishap, he said the wrong name. Constance, Rozanne, Nadine, Alison, Deborah, Janny, Vonda, Gabby, Ebony, Kendra, Betty and Orb received carnations and remain in the 'Candidate House'.

The early dates are group dates, and dark beauties Nadine and Constance appear to be Anthony's favourites; along with blonde bombshell Betty. At the next carnation ceremony, doctor of philosophy candidate Ebony and activist Orb, do not receive carnations, because they have not developed meaningful connections with Anthony.

Rozanne misses out on a single date and her intense disappointment is overwhelming to the emotionally reserved Dr. Anthony, who sends the woman home to find her equilibrium. Outgoing Gabby admits that the sober Anthony is not her type and is obliged to leave during an 'elimination date'.

Anthony looked for a response from the beautiful Betty; and failing to receive sufficient encouragement, allowed her to leave on the arm of a charming male model! Anthony then attempted to show model girl Alison that he respected her mind, but Alison decided to focus on the next stage of her career and move into television production.

Early favourites Constance and Nadine developed an unhealthy rivalry, resulting in conflict between the pair. Anthony was attempting to keep the peace, and hold on to both girls, when Constance assertively resolved the situation by refusing to accept a carnation. As she left, Simon Steeple, the cameraman who had been admiring her from afar, indicated that he would be interested in pursuing a relationship once she was free from her contract.

These events have left Anthony with a top five selection including: the feminine Nadine, challenging socialite Deborah, mercurial ballerina Janny, peace-loving graphic artist Kendra, and sensitive musician Vonda. However, Deborah has been conducting clandestine assignations with the other cameraman George — so she doesn't really count; and Anthony now appears to favour Vonda, in whose quiet determination he recognises his own reflection!

Meanwhile, Leticia who is unaware of the contestant's secret activities, concludes that the remaining girls all get along too well, and look like causing too little on-screen drama. The hostess is considering what can be done to sensationalise the remaining episodes of **The Charity Dating Show**...

CHAPTER ONE: A SURPRISE VISITOR

When Anthony arrived at the Candidate House the next day, he was accompanied by a tall dark haired man, whom he introduced to the girls as Abraham. Abraham was classically good-looking with neat masculine features and a short beard. The ladies all eyed him curiously.

"Abraham is my best friend," Anthony said. "He has known me since we were in primary school together, and if anybody knows who is right for me, I think it might be him. The final decision is mine of course, but Abraham has agreed to talk to you all, and nominate the two ladies he deems most compatible."

"In other words, you have asked him for a second opinion," Deborah observed with wry amusement.

"I guess I have," Anthony admitted. He turned and led the way towards a mini-bus. similar to the one they had used to transport the group to the Rose Farm on a previous date. "Hop in ladies, I am told there are some good water-ways at the Wollongong Royal National Park."

"I love getting out amongst nature," Kendra said, and Anthony gave her a warm glance.

"I know you do," he said.

Abraham, observing this by-play, followed Kendra to her seat in the bus and selected the seat next to the graphic artist. "It's a lovely day," he remarked.

"Yes it is," Kendra replied.

"What do you do?" Abraham asked.

"I am a graphic artist," Kendra said. "I do some creative stuff and some commercial work."

"That is interesting," Abraham said. "I work in promotions myself."

"The artists are a bit remote from the marketing department," Kendra said. "We design things to order, whether they be for children's books or television advertisements. I personally like to create greeting cards and giftware."

"Do you dream of serious Art?" Abraham asked curiously.

"In my spare time," Kendra answered modestly. "Anthony can tell you we have discussed Art as therapy."

"That sort of thing would create a common ground between you and Anthony," Abraham said.

"Yes," Kendra said. She blushed and looked down at her long slim fingers where they rested upon the seam of her jeans.

"How do you feel about Anthony?" Abraham asked very directly.

Kendra jumped. "I am sorry," she said. "I am only prepared to answer that question to Anthony himself, and not on a crowded bus."

"Fair enough," Abraham said. He was silent for a moment, assessing Kendra as quiet and firm; with a possible degree of emotional depth. "It is my job to ask nosy questions," he added gently.

"I know," Kendra sighed. "However, I am not prepared to do or say anything on this show that I would not do in real life."

"So what do you do on dates?" Abraham inquired.

"Be honest," Kendra replied, "And have fun."

"You pass!" Abraham commented and Kendra smiled.

"I may have become a bit cautious because of what I saw happened to the girls who got emotionally involved too quickly," Kendra admitted.

"Ah," Abraham said. "Anthony said something about that. What do you think happened?"

"The girls became insecure, and Anthony felt pressured," Kendra said. "After all, he had only just met them."

"It sounds like you are on Anthony's side," Abraham commented cannily.

"I don't know," Kendra said. "I think they were all very nice girls."

"I am sure they were," Abraham remarked. He considered asking the light-brown haired girl to identify the lady Anthony had confided was worrying him, but decided to wait and get the information directly from the Charity Eligible.

The bus pulled to a halt in the Royal National Park, and the party climbed out to look around. As the party had been promised, there were extensive water-ways with boats for hire, shady trees, outdoor tables and stone fire places.

"We are only allowed to use the gas barbeques because of the fire danger," Anthony remarked.

"That is a bit of a pity," Abraham said. "However, I understand we don't want to start a fire."

"We should be able to cook up a good barbeque anyway," Anthony said.

"That is cool," Abraham said. "Are we hiring boats?"

"Yeah," Anthony said. "How many do you think we should get?"

"Two boats," Abraham said. "There are seven of us, and we can double up a bit."

"I love the way you guys club together to organise things and ignore us girls," Janny remarked playfully.

"I am sorry," Abraham retorted. "I didn't realise it was possible to ignore such a scintillating beauty."

Janny looked set to make an ironic retort, but Anthony intervened.

"Janny is a great joker," Anthony remarked diplomatically.

"That makes two of us," Abraham said. "Come on Janny, help me collect the life-jackets." He took Janny by the hand and led her away towards the brick building which formed the rangers' office. Janny followed obligingly.

"You are a pretty girl," the dark haired Abraham commented. "What do you do?"

"I am a dance teacher and sometime performer," Janny replied modestly.

"Ah that is where that air of confidence and glamour comes from," Abraham said. "I bet the men fall for it all the time."

"They do," Janny admitted. "Unfortunately, they are always after the wrong thing."

"Whatever is the wrong thing nowadays?" Abraham mused.

"A brief encounter," Janny remarked. "Times have changed since the sexual revolution, but deep down people haven't, and a smart lady like me is looking for a long-term relationship, not just a fling."

"Do you think Anthony is after the wrong thing?" Abraham asked searchingly.

Janny shook her head. "No! Anthony is a good guy," she said. "I just don't know yet whether he is THE ONE if you know what I mean."

"Only time would tell a thing like that," Abraham observed. "You are however – interested – in finding out aren't you?"

Janny nodded. "Of course," she said. "There are other things I could be doing, and people I could be with if I were not at all interested in Anthony."

"That is a given with a beautiful and talented lady like you," Abraham observed.

They came to the water's edge and a group of swans swam past. "Oh - look at that," Janny exclaimed.

"Yes," Abraham said. He came to a halt beside the ballerina and pointed across the water's expanse. "There are some ducks over there with ducklings too."

"They are so beautiful," Janny breathed.

"That mother duck has a string of followers," Abraham said.

"Yes," Janny said. "It is so sweet, and the swans do remind me of *Swan Lake*."

Abraham and Janny stood for a few minutes looking at the water-birds. The ballerina was highly imaginative, and even the commercially minded advertising executive found himself inspired by the beautiful lake view.

After a while all the ducks swam past and Abraham turned to Janny. "Let's get those life jackets," he said. "The others must be wondering where we are."

When Janny and Abraham arrived back with the life-jackets, they found that Deborah and Anthony had started preparing the barbeque for use, and Kendra was chopping onions. Vonda was buttering slices of bread, and Nadine had wandered down to the water's edge to inspect the boats.

"Is there anything I can do to help?" Abraham asked.

"No, you can just sit back and be waited on," Deborah said briskly. She put a plate on his lap and a cup of sparkling cider in his hand.

"Are you always this bossy?" Abraham asked.

"Pretty much," Deborah said. "What you see is what you get around me."

"I understand," Abraham said, wondering briefly whether this was the woman who was causing Anthony all the problems.

"I didn't hear a 'thank you' for the food!" Deborah observed.

"I AM grateful, but it's not my job to be polite," Abraham retorted, "It's my job to check you out."

"I'm not for sale," Deborah said. "Anthony understands."

"I can see that," Abraham said. Indeed, if Anthony and this woman had developed an understanding, the socialite might not be the problem woman. "In fact, you two make a good team."

"Depends what we are working on," Deborah said. "I'm pretty task oriented anyway."

"I think it is safe to say Deborah and I are friends," Anthony said. "Leave it at that." He dropped some chops onto the barbeque and the meat made a satisfying sizzle.

"None of us are really for sale," Vonda added shyly, and Abraham's attention was attracted towards the slim blonde.

"What do you do?" the Charity Eligible's Friend asked.

"I am a musician," Vonda said.

Abraham looked curious. "Might I have heard you play?" he inquired.

"It depends on how often you go to the symphony, and in which theatres," Vonda replied.

"I bet you are good," Abraham said.

Janny accepted the compliment gracefully. "Thank you," she said. "I believe I am."

"I am curious as to why you would leave something like that to come on a dating show," Abraham said.

Vonda shrugged. "The orchestra will wait," she said. "But I am very shy. Occasionally I do something really crazy to break out of the quiet existence I settle into."

"Anthony can be something like that too," Abraham said. "Quiet-like I mean."

"We've talked about it," Vonda said. "Anthony has encouraged me to get as involved in all the activities as possible."

"Good for him," Abraham said. "And how has it been going?"

"Really good," Vonda said. "Except when I met that creepy guy at the opera."

"What creepy guy was that?" Abraham said.

"Some guy called Roy who wouldn't believe I was there with Anthony," Vonda said. "He kept grabbing me."

"That sounds pretty dramatic," Abraham commented.

"I'll say!" Anthony interjected. "I almost had to fight him off her."

"We were all worried when we heard about the bloke," Kendra said.

"Yeah," Deborah said. "Luckily Anthony found her in time."

"I'm glad nothing went wrong on any other dates," Janny said.

"Don't speak too soon," Kendra said. "The dates have mostly been well organised, but there could always be a first time."

"Where's Nadine?" asked Janny, and everyone looked around in alarm.

"I think she is just being solitary," Anthony said, and Abraham pricked up his ears. "She didn't really like my warning yesterday."

"I'll take her food over if you like," Abraham said.

"Okay," Anthony said. He piled a lamb chop, some onion and some salad onto a plastic plate and handed it to Abraham. "I hope that is to her liking."

Abraham made his way across to the pier, where Nadine had last been seen. As he approached, he saw a petite brunette with a beautiful face. She was sitting in the sun, looking mildly pensive.

"Hello," Abraham said.

The brunette turned, and Abraham felt a flicker of interest as he noticed her liquid brown eyes. "You must be Nadine," he said. "I barely caught your name earlier."

"Yes I am," Nadine said. "Forgive me for seeming snobbish, but Anthony told me to tone it down a bit."

"I don't think he meant for you to be left out altogether," Abraham said. "Here is your food for instance."

"I know," Nadine admitted accepting the plate, "But I don't want to do anything wrong again."

"Do you know what happened?" Abraham inquired.

"One of the other girls thought I was a bit too pushy and blamed me for the failure of her relationship with Anthony," Nadine said. "I can't see how it would have been my fault though. It takes two to form a relationship."

"I think there would have been a few factors involved," Abraham said. He was warming to the honesty in the woman's attitude. "You look like a lady who expects the men of her acquaintance to be protective and attentive."

"I have a warm heart," Nadine admitted, "And my school friends always said I had a strong personality. But I wouldn't do anything silly."

"There are cultural differences among us," Abraham said. "You are Macedonian aren't you?"

"Several generations back," Nadine admitted. "My family is Australian now."

"I am Italian and there are some cultural similarities," Abraham said. "We are also very family oriented."

Nadine shrugged, and Abraham could tell that he was not impressing her in the manner he had hoped. "I am sorry," he said. "I didn't mean to focus on your ethnicity or anything."

"It just doesn't seem relevant to me," Nadine said. "I have never been to the old country."

"I have to travel to Europe and toured the Mediterranean for my company," Abraham said.

Nadine looked intrigued. "Now that you mention it - travel would be interesting," she murmured.

"I might be able to escort you back there sometime," Abraham suggested, laying a hand upon her knee.

Nadine looked mildly shocked. "I am here to date Anthony," she cried, pushing Abraham's hand away. "You have only just met me, and you are trying to take advantage of the situation."

"I got carried away," Abraham said humbly. "Please forgive me."

Nadine looked appeased. "Now you are confusing me," she said.

"I am confusing myself," Abraham said. "I must have somehow forgotten the exact situation. Would you like to take one of the boats out on the river after you have finished your food?"

"I guess," Nadine said. "It is lovely weather."

"I'll tell the others," Abraham said. He walked across to the barbeque area, and returned with Janny and Vonda, who had volunteered to join the boat. "We are all going out on the lake," he said.

Anthony, Deborah and Kendra arrived shortly after and took the other boat out on the stream. They rowed out towards Abraham and the girls, and challenged them to a race.

"Are you sure you want to?" Abraham said. "We have one more oars-person."

"It's only for fun," Anthony returned, and they lined the two boats up the best they could. The attempt at racing was hilarious and short-lived, with Anthony and his crew drawing ahead, and

Abraham's boat going around in a circle because the girls failed to row evenly on both sides.

"Give up," Anthony cried.

"Sure," Abraham cried. "I have too attractive a cargo to risk it racing with you."

The boat rocked as Janny and Nadine attempted to silence the dark haired man, and Abraham ducked low to the seat.

"Take care we do not capsize," Vonda said, and Abraham reached out to take control of the oars.

The shadows lengthened, and Abraham's boat eventually turned around and the occupants took turns rowing back to the pier, where they found that Deborah and Kendra had cleaned up the picnic area with Anthony's help and the bus was ready for the return journey to the Candidate House.

"Thank you for a good day," Abraham said. "It was lovely to have met you."

Abraham shook hands with all of the ladies in turn, and noticed that Nadine did not resist when he attempted to sit next to her on the bus-ride back to the Candidate House. After the bus had dropped the ladies off, it continued onwards towards the Eligible Quarters, where Anthony and Abraham settled down on comfy chairs in his accommodation, to begin their all-important discussion of the girls.

Anthony looked at Abraham. "What do you think?" he asked.

"Well, for starters mate," Abraham mused, "You must be one of the most blessed men on earth!"

"I sort of agree," Anthony said. "Except I only get to keep one lady in the end."

"Does your contract contain any ban on remaining friends with the others?" Abraham inquired.

Anthony looked thoughtful. "Technically no," he said. "The trick is to part with them without creating any sort of offense. The ladies have all made it clear that they prefer exclusivity, so I wouldn't dare play a double game."

"It isn't in your nature anyway mate," Abraham said. "I am somewhat surprised you are dealing with all of this."

"It is in a good cause," Anthony said. "There is that donation to the hospital remember."

"Ah yes," Abraham said. "But there must be a limit to what you would sacrifice for medicine."

"Of course!" Anthony said. "We have already established that dating the girls is no hardship."

"It might even have done you good," Abraham speculated. "I bet you have gone places and discussed topics that are outside your normal range."

"I have certainly heard more about female emotional issues than I had hoped to in an entire life-time!' Anthony exclaimed.

Abraham looked amused. "There is no getting away from that mate," he said.

"Thank goodness for surgery," Anthony said. "It has sheltered me to a certain extent."

"You don't have to deal with your patients as equals anyway," Abraham commented shrewdly. "These girls are all definitely your equals."

"They are very real," Anthony said. "And there seems to be more at stake at every elimination, which is one reason why I am asking you to give me an opinion."

"Okay mate," Abraham remarked. "Firstly, I am surprised to find you so pally with the she-wolf."

"Deborah is great when you get to know her," Anthony declared.

"I personally think that you like the fact you are not dealing with the risk of a relationship with that one," Abraham surmised.

Anthony grinned. "No comment," he said. "Actually, I really enjoy her company!"

"Moving along," Abraham continued: "It is obvious that something is developing between you and the mousy blonde."

"Kendra is very sweet," Anthony said. "Mousy indeed!"

"It is just a word my mother used to use for that hair colour," Abraham said. "I didn't mean anything by it."

"Sure," Anthony said. "So are you recommending Kendra for one of the 'most compatible' dates?"

"I think Kendra is a certainty," Abraham concluded.

"And who would be the second one?" Anthony inquired. "I am thinking about Janny," Abraham said.

"Janny?" Anthony exclaimed. "Not Vonda?"

"I can tell you prefer Vonda," Abraham said. "But she is very quiet, and I honestly don't believe she will be at all relationship-ready by the end of this show."

"Janny is something of a tease," Anthony said. "She is very attractive, but I somehow cannot read her intentions."

"I think Janny has trust issues," Abraham remarked. "If she got over those she would be a lovely companion."

"I don't know what to do about that," Anthony commented.

"Try taking her somewhere really romantic for the next date," Abraham advised. "And covering her with chocolates and flowers."

"It's worth a try," Anthony said. "So you recommend Kendra and Janny get the next two individual dates?"

"Yes I do," Abraham agreed.

"And what do you think of Nadine?" Anthony asked curiously. "She has been causing dramas amongst the other girls."

"I guessed she was the one," Abraham said. "To be honest, I think Nadine is lovely. If you are thinking of eliminating her, I would like your permission to date her myself."

"WHAT?" Anthony cried.

"I know you've found she doesn't relax around the other women; but I like someone who is very feminine myself, and I don't mind if she gets a bit high maintenance," Abraham said. "It is the southern European way."

"But you have never settled down," Anthony exclaimed.

"I hadn't found the right girl," Abraham said with matter-of-fact assurance. "Nevertheless there is a first time for everything."

"But," Anthony gasped. "One of my candidates?"

"Enough buts," Abraham said. "Have you finished with the lady?"

"Yes I have," Anthony said firmly. "I still don't want to see her trifled with, however."

"Nadine said something in the same vein," Abraham said. "She thought I was taking advantage."

"You have discussed it with her?" Anthony exclaimed.

"Not in so many words," Abraham said. "I am waiting for your permission."

"We will think of an excuse for you to spend tomorrow with the ladies I am not dating," Anthony said. "I don't want to see you rush into anything."

"Okay if you say so mate," Abraham said. "I think I know my mind already, but I won't turn down more time with the ladies."

Elsewhere, Deborah was waiting anxiously in the shrubbery. It was one thing to have agreed to meet George, but it was quite another to be standing outside in the dusky evening. Despite being summer the dark was falling, and the hedges loomed darkly. Deborah thought briefly of the cowboy type who had accosted Vonda at the opera and imagined what might happen if he had somehow managed to follow the musician home to the Candidate House.

The socialite shivered, and reined in her wandering thoughts; she was Deborah, who was rarely afraid of anything - even love. However, now she glanced at her watch, activating the little light. George was late, and it would be humiliation itself to be stood up by some ordinary looking guy at whom she had practically thrown herself.

A shadow appeared at the entrance to the shrubbery and a low whistle sounded. "Is that you Deborah?" someone whispered.

"George?" Deborah hissed.

The shadow nodded and approached more confidently. "Put out your hands," George said, and Deborah found herself holding the silver paper surrounding a large bunch of mixed flowers such as one could purchase at the florist.

"They are lovely," she said, inspecting what she could of the blooms in the dark. "You didn't have to!"

"I did," George said. "I want to court you properly, despite the difference in our finances."

"Don't ever mention it again," Deborah said firmly. "You have obviously always paid your way."

"Of course," George said, "That is not what this is about."

"Glad to hear it," Deborah said. She reached out to give George a hug, and found he was carrying something else. "Whatever is that?" she asked in surprise.

"Donuts," George said. "I thought we could have a mid-evening snack."

"Out here in the bushes?" Deborah asked incredulously. "I feel like a teenager once again."

"Then you have aged considerably since the day I found you playing with Parker," George said jovially. "You looked like you felt his age just then."

"My age seems to be a bit fluid just now," Deborah remarked. "As are my legs, I feel I have been standing around for long enough."

"Well, why not sit on the bench?" George suggested.

"I didn't notice it," Deborah said. She settled down on the afore-mentioned bench and turned to George. "How many other ladies have you brought out here?"

George would have looked amused, if Deborah could see his expression. "How like a woman," he said. "You are jealous already."

"No," Deborah said. "Just very territorial once I stake a claim." She paused, holding her breath to see whether her accustomed candour would go down badly this time.

"I normally stick to my job," George said. "However, you are the most unruly of the unruliest bunch of contestants I have seen for a long time."

"What do you mean?" Deborah said. "Are we fighting more than usual?"

"The fights are nothing compared to what we usually get when a bunch of women are after one man," George said. "On the other hand, you girls are down-right subversive. With a few notable exceptions, you stick together and encourage each other to cut Anthony down to size."

"I think Anthony likes being a certain size," Deborah remarked.

"I do too," agreed George. "He tries to be a gentleman, and keep things within reason."

"Have you had other types of eligible men?" Deborah asked curiously.

George crowed softly. "My word we have. However, the creepy ones usually get weeded out in the auditions. Leticia is a pretty good judge of character."

"Should I trust her judgement in employing you?" Deborah inquired teasingly.

"Only if you want to employ me," George said cheekily.

Deborah laughed softly and tickled him under the ribs.

The Camera Operator twitched and squirmed. "Two can play at that game," he said, tweaking Deborah at the back waist. Although George was aiming for a neutral zone, his wrists brushed against the sensitive skin along her side and Deborah felt a wave of excitement. She twined her arms around him and reached her face up for a kiss, but George pulled back.

"Steady on," he said. "I can't just get involved, I have a son."

"I think that must be part of your appeal," Deborah said. "I felt something for Parker from the day I met him."

"Still, I am cautious," George said. "Girlfriends could come and go, but I would still be responsible for my boy."

"Oh," Deborah said musingly. She pondered for a moment, trying to think of a way to make things right.

"I have an idea," George said. "Let's see if we can sneak our way around into the private studio, I have a hankering to watch a horror movie."

"A horror movie?" Deborah queried.

"Sure," George said. "Are you into that sort of thing?"

"Sometimes," Deborah said. "I don't usually have someone with whom to watch horror."

"Well, tonight you do," George said. "And I know just where the best titles are stored."

The pair crept through the side door, across the hall-way and skirted around the edge of the dining room. Luckily, almost all of the contestants were playing billiards or watching television in the large lounge, and Leticia was working in her room.

At last they came to the dark door of the private viewing theatre. George switched on the light and shut the door behind them, making sure the latch fell into place from the inside.

"We are safe inside!" he said. "If anyone approaches we will have plenty of warning."

"You are not that ashamed of seeing me are you?" Deborah asked cagily.

"Of course not," George said. "However, if someone decided to join us, we lose all our privacy."

"I see," Deborah said. "By the way, where is Parker tonight?"

"My mother is sleeping over," George explained. "She often does that when I have to work at night; other-times, Parker sleeps at my parent's house. He could sleep there all the time, but I like him to feel he has a home with me."

"I think you are right," Deborah said. "How are you going choosing a movie?"

"I've found just the one," George said. "*Werewolves and Haunted Castles* #13."

"What happened to the other twelve?" Deborah asked.

"Never made," George laughed. "Darkness and atmosphere,

what else could you want?"

"A warm arm around me," Deborah said.

"At your service ma'am," George said. He activated the projector and a picture appeared on the big screen. George then turned off the main light and sat down on the plush seating beside Deborah. The Socialite sighed and settled down to savour the movie. She was especially pleased when George reached out his arm and put it around her shoulder, pulling her close towards him.

Two hours later, the last scene flickered into obscurity and George stirred. "I've gotta go," he said. "Pizza at my place next time okay?" He sounded somewhat diffident, as if he believed that he had nothing to offer.

"It sounds fine," Deborah said, heartily glad to hear that there was to be a next time. "What would you normally do on a date?"

"It's been a while," George said, "But if I had baby-sitting arranged I would fancy going to see a band."

"Beer and live music," Deborah said. "I could go for that! However, I had a good time tonight."

She leant forward, and this time George did not dodge the kiss. Instead he tightened his arm around the socialite and returned her kisses with ardent pressure. Deborah was shaking and longing for more by the time they stopped, but she knew that all good things were worth waiting for.

George excited and interested Deborah more than anyone she had met during her university years or through her work at the library. He was also far easier to relax around than her father's rich friends or the sons of her mother's high society connections. She hoped it meant the relationship was going somewhere.

CHAPTER TWO: A SECRET ROMANCE

When Anthony arrived the next day to collect Janny for her individual date, he was carrying a bunch of flowers and box of chocolates for her. The ballerina squealed in delight and hastened to deposit the chocolates in her room and set the flowers in a vase.

Anthony was also accompanied by Abraham. The other candidates, the majority of whom had collected around the front door, looked at the visitor in surprise. They had clearly expected Abraham to return home after the previous group date.

"Abraham is staying with me a little longer," Anthony said. "And I don't want him left alone at the Eligible Residence all day, so I asked Leticia whether he could spend the day over here with you girls."

"I guess that is okay," Vonda said, and the other girls exchanged glances. It was obvious that while they considered Abraham something of an outsider, and a very different proposition than Anthony himself, he would not be completely unwelcome. Indeed, Nadine who was currently finishing her breakfast, might even be glad to see him.

Anthony exchanged a few pleasantries with Deborah and Kendra, and then took Janny by the hand. As Anthony drove off with Janny, Abraham turned to the date-free girls: "I appreciate your keeping me company," he said. "Why don't you show me around? If your accommodation is anything as good as Anthony's, I expect this is a real mansion."

"Sure," Deborah said, and she and Kendra turned to lead the way. Vonda followed along in a more leisurely fashion. They entered the hallway and progressed towards the living area, passing the kitchen, from where Nadine appeared, wiping her hands daintily. The brunette stopped and blushed when she saw Abraham.

"Hello Nadine," Abraham said.

"Hello yourself," Nadine replied. "What are you doing over here?"

"Apparently we are baby-sitting the best friend today," Deborah said dryly.

Nadine coloured. "Well you should be getting good at babysitting," she retorted, pointedly referring to Deborah's antics whenever Parker was at the Candidate House.

"Tut tut, we are getting clever," Deborah remarked, not in the least abashed.

"Why don't you join us Nadine," Kendra asked. "I believe we ought to take Abraham down to the pool - there is no need for him to see our bedrooms."

"Most of us have swim-suits out there in the change room," Vonda added in a matter of fact fashion.

"Even I was warned to bring my boardies," Abraham said, indicating the small bundle draped across his arm.

"Okay," Nadine said. She fell into step beside Vonda and surveyed Abraham while he marched along with Kendra and Deborah. The dark bearded man turned around once or twice, and caught her bold eyes, which immediately dropped in confusion.

"This is the large lounge," Deborah said as they entered the airy room. "It is where we hang out and watch television in the afternoon. See those double doors? They open onto the patio and pool area, where we usually have a swim in the mornings if we are not out on a date."

"I am happy to do whatever you usually do," Abraham said. "I don't want to disrupt your routine."

"The presence of a male will of necessity change things," Kendra said. "We have developed a real female republic left here to ourselves."

"A change is as good as a holiday," Vonda said cheerfully. "So long as you excuse me this afternoon, I was planning to practice my violin."

The party arrived at the pool area and Abraham exclaimed in delight at the size of the pool, and warmth of the water. "You could maintain an excellent exercise programme here," he said.

"Janny does," Deborah remarked, "The rest of us swim more for fun."

The four ladies and one gentleman took turns using the changing room, and soon they were all ready to swim. Abraham dived assertively into the pool, and Nadine followed him more gingerly.

Vonda climbed into the shallow end using the ladder, while Deborah perched herself upon the ledge and dropped in slowly. Kendra slid neatly into the water from one of the blocks up the deep end, and they all started swimming laps up and down, occasionally being forced to circle around out of each other's way.

Vonda was the first to climb out of the pool. "I will see the housekeeper about our lunch," she said. "Would you like to have something brought outside?"

"I am coming too," Kendra said, after swimming swiftly to the side. "Shall we have the barbeque set up in the rose and herb garden? We have never yet eaten there."

"Good thinking," said Deborah, who was bobbing around in the shallows. "I shall have a shower and then come to join you."

"That seems to leave just you and me here," Abraham said, swimming close to Nadine.

Nadine stopped swimming and began to tread water in close proximity to the best friend of the Charity Eligible. "So it does," she said coyly. "How about that?"

"You cannot go inside and leave a guest out here alone," Abraham said. "Perhaps we could get into that spa thing and luxuriate until the others call us."

"That sounds like a plan," Nadine said. "I think I know where the operation switch is by now."

Abraham climbed into the spa, and Nadine made a brief trip into the service room, located next to the changing room to hit the activation switch. The babbling mechanism began to work, heating the water as it agitated and circulated.

"This is peaceful," Nadine said, sliding in beside Abraham.

"I am glad that the others went inside," Abraham said. "It was really you that I came to see."

"I guessed as much," Nadine said. "Does Anthony know?"

"He was a bit shocked, but he gave his blessing," Abraham said.

"I feel privileged," Nadine said. "Your attentions are so much more focused than Anthony's."

"Anthony hasn't really been in love with anyone up to this point," Abraham said neutrally.

"I don't know what happened in my case," Nadine said. "I thought I was doing the right thing, getting to know him and everything. Then boom - the other girls all hated me! I really felt hurt."

"I am sorry to hear that," Abraham said. "I hope it doesn't put you off of developing another relationship."

"I think I am too smart to let myself get disillusioned," Nadine said calmly. "I would look for a different situation though. Twelve girls and one man really isn't what nature intended."

"Of course," Abraham agreed. "And in case you should agree to consider me, I must warn you that I have been something of a rat in the past. If the girl I was seeing wasn't right for me, I would move right on without bothering to finish things up with her."

Nadine wrinkled her nose. "The girls would have wondered what had happened. Should I be nervous?"

"No!" Abraham said firmly. "I think I am past that stage, and I have a different set of priorities this time."

"I expect I will be out of here at the next elimination," Nadine said thoughtfully. "I believe I barely survived the last one."

"Hmm," Abraham murmured. The thinking noise was designed to cover his confusion at being in possession of the inside story. "I am glad that I got to meet you anyway."

"I am actually wondering whether I should leave early," Nadine said. "Then I would be free to go out with you, if that is what you are asking."

"On no, don't do that on my account," Abraham said. "You might get me into trouble for spoiling the show!"

"We are risking having a camera pointed at us even now," Nadine pointed out logically.

"If they did film us, they wouldn't air it until the secrets and scandals episode," Abraham laughed.

"I guess so," Nadine conceded. "If I am not leaving early, then what will we do?"

"I am prepared to stick around," Abraham said. "The elimination will have to be tomorrow or the next day at the latest."

"Do you really want me to stand there and let Anthony dismiss me like some unwanted baggage?" Nadine asked. "That would be humiliating to say the least."

"You will have our secret to keep you in good spirits," Abraham said clasping both her hands. "And I am sure that Anthony will be polite enough to allow you to keep your pride. He is my best friend after all."

"I will try to give it another day," Nadine said. "It won't be so tough if you are around."

"That's my girl," Abraham said reassuringly. He put his arm along the edge of the spa just behind Nadine's shoulders, but refrained from making the gesture any more possessive out of respect for the procedure that had to be undertaken before Nadine was free to leave the show.

Just then Deborah poked her head out of the large lounge door and called to them. "Come along you two," she said, "We have almost finished preparing lunch."

Nadine climbed out of the spa and reached for a large towel, which she wrapped around herself sarong style. "I will wait a minute if you want to get changed," she said in acknowledgement of the fact that Abraham was not used to the relaxed life-style of the Candidate House.

Abraham said, "Thanks," and headed into the change room to dry himself thoroughly. He emerged wearing his shirt and trousers once again, and allowed Nadine to lead the way out to the herb garden.

"This is great," he said surveying the portable barbeque set up amongst the rose bushes in the centre.

"I love the way they have mixed native plants with the cultivated varieties," Kendra said. "It is so common to separate the two, or treat one as less important as the other."

"They must have a hard time watering some plants more than others," Abraham exclaimed. "Some of the plants must have very different needs."

"It would be labour intensive," Deborah said. "However, all we have to do is enjoy." She lifted the lid of the barbeque, "Garlic kebab or marinated chicken wing anyone?"

"Yes sure," Kendra said. "We are all very hungry!"

The party settled down to eat, and managed to use so many plates that the housekeeper threw her hands up in despair when she came outside to tidy the area.

"I am sorry," Deborah said, "We were very naughty." The socialite was perched on a garden seat and made no move to clean up, for she was too full and happy.

However, Kendra and Vonda scampered around helping the housekeeper collect the stray crockery. They became competitive in their zeal, and began to argue about who was going to help with the washing up. In the end, Kendra reminded Vonda that she had wanted to practice the violin, and the musician retreated from the fray.

"We have the whole afternoon to ourselves," Nadine said to Abraham. The couple selectively excluded Deborah, who nodded at them lazily.

"Go on," Deborah drawled, "Find something to do. Don't mind me, I am going to have a nap."

"I have an idea," Abraham said. "Do you play chess?"

"Occasionally," Nadine replied.

"I think I saw a chess-board inside," Abraham said. "I will bring it out here, and we can play in the relaxed atmosphere of the outdoors."

Abraham and Nadine dragged two comfy chairs away from the pool area and set up the chess board on an ornamental table. They played against each other several times, and when Kendra returned from helping the maid in the kitchen, she played against the winner.

Deborah then joined in, and Abraham demonstrated a few puzzles that had even the best players amongst the girls mystified.

When the afternoon sun dropped low to the horizon, it penetrated the tree line and began to glare in their faces. The girls decided to pack up the chess set, and asked Abraham to carry the arm-chairs back into the pool area. The housekeeper prepared an early tea of soup and herb bread, which they ate in front of the television.

Finally Abraham exclaimed regarding the time. "I had better be going," he said. "Thank you all for having me over to visit." He then asked permission to use a phone and call a taxi to take him across to the Eligible Residence. Nadine saw him to the door, and remained for a few private words.

"Stay strong," Abraham said. "I won't come over tomorrow in case I wear out my welcome."

"Perhaps you could come by for a little while," Nadine suggested. "I would really love to see you."

"I think I will give you a call," Abraham said. "That will have to suffice."

"Okay," Nadine said. "I will talk to you then."

They exchanged a discrete hand-clasp, and Abraham got into the taxi. "Goodnight," he said. "Sweet dreams my sweet."

Earlier that day, Anthony led Janny out of front door and walked towards the limousine, stopping to open the automobile door and make sure that the dancer was settled comfortably. "I have a surprise for you today," he said. "Abraham though we ought to try something more interesting than a simple lunch date."

"Oh - what will we be doing?" Janny inquired.

"We are going on a helicopter ride to a glorious ranch on the other side of the mountains," Anthony explained. "They specialise in bed and breakfast holidays."

"Are you asking me to stay away the night?" Janny's eyes were as huge as saucers. "I am not sure that I am ready for that - it isn't even the end of the show!"

"Don't worry," Anthony said. "We will fly back this very evening if you wish!"

"Okay," Janny said. "I can go for something like that – if my options are truly open."

The pair joked gently for the rest of the limousine ride, until they arrived at Bankstown Airport; where they climbed out of the automobile. They were greeted by some official looking staff in uniform, and directed towards a field designed to serve the lighter aircraft.

With the camera crew in close pursuit, the Charity Eligible and his companion crossed the tarmac the waiting chopper, which was a six seater to comfortably accommodate the pilot and co-pilot, Anthony and Janny, and two camera-men.

Janny exclaimed in delight, as she had never before been on a helicopter ride, and Anthony hurried to re-assure her it would be extremely safe. Then they settled into the leather seats and fastened their safety belts.

The camera crew settled opposite them and promised to be as unobtrusive as possible. "Concentrate upon each other," Simon Steeple said. "You will never know we are here."

"That could be difficult," Janny whispered to Anthony, as the camera seemed to be right in her face. However, when the helicopter rose into the air, she began to exclaim over the map-like view of main roads and houses on the ground below.

When they cleared the suburbs, the aircraft gained altitude to pass over the western mountain range, and the passengers found themselves surrounded by some light misty clouds. The pilot frowned and talked to someone on his radio, but it turned out to be mere minutes before they cleared the cloud cover and began to fly over some pastoral land.

"Have you flown often before?" Janny asked Anthony, who was obviously comfortable with the flight procedure, and appeared quite undisturbed by the cloud cover.

"I did a few months' work with a remote area medical centre," Anthony said. "I had to fly around a fair bit then."

"Was it like this?" Janny inquired, and Anthony shook his head.

"It was always lot tenser," the Doctor replied. "I was usually travelling post haste to an emergency situation."

Janny looked suitably impressed, and asked a couple of questions about the surgeon's work with the out-back community. Anthony answered each query to the best of his ability, and then decided to steer the conversation into a lighter direction and daringly told her that he found her attractive.

"The way you move reminds me of a cat," Anthony said, and Janny giggled irrepressibly.

"Almost twenty years of training, and you call me a domestic animal," she cried. "At least I get nine to have lives and always land on my feet!"

"I meant that you are always light and graceful," Anthony said indignantly.

"I know what you meant," Janny returned, patting the Charity Eligible on the hand. "And I was just teasing."

Anthony was just getting around to gazing deep into the ballerina's eyes, when the pilot announced that they were going to land.

The helicopter pilot opened the door and the couple found themselves facing a huge stone homestead situated about fifty meters away from the landing field.

"Is that our ranch?" Janny asked.

Anthony nodded, "I guess so," he said. "There is nothing else around here, except cattle and trees."

"Let's go then," Janny said. "I am curious to see everything."

The pair linked arms loosely and tramped up to the station-house, where they found that the interior was every bit as impressive as the exterior. There was a rich wooden floor, nineteenth century style paintings and wall plaques, and a huge antique grandfather clock. The proprietor bustled out of a huge kitchen tucked behind a well-stocked bar and greeted them.

"Please call me Mrs. Buchan," the station owner effused. "I will be doing everything I can to make your visit enjoyable."

"Thank you," Anthony said. "We appreciate your hospitality!"

Mrs. Buchan beamed. "Don't worry about it," she said. "It is a pleasure to serve you."

Mrs. Buchan then offered to show the pair to their rooms, and led the way to two inter-connected chambers, both featuring huge oak double beds. Crossing to the wall in one room, the woman threw open the door of an antique wardrobe where they could stow their things.

Janny was about to object that she had no luggage, when she saw the helicopter pilot arrive with her small case, which Leticia had obviously packed in secret and included in the baggage.

Janny turned to Anthony: "I thought you said I had a choice?" she exclaimed accusingly.

Anthony looked abashed. "Leticia thought that you might like to freshen up or get changed sometime during such an extensive day-trip," he declared contritely. "Like I said, we will fly back home tonight if you wish."

"It is rare that a male goes to so much trouble without expecting something in return," Janny continued suspiciously.

"I admit that it was Abraham who gave me the idea," Anthony said. "He suggested you had trust issues and that I should show you that you were worth every effort a man could make."

"Did Abraham mention what sort of trust issues?" Janny inquired.

"Men only after one thing I presume," Anthony replied.

"And you two thought it would fix things if you appeared to put the hard word on me too?" Janny scoffed with a fearful glance towards one of the double beds.

"Absolutely not!" Anthony said. "I promise you that although I do find you attractive, this date is not about sex. It is about romance, and there are no strings attached."

Janny looked suitably impressed. "I almost believe you," she said gently. "I am always working, and until now, I don't think I knew how much I missed being treated like a real woman."

The couple were interrupted just then by a station hand who led them out the back door and to a paddock where two friendly looking horses were grazing.

"Has either of you ridden a horse before?" The station hand, who said his name was Jeremy Buchan, inquired.

Both Anthony and Janny shook their heads. However, Janny announced that she was suddenly very glad she had worn jeans.

"Please don't be concerned," Jeremy Buchan continued, "These horses are very docile."

Jeremy showed them how to pat and greet the horses before saddling up and leading them out of the yard along a bush track. The natural scenery was beautiful as they passed through light eucalyptus scrub. The day was warm, but the sun was filtered by the trees that lined the path and a fresh breeze played on their shoulders.

After a few minutes, they came to a grassy clearing where a picnic blanket had been spread out. Mrs. Buchan had provided a pleasant meal of cold smoked beef and Cesare salad, finished with passion-fruit sponge-cake and washed down with coffee from a thermos flask.

Janny expressed herself too well fed to ride back to the ranch house immediately and they sat on the picnic rug for some time conversing dreamily. Anthony, who was determined to show his companion that he could be a gentleman, made no attempt to pressure Janny for intimacy.

Eventually Jeremy, who had been hovering in the background sharing lunch with the camera crew, suggested Anthony and Janny ought to mount the horses again and ride back to the house. Janny then retired to her room to luxuriate in the deep bath; while Anthony read a book from the antique bookcase out on the balcony.

It was tea-time when Janny emerged in an attractive new summer frock, and knocked upon Anthony's bedroom door. "I began to wonder where you were," the ballerina said.

"I was being careful not to barge into you room and cause you to doubt my intentions again," Anthony replied.

"That was very thoughtful of you," Janny said. "However, I am getting hungry."

"I am sure Mrs. Buchan will have something cooked for us," Anthony said.

Hearing their voices, Mrs. Buchan appeared and ushered *The Charity Dating Show* participants to a dining area with an ornate carved dining table and antique wooden chairs. She then served an evening meal notable for its well cooked vegetables and rich meaty sauce. Desert was delicious homemade ice-cream and jelly.

After dark, Anthony and Janny took a walk outside to see the rise of the first stars, and they each made a secret wish. Anthony finally managed to kiss his companion on the lips, and whispered that his wish might be coming true.

Janny allowed Anthony to explore her mouth briefly before turning her head, and nestling her face into the hollow of his shoulder.

"What is wrong?" Anthony whispered, puzzled by the mixed signals the ballerina continued to give him.

"Nothing," Janny whispered. "I am very happy."
Anthony reflected that he was still a long way from understanding women. "Are you sure there is nothing else bothering you?" he inquired.

"A little," Janny whispered. "I think I need to work something out."

"Is it about me?" Anthony asked.

"No, it's about me," Janny replied. "I will tell you sometime." She raised her face to his kiss again, and Anthony covered her mouth with his once again.

Anthony had a slight suspicion that Janny was allowing the kisses to distract him from asking further questions, and found it hard to get back into the mood.

"You don't really want to stay here tonight do you?" he whispered.

"I don't really mind," Janny began. "But it might be better if we went back to the others."

"Alright," Anthony said. "I guess we don't need the other girls all jealous because we stayed over anyway."

It was late at night when they boarded the helicopter and flew back to the city.

Janny fell asleep against Anthony's shoulder soon after the chopper started, and the Charity Eligible had to content himself with gently placing a kiss upon her drowsy forehead.

Janny stirred and murmured something indistinguishable about "Kindness" and "Thanks". It seemed that she had become more thoughtful than was her usual custom. The day had obviously initiated some significant thought processes for the girl, but Anthony was unsure exactly what those had been.

CHAPTER THREE: AN UNDERGROUND ADVENTURE

Early the next day, Anthony arrived all spruced up in designer jeans and a cotton shirt to take Kendra out on their date. Kendra was like-wise sportily attired in a striped top and cargo pants. They hugged each other warmly and climbed into the limousine together.

"Where are we going?" Kendra asked.

"I thought that you would like to see some of the scenery in the Blue Mountains and even go into the caves," Anthony said.

"Would I ever!" Kendra exclaimed. "You do know how to treat the artist in me."

"Do you have your sketching materials?" Anthony asked, and Kendra shook her head.

"I had better go and get some," she said. They tapped on the glass and asked the driver to wait for a moment, and Kendra ran back into the house, returning with a small satchel. "I don't know why I haven't been bringing these along," she said.

"Maybe there was less to draw," Anthony suggested, and Kendra shrugged.

"There is always something to draw," she said. "It's just that sometimes I am able to keep it in my head until we get home."

The limousine drove the couple west into the mountains for about an hour, and through the town of Katoomba. It finally pulled up along-side a miniature rail siding at Scenic World. Kendra climbed out of the car and exclaimed in delight.

"Is it a real train?" she cried.

"I believe it is an adventure railway," Anthony informed her. "If you are game, it will take us down the side of the mountain just like a roller coaster - only for real."

Kendra crossed to the look-out rail, surveyed the train track, and shuddered. "It will actually go down there?" she said.

"Yes," Anthony said. He glanced at his companion's face and became concerned. "You are not frightened of heights are you?"

"Not normally," Kendra said. "However, the train must gather up a lot of momentum on the way down."

"You will have to hang onto me," Anthony said, hovering close to her side.

"Yes," Kendra agreed amicably. "I will most certainly hang onto you all the way."

The graphic artist took one more long shuddering look at the view from the top of the cliff, and whipped a notebook out from her satchel. A few pencil lines and she had the outline of the ranges around them, and the drop into the valley was marked very clearly.

Anthony was impressed. "You are exceptionally good," he said, peeping over her shoulder.

Kendra shut her notebook with a snap and put it away in her bag. "It's just a sketch for my personal use," she said.

"You really are shy about your painting," Anthony said in amazement. "Aren't you?"

"I have never been paid much for my drawing or 'serious Art' as you could call it," Kendra said. "Unlike my commercial work, for which I receive a wage. I guess you could say I remain a little insecure about it."

"That is a pity," Anthony said. "I think you should be very proud of your creative work in addition to your commercial."

Just then the train arrived. It was about a third of the size of a standard train, and ran on a much smaller gauge of rail. When Anthony and Kendra climbed in and sat side by side, they were quite crowded. The sides seemed to enclose them and the row of windows made the view seem very close.

The train began to travel gently at first, but then it rushed down the hillside with an almighty whoosh. Kendra hid her face in Anthony's shoulder and clung on tight. The Charity Eligible put a protective arm around her shoulder and murmured to her gently. To tell the truth, the drop was impressive enough to unsettle anyone, male or female, and he was very glad of her feminine presence.

The trip lasted about ten breathtaking minutes, and then the train came to a halt at the foot of the mountain. Anthony and Kendra clambered out, and crossed gingerly to a wooden seat at the side of the valley. Kendra sat down gratefully and rested her head in her hands for a few minutes. Anthony stroked the line of her hair where it rose from her forehead, and waited for her to recover her equilibrium.

"That was magnificent," Anthony said. "Thank you for coming with me."

"It was pretty amazing," Kendra said, raising her face to his, "But I would never have gone alone."

"That's what a friend is for," Anthony said, kissing her lightly upon the lips, "Or boy-friend, whichever you prefer."

"I'm not prepared to put a label on you at this stage," Kendra said. "Not when you are dating other women."

She lifted her face away from his, and reached into her satchel once again, pulling out a notebook. Bowing over the page, she created a pattern of lines and shading.

Anthony was perplexed. "That is pretty abstract," he remarked.

"It represents our trip down the mountain," Kendra said.

"But you didn't look," Anthony exclaimed.

"I've drawn what I felt," Kendra said.

"Interesting," Anthony said. "May I?" He extended his hand and Kendra reluctantly handed over the notebook. Anthony thumbed through the pages, blushing slightly as he came to sketches of himself and the places they had been together.

"You have drawn something every day," he remarked.

Kendra nodded.

"I am glad you are drawing in front of me now," Anthony said. "I feel like it is the real Kendra coming out. In fact, I would like to join you. Would you mind if we stopped in the township on the way to the caves and got me a pencil and paper?"

"That would be fine," Kendra said. "I would like to see the town anyway."

The pair got up and crossed to the small car park where the limousine was waiting for them. "The main street please," Anthony said to the driver.

The main street proved to be long and narrow, and placed upon the slope of a hill. However, it was very picturesque and they found a novel little newsagent at which to purchase a sketch pad for Anthony; and a take-away food shop where they could have coffee and sandwiches. Then they climbed back into the car and allowed the driver to transport them to Jenolan where they could visit the caves.

Upon arriving at the cave-site, Anthony and Kendra jumped out of the car. Kendra made sundry sketches of the trees and plants around the edge of the surrounding mountains, and a separate picture of the cave entrance itself, which formed a dark mouth in the side of the hill.

Anthony attempted to draw something similar and found that his sketching skills were something untutored. Focusing closely on a nearby plant, Anthony produced a rough drawing of its various formations.

It was a simple line drawing, minus the perspective and realism of Kendra's still life and landscapes. Kendra however, on inspecting the picture, congratulated him on its execution.

"I would love to be able to do all that shaping and shading you do," Anthony said.

"I can give you some hints someday," Kendra said. "I observe things closely, and create effects and impressions. I enjoy creating greeting cards at work, but I would also like to be able to display a set of oil paintings or publish a book of water-colours."

"If you persist in doing both, it should happen," Anthony said.

Kendra laughed. "You are stirring up ambitions that have lain fallow since I graduated from university and obtained paid employment," she said.

"I am glad," Anthony said. "And I hope that is not all I am stirring in you..."

"No fair," Kendra said. "You were out with Janny yesterday."

"That went well enough," Anthony said. "Although I am not sure why Abraham recommended her as compatible. She definitely does have some trust issues to work on."

"Those could be overcome," Kendra said lightly. However she sounded relieved to hear the news. "You were away for a long time."

"It was a busy date," Anthony said vaguely.

Kendra let the subject drop. "Are we going to go into the caves now?" She inquired.

"Sure," Anthony said. "If you have finished looking around the outside."

"I finished a while back," Kendra said. "It's just that we got talking."

They entered the cave mouth and the rocky walls closed quickly around them. Wooden sleepers had been used to strengthen and even out the main path through the cave, and rails had been placed on either side of the main walk-way to prevent people wandering unaccompanied through the more treacherous caverns.

"The cave system must stretch for miles," Kendra whispered in awe.

"It is possible that the fissures could reach through the entire mountain range," Anthony agreed.

"I wouldn't like to get lost," Kendra whispered.

"No," Anthony said, putting an arm around her. "Nor would I."

"It sounded very romantic for Tom and Becky in *The Adventures of Tom Sawyer*," Kendra said.

"It sure did," Anthony said. "But that was a story."

"I am cold," Kendra said with a shiver. "I didn't expect that today, even in the shade."

"I have got a jacket," Anthony said. "I'll lend it to you." He unfolded his lightweight sports-coat and draped it across Kendra's shoulders. She pulled it around her gratefully.

"That is better," Kendra said. "It is far too big though."

"You look adorable," Anthony said, "Like you are playing dress up in my coat."

The couple traversed several hundred meters of cave fissure, sometimes climbing slightly upwards, and other times descending into the earth. As they progressed, the light from the entrance disappeared, and they became reliant on electric lamps mounted at intervals upon the cave wall.

"I am starting to wish we had a torch," Kendra commented as they passed one particularly dim corner.

Just then a couple of bulbs blew a few steps ahead, and they were plunged into darkness. Anthony placed one hand upon the guard rail and gave the other hand to Kendra. "Hold on tight," he said.

"Do you think we ought to go back or forward?" Kendra said.

Anthony glanced at the dim recess behind them, and then peered further into the cavern. "We are in pretty deep," he said. "Unless there is a full black-out, we should be able to pick up some lighting ahead."

"Okay," Kendra said, and they padded carefully forward with Anthony following the rail for some distance.

"I am getting really nervous now," Kendra said after a while.

"So am I," Anthony said. "But I know we haven't left the main track."

"Well then why haven't we come to any lights?" Kendra asked.

"It must be something to do with the way they are wired," Anthony said. "Shall we talk about something else to get us through?"

"Yeah sure," Kendra said. "So long as it doesn't make you let go that rail."

"You can trust me," Anthony said. "I don't want to fall to my death any more than you do."

"I won't say the proverbial about dying together," Kendra said.

"You wouldn't," Anthony laughed hollowly. "It's not your style."

"That sort of romanticism is very dark," Kendra said. "I would rather live together to enjoy another day."

"I assure you, we will live through this," Anthony said.

"What if there are – er steps – and we don't see them," Kendra moaned.

"Now who is being negative?" Anthony said. "I promise you I am holding this rail very tight!"

"I trust you," Kendra whispered. "Even with my life."

"Thank you," Anthony said. He tried to change the topic. "Do you remember how we talked about using art as a form of therapy?"

"I do," Kendra said. "Albeit, I can't do anything about it while I am here in the dark. When I leave this cave, I will read up a bit."

"I will too," Anthony said. "Although I have little ambition towards psychiatric practice. I think it would be best to stick to a sort of occupational or physiotherapy approach."

"I agree that is the most accessible," Kendra said. "Although I have always been aware of the function of art as a form of self-exploration and communication with others."

"Perhaps we had both better approach it from our individual areas of expertise," Anthony said.

"I agree," Kendra said. "Is that a light up ahead?"

"I believe it is!" Anthony said. He began to pull Kendra forward more quickly, and they descended a dip into a passage from which a faint glow emanated. "There is something up ahead."

"It doesn't look connected to those other light bulbs," Kendra said observantly.

"That is why it is still glowing," Anthony surmised. They reached the bottom of the dip, and climbed upwards for a few paces, entering a large cavern, the far end of which was lighted.

"At last!" Kendra exclaimed. They ran forward, and found that the lighted end of the cave led into an even larger cavern, which was strung with strings of white light all around the edge.

"It is like a Christmas display," Anthony remarked.

"It is absolutely beautiful!" Kendra exclaimed, looking around. "And it is so big!"

"It is almost endless," Anthony said, looking around and blinking. To tell the truth, the brilliantly lighted cave was dazzling after the dark corridors they had traversed. It was also pleasant to be able to wander at will, and not remain cautiously beside the guard rails.

"We have found some lights," Anthony called out to the camera crew, who had been attempting to follow, but were hampered by their equipment in the darkness.

"I want to dance," Kendra said grabbing Anthony by the shoulder in excitement. Anthony linked his left hand in hers and led a skipping romp around the broadened area.

There was no music but the rhythm of their exuberance, and they paid no attention to step patterns or timing, falling naturally into a loping pace suitable to them both, and circling around the cave until they tired.

At last the couple slowed to a halt, and Kendra remained standing, with her arms sliding around Anthony's neck. Anthony gathered her towards him with his arms around her waist. "This feels so right," he said.

"Oh aye," Kendra murmured in agreement. She buried her face in his neck for a long moment, and then raised her mouth for a kiss.

Anthony held the kiss until it deepened, and then stopped for breath. "It's been too long," he muttered. "The group dates are very pleasant, but I don't get to concentrate on developing a relationship with any one girl."

"We don't get to spend much time alone," Kendra murmured. "Not even on our individual dates if you count the cameras."

"Would you like to start seeing more of each other in secret?" Anthony asked in a whisper.

Kendra considered this seriously for a moment, and then shook her head. "It wouldn't be fair," she whispered in reply. "And I don't believe you want to give up exploring your relationship potential with the other girls yet."

"You may be right," Anthony said. "Although, I think Vonda is the only other serious contender."

"In that case," Kendra whispered, "I will let you know if and when I am ready to take things further."

"And I will continue to be honest with you," Anthony murmured. He gave Kendra one more kiss, and then stepped back.

"I am worried about attempting the walk back with the lights off," he remarked in a louder voice to Simon, and the rest of the camera crew, who had caught up with them. "There is no telling how much of the corridor behind us is blacked out."

"Good thinking," Kendra said. "There might be a service phone or something around here."

"I expect the camera crew have mobiles, but they might not be able to transmit through all this rock," Anthony said.

"It would depend how deep we are and how far from any towers," Simon agreed. "I know I have trouble getting reception from the basement at the studio sometimes."

After a circuit of the cave, Anthony discovered a cable phone installed in the wall, and lifting the receiver, found himself in contact with the cave maintenance office. "The lights are out in the corridor," he said. "At first we thought it was the bulbs, but then there were so many dark places we concluded it might be the wiring."

"We are terribly sorry to hear that," the Service Manager said, crackling down the line. "Are you in the main cavern complex?"

"Yes we are," Anthony said, "And there are lights on here."

"Good," the Manager said. "Stay put and we will send someone after you with a strong torch."

Anthony hung up the phone, and turned to Kendra. "What do we do now?" he said.

"I don't know about you," Kendra said, "But I am going to do some sketching."

It was an hour before the maintenance crew arrived, and then they found them, with Anthony sprawled out asleep and Kendra tucked up between his legs for warmth, drawing her fifteenth impression of the cave and lights.

The camera crew, who had turned off their equipment to save the batteries, rose to their feet and filmed the rescue. They swore that the blackout had not been a set-up, although it had made very good drama.

Kendra arrived home that evening looking exceedingly dirty and raced into the shower, explaining that she had spent some of the date sitting on the ground. Her house-mates looked at each other and raised their eyebrows.

"On the ground she says!" Deborah commented to Nadine. "Did you happen to sit on the ground during your date with Anthony?"

"No," Nadine commented, blushing slightly. "Mine was only a first date...and Kendra looks a bit like she has been rolling in the dirt!"

"Maybe there is a perfectly innocent explanation," Vonda ventured.

"I'm sure," Deborah remarked. "Perhaps they had no chairs at their particular restaurant!"

"Do you know what sort of date it was?" Janny asked, thinking about the horse ride and outdoor picnic she had been on the day before. "The dates are getting more adventurous and it might have been a picnic after all."

Deborah shrugged: "I have no idea what was planned," she said.

"We will hear soon enough," Nadine said. "Talk to Kendra as soon as she gets out of the shower."

When Kendra emerged from her bathroom, she was slightly embarrassed to find three girls waiting to interrogate her. Begging for a moment of peace, she shrugged into a light-weight robe and sat on the corner of her bed.

"We went caving," Kendra said. "There wasn't any extreme sport type spelunking, but it was the real thing for all that."

"How exciting," Vonda said. "I bet you just loved being alone in the dark with Anthony."

"Actually, I preferred the light," Kendra said, and explained about the calamity with the electricity. Deborah laughed and Nadine shivered, while Vonda seemed enthralled.

Tea was a cosy affair that evening. Anthony arrived accompanied by Abraham, who was still staying at the Eligible Residence. The Candidates were becoming accustomed to Abraham's presence and several speculated whether he would have a further role in *The Charity Dating Show*.

"He could even be next year's Eligible Candidate," the innocent Vonda whispered.

"I expect he will be planning more of our dates," Janny suggested, mindful of the role Abraham had in her recent date.

Nadine frowned slightly at Vonda's suggestion that Abraham might be a future Eligible Candidate, and hurried to greet him with a secret smile. She then led the way into the dining room.

Deborah and Kendra exchanged glances. "I thought I saw something happening between Abraham and Nadine yesterday," Kendra whispered.

"Yeah, the wind is definitely blowing in a certain direction," Deborah agreed. "And why not indeed?"

"As long as Anthony is happy," Kendra murmured.

"It is one less rival for you, if it is true," Deborah whispered.

In acknowledgement of the dwindling numbers, Leticia had arranged for a smaller table to be installed. None of the contestants knew where the large table had gone, although some speculated that the shed at the back of the garden might be stacked with an absolute assortment of furniture and equipment.

Despite being set up for a small group, the background music was pleasant and romantic, 'easy listening' in style. Vonda found herself humming along; and Janny also began to relax and sway along with the music. Deborah was her usual cheery self, Nadine seemed pleased to talk to Abraham in the corner, and Kendra looked tired, but contented.

The table was decorated with some colourful potted geraniums, prompting Anthony to ask each of the girls which species of flower were her favourite.

Nadine predictably volunteered that her favourite flower was the rose. As she said this, she peeked shyly under her eyelashes to see whether Abraham was taking note. The Charity Eligible's best friend was attentive as usual.

"The mixed bunch you gave me yesterday was absolutely perfect," Janny said to Anthony. "Although I must say my absolute favourite flower would be the lily."

"Some people say that lilies are for funerals," Anthony frowned.

"Weddings too," Janny asserted. "They are a deeply symbolic and emotional flower."

"To match an emotional girl," Anthony deduced, and Janny

flushed.

Anthony then asked Vonda which flowers were her favourite, and seemed pleased to hear that she liked tulips. "They are nice bright flowers," he commented. "And easy for a fellow to find in the florist."

"They also come in many colours," Vonda explained. "I like to think that even though I am quiet, I have many aspects."

"Carnations are a little overdone on this show," Deborah remarked, "So I am going to pick dahlias."

"I like daisy-type flowers," Kendra replied. "From the tiny white wild-flower, to the huge double gerbera. I also quite like the huge sun flower."

Anthony took note, and promised to give her a bunch of daisies at some stage during the dating process. Over-hearing this, Deborah laughed and asked whether they would be everlastings; and Anthony parried by saying he did not know what the florist would have in stock at the time.

CHAPTER FOUR: JANNY'S BIRTHDAY PARTY

Janny was usually the first girl out of bed and into the pool for a swim. However, the following morning, Kendra and Vonda noticed their room-mate, who was usually full of mischievous energy, was abnormally withdrawn. The ballerina did not stir while her room-mates showered and dressed, and drew the sheet even closer around herself when they suggested she accompany them to breakfast.

"Are you alright Janny?" Kendra asked when they returned from breakfast and found that Janny still had not moved out of her foetal position.

"I'm not sick," came the reluctant reply from Janny. "I just don't feel like being sociable today."

"What's wrong?" Vonda inquired. "Is it Anthony?"

"It's not really Anthony," Janny replied. "Although I hope he hasn't planned a group date for today. At least not one I am involved in."

"I think we are due to film a carnation ceremony," Kendra said. "But it's later in the day luckily."

"Just what I always wanted," Janny muttered somewhat cynically.

"Is it the time of the month?" Vonda asked.

"You could say it is something like that," Janny muttered gloomily. "If you MUST know girls, it is my birthday today!"

"But that is great!" Vonda exclaimed.

"Is it really?" Janny cried. "I'm turning twenty-six today and I'm stuck on *The Charity Dating Show* because I cannot find a good boyfriend the NORMAL way."

"When you put it that way, I do see the problem," Kendra agreed. "But aren't we all in a similar situation?"

"I will also be spending the day without any celebration because filming the show is more important than my birthday," Janny declared.

"I would hate to spend my birthday without my family and friends," Vonda exclaimed. "And you must do something to celebrate."

"There are a few things I would do if I was home," Janny agreed.

"Let us see whether anything special can be arranged while you are in here," Kendra said.

"I am willing to do something with you girls," Janny said, "But please do not tell Leticia or Anthony."

"I don't quite understand why not," Vonda said.

"Because I'm feeling emotional and don't want a huge fuss," Janny said. "I also don't want my birthday to become part of the show. I don't want to be used for publicity."

Janny climbed out of bed briefly and stared at her twenty-six year old self in the mirror. Then she decided that getting out of her pyjamas was too much effort, and climbed mournfully back into bed admitting to feeling depressed.

Kendra and Vonda decided to serve the ballerina breakfast in the room to try to cheer her up. They ran down to the kitchen and brewed hot coffee, toasted some muffins and spread them with Janny's favourite marmalade.

When they returned to the bedroom, the girls noticed that Janny had begun fiddling with her mobile phone, which was meant to have been packed away for the duration of the show. However Kendra whispered that since it was Janny's birthday, she could be excused for breaking the rules.

"Did you call your mum and dad?" Kendra, who was very family oriented, inquired.

Janny shook her head. "I read my birthday messages," she admitted. "But my family know I am on this show and do not expect any answer."

"What about your friends?" Vonda asked innocuously.

"My best friends are cool with it too," Janny said. "But I haven't told everyone else where I am of course."

"Of course not," Kendra agreed. "Not everyone would understand. At least not at first!"

"That food looks good," Janny said catching sight of the tray Kendra was carrying. She struggled to sit up in bed and Kendra placed the tray on her knees. "Mm coffee – I don't usually need the pickup, but this is delicious."

"We are glad you like it," Vonda said anxiously.

Janny picked up a muffin and bit into it, clearly enjoying the buttery taste and slight tang of the marmalade. When she had finished the food and drink, she pushed the tray aside.

"Honestly girls, I am twenty-six today!" Janny burst out. "Twenty six years old - and I haven't had a relationship of any substantial length or depth."

"What do you mean?" Kendra inquired. "Everyone dates. I've even had a couple of serious offers I had to turn down. But I haven't found the right guy – unless it is Anthony!"

"The guys I dated got keen quickly," Janny said. "They said they loved me and everything, but their interest didn't last very long."

Vonda nodded thoughtfully: "Those guys just weren't right for you."

"Do you think that was because you were focusing too much on your work?" Kendra asked practically. "I've been led to believe dancing is a very demanding sort of career."

Janny shrugged. "That might have been part of it," she said. "But most guys just seemed to be after sex. If I gave it to them, they were off, forgetting they loved me as fast as they declared it."

"That sounds awful," Vonda exclaimed.

"That is why I normally joke around and keep things light with men," Janny explained. "There was only one guy who sort-of understood my career."

"And what about happened with him?" Kendra asked.

"I left him," Janny said. "He had the opposite problem. He was possessive and controlling...and it was complicated."

"How long ago was this?" Vonda inquired.

"Just before applying for *The Charity Dating Show*," Janny admitted. "I thought it was for the best at the time, but dating Anthony has made me think more about commitment and stuff."

"Do you regret breaking up with this guy?" Kendra asked.

Janny shook her head. "No. On the contrary - I wish I had broken up with him sooner. Confronted him about a few things he did! Made things clearer - I don't know. Anthony has been so nice, that now I feel weird."

"Dating Anthony seems to have stirred things up for a few of us," Kendra said. "I also began this process with a number of assumptions about relationships and what I wanted. I have had to give some of them away."

"I don't want to be unsympathetic Janny," Vonda said, "But I am finding it hard to perceive you as a victim - you are so beautiful and you seem so confident!"

"Being positive about yourself doesn't always help you find the right guy," Janny murmured.

"It would appear to be a bonus in most cases," Vonda commented. "My relationships never even get off the ground because I am so unassuming."

"I can see how it might be like that for you," Janny said shortly. "But please don't assume these things come easily for me either...you know nothing about my personal life."

The dancer gave the musician a resentful look, and for the first time in the record of their friendship, a note of chill entered the air. Vonda knew she had gone wrong somehow. She looked hurt and baffled.

"I was just trying to understand you Janny," Vonda said. "Don't let's fight."

"We are not fighting," Janny declared. "I'm merely upset over your assumption that because I am more outgoing, relationships work out for me. Relationships are not easy - you begin to lose yourself - and hearts can be broken."

"I'm sorry, Janny," Vonda said. "It does sound as though you have been hurt."

"It doesn't really matter," Janny said sulkily. "We haven't known each other that long and we are obviously very dissimilar."

"I think that it does matter," Vonda said. "We have been good friends up till now."

"Maybe we will be friendly again soon," Janny said. "I don't know." She turned to Kendra: "Thank you for the understanding you have extended."

Kendra took that as her cue to leave the bedroom and only Vonda remained.

"I'm really sorry Janny," Vonda whispered. "You and I have clearly had different experiences."

Janny pointedly ignored Vonda, and turned to fiddle with her mobile phone once again. As Vonda left the bedroom, she noticed that Janny appeared to be typing some sort of message on the key-pad of her electronic phone. Vonda wondered who Janny might be contacting as the ballerina had said she did not intend to answer her family's birthday wishes.

However, the musician carefully refrained from making any comment as there was too much difficulty between her and Janny already. Vonda picked up her violin case and discretely withdrew to the projection studio, which she had discovered was sound-proofed and afforded her the privacy she required to play music. An hour's practise would suffice to soothe her strained nerves.

As Janny had refused to allow Leticia or any of the television crew be told, and begged that Anthony not be informed, Kenrda confided in the outgoing Deborah; and the girls decided to arrange something private between themselves. Nadine, who was looking surprisingly serene and satisfied after a long telephone conversation with the Charity Eligible's friend Abraham, agreed to help with the birthday preparations.

Deborah and Nadine asked the housekeeper to allow them to use the kitchen for the morning, and resolved to bake a birthday cake and chocolate peanut cookies. They raided the refrigerator for salad ingredients, preserves and cold meats, before purloining sparkling cider and a bottle of white wine from the bar. They then set up a secret celebration in the privacy of the pool house.

The only mishap occurred in the kitchen when Nadine and Deborah loaded the dirty utensils into the dishwasher in blissful ignorance of the fact it had stalled and a repairman had been called. This resulted in a substantial flood emerging during the wash cycle. Howling in horror at the result, the girls mopped up the water and suds, trying to disguise their error from Leticia.

Once the party food was ready, Kendra called Janny into the pool house. She was relieved to see that the ballerina had showered and dressed and was sitting watching some television.

"Come and see your party now," Kendra said. "Deborah has almost finished setting up."

Kendra led the way to the pool house where Deborah and Nadine had cleared away the scattered clothes, set up a table and hung some streamers. The slender dancer cried a few tears of gratitude, hugged and thanked the girls, and ate a piece of her cake.

"I can hardly believe you did all this for me," Janny declared.

"On my part I can't believe we have only known each other for Just over a month!" Nadine remarked.

"Is it that long?" Vonda exclaimed. "It seems like time has flown."

Deborah began to count upon her fingers: "It has to be," she concluded. "But we have been together most of the time, and had a lot of activities planned."

"It is weird," Janny said. "I feel like I have known you girls forever, and yet I feel like you are all very new to me as well."

"It's an unrealistic situation," Nadine said. "We had nothing in common at first except that we were dating the same guy. However, we have been locked up together all the time."

"That's normally a recipe for trouble," Deborah said. "I am glad that some of us were able to shift the focus off the Charity Eligible and onto our lives in the Candidate House."

Anthony arrived at the Candidate House soon after that and inquired why they were eating lunch in the pool house instead of in the dining room or on the patio. There was much nudging and winking between the girls on his arrival, and despite the injunction regarding secrecy, Nadine let slip that it was Janny's birthday party.

"Why ever didn't you tell me it was your birthday?" Anthony inquired. "We were meant to be getting to know one another."

Janny sighed. "Twenty-six is one past twenty-five," she said. "I am no longer young and beautiful."

"Twenty-six is still a good time to be having fun," Anthony said. "And you are very beautiful in my eyes!" He helped himself to some meat and salad, before trying a peanut chocolate cookie. "Someone around here is a very good cook."

Nadine, Deborah, Vonda and Kendra clustered around the birthday girl holding their glasses high. They explained to Anthony that they had not had the birthday salute yet.

"What shall we drink to?" Kendra asked.

"To love," Janny replied with some hesitation. "I want to see the world full of love and peace."

"Love and peace it is," Deborah said.

"Peace for the world and love for us," Vonda added slyly.

"I think we are all here for love!" Kendra cried. "And peace and love for the rest of the world."

"All for love," Anthony cried, raising his glass. "And the best possible future for our Janny!"

The group clinked their glasses together and completed the birthday toast. Deborah then collected the glasses together and began tidying up, as she instinctively adopted the role of hostess even though the mansion was not her home.

Anthony and Vonda left Deborah to the cleaning, and moved the party across to the large lounge. Nadine collected up the clean crockery and some of the chocolate biscuits to take with them, while Kendra picked up her sketch pads and followed soon after.

Janny disengaged herself from the conversation, and wandered over to the stereo in the lounge, fiddling for a few minutes until she found a classical recording she liked. The strains of a Viennese waltz filled the room. When that piece of music came to an end, a regular waltz commenced.

Anthony approached Janny and invited her to celebrate her birthday with a social dance. However the ballerina refused his invitation, preferring to sit on the sideline looking pensive.
She shook her head, "Go to Kendra or ask Nadine, they both like to dance socially."

"I would especially like to dance with you," Anthony returned.

"I'm not really in the mood," Janny said. "Thank you all the same Anthony."

Anthony was puzzled, wondering whether he had read the cues all wrong the last time he had been out with the ballerina. He excused himself from the group and slipped out to the florist to buy Janny a bunch of native flowers and anything else he could find suitable for a present.

He returned from his shopping errand with a bunch of Australian flowers, featuring a huge waratah and some minor brush and foliage. He also had a leather bound diary. He presented these items to Janny with a gentle air of courtesy, and she thanked him with coy embarrassment.

"I'm afraid there weren't any lilies," Anthony said. "Someone had just put in a huge order."

"These are lovely anyway," Janny said. "I don't want to seem ungrateful – I know you got me flowers for my birthday and all - but I'm not feeling festive this moment. I'm missing my home and family too much, and I did ask the girls not to reveal my birthday on the show."

"Ah," Anthony opened his mouth to express understanding, but Janny's phone beeped. He glanced at it in surprise. "I thought we weren't supposed to have those out during the show?"

"It's my birthday," Janny cried, twirling away coyly to view the small screen. "I have to check my messages."

"Of course," Anthony murmured, accepting her logic at face value. Anthony was standing waiting patiently for Janny to return when Leticia, who had been hovering around watching for a suitable break in proceedings, asked him to sojourn into the deliberation room.

Bidding the women goodbye, Anthony reluctantly complied. Once in the deliberation room, he felt a sense of solitude and silence settle upon him. He realised that for an earnest young doctor, who had never been much of a party-boy, the celebratory scene he had just vacated was rare and precious. At this point, he valued the company of each and every lady and was reluctant to let any go, even though he suspected one or two were not seriously interested in him.

Kendra was a certain selection. While she was not progressing into a relationship with him as quickly as he would have liked, Anthony felt that he understood her point of view. Her caution might well be a necessary provision in a situation of non-exclusive dating.

Vonda was gentle and sweet. Her ability to face situations that clearly intimidated her, and her love of travel intrigued the Charity Eligible. She was blossoming like a flower with each day upon the show, and Anthony felt that she was worth keeping around as long as possible.

Deborah was still his friend. However, she was becoming less predictable as her alternate interest grew in strength and commitment. At the moment the Charity Eligible felt she was in solid with him, but he was not sure how much longer he could count upon her forbearance.

All said and done, the two girls whose selection was in question seemed to be Nadine and Janny. Nadine, who had been such an irritant in the previous rounds, had calmed down immensely since she had Abraham to talk to on the side. If her current pleasant style of interaction with the other girls were to continue, it would be possible to keep her on the show.

Anthony had half-promised Abraham he would release Nadine so his friend could ask her out. However, he knew Abraham well. A small wait would not hurt him. It might even be good and give his mate the chance to make sure of his feelings. Unlike the Charity Eligible, Abraham had been something of a ladies' man over the years.

Janny, on the other hand, was presently the most restless. The lady who had once perplexed the Charity Eligible with her vivacity and teasing, now confounded him with her sighing and moping. Her reaction to his attempts at gallantry had been both gratifying and confusing; and Anthony was at a complete loss as to where he stood with her.

On the other hand, she was bright and attractive and it had come to light today was her birthday. It would be unthinkably bizarre to reject someone on their natal day, unless she really wanted to go home and celebrate with family.

Anthony struggled with this concept for a few minutes more, and then he made up his mind. When Leticia arrived to escort him into the small reception room, his mind was thoroughly and solidly resolved.

Once in the small reception room, Anthony faced the dwindling line of women, who all eyed him apprehensively. A brief memory of the previous carnation ceremony where the power was taken from his hand and a girl left of her own accord flashed across his mind, and the Charity Eligible stood as tall and straight as possible. He picked up a carnation.

"Vonda," Anthony said. "We haven't had a real chance to talk this round. However, I hope you are still having a good time on the show."

Vonda stepped forward and gave Anthony a brief hug. The gesture left her slightly pink, but it was nothing compared to the embarrassment she would once have suffered following a gesture of public affection.

"Of course I am having fun," she said. "You can be certain of me."

"I am glad," Anthony said. He gave Vonda a peck on the cheek and presented her with a carnation. "Will you accept this carnation?"

"Thank you Anthony," Vonda returned shyly. She returned to the line.

Anthony selected another carnation. "Kendra," he called. "Come here please".

Kendra stepped forward in a confident manner. "Yes Anthony," she said.

Anthony extended the carnation towards the graphic artist. "I hope that you will continue to say yes to me," he said in a humorous fashion.

Kendra laughed. "Whenever possible Anthony," she said. "Whenever possible."

The pair exchanged a warm hug and then Kendra stepped back into line with the other ladies.

"Deborah," Anthony said. "It is about time you and I went out on an individual date."

Deborah stepped forward and collected her carnation from the hand of the Charity Eligible. "I have been a bit neglected in the date stakes," she said laughingly.

"You don't seem particularly worried," Anthony hinted jovially.

"Well I am so bossy I can make every group date my particular event," Deborah responded cleverly.

"Then I don't owe you a date after all," Anthony said with mock severity. "But I will think of somewhere interesting to take you this round if possible."

"You do that Anthony," Deborah responded stoically.

Deborah returned to her position and Anthony picked up the last carnation. "Nadine," he said.

Nadine stepped forward and faced Anthony squarely. Anthony fumbled with the carnation and it dropped to the floor.

"It's an omen!" the girls all exclaimed.

Anthony bent down and picked up the carnation. As he straightened, he looked into Nadine's eyes. They were eloquent and pleading. He put the carnation back onto the table.

"I'm sorry Nadine," Anthony began haltingly, but then his voice gained momentum. "I was going to say that I appreciated your sticking around and making an effort to join in with the other girls."

"Thank you Anthony," Nadine said firmly. "It has been my pleasure."

"However," Anthony continued circumspectly: "I was wondering whether you really would prefer to go home now?"

"Yes Anthony," Nadine replied calmly. "I will miss you but it seems to be time for me to leave now. I will respect your decision in the matter of course."

"I wish you all the best for your future then," Anthony commented.

"You too Anthony," Nadine said. "I hope you find the right girl."

The pair shook hands formally and Nadine turned to walk away.

"Janny," Anthony said anxiously. He was hoping that the girl would not be offended because he had called her last, and incline towards turning him down on those grounds. "I have enjoyed all our outings, and while I am never quite sure what is happening for you, I would like to continue dating you."

Janny did not hesitate, but stepped forward and seized the carnation. "Thank you Anthony," she said giving him a fierce hug. "I am sorry about the mixed signals. Going out with you has been teaching me a lot about love. I would be happy to stay here with you."

If the petite blonde suspected that Anthony had almost let her go, she did not say. Anthony gave Janny the carnation and a kiss on the cheek. "Thank you!" he said.

The girls clustered around Nadine, who was now hovering beside the exit. Everyone wanted to wish her farewell and good luck in the outside world. They all exchanged hugs and made discrete small talk for the cameras.

Only Deborah put her face close to Nadine's ear and whispered what everybody else was thinking. "Clever girl," she said. "Have fun with Abraham!"

"Oh I intend to," Nadine asserted quietly.

"Where is he?" Deborah asked. "Waiting in the limousine with a bunch of roses?"

Nadine shook her head. "More like the airport if the truth be known," she admitted. "We both have homes to return to – and then – let the romance begin."

Nadine left the Candidate House and crossed the lawn to climb down the small set of steps leading to the drive way. She allowed herself to be seated in the limousine and then spoke for the cameras:

"I did really like Anthony when we met, but somehow all the drama got in the way of our connection…It wasn't meant to be and I am a little disappointed…I hope that he finds happiness with one of the girls left in the house."

Nadine lowered her eyelids and looked down at her hands modestly. "If you are looking for any tips, the front runner is Kendra, although I notice that Anthony does jump and run at Janny's beck and call. Janny also has received two bouquets of flowers and Kendra none so far!"

CHAPTER FIVE: A DAY AT THE BEACH

Deborah greeted Anthony with a warm hug when he arrived at the Candidate House. Her eyes were shining with mischief, as the socialite figured this would probably be her only legitimate opportunity to make George mildly jealous, and all public transgressions could be paid for in sweet privacy later.

Seeing Deborah's expression, Anthony suppressed a sigh. Something that would have been an awkward situation for the average person, obviously appealed to the stubborn constitution of the socialite. He suspected that while Deborah did not want to provoke George into a state of all-out jealousy, she might believe that an extra dose of sensual tension would not hurt her situation.

"Where are we going today?" Deborah asked coquettishly. "Remember you promised me something different." Her eyes were brilliant and her smile sparkled for the camera.

"We are going to the beach," Anthony said. "I hope that you have brought your swimmers, and packed some sun-screen."

"Oh I have," Deborah said boldly, rolling back the edge of her high-fashion sarong to reveal the lycra edge of a piece of designer swim-wear. A shapely length of thigh was also revealed.

"Who are you and what have you done with my best friend?" Anthony exclaimed in shock.

"Oh no – have I been friend-zoned?" Deborah cried. "We can't have that! I must make you see me in a more romantic light." She clutched at his arm and fluttered her eyelashes appealingly.

Anthony stepped in closer and whispered in her ear: "I see you are a good actress! But for mercy's sake tone it down a bit before George bursts a blood vessel."

Deborah laughed happily. Clearly the opportunity to indulge in flirtatious behaviour towards the Charity Eligible in front of her secret paramour, George, struck Deborah as highly amusing.

"I genuinely enjoy your company, and am glad to be out on a date with you." she assured Anthony loudly. "Please, don't friend-zone me, please."

Anthony attempted to glance sideways at George, but the fashionable female was taking no hints. The Charity Eligible wondered briefly what it took to provoke someone of George's pacific nature, and then decided to wait and see how the day progressed.

"Okay, let's get into the car," Anthony said gallantly.

The couple drove through the city talking animatedly about the weather, which Deborah declared was "Just perfect" for a beach picnic. And that it had been "So clever" of Anthony to choose such a great Australian icon to share with her.

Anthony ventured to suggest that it might be a little hot by midday, but Deborah declared sturdily that they would be able to find some shade for a romantic siesta. After about three quarters of an hour, they drew up alongside a sandy inlet lined with cultivated palm trees.

"It is lovely," Deborah gushed, linking her arm through that of the Charity Eligible. "Do show me around."

"I don't really know the place myself," Anthony observed skeptically. He was missing the normally practical Deborah whose company he found so comfortable. "I heard that it was popular with the tourists, and attracted the occasional circus."

"Better and better!" Deborah declared amiably. "We can pretend we are tourists and explore the beach together. You lead the way."

Anthony bared his teeth in a smile of polite exasperation. "We actually are tourists," he observed. "And I would be surprised if my leadership lasts past the first few steps."

"I can be feminine and submissive if I like," Deborah replied sweetly.

"Ah," Anthony said. He was beginning to see the funny side of things himself: "You will be submissive if you like, when you like, and for as long as you like, but only if you like!"

"Something like that," Deborah admitted. "I have many facets to my personality."

"I am actually more comfortable with the other Deborah," Anthony complained lightly. "The one who is my best mate."

"She is not here today," Deborah replied firmly.

"I cannot believe you really act like this on a date!" Anthony exclaimed. "Maybe I should ask someone with whom you have gone out."

"You wouldn't dare," Deborah retorted.

"Maybe I wouldn't," Anthony said ominously. "I don't know any of your old boy-friends anyway...and it wouldn't do to ask anyone around here would it?"

"No it would not!" Deborah retorted, suddenly turning pink and sounding less amused.

The hunter was becoming the hunted, and there was a national television audience ready to observe any embarrassment she displayed. The socialite was not easy to embarrass, but then she had never been seriously in love before.

"Cut!" Simon Steeple called firmly, and both he and George turned off the power in their photographic equipment. "What has gotten into you Anthony?" Simon demanded. "You seem to be skirting around some dangerous territory."

"Deborah is not your typical reality television date girl," Anthony retorted. "It is what I like about her - normally."

"There is still no need to question her past on national television," Simon said frowning.

"How gallant you are Simon," Deborah remarked defensively. "You are quite the knight in shining armour to defend my honour like that! How is Constance by the way?"

It was Simon's turn to blush bright red. "Constance is very well," he replied. "She has gone back to her home town, and I have driven over for the occasional visit. How did you know about that?" The camera operator's manner was carefully understated.

"I am a good guesser," Deborah said smartly. "Nothing else can happen until after the show has gone to air, can it Simon?"

"Of course, not," Simon said. "We do have to observe some proprieties, including the terms of her contract."

"Turn the camera back on Simon," George interjected, also looking mildly flushed. His workmate meant well, but was in danger of uncovering the truth in his zeal. "We are wasting valuable filming time."

"Sure," Simon said equitably. "Where were the love birds when we left off?"

"They were passing the rock garden and talking," George supplied firmly. "Then you said that they were getting into dangerous territory and called cut."

"All territory is dangerous around me," Deborah said lightly. She had apparently recovered her equilibrium. "Do turn the camera back on Simon. I promise I will get things back on track."

"Okay," Simon said, "Over to you Deborah!"

"Yeah," Deborah said cheekily striking a pose for the cameras, which were rolling once again, and looking across at the Charity Eligible. "Go and ask the man at the ice-cream stand to sell us an ice-cream. I want a double-choc if they have one."

"The ice-cream shack appears perfectly clean," Anthony granted. "Come on Deborah, we will go inside together, you know how you like ice-cream."

"I do," Deborah said, allowing herself to be dragged into the shack and seated at a minuscule table. The ice-cream stand was just within range of the sound of the festive music from the fair, and her face was enthralled as she turned to look in that direction. "A circus is just perfect for the repressed child I have discovered lives inside me."

"I am glad you are happy!" Anthony said. "I warn you it will be gaudy though."

"That is okay," Deborah said. "A circus is meant to be gaudy."

Anthony was amused. "Stay still while I get our ice-cream," he said. "Double-choc was it?"

"That is right," Deborah said.

A few minutes later, the couple sat contentedly consuming ice-cream, and Anthony viewed his companion with conjecture. It amazed him how easy it was to please the heiress, and he was genuinely astonished no man had discovered this before.

A sly glance at the camera crew showed Anthony that even George was surprised to see Deborah was satisfied by the simple ice cream on the beach. Anthony's heart glowed with a sense of pride. It turned out that he could provide his high society date with something special after all!

"I thought we would go for a walk along the water-line later," he remarked gently.

"Okay," Deborah said, but she was gazing in fascination at the row of carnival attractions along the esplanade. "I want to go over there," she said.

"We can pass through the fair if you like," Anthony suggested.

"Oh yes please," Deborah said agreeably. Her manipulative mood appeared forgotten.

The television couple stood up and walked hand-in-hand across the pavement to the grassy area where the side-show tents had been constructed. Anthony was looking around for a suitable game with which he could demonstrate his prowess and impress Deborah, when he felt her tugging excitedly at his hand.

"What do you do to those?" The socialite cried, pointing to a stand where a number of gaily wrapped boxes were laying in close proximity to a large wooden mallet.

"I don't know," Anthony said. "It almost looks like you smash the boxes." He addressed a question to the burly stall-holder and received an answer.

"They are piñata," the Carnival-Worker explained. "Some of the packages contain old junk, while other packages contain prizes or tickets."

Anthony glanced across at Deborah, fully expecting her to have lost interest, but she looked as eager as ever. "Buy me a turn," the socialite pleaded.

"Sure," Anthony said, and paid the Stall-holder.

Deborah picked up the wooden mallet and struck out at the nearest package. It shattered with the sharp clink of breaking crockery, and she crowed in delight. The socialite aimed the mallet at another package and it too went clunk and crumpled under the blow.

"You must really like smashing things," Anthony remarked in surprise.

"Oh yes!" Deborah exclaimed. "Whenever I accidently smashed anything at home, the housekeeper became very angry."

"Amazing," Anthony said. "So in effect, you were subservient to the hired help?"

"I was a child," Deborah said. "And the staff were in charge. They were also very well paid. My father expected the best."

"How do you feel now?" Anthony inquired.

"I prefer to phone out for delivery or take my clothes to a dry-cleaner than employ live-in domestics," Deborah replied. "I was happy to see that the housekeeper and chauffeur on the show go to their own homes at night."

"What about security staff?" Anthony asked.

Deborah shrugged. "Sometimes they are necessary. I assume they work shifts."

"I hope all stays peaceful around the mansion," Anthony said. "I would hate to see you girls threatened by anything."

Deborah aimed a deliberate blow toward another package and it popped, resolving itself into thin air. "That one must have contained a balloon," Anthony said.

Deborah spied a round parcel with a bright green wrapper and brought the mallet down with a thud. The package crumpled into a limp pile of cardboard.

"Cereal packet," Anthony observed. "The fellow really meant it about junk!"

"I think it is cool," Deborah said. "Buy me some more!"

Anthony paid the stall-holder for another round of smashing delights and returned to Deborah. "Go for it," he said.

"Thanks!" Deborah replied. She selected a bright red package, which split open to spill white grains of flour.

"Tasty," Anthony remarked, blowing his nose, which was always affected by dust. "Are you sure you don't want to move on now?"

"One more package," Deborah begged. "If I was at home or work, I would be fixing and tidying things. It is such fun to make a mess."

The last package, an orange spotted one, burst open to reveal an absolute mass of bridal confetti. A sudden wind blew to scatter it amongst the hair of the socialite and over the shoulders of the Charity Eligible. A few stray fragments even reached the camera crew.

"Is that some sort of omen?" Anthony asked, brushing the offending paper off of himself.

"Maybe the television station told someone we were coming," Deborah suggested.

"They weren't to know you would like smashing the parcels," Anthony said logically, "And nothing of the sort happened on any of my other dates."

"You are a winner," the Stall-holder said, appearing beside Anthony's left shoulder. "If you sort through the confetti, you will find a numbered ticket."

Anthony searched through the confetti until he found the prize ticket. He picked up the various wrappings and smashed parcels and dropped them in the large council bin parked not far away. "I wonder what we have won?"

The couple approached the prize-collection station and presented the ticket. They were given a little glass statue shaped to represent a dolphin.

"Interesting," Anthony said, inspecting the prize. "Machine cast in a couple of seconds I expect."

"There's more," Deborah said, pulling at his arm. "I think I see a new age stall over there."

"I'm not into all that stuff," Anthony said, but he indulgently allowed Deborah to rifle through the merchandise, finally selecting a scented candle and a dream-catcher.

"The lady said we were entitled to a free fortune telling session with our purchase," Deborah exclaimed.

"Now that's a bonus indeed!" Anthony chortled, but he permitted himself to be led into the interior of the Psychic's tent, where they both sat down expectantly.

The Psychic was a pleasantly plump woman in a batik printed kaftan and silk scarf. She was hung with innumerable strings of beads, and every finger of her hand boasted at least one ring. Her hands were clasped over a large glass ball that glowed with changing colours. The crystal ball was clearly battery operated. Moreover, the incense in the tent made Deborah purr appreciatively and Anthony sniff uncomfortably.

"I am Deborah, and this is Anthony," Deborah said boldly.

"I am Madam Helene," the Psychic replied. "Please do not tell me any more my dear, as it interferes with my gift."

Anthony raised an eyebrow, and Madam Helene smiled. "I see you are a sceptic," she said. "And you too, Deborah, although you would love very much not to be. You are very confused... for the man you are with... is not the man for you... but he is your friend. The right man for you... is very close.... very close indeed."

The Psychic turned to Anthony. "You like the lady you are with very much," she said. "But you have many choices. I see you ending up with someone artistic. Maybe an artist, a musician or a dancer. Any of these would be a good compliment for you."

"Someone has told you who we are," Deborah exclaimed, and Madam Helene laughed.

"It is true that not all my customers bring a television crew into my tent with them," She declared. "This tells me you may be acting some sort of part... however... don't we all?" The psychic laughed throatily. "Think about what I said," she added, "For it might come true when you least expect."

"Do you see anything else?" Anthony asked, becoming curious in spite of himself.

"I do not know," Madam Helene said considering. "There may be something else. There may be something wrong in the house in which you now live Deborah. I cannot say what it is, but your friends should stick together, especially at night."

Deborah gulped, and her mind went back to those moments when she was frightened of the dark, waiting outside for George. It was true that anybody could have come by at that time. The garden was after all barely guarded, with respect for the girl's privacy being finely balanced with security.

"I will tell my friends to stay inside after dark," she said.

Anthony sensed her mood, and grasped the socialite by the hand. "It has been interesting talking to you Madam Helene," he said, "And I am sure that you are a very intuitive and observant person. However, I do not believe you know the absolute future. Please do not frighten my lady friend anymore."

"Do not concern yourself too much my dear," Madam Helene said comfortingly. "It will turn out all right in the end."

"You have just contradicted yourself, Madam," Anthony said sternly. That seemed like a good note on which to leave the tent, so they thanked the Psychic for her time, and said goodbye.

As soon as they were outside, Anthony turned cheerily to Deborah. "Let's check out the other attractions, shall we?" He said. Deborah nodded eagerly, and they continued their path through the fair.

The side-shows included the standard plastic clowns that opened their mouths with deceptive eagerness to devour a small white ball, which in reality always ran off to the side. A standard shooting gallery involved some air-rifles and a plastic coated target. Beyond the first row of attractions, the party found a mini ferris-wheel, a train of horrors and some dodgem cars.

Deborah also insisted on riding a merry-go-round which was obviously too small for her; with George and Simon choking back their chuckles as they filmed her couched spider-like on the back of a miniature pony. As soon as the ride came to a halt, Anthony climbed onto the carousel and offered her his hand as a form of assistance toward the uncurling of her long legs.

"We will go to the beach now," Anthony suggested.

Deborah nodded in agreement, and they laughed and splashed their way along the shallows of the fore-shore. The energetic Deborah threw her sarong down onto the sand and ducked into the water for a serious swim, with George trailing along after her with the water-proof camera. Anthony sat down on the warm sand, and was soon snoring in the sun, thus providing Simon Steeple with some thirty minutes of very boring footage.

About half-an-hour later, the damp shadow of Deborah appeared and shook the Charity Eligible awake. "I hope you had some lunch planned," she said. "I am starving!"

"Oh yes," Anthony said. "I believe there are some fish and chip shops the other side of the esplanade.

The couple ate a quiet lunch, with crisp chips, fresh fish and loads of cool drink. After lunch, they once again agreed to differ, with Anthony going to the end of the pier to try his luck with a fishing rod, and Deborah taking her fine features to a lounge underneath a palm tree, where she devoured a book purchased at a stand on the esplanade and taunted the long-suffering George with an array of provocative poses, the majority of which he would be obliged to edit out of the final footage.

At last Anthony decided to pack his hired fishing equipment away, and collected Deborah on his way to the car. The socialite leaned companionably against him in the back seat, for they were firm friends, despite their new-found tendency to go separate ways.

"I had a lovely day," Deborah murmured.

"I am glad," Anthony said. "Thanks for letting me fish too. I'm not a great fisherman, but I do find it relaxing."

"As I find reading a book," Deborah said with a smile. "Tell me, what made you think of bringing me to the beach and fair?"

"Well," Anthony said. "Choosing an activity for you was very difficult. I assumed that you were used to sophisticated functions and high class restaurants."

Deborah looked knowing. "Yes," she said. "To a certain extent... although I do have friends amongst my colleagues at the library. We enjoy simple outings like coffee together."

"Given that I can't really compete with high society, I thought where you take the girl who has everything, except for somewhere simple like the beach!" Anthony grinned.

"It worked," Deborah exclaimed. "It did so worked!" She leant towards the Charity Eligible and planted a kiss upon his cheek, quite close to the corner of his mouth.

It felt uncannily like a real kiss, and Anthony jumped, for it was the last thing he expected from their usually platonic friendship. However, Deborah was sliding back onto her side of the seat with a calm expression on her face, and he had to conclude it was nothing more than a moment of enthusiasm.

Soon after that they arrived back at the Candidate House and made some polite goodbyes especially for the camera. Deborah went inside the residence, and Anthony turned around to the limousine, heading home to his own assigned quarters. It had been a pleasant and interesting day, and he wondered what the cameras would make of it in the end.

Upon entering the Candidate House, Deborah was greeted by Vonda and Kendra, who were both eager to talk about her outing.

"We went to the beach," the socialite said. "There was also a circus nearby. It was good fun."

"Did anything romantic happen?" asked Vonda, who was not in Deborah's confidence.

"Depends how you define romantic?" Deborah replied. "The palm trees were very nice and Anthony was a perfect gentleman."

Kendra laughed. "No awkward moments then?"

"Quite a few actually," Deborah said. "I specialise in awkward." She described her ride on the merry-go-round. "Oh and girls, there was a psychic!"

"What did she say?" Vonda asked eagerly.

"She said Anthony would pick one of you three," Deborah replied. "But that's pretty obvious isn't girls? She said some other things, but I reckon she was a fraud."

"What other things?" Kendra inquired curiously, but Deborah shrugged.

"Just that the right man for me was very near and that we need to stay inside at night," she said. "I am tired and going to rest now. I think I'm also a bit dehydrated."

After a few minutes, Janny wandered into the room, and joined in the conversation with much less enthusiasm. The other girls noticed that the dancer still had her mobile telephone, despite the fact that her birthday was over and the contestants were restricted to emergency communications only with the outside world.

The next date, which was designed to be a group date for the remaining three, was not due to commence until the following morning, when Anthony had said something about "Keeping a promise to Vonda".

Deborah said, "Good afternoon," to the other girls and retired to her bedroom, for she was weary and a little sun-burnt. The first thing she did was run a hot bubbly bath and settle down to relax with some soothing essence. She lay there sleepily listening to the soft echoes of music playing on the bed-side compact disk player. When she was thoroughly relaxed, she reached out for a towel, dried herself, and shrugged into a silky robe.

Now that Constance, Nadine and Alison had all left the show, Deborah had sole possession of the huge bedroom, and she allowed herself to behave very much as if she were at home. Closing the blinds against the intrusive beams of the late afternoon sun, she stretched out on the bed to catch a nap.

However, before the socialite could doze off, her attention was attracted by a soft thump on the outer pane of the window. Peering around the edge of the curtain, she observed the flushed face and ginger head of George, the assistant camera man.

Deborah was vastly flattered by this romantic gesture, but she decided to act surprised. Raising the blind, she slid back the screen and leant out: "Whatever are you doing there?" she whispered. "Auditioning for the part of Romeo in some modern drama?"

"I should think not!" George replied. "Actually, I would rather not be caught - let me in quickly."

Deborah stepped back from the window, and George clambered through, sliding the screen back into place behind him. The window shut with a click as it had an automatic latch. Deborah looked at the device thoughtfully, a mischievous idea forming in her head. She turned to George.

"Go on," she said, "Say what you want to say."

"You are not making my job easy for me," George complained. "I feel like you have been sending me some sort of signal all day."

"Maybe I have," Deborah admitted. "How long has it been since we shared that video evening?"

"Not very long at that," George said. "And we have seen each other pretty much every day since."

"Only while you are working," Deborah pointed out in a matter of fact manner. "Our second date seems not to have eventuated."

"Well, what did you expect me to do?" George cried.

Deborah shrugged. "Let me know how you feel," she said. "Are you still worried about the impact of our relationship on your son?"

"To be honest," George replied. "I think we could work that out. I am more worried that you will despise the way we live, and think my house is a dump."

"You are buying your own home," Deborah said comfortably. "That is an achievement whatever it may look like. I could put my so-called millions into a long term investment, and then I would be on an average wage, just like you."

George looked thunderstruck. "Would you really do that for me?"

"It's not like I would be losing the money," Deborah said in amusement. "Just learning how to live without it for a while."

"It would mean a lot to me," George said. "It's important to me to have a partner who accepts pizza, beer, and chipped wall-plaster."

"Well lead the way," Deborah suggested wickedly. "I am sure that we would be more comfortable at your place."

"Would you be missed?" George asked cautiously.

"Not till morning, I'm sure," Deborah said. "I told the girls I might be too tired to come down to tea."

"What if someone checks?"

"They are mostly too polite to do that, but if I'm not in here, I could be resting out on the terrace."

"It's your decision," George said, looking moderately keen. There was some risk to his job, but on the whole, he could not be held responsible for the antics of the head-strong Deborah.

"Okay," Deborah said. "Just wait a minute while I change into day clothes."

The socialite selected some comfortable jeans and a cotton top from her drawer, and retreated briefly into the adjoining bathroom, emerging casually dressed. Then she began to scrabble around for flat shoes.

A few minutes later, George and Deborah exited the room, having made sure that they were not being observed. They slunk around the side of the house, and sneaked out through the shrubbery. George had parked his car in an obscure corner, so they could climb in and drive off safely.

"This is exciting," Deborah said happily.

"Wait and see if you still feel that way when you see my place," George said soberly. "I know you think you would like working class life, but the novelty would soon wear off, not to mention the boring business of being a step-mum."

They drew up outside George's little unit. It was compact, and well placed toward the centre of the city, which made up for a certain amount of disrepair. The outer fencing was rough and the unit itself was locked in amongst a lot of other homes, however, the sparse little back yard was a luxury in a real-estate hungry neighbourhood. Deborah noticed a well weathered jungle-gym and slippery slide set up, and a goldfish pond, and then they were unlocking the front door.

The interior was small, with only a little space separating the fridge and stove from the dining table and chairs. The adjacent living room was overpowered by the comfortable lounge suite and sturdy coffee table that George said he and Parker often used, to eat in front of the television. Deborah noticed that they had to be careful to skirt around the furniture, or they would block each other's passage.

George went to the fridge, took out a frozen pizza, and put it in the oven. Deborah tiptoed into the short hall, and inspected the bookcase which had been cleverly attached to the wall.

The bathroom opened to the side, and one step beyond that was a small bedroom, which would be occupied by Parker when he was dropped home by his grandmother. A larger bedroom was crowded with a double bed, and built in wardrobes. There was a third bedroom, but it was full of computers and professional video editing equipment.

There was a knock at the front door, and George hurried to answer it, admitting Parker and his grandmother. Deborah caught a brief glimpse of a cheerful, bushy-haired woman, who looked intrigued by the new development in her son's life, but discretely made no comment.

"She seemed nice," the Socialite commented as they removed the pizza from the oven and sat down to a simple tea.

"Yeah, Granny is pretty cool," Parker remarked. The boy had been pleased to see Deborah, and cordially invited her to stay for a "sleep-over". Both George and Deborah laughed, relieved at the innocent interpretation the boy placed on their situation.

After pizza, it was time for Parker to be read a story and get put to bed. Deborah remained seated in the lounge during this proceeding; she was ostensibly watching a home renovation show, but in reality she was quietly admiring George's parenting skills.

After the couple were sure that the boy was settled, they fraternised on the sofa for a while before retreating to the larger bedroom, where George apologised for the crowding, and Deborah expressed her willingness to cuddle up underneath the rustic patterned cover on the double bed.

George turned off the main light, and the couple were both overcome with lust, reaching out towards each other and giggling as they attempted to make-out without creating any noise. They stopped short of going all the way because it was technically only their second date; and Deborah could not help but be self-conscious with a little boy sleeping in the next room. However, she enjoyed the feeling of George's hands running across her body and exploring above her waist.

A few minutes later, however, Deborah turned over restlessly. Something hitherto forgotten was bothering her mind. "George," she whispered sleepily, "Do you remember the Psychic?"

"That crazy old woman," George murmured. "I reckon she was just very good at picking up on the signals in the room. After all, no one would interpret you and Anthony as a real couple."

"She was right about us however," Deborah said.

"If you want to interpret it that way," George replied. "Maybe I looked at you or something more than usual for my job."

"But what about the trouble she foresaw at the house?" Deborah asked in concern. "I forgot to warn the other girls properly."

"It was probably just a lot of dramatic talk," George observed comfortingly.

"She said we girls ought to stick together," Deborah commented.

"It is certainly better than fighting, and a good solution in a lot of situations," George remarked.

"What about tonight?" Deborah asked anxiously.

"I don't think anything will go wrong tonight," George said. "The others are all together aren't they? And you are safe here with me."

There is that," Deborah murmured sleepily. "I will talk to them in the morning."

"Yes," George murmured, his tousled head resting against hers, "You do that."

CHAPTER SIX: ACTION AND REACTION

Janny declined to attend the group date the next day, saying that she was too tired to participate. Vonda and Kendra did notice that the dancer appeared quite pale, but she would not answer when they inquired as to the cause of the problem. After applying a polite amount of pressure, the other two gave in and went outside to await the Charity Eligible.

When Anthony arrived, he looked at the two girls with approval. Kendra was wearing a fitted tee-shirt and loose yoga pants which were tied at the hip; while Vonda was wearing a light blue tee-shirt and purple fitted stretch pants.

"You girls look pretty comfortable," he said. "Do you both feel like you can move around?"

Kendra grinned and kicked her right foot forward, while Vonda demonstrated that she could take a fairly broad step to the side.

"What did you have in mind?" Kendra asked.

"Well, I have arranged something in particular," Anthony replied. "It all started when I took Vonda to the opera. There was this jerk that dragged her down to the bar and began putting the hard word on her."

"I remember," Vonda said. She shivered: "After you rescued me, I said that I wanted to know how to deal with that sort of thing."

"And I promised I would organise a self-defence class," Anthony said.

"Oh yes!" Vonda exclaimed. She turned to Kendra: "I hope you don't mind Kinny."

"It could be interesting," Kendra said slowly. "In fact, it is a great idea for the two of you....Are you sure I won't be in your way?"

"Of course you won't!" Anthony exclaimed. "I had meant for Janny to come along too. Where is she?"

"She doesn't seem to be feeling well," Vonda replied. "We had to leave her in the house."

"I hope she feels better soon," Anthony said, his face displaying mild disappointment. During his previous visit, the ballerina had been pensive due to her birthday celebrations being masked by filming the show.

Anthony had been looking forward to seeing whether Janny had recovered her good spirits since. "However, we had better get on our way now."

Anthony opened the car door, and Kendra and Vonda both piled into the back seat. Anthony slid in beside the girls, and instructed the driver to head for the Eligible Residence.

"I hope you don't mind," Anthony said. "But I have arranged for the instructor to come to my accommodation."

"Cool!" Kendra exclaimed. "We will see where they have set you up."

"It is very nice," Anthony said. "I intend to ask you over for dinner sometime. One at a time - I mean. This visit is only a preview."

Kendra nodded, although she looked thoughtful.

The Judo Instructor had arrived at the Eligible Residence before the contestants and already begun to set up mats and equipment. He looked at the group in surprise: "I was told that there would be four," he said. "That would be perfect, as there would be two practice pairs. Never mind, I will join in to make the numbers even."

"That sounds fine," Anthony said, looking at the sportsman. Clad in a black uniform, the Judo Instructor was of above average height; furthermore, he was obviously very fit, and moved in a highly skilled manner. The Instructor's face was open and sociable, and his dark hair was closely cut.

Watching the sportsman exchange friendly glances with the two girls, Anthony found himself experiencing a pang of envy. It would be great to be that fit, and to impress the ladies so easily.

"Come along with me," the Instructor said, leading the way around the side of the building to the grassy area which he had been preparing for their lesson. It was cleared of all sticks and stones, and rubber mats were set out on one side.

"It looks interesting," Vonda murmured, and Kendra nodded in agreement.

"Some safety issues to discuss first," the Instructor began. "I will start by asking whether there are any injuries, knee problems or lower back pain?"

"No," Anthony replied.

"I'm fine," Kendra said, and Vonda also indicated that she was well.

"We have been swimming and playing sport all this month," the Musician said.

"I am glad to hear that," the Instructor said. "It will make a basic work-out that much easier. We will start by warming up."

"Yes sir," Anthony exclaimed, and began to march upon the spot in the same manner as the Instructor. This activity led into some gentle stretches and flexibility work, then the instruction in real manoeuvres commenced.

"Contrary to what you might expect," the Instructor said, "I am not here to teach you to fight! The basic principle is to deflect a blow, break the assailant's hold upon you, and then run away. That is if you have no choice in the matter. If you have a choice, it is better to avoid conflict by walking away immediately."

The Judo Instructor then instructed that the three participants form a straight line in front of him. "The first thing you have to learn is how to stand correctly," he said. "Straight back, legs shoulder width apart for good balance, arms loosely by your side, and your chin at ninety degrees to your neck."

Everyone shuffled into the correct position. They were suddenly all very aware of their posture. The Instructor gave them a moment to become accustomed to the new stance, and then he began to give further guidance: "If someone aims a blow at your face, you need to know how to block it with your own fist."

The Instructor deftly moved his right arm from his side, forward across his body, and up in front to shield his face. Then he asked each participant to practice until they were proficient at creating the right arc, and moving quickly enough to possibly intercept a blow. After that, the Judo Instructor showed the group how the same arm could be used to push a kick aside.

Anthony was impressed with the principle of defence, although he privately speculated that the arm could break under the pressure of a solid attack. It was better perhaps, to place an arm at risk than a jaw or internal organ, he reflected.

The Instructor then faced Kendra. "Grab my wrist like this," he ordered. Kendra placed her hand around his wrist, and with a quick twist of his arm, the Instructor freed himself.

"Wow!" Vonda exclaimed, and paired up with Anthony to

attempt the same feat. After a bit of practice, always taking care not to actually hurt each other, all the participants could perform the manoeuvre.

"Now I will show you how to break the most basic hold from behind," the Instructor said. "Put your arms around my neck please Kendra."

"I think you had better tell me your name first," Kendra said laughing.

"It is John," The Instructor replied. "Instructor John to everyone but you! Now go on, grab me."

Kendra approached the Instructor and linked her arms around his neck in an attempted choke hold. The Instructor neatly bent forward, lowered one shoulder, and levered Kendra off his back and down onto the mat.

Anthony and Vonda both cheered. Despite the undercurrent of flirtation with Kendra, the Instructor was impressively professional in his athletic ability.

"Show us how to do that," Anthony said.

The Instructor moved around, demonstrating the hold and escape, until the others could all wriggle out of each other's arms. Then he returned to Kendra: "Would you like to practice some more?" he asked.

Kendra nodded, and the pair reversed their positions so that Kendra could learn how to break free from the hold too. "That is amazing," Kendra volunteered as she became proficient. "I never thought I could get away from a robust man like you."

Instructor John laughed. "Do you really want to?" he asked swinging Kendra around in his turn.

"If you were actually attacking me, YES, I would!" Kendra giggled. "Why don't you show us another one?"

"Hey everyone," John called. "Pay attention to this. A more complex escape can be engineered after blocking a blow to the face. You grab the attacker's wrist, step behind their foot, and swing your arm across their chest. They should trip and fall at your feet."

The Instructor deftly swung Kendra around, and as he wasn't aiming to drop her roughly, the effect was reminiscent of a dance movement.

"Wow - you are strong!" Kendra exclaimed, relinquishing Instructor John's hand and relaxing to the ground. "I didn't for one minute feel as though you were really going to drop me."

There were many more laughs as the two couples practiced the manoeuvre, and the ladies discovered that due to the effect of gravity, they could also throw the heavier men down.

"I didn't know I was so strong," Vonda cried.

The Instructor nodded approvingly: "You can do a lot of things if you know how," he said.

Anthony and Instructor John changed partners so that John could get a better look at Vonda's technique, and then John pronounced himself satisfied. He worked for a few more minutes with Anthony, and then announced that it was time to do some 'cool down' exercises.

After the cool-down had been completed, Anthony and Vonda sat down on the patio sipping cool drinks. Kendra, who had shown amazing stamina throughout the work-out, went back to wrestling with the Instructor, asking him to review her on certain techniques, and show her a few more complex manoeuvres.

"Kendra is sort of fit," Vonda commented from where she was watching.

"She did well when I took her belly dancing, and caving too," Anthony commented.

"I think that she has a very well balanced personality," Vonda observed, eying Anthony thoughtfully.

"Yes," Anthony agreed. "I am fond of Kendra. However, I did organise this lesson especially for you, to keep the promise that I made to you."

"I appreciate that," Vonda said. "I do feel a bit more confident too, I think. Surprisingly, it helps to know that even a tough guy like that would run away from a fight."

"It sounds reasonable," Anthony said. "If he is not violent at heart, he wouldn't want to inflict any injuries on another person, even in a situation of self-defence."

"And one could possibly be charged with assault if they defended themselves too effectively," Vonda remarked.

"I cannot imagine you doing that," Anthony laughed, "Even with your newly learnt throw."

Vonda laughed and slipped a hand into Anthony's clasp. As usual, the Charity Eligible marvelled at the delicacy of the musician's touch. He glanced across the grass at Kendra, who appeared to be pre-occupied with the Judo Instructor.

"Do you want to come into the house?" Anthony asked. "I will show you around."

"Oh sure," Vonda said, and sliding to her feet, followed Anthony through the side door into the Eligible Residence. They passed through a well-appointed kitchen and dining area, past the guest bathroom and bedroom doors, into a medium sized entertainment room with a stereo and dance floor.

"Cool," Vonda exclaimed.

Anthony deliberately did not lead the way into the lavishly appointed bedroom; as he was reserving this room for a far more intimate type of visit. Nor did he linger in the entertainment room, but led the way into the main lounge, which was equipped with a poker table, two sofas, a variety of book-shelves and a comfortable woven floor mat.

"Let's sit down," he said.

Vonda complied and settled down on the sofa. Anthony sat beside her, and the pair relaxed in silence for a moment. Then Vonda turned to look up at Anthony.

"I really do appreciate your arranging the Judo instruction for me," she said.

"Once again, it was my pleasure," Anthony replied.

"Most guys don't bother with me once they find out I am shy," Vonda whispered.

"I'm not most guys," Anthony said. "And I must say, some girls can be like that about me when they find out I have a serious disposition."

"I like it," Vonda said. Her eyes were wide in the dull room, as the couple had not bothered to open the blinds or switch on a light.

Anthony leant forward and kissed the fragile blonde girl upon the lips. Vonda was obviously carried away by the moment, and returned the kiss. It was a few minutes before either of them surfaced, and when they did, both parties looked bemused.

"I am sorry," Anthony said as his senses returned to normal. "I completely forgot this was a group date. Kendra and the Judo teacher could have walked in at any moment."

"But they didn't," Vonda whispered. "And I for one, aren't going to get into a guilty state over one little kiss."

"I don't regret kissing you," Anthony said. "But I wish we had waited till our next single date!"

"Let's go and find the others," Vonda said, jumping to her feet. The musician reached out in a manner which was quite assertive for her gentle personality and took the Charity Eligible by the hand, pulling him to his feet. Anthony and Vonda walked through the house to the kitchen, where they found Kendra and the Judo Instructor unpacking a hamper.

"I hope you don't mind Anthony," Kendra said, turning around as they entered. "I've invited John to stay for lunch."

"I guess it is okay," Anthony muttered. He normally appreciated Kendra's hospitable streak, but the day was rapidly becoming more complicated.

"I really enjoyed the lesson, and three is a crowd and all that," Kendra said. "John does help make the numbers even."

Anthony grunted. He had actually been looking forward to having the two girls around his abode for the afternoon. Group dates had their odd moments, but he figured he had two arms and could manage to be equally attentive to two girls, within reason.

"You are a lucky man," John said diplomatically. "These two great girls are here to date you, and how many more waiting back at the house for you?"

"Two more," Anthony said. "The show actually started with twenty contestants."

"I wish I had been invited over then," John laughed.

"I half wish you had too," Anthony said, observing the light hand John laid upon Kendra's shoulder. "Then you could have spread your attentions around a little more evenly."

"Fighting words," John said light heartedly. "Luckily I am a pacifist at heart."

Vonda edged her way around the table and pulled Kendra outside. "Are you sure it was a good idea to ask John to dinner?" She asked.

"I don't know," Kendra said. "John seems like a nice guy, and I am sure Anthony and he will get along." Her eyes were glittering. "You and Anthony were gone a long time," she said. "That's one reason why I talked so much to John."

Vonda blushed, and the two women read each other's expressions.

"I thought so," Kendra said simply. "You kissed Anthony."

"He had organised this self-defense training especially for me," Vonda said. "How could I not feel grateful – and flattered and – more?"

"Of course you felt those things," Kendra acknowledged. "Like I felt I was a bit out of place doing your special activity."

"You have always said that one of us will be more suited to Anthony than the other in the end," Janny continued, "So you don't have to stress."

Kendra sighed. "I used to believe in that sort of thing, and then I got my heart involved," she said. "So I've become a quivering heap of emotions and you have become the practical one."

"You are especially vulnerable where Anthony is concerned," Vonda observed. "Which brings me back to the question, what on earth were you doing flirting with that John guy?"

"Just being friendly," Kendra said. "And filling in time while you were with Anthony. John seems very nice."

"Well make it clear you are winding things up with him," Vonda said. "Or you might end up with more attention than you expected. Being shy has kept me safe at times, as well as making me lonely."

"You may have a point," Kendra said. "Shall we go back to the lunch?"

As it turned out, lunch was quite a cheerful event. Instructor John proved to be interesting as a conversationalist as well as trainer. He was full of interesting facts about strength and fitness, and knew a lot of anecdotes from the sporting world. Vonda found herself warming to him almost as much as Kendra had, and was glad that the sportsman had stayed to lunch.

Anthony valiantly set aside his doubts about sharing his dates with a muscle-toned rival and joined in the conversation. The Charity Eligible found that his medical training made him quite savvy to all the talk of muscles and manoeuvres, and he could take some pride in sharing his knowledge on an intellectual level.

After lunch, Anthony suggested that they all sojourn to the lounge room for a few minutes relaxation. Instructor John however, shook his head.

"I must be going now," the Sportsman said regretfully. "It has been lovely meeting you people, but I do have other bookings."

"Oh do you have a large clientele?" Vonda asked with interest.

"Yes," replied Instructor John. "You would be surprised how many people book me to train them. Some people want to learn the Judo skills, others want to improve their general fitness, while still others need help with injury recovery and rehabilitation."

"You must have some sort of qualification then," Anthony said, frowning slightly at the reference to therapeutic work.

"Oh yes," John replied. "Apart from my black belt and coaching qualifications, I have Diplomas in Fitness and Disability."

"That is very interesting," Vonda exclaimed. "I would like to hear some more sometime."

"I need to pack up the gear," John said. He looked at Kendra. "Why don't you give me a hand?"

Kendra and Instructor John exited the kitchen door, from where they could be seen packing up the exercise equipment and chatting in the yard. Vonda looked at Anthony, who was staring after the pair.

"I feel like listening to a bit of music," Vonda said. "Shall we try out the stereo?"

"That is a good idea," Anthony said, transferring his attention back into the house. "There has been an extensive compact disk selection provided for my use. Do you feel like classical or popular music?"

"Actually, a bit of easy listening would be just fine," Vonda replied.

Anthony selected a country recording from the stack, and inserted the disk into the tray of the stereo. Mellow sounds filled the room, and Vonda began to visibly relax.

"I stayed up too late last night," the petite blonde confided. "Because it wasn't a date night, I sneaked into an empty part of the Candidate House to practice my violin."

"I am glad you are keeping your skills up to date," Anthony murmured.

"I have to," Vonda laughed. "There could be a whole musical season after this, and as far as I know, I am involved. If you don't mind, I will recline in this chair," the musician said, sinking back into the depths of the cosy lounge chair.

Anthony settled down into a chair just opposite and allowed himself to drift with the music as well. The tracks on the compact disk came to the end, and he rose quietly to select another album. Vonda appeared to be either asleep or lightly dozing, so he turned the volume down a notch.

Outside, Kendra gathered up the pile of rubber mats, which were surprisingly light in weight, and followed Instructor John who was carrying the heavier pieces of exercise equipment, to his car. They piled the equipment into the hefty boot of the white commodore wagon, and then John turned to face Kendra.

"I really enjoyed meeting you," the Judo Instructor began.

Kendra flushed slightly, but she returned the compliment in kind. "I've enjoyed meeting you too, and I have learnt a lot from your instruction," she said.

"I was wondering," Instructor John said cautiously, "Whether you could give me your home number for when this show is over. If that guy should be such a fool as to not choose you - I would be more than happy to take you out."

"I'm flattered," Kendra said. "I really am. But I think not. I am serious about Anthony, and if he does not choose me, I will need to take a break from the dating scene to get over my broken heart."

"What will you do?" John asked curiously.

"Throw myself into my commercial work and start afresh with my pure art," Kendra said. "I have been inspired by some of the talks I have had here with Anthony and the girls."

"I didn't know that you were an artist," John said. "But now that I do, it seems to suit you."

"Thanks, I think," Kendra said. "I mostly do graphic art and my employer pays well."

"But you feel the call of creative art as well," John said thoughtfully.

"Art that is created on commission is usually considered inferior to spontaneous work," Kendra said. "But I don't expect you to understand."

"Funnily enough I do," John said. "My most rewarding work involves a non-profit organisation for children. I don't do that for the money, so I have to keep it separate from my actual business."

"We do have some things in common then," Kendra said wistfully. Bearing Vonda's warning in mind, she did not want to give John the wrong impression. However, he seemed like a good man.

"I tell you what," John said comfortably. "I will give you my business card, and then you can contact me if you want to - no romantic strings attached if you don't want them to be."

Kendra began to protest, but the sportsman pressed a small white card into her hand, planted a hurried kiss upon her cheek and climbed into his car. "I hope things work out for you," he called through the open driver's side window.

Kendra, slightly bemused, waved as John drove away down the street. Then she turned around, and entering the front door, found Anthony standing alone, as if waiting for her. "What happened to Vonda?" she asked.

Vonda fell asleep listening to some music," Anthony said.

"She is well isn't she?" Kendra asked in concern.

"I think so," Anthony replied. "She said she had been practicing her music all last night."

"I believe she has a series of concerts coming up after the show," Kendra observed.

"I am glad she has plans," Anthony said. "It will be back to surgery for me."

"I am sure that my employer has been piling up contracts in my absence," Kendra laughed.

"I expect the show will go on for a couple more weeks at least," Anthony said.

"Yes," Kendra agreed. "You have four more girls to eliminate."

"Three girls to eliminate, and one to choose," Anthony corrected. He approached Kendra with a gleam in his eye. "What is that in your hand?" he asked.

"John's card," Kendra admitted somewhat bashfully. The exercise instructor did not seem half so impressive now that he had left and she had regained Anthony's attention. "I don't really need it." The artist tore the card in half and dropped it into a nearby bin.

"I am glad that you did that," Anthony said. "I wouldn't have wanted to wrestle you to take it away."

Kendra's face showed her delight at this playful show of possessiveness. For a situation in which exclusivity was impossible, she was yet cheered to feel that there was a growing degree of understanding between herself and the Charity Eligible. "John did show me some pretty cool wrestling moves," she said provocatively.

"Oh yeah?" Anthony muttered as he reached out for the woman and she deftly tipped him down onto the woven mat.

"How do you like that?" she laughed.

"This is much better," Anthony said, pulling Kendra down on top of him. The couple rolled over several times, and then the struggle dissolved into a mutual kiss. They remained locked together for a few minutes, and then Kendra blinked her eyes open. The glare from one of the cameras caught her line of vision uncomfortably, and she pushed Anthony to one side.

"We are on a television show remember?" she whispered.

"Oh yes," Anthony said sitting upright. "And Vonda is in the next room."

"Gross," Kendra murmured, referring more to her own behaviour than her fellow contestant. "And you have been kissing us both on the same date too."

"She told you?" Anthony looked mildly shamefaced.

"Nah," Kendra said. "I guessed. I guessed, and I'm still here unfortunately. More fool me!"

"I certainly don't view you as a fool," Anthony said. "The show won't allow me to make any commitments, and I must admit, Vonda is the sort of girl I always hoped to find."

"So, what am I doing here then?" Kendra inquired.

"I can't deny what I have with you either," Anthony said. "A man would be a fool to get himself into this position out in the real world, but it is something I must sort out while I am on the show with you ladies."

"That is about as clear as mud!" Kendra exclaimed.

"Let us wake Vonda and go back to the Candidate House," Anthony said. "I have had enough complications for one day."

Kendra agreed completely.

CHAPTER SEVEN: JANNY'S OTHER MAN

Deborah was stealthily attempting to gain entry to the Candidate House through one of the side doors early the next morning, when she bumped into a scruffy looking young man attempting the same endeavour.

The socialite regained her balance and looked the stranger over carefully. Alarm bells rang as she noted the knitted red cap pulled down low over his head so that obscured it his hair and a portion of his forehead. Trying to reassure herself that thieves usually wore black, she asked the guy if he were one of the maintenance men.

"No," the fellow replied, "I'm Sam."

"I beg your pardon," Deborah said. "I don't think I heard you right."

"Sam - short for Sammy Davis Macpherson," the fellow explained. "I come from a show-biz family."

"I see," Deborah observed, reflecting that he might have some business around the Candidate House after all. "What are you doing here this hour of the day?"

"I could ask you that too," Sam said with a knowing grin.

"I went down to the 24 hour service station for some chocolate snacks," Deborah said firmly, and in fact she had made one or two purchases especially to support that assertion. She waved the package at the newcomer, who barely gave it a glance.

"So you are one of the contestants then," Sam said. "I am looking for Jandice. She must have mentioned me, after all I am her agent."

"Not in so many words - no," Deborah said. Her mind was working rapidly and the guy was beginning to register high on her creep-o-meter.

"Maybe she didn't at that," Sam admitted. "She certainly forgot to tell me she was coming here."

"I guess she is entitled to some leave," Deborah ventured cautiously.

"Yeah some," Sammy Davis MacPherson admitted. "But we usually negotiate that."

"Janny is not dancing here," Deborah said carefully. "Maybe she thought it did not concern you, if what you usually manage is her BALLET CAREER."

"We have been together a long time," the Agent said. "At one time you could say I was...the man in her life."

"Oh," Deborah said, as if things were suddenly becoming clear: "I guess that is why she did not mention being on a dating show to you."

Sam shrugged. "She gave me some story about a trip," he said. "That is between the two of us."

"Of course," Deborah acknowledged, although she was rapidly coming to the conclusion that she did not approve of Janny's previous taste in men.

"Is there any prize money involved in this show?" Sam asked, changing tack suddenly.

"Yes - but it all goes to charity!" Deborah replied. Her suspicions were fully confirmed now.

Sam was the exploitative sort of person who often hung around people with successful careers. Moreover, he was not above mixing business with pleasure and controlling his victim through a romantic relationship. The sooner Janny saw through him, the better.

"I think you should wait here until I find Janny," Deborah said. "The house has fairly strict security arrangements."

"Oh sure," Sam said, obviously knowing when to appear easy going. He subsided onto an outdoor bench. "Go on inside then. Jandice can come out here to me."

"I'll be certain to tell Janny," Deborah said over her shoulder. The socialite entered the side door, making sure that it latched securely behind her, and then began to sidle along the corridor towards her room. She was congratulating herself upon having successfully negotiated the office area, when Letitia appeared coming along the opposite direction.

The hostess greeted Deborah cordially and then indicated that the socialite should follow her into the bed-sitting room Leticia used as a study.

"Miss Markham," Leticia began brusquely. "I have had a call from your father."

Deborah groaned. If there was anyone in the world whom she feared, it was her rich and powerful paternal parent. "What does he want?" she inquired.

"Mr. Markham wants you to have dinner with him tonight, accompanied by the Charity Eligible."

"Tell him we are busy filming," Deborah returned.

Leticia looked mildly uncomfortable. "When someone owns shares in the network, we have to make certain concessions," she began.

"My father did not have any shares in this channel the last I knew," Deborah murmured regretfully. She had some idea where this was heading.

"Soon after you applied to be a guest on the show, he purchased some," Leticia observed.

Deborah looked bleak. "He would," she said. About the only thing her father had never managed to purchase was the library in which she worked, and that was largely because it was government funded. Moreover, because it was such a respectable institution, it had his approval as a suitable venue for her 'hobby' of working.

The socialite sighed. "Tell my father I will have dinner with him at a time the station deems suitable and the Charity Eligible will accompany me if he can be spared from filming. If Anthony is not available, however, I may need to be accompanied by one of the station employees instead."

"Very good, Miss Markham," Leticia said. The hostess looked pleased she could carry an affirmative response back to the powerful tycoon.

"I need to return to my room," Deborah said. She jiggled the bag of chocolate which was designed to provide her alibi in front of the hostess. "Sweet cravings".

Leticia laughed, "Don't we feed you enough?"

"You provide an excellent breakfast", Deborah returned diplomatically. "I'm just a girl who likes her chocolate bars!"

"I will let you go then," Leticia conceded and turned to head towards her office.

Deborah hurried towards the bedrooms and sought out the suite now occupied by Janny. "Here", she said, handing the chocolate to the other girl. "You eat these – you exercise so much the calories will not make you put on an ounce of weight."

"Thanks," Janny said, opening the bag. "Where have you been?"

"Around," Deborah said. "What about you? I hear you missed a date you were meant to go on."

"I had to see somebody," Janny said. "Get some things clear in my head. It seems the more I like Anthony – the more I see other things differently as well."

"Well, you better look sharp", Deborah said, "Because if that someone is Sam, he seems to have tracked you down here... and if you ask me, he is not exactly a gentleman of the top drawer."

Janny laughed. "Once I would have been offended to hear you say that!" she said. "But I've come to realise Sam is just an agent. It's their job to be a bit – um, persuasive."

"He is looking into whether you are making anything from this show," Deborah informed her moderately.

"I don't owe him a commission for *The Charity Dating Show*," Janny said. "I applied for this all on my own. If I hedged about what it was at all – that was because I was embarrassed to tell him I would be dating on the show."

"He is waiting for you outside," Deborah said. "Sitting down near the side door in the shrubbery. He tried to use me to get inside, but I promised to get you instead. Take care if you go out there to him."

"I will, thanks", Janny said. "And thank you for the chocolate too."

"Good luck," Deborah said and continued down the corridor to her room. Sprung at least twice on the way into the house – that was living dangerously. Of course, the socialite didn't care about staying on *The Charity Dating Show*, but she did care about George's career too much to cause a scandal amongst the staff.

Meanwhile, Janny ran out to the side door closest to the shrubbery as Deborah had instructed. Sam was sitting on a wooden garden bench waiting determinedly for her. "You made it!" she cried, giving him a brief hug. "I hardly expected you here so soon."

"I am glad that you are pleased to see me," Sam said, returning her embrace. "When you were so mysterious about your whereabouts, I began to wonder whether our partnership was in trouble."

"You have always been my agent," Janny said, "But I wanted to do this for myself."

"You told me you wanted a holiday," Sam said. "Because you feared I would be upset if I thought you wanted to date this Charity Eligible fellow."

"Actually, I truly did want to meet him," Janny said. "And I am really beginning to like him. That is why I thought I ought to be straight with you."

"I think we can make the situation work for us after all," Sam remarked. "It sort of does make sense in show-biz terms. The publicity of being on television can't possibly hurt your career."

"I didn't look at it that way," Janny murmured demurely, although she knew the thought had crossed her mind once or twice in the early weeks.

"Well, try to start thinking in commercial terms," Sam said. "The first thing to do is get you back dancing, and the second is to arrange for you to do a performance on camera."

Janny laughed: "I have been dancing since I was four," she said. "I assure you that I can still put together a routine."

"Even so," Sam returned. "Is there anywhere you can practice here? I have some great plans for you. There are lots of auditions coming up in the New Year. Some of them are with the ballet company, and at least one is with a major international production!"

"There is the ballroom," Janny said. "If we roll back the carpet, it has the right sort of floor. I don't need mirrors if you are watching my moves."

"How would we stop anyone else coming in?" Sam asked.

"I will go and tell Leticia I am preparing a surprise for Anthony," Janny suggested. "I think he did ask to see my dancing once."

"Okay," Sam said. "You just have to get me safely through the corridors then, tell this Leticia person that you are practicing, and lock the doors."

"How simple you make it sound," Janny exclaimed. "You must be a master of intrigue!"

"I know how to get things done," Sam said practically.

The pair retreated into the change room, where they borrowed a flowery cover-up off the hook, and wrapped it around the theatrical agent. The garment was loose and flowing, with a hood that they pulled across up over his head and across his face. Hopefully, any staff members that saw them would assume Sam was one of the taller girls.

Sam remained hidden in the change room until Janny had spoken to Leticia and arranged to use the ballroom for a private 'practice session'.

It was arranged that the following evening could be a 'talent night' in which each girl presented something of interest to the Charity Eligible, for Vonda was known to play the violin and Kendra could surely come up with something.

Janny returned to her bedroom to change into a pink leotard, and collect her pointe shoes before repairing to the cubicle in which she had secreted Sam. She knocked gently on the door to signal the 'all-clear'. The pair then slunk their way through the main lounge, down the hall-way into the ballroom; where Janny locked the main door, and bolted the alternate entrance from the inside.

"We are set," the Ballerina said to her agent, who immediately began to push the furniture aside and roll back the Persian carpet.

"It's a good floor," Sam commented, surveying the polished boards.

"Yes, it is quite suitable," Janny agreed. She checked that the surface was not sticky from the wax which had been used to create a smooth finish, before dropping to the floor and going through her regular routine of stretches and warm-ups. Then she laced on her ballet shoes and stood on her toes.

"You are shaking slightly," Sam commented. "Are you sure you have been doing your leg exercises?"

"I have been doing ball of foot rises and other exercises in my room," Janny returned sharply.

"Well you had better do an extra twenty tonight," Sam commented, and Janny grimaced.

"It's just that I haven't worn the shoes lately," the lithe Blonde said. "I will be fine when I have danced a little."

"Let's hope so," Sam returned. "Show me something you are thinking of doing."

Janny poised herself with her arms raised elegantly, and then launched into a graceful series of steps. "One, two, three, pirouette - one, two, three, forward kick - one two three, four - slow arabesque."

"Very pretty," Sam commented. "Keep practicing. This will be your first fully televised performance, and unlike a live audience, the camera will be able to zoom in on you. There will also be no one else on the floor to share the lime-light."

"I am envisioning it as more of a private viewing," Janny said. "I am sure the camera crew will cover the Charity Eligible's reaction as well."

"We will choreograph for a reaction then," Sam said. "Nevertheless, it is your chance to show film and television producers what you look like on celluloid. You must do your absolute best!"

"Hush - I can't concentrate," Janny said. While she appreciated Sam's perfectionism in regards to her career, she reflected he could be a little intense.

The dancer swirled around until she was quite exhausted, but Sam was not satisfied. "I am wondering if we can make it a bit sexier," he said.

"I was going for the classical look, so that I stood out as a fully trained ballerina," Janny returned patiently.

"Classical is okay, but you won't get really noticed that way," Sam said.

Janny came to a halt and slumped against the wall, panting. "I get to use so few of my moves with that other stuff," she said.

"We will mix the two," Sam said, "Send someone out for some contemporary music."

Janny sighed: "You win, I know of some very light techno music that will fit the classical steps."

"I think you should add a cartwheel or tumble," Sam ordered.

"And where do you propose I put that?" Janny muttered darkly. A tumble was not really her style, but she had to admit that Sam was usually good at his job.

"Right at the beginning, and every time you come to the point of repeating the choreography," Sam said.

"Yeah, it would fit as long as I time it over four beats," Janny said, mentally checking the choreography against the music she had in mind.

"You could do the splits too," Sam said. "That never fails to impress."

"It is meant to be a dance, not a school gymnastic demonstration," Janny remarked in exasperation. "I suppose you want me to replace one of the arabesques with the splits."

"That is exactly what I had in mind," Sam said.

"The splits takes more counts than most moves," Janny said. "Because you have to go down, hold the position and then come up again. I will have to figure something out regarding the timing of that segment."

"I am sure you will do just fine," Sam declared.

Janny frowned, "I know what you are doing," the ballerina said. "You want me to demonstrate my range, but it will need careful styling work - or it will look like a fruit salad."

"Well I have dedicated my time to you," Sam said. "So we may as well keep practicing."

"I like the way you include yourself," Janny returned petulantly. "When I am the one getting tired!"

"That serves you right for slinking off on me," Sam remarked acidly. "I have no sympathy with you for letting you skills lapse."

"When have you ever had sympathy for me?" Janny inquired ironically.

"I have never been an easy mentor!" Sam stated irrevocably. "And you used to love me for it."

"I actually always loved your business skills," Janny said reasonably. "I just worked with your bossiness."

"Well now you have everything in one package babe," Sam said firmly. "Get back to work."

Janny returned to her dance practice, despite every muscle in her body registering an ache. Sam kept quizzing her on stylistic options and drilling her in the chosen moves until she was well beyond the point of exhaustion. When he finally allowed her to stop, they rolled the carpet out across the floor again, and returned the furniture to its customary place.

"I hope you are satisfied," Janny said, slumping across the large table which had just been returned to the centre of the room. She reflected that Sam had always been a hard task-master, but she somehow had expected some consideration to develop upon the commencement of their personal relationship.

"If we have another day to practice, you may have something worth presenting," Sam responded grudgingly.

Janny resisted the impulse to remind her agent that she had performed before a live audience hundreds of times. "What if Anthony asks me out on a date?" she asked with some concern.

"Are you allowed to refuse?" Sam suggested.

Janny shook her head, "I can't refuse the date if I want to stay on the show," she said. "But am guessing that I am not due for elimination or Leticia would not have given permission for me to prepare a talent show."

"Who do you think the Charity Eligible prefers?" Sam inquired curiously.

"I don't know to be honest," Janny replied. "I sometimes think Anthony seems to be the keenest on Kendra and Vonda."

"I am worried he will get keen on you," Sam said with hackneyed possessiveness. "Then I will lose my little dancer". He stepped up behind the dancer and encircled her with his arms. "Let us go to your room," he said.

Janny laughed, glad to have the perfect excuse to refuse. "Actually, I am sharing a room with two other girls," she said.

Sam looked surprised. "How come? There must be enough spare rooms in a place like this. It is practically a mansion."

"There were originally twenty of us girls," Janny explained. "And most of those eliminated were from the other rooms."

"You have done well to get this far on the show," Sam said considering. "It must be time to request your own room."

"Leticia might get suspicious if I request a change," Janny said. "I will talk to Kendra and Vonda when they get home."

"As you think best," Sam conceded. "We had better smuggle me through to one of the spare bedrooms for now though."

Sam donned the colourful beach wrap and pulled the material up over his head once again. "Let's go," he said. They sneaked through the corridors till they reached an empty bedroom beyond the one Janny shared with the girls.

Janny retreated into the ensuite bathroom and attempted to soothe her body with a bubbly soak. After about twenty minutes, she wrapped herself in a towel and progressed back into the bedroom, where Sam offered to give her a massage with some aromatherapeutic lotion. This proved to be soothing for the stinging muscles, and the dancer began to hope that the care routine would make it easier to move around the next day.

Janny also found herself forgiving the agent for all the impatient and churlish words he had spoken as he was supervising her dance practice. He was very good at his job as an agent and had been a friend until she made the mistake of allowing him to believe he was something more than a friend to her. She was about to say something when there was a knock at the door.

Janny struggled upright and created a tighter wrap of the towel around her torso. Motioning Sam to duck under the quilt on the bed, she unbolted the door and peeked out a crack. It appeared to have been Vonda knocking.

"Hello Vonda," Janny said, attempting not to appear too guilty.

Vonda looked puzzled: "We could not find you anywhere," she said. "What are you doing locked away in this bedroom?"

"I needed to rest," Janny replied ambiguously.

Vonda looked concerned. "This isn't about that fight we had on your birthday - is it?" she asked.

Janny shook her head: "No," she said. She glanced around the corridor and lowered her voice, "Come inside".

Vonda appeared confused, but she complied.

Janny shut the door tightly behind the musician and shot the bolt. "I would like you to meet someone," she mumbled. "Sam - you may show yourself."

A tousled male head appeared from amongst the bedding, and Vonda gasped. "You have a boyfriend," she exclaimed. "Isn't that against the rules of the show?"

"He is a man friend, not a boyfriend," Janny corrected. "Sam is my agent, and I need him here to help me prepare for the talent act."

"Why don't you just introduce him around as part of the staff then?" Vonda asked reasonably.

"It is not what Sam wants," Janny explained. "Besides, the television station might try to keep us apart for the next week... because they have a contract with me. And its Sam's job to get me other contracts after the show is finished."

The dancer turned to face Vonda and fixed an appealing look upon her face: "Please Vonda, I need a favour. I have already made too many requests from Leticia for one day – so I need you to go to her and ask for separate rooms for the lot of us. Say you can't sleep or something."

Vonda looked perturbed. "You are involving me in your intrigue," she said doubtfully. "I don't know if I like that."

"Please Vonda - please," Janny begged.

"I will think about it," Vonda said.

Vonda went back to the lounge and told Kendra, who looked concerned. "I don't really like the sound of this Sam guy," the artist said. "From what you say, he has been here for less than a day, and already has begun to monopolise Janny's time and separate her from her friends."

"It doesn't seem right to me either," Vonda said. "But what can we do?"

"Nothing," Kendra said frowning. "We have to respect Janny's wishes."

"So I will make the request to change rooms then?" Vonda asked anxiously.

"You had better," Kendra said. "We certainly don't want this guy coming into OUR room at night."

"I will say that I am afraid of waking you and Janny up with my violin practice," Vonda resolved gloomily.

"I will back you up on that," Kendra rejoined. "But Vonnie, I will miss you!"

"I will miss you too," Vonda said. The two women exchanged a hug, and Vonda withdrew to speak to Leticia.

"What is all this about?" Deborah inquired, entering the lounge softly on slipper clad feet.

"We are just organising separate bedrooms," Vonda said quickly. "You are lucky, the rest of your room-mates have all been eliminated and you already have a room to yourself."

"I thought you two were good friends...." Deborah mused. "Is one of you planning to entertain Anthony at night?"

Kendra went pink. "We could go across to the Eligible Residence for that," she said.

"We are still friends," Vonda said. "We just need a bit more privacy for doing our make-up and things for these last few dates – we are the final four after all!"

It sounded reasonable enough, but the shadow of a memory passed through Deborah's mind.

That silly Psychic had said: "You girls must stay together – especially at night!" However, the socialite was too busy with other thoughts to pay much heed.

The change of rooms was officially effected in the morning. Kendra bundled up her belongings and moved into the suite vacated by the earlier candidates; while Janny collected her remaining clothes and transported them into the room she had begun clandestinely sharing with Sam. Vonda was left in lonely possession of the suite she had originally shared with Kendra, Janny and Rozanne.

There were to be no dates the following day, because all the girls had been granted time to prepare something for the talent show the next evening.

CHAPTER EIGHT: DEBORAH'S SUBTERFUGE

Deborah knew that she would not be able to put off her father's invitation to dinner for too long. Moreover, if she took Anthony, she would be perpetuating a lie, as she was not romantically interested in the Charity Eligible. On the other hand, if she took George, her father would be disappointed he was not meeting the Charity Eligible, unless he understood that he was meeting the man in her life. Then the cat would truly be out of the bag!

"You had better go and call your father," Leticia ordered, appearing in the doorway.

"I guess I had better," Deborah agreed, her mind was racing, scheming and searching for a solution. The socialite was aware that she had only just convinced the bashful camera operator that he was truly the man of her choice; and here was her father coming along with the heavy patriarch act. It was enough to set any suitor running.

Augustus Markham did not have a good track record in the listening department. However, she had never met a man as genuinely honest and unselfish as George before... and he did have his career and the title to an inner-city Sydney unit. There was a slight chance that her father would respect him for these things.

"Leticia," Deborah said, "If Anthony comes out for dinner with me, it might be perceived by the other girls as an extra date. That would be unfair."

"I know miss," Leticia replied. "But if Mr. Markham wants to meet the Charity Eligible?"

"If my father wants to meet the Charity Eligible he could come to the launch party!" Deborah said. "I think tonight should be about him and his daughter."

"I will send Mr. Markham an invitation to the launch party immediately," Leticia agreed. "And you will organise to have dinner with him tonight. Where will that be in case he asks me?"

"I will meet Mr. Markham over at the Markham Corporation office if I am not needed for filming this afternoon," Deborah replied.

Deborah returned to her room and changed quickly into a summer frock. Then she picked up the telephone and called her father. A taxi was ordered immediately, and the socialite was shipped across to the Markham Corporation, along with her bag which contained a change of clothes. Once there, she was ushered into a side office and asked to await the arrival of her father. Deborah sighed and sent the receptionist off to purchase a bestselling novel and some sandwiches with which to while away the time.

The door eventually opened and Deborah's father entered the room. A tall balding man, Augustus Markham was well built; and the hug he gave Deborah was crushing.

"It seems like ages since I saw you," he cried.

"Two months Daddy," Deborah replied precisely. "I had lunch with you and Mummy just before starting on *The Charity Dating Show* remember?"

"Ah yes," Augustus reminisced. "And you thought you would fancy this young doctor. Now I hear I am not going to meet him yet after all... what is going on Deb?"

"Anthony is busy filming," Deborah replied. "And there are three other girls who are much more interested in him at this stage."

"And you?" Augustus queried. "I know you too well to believe you would just give up on the Charity Eligible!"

Deborah flushed. "With your permission sir," she said, "I would like to invite someone else to meet you."

Augustus looked mildly affronted. "What sort of person is he?" the tycoon inquired.

"A working man, and a family man," Deborah replied.

"A family man, what does that mean exactly?" Augustus inquired sharply. "You know I won't countenance you carrying on with a married man, although goodness knows it has been done often enough in our circles."

"George is a widower with a young son," Deborah replied.

"Oh?" Augustus continued with the interrogation. "Interesting! How do you get along with the boy Deborah?"

"Just excellent," Deborah answered. "You could say that Parker brought us together."

"You have got yourself in deep then," Augustus said thoughtfully.

"I know father," Deborah replied. "I am actually glad to have it happen to me at last."

"This is going to change a lot of things," Augustus blustered. "The fellow is going to have to sign a pre-relationship agreement."

"I'm pretty sure he will do that!" Deborah exclaimed.

"And I'm not going to sign the rights to your shares over for a few more years," Augustus continued: "In fact Deborah, I might make it so that you can't touch the Markham shares, except to draw on the profits and pass them on to your biological children."

"We have already discussed something like that," Deborah said. "George is very honourable."

"A young man needs to be," Augustus remarked sternly. "You are quite a catch Deborah, and not just because of your inheritance. I have always loved you girl - even when you made me angry by renouncing your rightful place in society."

"I take a holiday with you and mother every year," Deborah returned defensively. "That is enough cruising the seas in luxury liners, and partying in European resorts to last me a lifetime."

"So you said," Augustus returned. "I thought it particularly ungrateful of you. After my slaving for years to make our family fortune!"

"I was actually never ungrateful Father," Deborah replied, stung to indignation. "I just had my other interests."

"Yes," Augustus replied. "You have successfully lived a double life for years. Now you are going to have to integrate that into one life, together with a ready-made family. I don't envy you one bit!"

"Some of it will be hard work," Deborah said, "But I expect a lot of fun as well."

"Well, you better contact this George guy and see whether he is man enough to face up to me," Augustus said. "I have a couple more business meetings to conduct, and then I will be free to take you out to dinner. Your mother is keen to come along too."

"I look forward to seeing Mummy," Deborah responded, genuinely relieved at the manner in which her father had taken her news.

About four o'clock in the afternoon the door opened and a bemused looking George was ushered into the room. He put his camera bag down on the desk and looked around.

"This is some establishment!" he said. "Is this the main office building?"

"Err sort of," Deborah admitted. "The Markham Corporation has at least one branch in every capital city. They Sydney office is the headquarters."

"Marrying into the mob then am I?" George seemed mildly amused. It was a coping mechanism that had stood him in good stead during other awkward encounters.

Deborah rushed across to his side: "I am so sorry," she babbled.

"Calm down Debs," George said, holding the socialite out at arm's length. "What has happened to my tough girl?"

"All gone," Deborah burbled. "Summons from my father tend to destroy my confidence."

"Luckily I have seen most of your moods," George said. "I reckon that if I can deal with you, I can deal with your old dad!"

"No you don't know half," Deborah cried. "He could be watching us through a security camera right now."

"Oh in that case..." George said, "We had better give him something to look at." The cheery cameraman caught Deborah around the waist and pulled her towards him.

Deborah gasped. "You wouldn't dare," she whispered.

"Oh yes I would," George laughed. "I love your daughter Mr. Markham," he announced to an imaginary surveillance camera and the proceeded to kiss the socialite very thoroughly.

Deborah relaxed into George's arms as the affection was very reassuring.

"I somehow don't think that your father is watching," George remarked after a reasonable interval.

"I don't either," Deborah said. "But you may have shocked some of the security staff."

George glanced around the room, and his eyes lit upon a portable television. The unit was meant for the viewing of business presentations and probably had no aerial connection to the outside, however it was better than nothing.

"I am going to see what reception I can get on that," George remarked.

He pulled the mini-television off the storage shelf and placed it upon the office table. After much fiddling with the dial, he managed to get a blurry picture from one of the commercial stations; the network was playing a repeat of a situation comedy that had run well through the nineteen-seventies, but it was better than nothing.

George pulled a pair of comfortable chairs out from against the wall, and motioned to Deborah to sit down. "We might as well be comfortable as we wait," he remarked.

"I can't believe your reaction," Deborah said with a snigger. The socialite was fast regaining her equanimity, and was feeling better about facing her father than she ever had before.

"I know you are scared of your dad," George replied reasonably, "But the simple truth might be that he is a very busy man."

"Things are never simple with my father," Deborah continued skeptically. "It comes of being half-Irish Catholic, half-Australian and a quarter Jewish."

"I reckon he would be so used to running a business, that he tries to run his family in the same manner," George said. "Actually, a lot of men get like that. The thing they understand the best is their work."

"I am glad you are not like that," Deborah murmured, and George laughed.

"Actually, I am a bit!" he said: "It's just that I work in the Arts. I see below the surface and make connections for a living. It's a slow old career field too. I would be a manager at least if I wasn't in the film industry."

"Whatever it is," Deborah said. "I am glad you are exactly who you are."

"Keep thinking that way," George murmured. "I have the feeling it is about to be tested."

Augustus Markham arrived some half-an-hour later. The tycoon strode up to George and shook the younger man's hand with the supreme confidence of someone who knows he can safely condescend to the majority of the population. "I am pleased to meet you, young fellow," he said.

"I am a bit surprised to be meeting you sir," George returned. "However, I am also very pleased."

"So you didn't seek my daughter out with the intention of advancing your career then," Augustus Markham observed.

"Err no sir," George stammered. "Indeed it was your daughter who sought me out."

"Just as I thought," Augustus said, "But you have been pretty quick to fall in with her wishes - haven't you?"

"Your daughter is a lovely young woman sir," George returned. "Lovely, and determined - no man can resist her."

"She takes after me in her determination," Augustus said. "Look around you boy, everything in this company has been built up by me. It was a lot of hard work."

"Very impressive sir," George acknowledged. It was impossible to tell where Augustus was leading with this discussion, so it seemed politic to agree.

"I have had to give up a lot over the years, including time with the family to build this business," Augustus said. "I did it so that Deborah and her mother could have everything of the very best."

"I am sure you did sir," George returned. His role in the conversation so far seemed to be that of mirror to the older man.

"Deborah has been courted by the richest sons of this country, and a foreign prince or two," Augustus informed the young man. "What do you think of that?"

"It err - seems quite natural, your family being in society and all that," said George. "Do you mind me asking what happened then sir?"

"She turned them all down flat!" Augustus exclaimed. "She turned them all down, and somehow settled her mind on you. How do you explain that?"

"Maybe she wanted someone different sir," George replied.

Augustus snorted. "Don't you be funny with me! If she turned them down... obviously she wanted someone different. What do you think she saw in you?"

"I am a hard-working man sir," George ventured. "A working man who has developed something of a career. If these other men were born rich, they may not have seemed as reliable to Deborah."

"An interesting theory," Augustus said. "But Deborah has gone out with her share of working men, and none of them have had any great effect upon her."

"Can't we ask Deborah her opinion?" George cried. "It seems rude to be talking like this in front of her."

"Deborah knows me," Augustus said. "I like to get to the bottom of things. I don't care who is listening."

"You are bit like Deb in that too then," George remarked.

"Am I then?" Augustus asked sternly, but he seemed amused.

"Deborah and I will manage," George said, taking Deborah by the hand. He judged it to be time for some show of unity. "We will build a life for ourselves and my son. Your blessing would be nice too sir, if you can see your way free to give it in time."

Augustus gave the camera assistant a hard look: "I guess I had better do the civilised thing and take you two lovers out to dinner. Deborah's mother is waiting for us in one of the better Sydney restaurants."

The business man turned and led the way out of the office, through the Markham Corporation building and into the street where a company car waited.

Deborah and George followed more slowly, with George putting one arm around Deborah. "That wasn't so bad after all," he whispered.

Deborah shrugged. In her experience of some twenty-and-four years being the only daughter of Augustus Markham, she understood it was highly likely that her father had only just begun to assess them. However, the socialite was not going to depress her gallant escort with such speculation.

"You did very well," she murmured. "Thank you for standing by me."

"I lost someone I loved once," George muttered, "And I am not going to let it happen again. I don't care whether it is through death or simple neglect."

The well-appointed car belonging to the Markham Corporation drove up alongside the group, and the professional driver beckoned for them to enter the vehicle. Augustus Markham sat in the front, while Deborah and her partner climbed into the back.

Augustus Markham ordered the car to drive straight to the harbour and park in an exclusive club area. They climbed out of the car, up a narrow flight of steps and into the foyer of a comfortable restaurant.

Recognising Mr. Markham, all the staff came running.

"Lady Ellen is at your usual table," the Manager informed Augustus.

George jumped, and cast Deborah an inquiring look. He had not known that her mother was a woman of title.

Deborah quickly told the camera-man not to worry, for Ellen Markham had been the daughter of an English Baronet, who was sufficiently impoverished not to concern himself as to whom the daughter married. There was little danger of Deborah inheriting a title, as her mother had a younger brother, who might still have children. Moreover, British rank did not traditionally pass through matrilineal inheritance. However, George continued to look intimidated as they approached the assigned table.

Lady Ellen Markham proved to be a woman with fair hair and a love of silvery lace outfits, the effect of which was somewhere half-way between elegant and subdued. All in all, the lady was difficult to read. Courteous with her husband, and cordial toward her daughter; she took very little notice of George at first, which created the impression that she might not like the young man very much.

After the initial introduction, when George tried unsuccessfully to endear himself to Lady Markham with flattery, the party fell silent. Deborah was earnestly reading the menu, Lady Markham was looking at the desert tray, and Augustus was in the men's room.

Finally, Deborah broke the silence: "How is Uncle Edward doing in parliament?" she said.

"He had a good run in the election," Ellen Markham replied nervously. She turned to George: "My brother was not satisfied with a seat in the House of Lords," she explained. "So he campaigned for the House of Commons in the manner we do over here in Australia."

"Good on him," George remarked.

Lady Markham was obviously someone around whom you watched your manners, but the difficult thing seemed to be gauging how positive to make his demeanour. Apparently, it was as uncouth to be overly enthusiastic, as it was to be surly.

Lady Ellen gave the camera-operator a patient look, and Deborah rushed back into the breach. "I think I will have steak with that wonderful pepper sauce," she said. "What about you mother?"

"I will have chicken and mushroom," Ellen said. She turned to Augustus, who had just re-joined them at the table. "What will you have dear?"

"I feel something different," Augustus said. "I will have their steak with garlic sauce and blue cheese exclusive special. Have you ordered yet George?"

"I will have steak with pepper sauce too if I may," George replied.

Augustus duly relayed their order to the waiter and requested a selection of drinks for the party. Then he sat back and surveyed everyone with a satisfied smirk upon his face.

"I believe we are having some entertainment tonight," he said.

Lady Ellen looked surprised. "I didn't think it was that sort of place," she ventured dubiously.

"It is not," Augustus replied. "It is a high quality restaurant. However, one can book a cabaret singer for a special occasion."

"Whatever you think best, Augustus dear," Lady Ellen subsided and turned her attention to the entree that had just been delivered.

Deborah frowned slightly as the band struck up a well-known tune and an exotic looking Italian performer appeared from behind a curtain. She was a burlesque singer who often appeared at the state theatre.

"Daddy, you didn't have to go to so much effort," Deborah said.

"Only the best for my daughter," Augustus said. "And I did think I was meeting the Charity Eligible tonight. He is a celebrity of sorts."

Augustus was clapping in time to the music, and even her own George was looking amused, as the cabaret singer tickled his face with a feather from her cape. The entertainer then moved on and repeated the procedure with Augustus Markham, who laughed and shooed her out into the centre of the room.

The main course arrived, and Deborah began to consume her steak in a determined fashion. The performer circled around George once again, displaying a lot of bosom as she warbled the throaty notes. The cameraman dropped his eyes to his plate, and Deborah felt her colour begin to rise.

"George," she said, "Would you go and get me a beer?"

They weren't up to the stage of after-dinner drinks, but George knew that his Deborah liked her beer, so he obediently tracked his way to the bar, returning with a nicely brewed lager. This activity had the desired effect of dislodging the performer from the camera-operator's back, and Deborah breathed a sigh of relief.

"Thank you George," she said, accepting the beverage.

"Glad to be of service," the George said, sliding back into his seat, and patting Deborah on the arm. "It is actually a novelty to be your official escort for once!"

"Yeah, what has that been like to hang around while Deborah goes out with that Eligible bloke?" Augustus Markham asked curiously.

George snorted: "Entertaining - on the whole," he replied. "She hasn't really been anything more than friendly toward Anthony."

"And yet he is a nice educated young man," Lady Ellen Markham murmured. "And with such a respectable job..."

"If it is education you are looking for in a son-in-law, I have a degree in History and a Masters in Communication," George remarked.

Augustus looked surprised: "I thought you were some sort of technical assistant," he barked.

"They refer to the second camera operator on set as the assistant," George acknowledged. "However, that is because there is only ever one maestro in any production."

"Do you work full time?" Ellen asked curiously.

"More than full time sometimes," George said. "I have been filming some ten hours a day, six days a week on this show. The only breaks I got have been arranged by swapping a solo shift with Simon Steeple."

"You must have a break in employment between productions," Ellen commented.

"Sometimes," George admitted. "Early in my career, there were periods of unemployment. However, now my skills have made me quite indispensable around the network."

"I am thinking that you could buy a house on that sort of work," Augustus commented. "Especially if you receive over-time."

"Actually," George said, "I am a fair way through paying for a unit in the city."

"In inner Sydney?" Augustus, who was well aware of the value of property in the inner suburbs, exclaimed.

"Err - yes," George said. "Near the bay. I got in during a lull in the market."

"Shrewd," Lady Ellen remarked, she looked at Augustus. "He isn't so very poor after all dear."

George looked embarrassed. If there was anything more disconcerting than being tried and found wanting, it was being examined and grudgingly accepted. Now that the pressure to impress his girlfriend's high-powered parents appeared to be resolved, the cameraman needed a moment alone to regain his equilibrium.

"I am going to the men's room," George announced.

The musical accompaniment came to an end, and the singing ceased. Deborah, who was mildly indignant whenever the heavily made-up cabaret singer approached George in a seductive manner, had firmly expected the woman to retire from the restaurant floor at the end of her show.

Unfortunately the performer appeared to have a reason for remaining in the restaurant, and continued to float vivaciously around the room, chatting idly to diverse diners. When she saw George move, the singer appeared to gravitate towards the general direction of the men's room door; chatting to unsuspecting patrons as she progressed.

As George re-entered the dining area, the exotic performer sidled up to him and looped her arms around his neck. George stood stock still in conspicuous surprise, while the entertainer kissed him flirtatiously on the cheek.

"Excuse me Senorita," George stuttered. The cameraman ducked out from under the woman's encircling arm. His whole attention was focused on Deborah, who was rapidly crossing the restaurant floor. It was obvious there was only one woman who interested him.

Deborah faced the opera singer. "Please stop it," she said. "This is my boy-friend George".

The opera singer looked mildly confused. "I was told it would be the Charity Eligible and to give him a kiss," she said. "Are you sure, that is not him?"

"No, he is not the Charity Eligible!" Deborah replied heatedly. "And there are a couple of other girls on the show who would be objecting to your kissing him if he were!"

"My mistake, Miss Markham," the Burlesque Singer murmured discretely, looking to retreat to the rear of house.

"I am sorry darling," George exclaimed. "I am really not used to being important enough for women to behave like that around me!"

"You need to learn to be more assertive," Deborah remarked

sternly. "That was obviously set up by my father. However, it could happen again in the future - especially if we are out at a society party."

"Point taken," George said. He took Deborah in his arms and gave her a brief public kiss. "Let's say goodbye to your parents," he suggested. "They must have made up their minds about me by now."

The young couple made their way back to the Markham family table and said, "Fare-well," to Deborah's parents. There they found that the tone of the evening had changed.

Lady Ellen, who suspected Augustus of having looked a little too closely at the cabaret singer, had become more animated. Usually a very gentle person, Lady Ellen had asserted herself, prevailing upon Augustus to pay the entertainer off and release the woman. The string band however, was to remain and play waltz-like music, for Lady Ellen loved to dance, and rarely had the opportunity to do so with her own husband.

Augustus and Lady Ellen Markham intended to amuse themselves in the restaurant for an hour or two before retiring to their luxury penthouse for the night. The couple invited Deborah and George to stay with them, but appeared to accept 'No' for an answer readily enough.

Looking over his shoulder as they passed the exit, George could see Lady Ellen Markham looking adoringly into the eyes of her husband Augustus, who was extending a gentle hand to touch his wife's grey-clad shoulder. It was evident that despite all the trappings of the society marriage market, the Markham's union had been very much a love-match.

The Cameraman pulled Deborah to a discrete halt. "Look back at your parents," he whispered.

Deborah appeared puzzled, but when she angled herself against the door frame, her eyes widened in surprise: "I have seen something tonight that I never once saw in my entire childhood," she exclaimed.

"I think we won this round if not the battle," George said. "There are forces in your parents' lives which could operate in our favour."

"It certainly looks like it," Deborah agreed. "I rather expect an encore or two though - my father is a creature of habit, and my mother rarely demands his attention."

CHAPTER NINE: THE TALENT SHOW

When the ladies arrived at tea that evening, they were surprised to find Deborah did not join them. Although none of the contestants had seen the socialite all afternoon, they had fondly imagined that she was somewhere around, doing some uniquely Deborah-like thing. They knew she was not with George because he had been working hard alongside Simon Steeple and the rest of the camera crew.

Anthony arrived to join them for tea that evening and there was still no Deborah, and after a while, George was not with the camera crew anymore. The contestants who knew Deborah had a few secrets exchanged puzzled looks.

"Something must have happened," Kendra whispered. "I don't think Deborah would leave without telling us."

"Unless she was told to go," Vonda ventured.

"Surely not," Anthony said, "She was bearing up quite well."

He frowned, reflecting that notwithstanding the fact he knew he should have eliminated Deborah and concentrated solely on the girls with whom he felt a romantic connection, he had by no means been ready to bid farewell to Deborah. It had been good to have an ally on the show, someone practical and able to be relied upon as a friend.

Anthony considered Kendra to be a good friend too, but there was also the very real possibility of breaking her heart, and he could so easily do it just by following the conventions of the show and exploring the genuine attraction he felt toward Vonda.

Vonda herself was lovely, but she kept him working to build up her confidence and bring her out of her shell; he supposed these skills were good for him to develop, but he did hope they would eventually achieve a comfortable level of openness in their interactions.

If anyone lived on the edge of elimination, it was the mercurial Janny. She was always teasing Anthony with her affections one minute and withdrawing sulkily the next.

Janny herself looked mildly relieved. She was functioning in blissful ignorance of the extent to which her behaviour perplexed Anthony, and mildly confident of her security upon the show.

However, with the upcoming publicity stunt planned for her by her agent Sam, the stakes had risen, and she did need to ensure her succession for at least one more round.

"I think Deborah might have gone out," the Ballerina ventured, "The house has been very quiet all afternoon."

"As if you would know," Kendra remarked with uncharacteristic irony.

Anthony picked up on it at once. "Is there something I should know?" He asked.

"No," Janny said firmly. "I've been busy practicing my dance for you."

"It's just girl stuff," Vonda added diplomatically.

Janny smiled sweetly and patted Anthony on the leg. "You have heard about the talent night, haven't you?"

"Oh yes," Anthony said, unaware that he was being effectively side-tracked. "I am so looking forward to seeing you dance!" He turned to Vonda: "And you play the violin. I thought you were going to avoid giving a recital forever."

Vonda laughed: "I may appear shy, but I always perform beautifully at the right time," she returned.

"Are you going to paint as your talent?" Anthony asked Kendra, and she shrugged.

"I don't know," the Graphic Artist replied. "Painting isn't something you can exactly do in front of people."

"I take it this idea doesn't suit you as well as the others then," Anthony deduced.

Kendra again shrugged: "I will work something out," she said. "I have quite a few hours."

The main course concluded and desert was served, it was deliciously cool and creamy. Leticia entered the dining room and perched herself at the head of the table. Everyone looked at the hostess expectantly.

"Deborah is not with us this evening, because she has been called away on urgent family business," Leticia announced. "There will be no carnation ceremony this evening, and you will go ahead and prepare for the talent show without her."

Kendra and Vonda exclaimed gently, and Anthony expressed his disappointment. However, no one pushed the issue in front of the cameras, preferring to all draw their private conclusions. The group ate their tea in a subdued mood and then repaired to the lounge room.

Anthony invited Janny outside for a walk in the gardens, as there was something in particular he wished to ask her. Standing outside near the pool, he thought the ballerina looked very attractive.

"I am very much looking forward to seeing you dance tomorrow," the Charity Eligible said, repeating his earlier thought. "I am sure that you are an excellent dancer, and your performance will be a real treat for all of us who get to see you."

Janny giggled nervously. "Good," she said. "I will try to present something special."

"However," Anthony continued in a lower voice, "Despite our occasional kiss, I wonder how you really feel about me as a man. Do have any real interest in dating me?"

Janny drew a deep breath and composed her expression. Leaving the show at this point was the last thing on her agenda, and yet it sounded very much as though Anthony was asking her to make a decision.

"I like you very much Anthony," she said.

"Why then did you miss todays' outing?" Anthony asked.

"I was tired and confused, until I had the idea about dancing for you," Janny replied. "I don't know how to show my feelings. Then I decided to use my time to practice. I am sorry if it meant that you, Kinny and Vonnie had an awkward triple-date."

"It was a bit awkward," Anthony admitted. "I stuffed up and kissed both Kendra and Vonda. At different times – of course."

"Lucky they don't know you have kissed me as well," Janny giggled. "You are going to get yourself into so much trouble Anthony, my boy!"

"I know!" he said. "I will have to make amends one day."

Anthony thought about Janny's explanation for her absence. It seemed to make sense and he could hardly fault it. Something was still a little weird, but he could not put his finger upon his suspicions, however.

"I don't know what to do," Kendra said as she and Vonda emerged from the lounge. "I am worried that my talent is the quietest one, and it will be difficult to make an impressive presentation," the graphic artist confided in a low voice.

"Hmm it would be hard to make a showing with a bunch of sketches," Vonda agreed empathetically. "Unless you tried going high tech... like a slide-show."

"I would need equipment," Kendra objected.

"Check out the projection room," Vonda suggested. "There is a lot of gear along the wall. I've noticed it as I went in there to play the violin in sound-proof conditions."

"Won't you be using it yourself?" Kendra asked.

"Not necessarily," Vonda said. "Remember the excuse for us to all have separate rooms? It was supposedly so that I could practice in comfort."

"Okay," Kendra said. "Thanks for the tip, and good luck!"

"Good luck to you too," Vonda said, and the two girls shook hands.

Around nine o'clock the next morning, Janny emerged from the bedroom to meet Sam at the front door. They made their way discretely to Leticia's office; where Janny officially introduced Sam as her technical support for the act.

No mention was made of their former relationship, or the fact that Sam had already been in the vicinity of the Candidate House for a day. Leticia accepted Sam's presence at face value and inducted him into the occupational health and safety aspects of show. The hostess appeared happily ignorant of any emotional undercurrents.

Janny and Sam then repaired to the ballroom and practiced openly all that day. The required piece of music arrived by courier, and they began to match the choreography to the rhythm and phrasing of the piece. Sam proved to be even more demanding than he had been the previous afternoon, calling for Janny to repeat dance manoeuvres until she was blind from exhaustion.

At last the Ballerina called for a respite. "I must stop now," she said. "I am afraid that if we practice any more, I will not have the stamina to actually perform this evening."

Sam looked disappointed. "I want everything to be perfect," he said.

""I am sorry, but I really do need to eat and drink and rest a bit," Janny said reasonably. "I am flesh and blood after all."

Janny was wondering vaguely why it was her doing the apologising, and not her inhumane slave driver of an agent, but such was the regular pattern of their interaction. The dancer knew that Sam believed that he was drawing the best out of her as a performer. Sam had an excellent reputation as an administrator, and his artists always obtained contracts.

He was also very handsome, and Janny was well aware that should she displease him, she would have competition for his attention. In all it was a situation that placed all the power in Sam's hands and left Janny insecure.

In the past the ballerina had been blinded by loneliness and infatuation, and her apparent incompatibility with anyone outside the entertainment industry. Now that she had begun dating Anthony, she saw things slightly differently, but established habits take a while to die.

"You aren't going to get rebellious on me are you?" Sam asked, obviously not satisfied by any apology which was accompanied by an excuse.

"Of course not," Janny said, giving the agent a kiss on the cheek in the deluded belief that physical contact softened him and improved his mood.

"Good," Sam said grinning broadly. He caught Janny around the waist and gave her a rough squeeze: "I do have other clients you know."

A dazed Janny responded in confusion, "Yes, I count myself very privileged to have you give so much time to my career."

Deborah might have pointed out that Sam was well paid with an above average percentage of commission, but the worldly-wise girl had barely left her room since she returned late the previous evening. The other contestants assumed it was something to do with the 'family matters' Leticia had mentioned and maintained a respectful distance, although they were curious as to why George had eventually disappeared the previous evening too.

Anthony arrived at the Candidate House in the evening wearing a tuxedo. He was seated on a special sofa in the ballroom, which had been decorated for the occasion with red velvet curtains and gold embossed screening; and being plied with champagne and lemonade like a prince at a royal command performance.

"This is the life," the Charity Eligible remarked, proposing a toast to the coming presentation and looking impressed that Leticia had remembered his moderate stance regarding alcohol.

Vonda was privileged to give the first performance. The musician arrived wearing a medieval style purple and gold gown that consisted of a chemise with surcoat and reached the ground. The far-away expression upon her face told Anthony and the other girls that she had switched into professional artist mode.

Seating herself on the cloth draped stool, Vonda lifted the violin to her chin and raised the bow. Liquid clear notes ensued from the instrument, and there was none of the squeaking associated with a small string instrument played without accompaniment.

Everyone listened spell-bound, and then broke out into spontaneous applause.

"I can see why you are in the State Orchestra," Anthony exclaimed.

"How did you get the notes so clean and pure?" Kendra inquired.

Vonda returned briefly to the here-and-now and smiled.

"I have been trained in the genuine historical methods of playing the instrument," she explained. "I can play as solo fiddle, orchestral ensemble, classical, Celtic or contemporary."

"Bravo, bravo," Deborah exclaimed. "It just shows what you can do when you get serious about a skill."

Anthony glanced at the socialite in approval, for she seemed to be regaining her positive attitude towards being on *The Charity Dating Show*. Then he turned back to Vonda: "Play us an encore," he demanded.

Janny clambered to her feet from a place on a cushion beside the sofa. "You will have to excuse me now," the dancer said. "I have to get changed for my act."

"We will let you go," Anthony said, and the group turned its attention back to Vonda with the violin. The light pure notes filled the room with a variety of melody for the next ten minutes.

Janny returned shortly afterward wearing a short bell shaped tutu in green and gold net. A pair of paper wings were attached to her back, and she looked remarkably like a sensual version of Tinker Bell. The ballerina stepped into the room and posed to one side of the lighted area poised gracefully in a flattering first position with arms curved above her head.

Sam, who was playing the part of stage manager, had politely removed the stool and cleared a section of the floor from its customary carpeting. The ballroom had been vacuumed earlier that day, so no dust rose as the agent rearranged the soft furnishing. Then Sam crossed to the stereo and began to play the chosen music.

Janny tiptoed her way into the centre of the room and did a beautiful curtsy. Raising herself en-pointe, she began to dance. The audience was enchanted by the blending of modern music and classical dance, and highly impressed by the flexibility and grace of the arabesque and floor level splits.

Round and around Janny whirled, gathering momentum as the music repeated its theme and increased in speed, for Sam had made the original score a couple of notches faster for each verse. The watchers became breathless and almost dizzy, as Janny spun before them, displaying her beautiful pirouette and lifting her well-formed leg in the arabesque.

With her arms outstretched and circling gracefully, the ballerina truly seemed to be flying, except in the grounded moments of the tumble and roll. The music came to a halt, and the watchers broke out into spontaneous spurts of clapping. Janny hovered before them graceful en-pointe, before dropping into a deep split.

"That was wonderful," Anthony exclaimed. "Beautiful, wonderful, out-of-this-world."

"Such exquisite balance!" Kendra added.

"The timing was good too," Vonda observed. "I have never seen such dancing to that music, was it your own choreography?"

Janny looked abashed. "Some of it was my own choreography," she said. "Sam also has a lot of ideas when he watches me practice."

"You should give yourself more credit," Deborah remarked cautiously. The socialite had not forgotten her initial encounter with the agent, when he looked like a crook trying to sneak in the side door. Now she found him officially admitted to the mansion, but she was still not convinced. Sammy Davis Macpherson indeed!

"I think you need to be strong as an individual artist and not just as a team," Deborah remarked.

"Sometimes being part of a group is important," Janny explained. "I have many more work-mates that you have not met at the ballet company."

"Hush Deborah," Vonda said anxiously. While she did not really approve of Sam either, she knew that the ballerina would not easily be persuaded against her agent. "That is show business for you."

Anthony was still staring at Janny in delight. Being at the centre of the show, he had a sense of entitlement which protected him from detecting her involvement with Sam.

"I would love to see you dance again sometime," he said.

Janny breathed a tortured sigh: "Don't ask me to do it again," she said, but it was too late.

Sam started the music and cranked up the volume insistently. Janny began to step and spin, but as the tempo increased in subsequent verses, she began to stumble.

Vonda glanced expectantly across at Sam, believing he would stop the music, or at least slow the timing down a notch or two; but he kept the track playing relentlessly. Janny stumbled during her lunge and failed to rise fully, relaxing into the swan position.

"Enough, enough," called Anthony, crossing the floor to pull the exhausted ballerina into a vertical position. He turned to the agent: "Can't you see that she is tired?"

Glaring at Sam, the Charity Eligible supported Janny across to the sofa and placed her in a comfortable position at his side.

"Get her a drink," Anthony ordered, and Leticia obliged, running to the kitchen and returning with a glass of cool water.

"Thank you, thank you everyone," Janny said, sipping at the drink. "I will be fine now. It was just too much intensive practice."

Sam brought the music to an end with a discordant crash. He left his post as disk jockey and ignoring Janny, crossed the room to Vonda's side.

"You were great!" he said to the musician. "I loved your performance."

Vonda said "Thank you" politely, but she looked distressed. Her recital on the violin had been designed to please Anthony and not compete with Janny's routine on the dance-floor.

Moreover, Vonda felt that Sam had no business being more attentive to her than to own his client. "It is what I do for a living," she added modestly.

"I am an agent," Sam said with a leer. "Do you currently have an agent?"

Vonda frowned: "My father usually takes care of that sort of thing for me," she said.

"Fathers aren't agents," Sam said, and he was laughing. "You could do better with a professional."

"I don't see why," Vonda replied, turning her shoulder resolutely away from Sam. "My father has always been a very good agent."

"You've got to be kidding," Sam said attempting to lay his hand on her arm.

Vonda pushed the marauding hand away firmly. "Please don't."

They were saved from further awkwardness by Kendra, who had the junior members of the camera crew wheeling a notebook computer and large screen television into the room.

"Whatever is that?" Anthony exclaimed as the graphic artist arranged the hardware and drew the curtains against what was left of the daylight.

"I didn't want to be showing you a bunch of still pictures, so I have prepared us a cartoon," Kendra said. "Settle back and enjoy the show!"

"This is cool," Janny exclaimed as a caricature of the group left in the Candidate House appeared upon the screen.

"I especially like the way you have done me," Vonda said, pointing to a female viking figure on the screen.

"That was the hard part," Kendra said. "As I actually knew you guys, I had to make a decision as to whether I portrayed you realistically or comically... please don't be offended anyone."

"There is no fear of that," Janny said, laughing heartily at a portrayal of herself as a willowy sylph-like figure floating around the screen.

"I knew you could take a joke Jay," Kendra observed.

"I'm not as sure about myself as Frankenstein's Monster," Anthony said. "All the girls are running away from me instead of trying to date me."

"An ironic reversal of *The Charity Dating Show* premise," Kendra returned. "And I only had one day in which to develop my ideas. You will have to forgive me for being a bit derivative."

"I think it is cute," Deborah said. "You have been especially horrid giving me the head of a donkey."

"It is a reference to Shakespeare's *Midsummer-Night's Dream*," Kendra explained. "And as you see, the ass gets their man in the end."

"Very generous of you," Deborah murmured dryly. "However, the Anthony monster is on his last legs and I expect his batteries will run out very soon."

"I do believe she is right," Anthony exclaimed. "Look - you extinguished the fake me."

"Not really," Janny observed, "Look there the monster gets packed away for re-animation another day!"

"I like it," Leticia who was hovering around the back of the room making sure that everything ran according to schedule, observed. "Congratulations Kendra, it is exceedingly clever. I especially get the irony of including me as Doctor Frankenstein."

"Yeah I liked that one," Kendra said happily.

"It is my turn now," remarked Deborah. "I am afraid you will have to give me a few minutes to prepare because I stayed to see the end of Kendra's show." The socialite stood and walked smartly out of the room, while the junior members of the television crew helped Kendra remove the electrical equipment from the centre of the floor.

Deborah returned about twelve minutes later wearing a neat conductor's costume. The outfit was red and black and fitted very snugly. She was accompanied by a snowy white poodle, who had his hair clipped and styled.

Anthony whistled in appreciation. "Sexy get-up," he said.

Vonda reached out a hand and patted the poodle. "What a cute puppy," she exclaimed.

Deborah whistled to her dog and threw it a pet treat. The animal caught the treat in its mouth and chewed the meat flavoured ring with glee.

"There," Deborah said. "The secret to training an animal is to keep it well rewarded." She gestured to the poodle: "Say hello to the people Moppet."

The dog rose up on his hind legs and trotted a few steps towards the audience. His balance was excellent, and he appeared to have no difficulty maintaining the up-right position. When the dog was positioned directly before the group of watchers, he dropped onto all fours and gave a short little bark.

"How cute," Vonda exclaimed and the white poodle ran up to her and thrust his nose into her hand. "I am sorry I do not have a biscuit for you," she said. "Go back to your mistress."

Anthony made a slight movement, and the poodle ran up to him. The Charity Eligible patted the dog on the back. "What a well behaved animal," he said. "It hasn't jumped up on me once."

Deborah clapped and the dog trotted obediently back to her, he was now manoeuvring on all fours like a normal canine, but his poise and grace were delightful. The socialite then put the dog through its paces, demonstrating how he was able to sit and stay, beg and fetch. The high-light of the show was a hoop jumping demonstration.

Deborah rewarded the dog and gave him a brief pat, then she signalled to the television crew. A lively tune began to play through the stereo speakers, causing the poodle to pick up his nose: "Dance for me," Deborah ordered, and the dog looked pleased.

The poodle began to trot around in a circle around the socialite, who waved her arms in time to the music. Taking its cue from the trainer, the dog appeared to synchronise his steps with that of the music, which was some sort of carnival polka. Everyone clapped, and the dog seemed to skip around in an even more enthusiastic manner.

"He seems to love to perform," Janny said looking impressed.

"Some animals enjoy music," Deborah explained. "They also like to please people and look forward to the good meal they will be given later."

At the conclusion of the talent show, Leticia allowed Deborah a few minutes in which to attend to her dog, and then called Anthony onto the centre of the floor.

"You are now the judge," the Hostess said to the Charity Eligible. "You must choose two acts, one as the winner and one as the runner up. The winner gets to have some one-on-one time with you tonight, while the runner-up will get some one-on-one time in the morning."

Anthony accepted the red and blue ribbons from her hand. "I wasn't really prepared to do any judging,' he said.

"Ah, but you know you always have to make a decision or two," Leticia said. "It is all part of the game."

"Well," Anthony said, "Put on the spot like this - I have to declare Deborah's puppy the winner."

Deborah rose to receive her kiss and her congratulations.

Vonda leant across to Kendra: "You were the real winner," she whispered. "I didn't think Deborah was half as clever."

"Your music was really beautiful," Kendra whispered in return. "But who can compete with performing animals?"

"Certainly not me," Vonda replied.

"Of course," Kendra said. "I think the best thing to do would be to avoid taking this personally."

"And now for the runner-up," Anthony said. "I must choose the exquisite Janny."

The Charity Eligible crossed the floor to the spot where Janny was sitting on the sofa.

"I am really flattered that you would wear yourself out preparing a dance for me," Anthony said seriously. "It was beautiful and I look forward to spending some time with you in the morning."

"I look forward to spending time with you too," Janny said stoically accepting the praise. The ballerina had after all been nominated for dance industry awards and while she had won some, she had also lost others. This game was nothing new to her.

Sam, on the other hand, looked angry: "You should have won an amateur show," he hissed. He drew Janny off to one side, and practically dragged her out of the room.

"But," Janny stammered. "Vonda and Kendra hardly qualify as amateurs. They both work in the Arts."

"Don't you argue with me," Sam cried angrily. "That Deborah had nothing but a third-rate circus act with a woolly animal."

"It's not my fault Anthony liked act her best," Janny began. "They have always been good friends."

Sam raised his hand and slammed his open palm into the side of the Ballerina's face. Janny cried out in pain and clutched at her cheek.

"What is going on here?" Kendra asked calmly, coming up behind the warring pair. "Sam, I think you had better go to wherever you are staying for the night. We have had weeks to get used to the way things happen around here and you are taking a bit of fun way too seriously."

The agent blustered, but something about Kendra's manner betrayed an absolute lack of fear, and he had no choice but to obey her instructions.

Kendra gently led Janny to the kitchen and wrapped a plastic container of ice in a towel before applying it to the dancer's cheek.

"You had better spend the night back in my room," the Graphic Artist said. "Just in case Sam hasn't actually left the mansion. I will ask Vonda to bunk in with us as well."

"Thanks," Janny said. She looked embarrassed: "It wasn't as bad as it looked you know. Sam will be very sorry tomorrow."

"I will believe that when I see it," Kendra exclaimed.

CHAPTER TEN: THE WILD-CARD ROUND

Deborah woke up early the next morning and took Moppet for a walk around the garden. She had missed the well trained poodle far too much in her weeks in the Candidate House, and it had been really good of her mother to bring the dog over just in time for the talent show.

It had also been sweet of Anthony to name Moppet the over-all winner of the talent show, although he had spent most of his one-on-one time with her last night attempting to make her explain her 'family emergency' the previous day. A visit from one's father was not normally considered an emergency, but then Anthony did not know the powerful Augustus Markham.

The socialite secured Moppet in one of the garden areas where she had been assured he could run safely and turned to go inside the mansion. As Deborah entered the lounge, Vondra met her all a flutter.

"George has been summoned to Leticia's office," the Musician cried. "They say he might even lose his job."

Deborah crossed the intervening length corridor using swift steps. She did not bother to knock, but turned the handle and marched straight inside. Leticia was in the room, together with George and several administrative members of the television station.

"Whatever is happening?" she demanded.

Leticia blanched. "I am sorry Miss Markham," the hostess said. "However there have been some unsettling rumours that one of my camera crew has been fraternising with the contestants."

"What does that mean exactly?" Deborah inquired.

"All of the crew are strictly contracted not to interfere with the outcome of *The Charity Dating Show* by becoming romantically involved with contestants," Leticia explained. "It is also important that the television station offer contestants an environment in which they feel free from any form of sexual harassment."

"Are you suggesting that George might have done something inappropriate?" Deborah asked. "I thought he was a valued member of your team".

"George is a highly skilled camera man, capable of filming, editing and directing," Leticia said. "I would be very sorry to lose him. However, it is a matter of the terms of his contract."

"George may have showed his friendly face around the mansion," Deborah began diplomatically. "But I'm certain that no contestant felt harassed by his presence."

"George was reported absent from his duties two evenings ago," Leticia announced. "I am not sure of the whereabouts of all the contestants at the time... but I am told there have also been several mysterious absences by contestant Jandice."

Deborah began to laugh. "George attended the dinner with my parents by special invitation of my father that evening," she said. "If that is a problem, because I am a current contestant on the show, I will remove myself from *The Charity Dating Show* immediately."

Leticia looked mollified. "If Mr. Markham invited George, for whatever reason, then I am sure he was obliged to attend," the hostess said. "I could allow you to remain a guest on *The Charity Dating Show*, Miss Markham, but you cannot be allowed to run amuck with my staff. Please promise me that you will behave!"

"I am not sure I can do that Leticia!" Deborah said. "I must admit my interest in the Charity Eligible is beginning to wane. It was fun while it lasted, but I might be getting restless."

"If you are no longer interested in the Charity Eligible, Miss Markham," Leticia suggested uncomfortably, "Then perhaps then you ought to leave. I wouldn't want to keep you here against your inclination."

"If I am assured George's career is safe, I will be leaving," Deborah said. "You may replace me with another contestant if you please, but do not penalise George in any way."

"George's job is safe," Leticia replied. "To tell you the truth, I never wanted to lose him."

"That is good then," Deborah said. "Your vigilance regarding the safety of contestant Janny is also to be commended. You may be onto something there. However, I assure you that George is not the culprit."

"I will always put the safety of the people involved in my show foremost, you may rest assured of that Miss Markham," Leticia said. "You had better go and pack your things, if you are leaving."

Deborah returned to her room and packed quickly. Then she returned to Leticia's office and signed some brief papers releasing her from contestant status, and allowing the show to replace her with another contestant. The only condition was that she was to retain a low public profile until all the episodes with her in them had been sent to air.

The socialite did not see Janny, or have a chance to warn the ballerina about her role in the debacle. A quick call to the Markham Corporation ensured that a car was sent across to pick up the socialite along with her baggage.

Augustus Markham then suggested that the company car take Deborah and her little dog Moppet to George's flat, where she was planning to spend the next few days. After that, Deborah would have to return to her home town to sort out some business, and continue her work at the library until she could arrange a transfer to Sydney.

"There will be a carnation ceremony of sorts," Leticia announced the next day, after giving the remaining contestants the sad news that Deborah had chosen to leave the show. "I would like you all to repair to the small reception room immediately upon finishing your evening meal."

"Yes Leticia," the various members of the party murmured rather despondently, and the hostess gave them all a firm look before leaving.

"Oh my," Vonda exclaimed, "Whatever will we do without Deborah?"

"I wonder what happened?" Kendra speculated. "Did she get caught..."

"It sounds like it was her choice," Janny said, "But we will miss her!"

Deborah's departure felt like the end of an era, because amongst the original party, Deborah had been the backbone, if not the life and soul. Even Anthony seemed to agree he would miss her terribly.

A few minutes later, the group of three girls and one man arrived in the small reception room, where they were surprised to see a table bearing four carnations instead of three. "What do you think that is all about?" Kendra exclaimed.

"Perhaps we get to give Anthony a carnation too," Janny suggested.

Anthony laughed: "That is a cool idea," he said. "However, I can't see this sort of show going for such a role reversal - and I would expect three extra carnations if you were all giving them out."

"You are a greedy man," Vonda remarked jokingly, and Anthony gave her an approving glance. Given that they still did not dare talk openly about Deborah, the sensitive girl seemed to be holding her feelings together quite skillfully.

"You could give a carnation to Leticia," Janny said.

"Yes," Vonda agreed. "The hostess must feel very left out with no one to ever give her a carnation."

"Perhaps she sees too much drama running a show like this," Kendra remarked cautiously.

"We don't actually know anything about her personal life except that no man calls here for her," Anthony remarked practically.

"I think she is single," Vonda remarked. "Perhaps Alison found out, they seemed to be getting quite companionable."

The door opened and Heddy, Betty and Ilese entered the room. These three girls had all been eliminated in the early episodes, and no one had expected to see them around. The intruders were all elegantly clad and groomed in a manner designed to make the casually clad residents of the Candidate House feel dowdy by comparison.

Anthony looked surprised and delighted to see the newcomers; while Kendra, Vonda and Janny looked perplexed. The three girls were used to only having each other for competition, therefore regardless of undercurrents and rivalries developing between them, they were essentially comfortable.

Janny was the first to recover, for she had been through her share of auditions and rejections, before she had won a secure place in the ballet company. The pretty girl pasted a smile upon her face and began to circulate, greeting the newcomers.

"Hello Betty, hello Heddy, hello Ilese," the ballerina said. "How nice to see you again!"

The normally friendly Kendra seemed the most adversely affected; and Vonda, who was also used to performance situations, tugged gently at her arm.

"You must not let them see how you feel," the musician whispered. "Come along and help me say hello. Everyone knows I am too shy to work a room on my own."

Thus encouraged to shepherd the younger girl, Kendra managed to regain a semblance of her usual graciousness, and circled the room once before sitting down on a sofa to observe, for contemplation was also a strong component of her nature.

Anthony approached the girls somewhat shyly, for he had not gotten to know Heddy and Ilese very well during the debut ceremony, and Betty had been eliminated after the third round.

"I am happy to see you again," he said. "How are you Betty?"

"I am well," Betty said, smiling her Monro-esque smile.

"I was a bit worried the last time I saw you," Anthony said. "I really had wanted to offer you a carnation – but I ran out!"

"Nah, it turned out fine," Betty said with admirable good nature. "You were right - lots of guys have been happy to meet me. I'm selective, but I date all the time now."

"Is there anyone special?" Anthony asked curiously.

Betty laughed: "Give me time," she said. "It has only been a couple of months, and I don't want to rush things."

"You are very pretty Betty," Heddy remarked, stepping forward. "You are spoilt for choice whenever you are with a group of men."

"Don't you worry Heddy," Betty said. "Just as many guys like smart girls like you!"

Anthony looked puzzled hearing this exchange. "Have you two kept in contact?" he asked.

"Just a little," Heddy replied. "We thought we were off the show permanently and could do what we liked."

"Now you have got a call back," Anthony said. "I hope you don't mind."

"I for one am happy to see you again, Anthony," the beautiful African girl said.

"I really appreciated your understanding attitude regarding that first elimination," Anthony said. "I stuffed up a bit there I think!"

Heddy shrugged. "You had far too many girls and far too few flowers that day," she said. "I don't hold it against you at all."

"It - err seems like that every time," Anthony returned. "Too few carnations, I mean."

"Well we will see what happens tonight," Heddy remarked. "Leticia hasn't even explained the new rules to us."

"We have lost a lady," Anthony said. "I assume one of you will be chosen to replace her."

"Lucky you Anthony," Ilese said joining the trio. "You get a second chance with us girls."

"It is not you getting a second chance with me by any chance?" Anthony queried, turning to face the young woman.

"Certainly not," Ilese said. "I was here for the fun of it last time, and I am having a good time visiting once again. I have been given a flight, and a good meal and a lovely dress. If you pick me, I will consider the romance side of things, however, if you do not, I fully intend to enjoy the hotel they will book me into tonight."

"You sound a bit mercinary," Betty remarked in her artless fashion, but Ilese was not the least offended.

"I am merely practical," the blonde girl in the flowing evening outfit said. "It is an adventure to fly, to meet people and to be on television once again. If you will excuse me, I will talk to Vonda and Kendra."

Heddy looked amused. "You have been told where you stand," she said.

"Yes," Anthony agreed. "I am getting quite used to being surrounded by females who have their own opinions."

"So not all the dates have gone the way you intended?" Heddy asked astutely.

Anthony nodded. "There is much I cannot say until the show has ended, but I can tell you that the outcome of some on-show relationships have not been flattering to what you ladies call my 'male ego'."

Ilese bubbled up to Kendra and Vonda, who were sitting quietly against the wall. "How has it been going?" she cried. "Have you been going on good dates?"

"It has been interesting," Kendra replied cautiously, "And some of the dates have been quite exotic."

"I've had fun and learnt from the experience," Vonda said. "The other girls have been good to live with too."

"So spill the beans," Ilese said. "How many of the girls have fallen in love with Anthony?"

"Quite a few thought they fancied him," Kendra said carefully.

"That is what the show was about wasn't it?" Janny said, appearing out of the peripheries of their vision and butting into the conversation.

"What about you three?" Ilese demanded. The blonde with the layered hair peered searchingly at Janny, Vonda and Kendra. Janny continued to grin, Vonda maintained the small smile she used to mask her nervousness on stage, and Kendra blushed.

"Ah!" Ilese exclaimed. "It is you Kendra... I somehow thought you might... do you think it is really love, or some sort of infatuation?"

"Time will tell," Kendra murmured, and Vonda gave her a reassuring pat.

"How do you feel about us arriving then?" Ilese demanded impertinently.

"It is all part of the show, isn't it?" Kendra replied, sincerely grateful for her pacific nature, which allowed her to at least appear to deal equitably with these things.

"Of course," Ilese said. "Well I expect most of us won't be here for very long, and then things will work out for you with Anthony."

"I'm not making any undue assumptions," Kendra said calmly.

"Of course not," Janny said. "That was what made trouble for the others!"

"Ooh juicy," Ilese burbled. "I am dying to see the all the dramas when the show goes to air."

"I must admit we are wondering what we will look like on television," Vonda remarked.

Just then Anthony approached the group, and greeted the girls all around. "How are you all going?" he said, and then he singled out Kendra in particular. "Could I please speak to you alone Kinny?"

"Yeah sure," Kendra said and got up to follow Anthony into the hallway.

Ilese and Janny made little whistling sounds, and Kendra blushed furiously. Out in the hall, Kendra allowed the door to slide shut, and faced the Charity Eligible.

"What do you think of the extra girls?" Anthony asked.

"It is a bit of a surprise," Kendra said, "But then maybe we had gotten into too regular a routine around here."

"If I am meant to select one to replace Deborah, who do you think I should choose?" Anthony asked.

"That is up to you," Kendra said. "As we are not in an exclusive relationship at this stage, I don't think I should be giving an opinion."

"You must feel something," Anthony said.

"Oh I do, I assure you," Kendra replied. "But you cannot date other women and expect to please me at the same time."

"I am sorry," Anthony said.

"So am I," Kendra re-joined impatiently. "Stop trying to be a nice guy in this situation, and make a decision that is honest for you."

"So who should I pick then?" Anthony said. "Someone who will be fun and fit in with you girls, or someone who brings the element of contrast back into the group?"

"Pick the girl you like best," Kendra advised firmly. "Thank you for the concern for my feelings, but I am going back inside now."

The blondette turned with dignity and headed firmly back into the small reception room, resuming her seat beside Vonda.

Anthony turned to follow Kendra back inside, but he was waylaid by Leticia.

"Deliberation room time," the hostess said.

Anthony groaned. "Am I picking one new girl, or replacing several with wild-cards?" he asked anxiously.

"You keep the three veterans, as is only fair," Leticia instructed, "And choose one wild-card."

"Okay that's clear," Anthony said, obediently allowing himself to be shut away in the deliberation room. So Janny, Kendra and Vonda were all safe; and he only had to make a selection between Ilese, Betty and Heddy.

The Charity Eligible mentally assessed the situation in his head. Betty had been on the show for a few episodes already, and had been ousted because a relationship did not appear to be developing. It was a total surprise to have a second chance with Betty, and a few short weeks ago, he would have leapt at the opportunity.

However, as he had gotten to know the women on the show, the Charity Eligible had felt a slight shift in his dating priorities. He had learnt that physical attraction could occur in a number of cases, but that intellectual and personality compatibility were far rarer.

Ilese, on the other hand, was a very pretty girl whose potential remained completely unexplored. Anthony believed that he would enjoy spending time with her, and that she would also fit in well with the other girls. He was very much inclined to choose her, and probably would do so, if it were not for Heddy.

Heddy was something of a challenge. She was physically attractive, and while he was not sure what she did for a living - he thought she once told him she was a veterinarian - they seemed to connect well on the intellectual level. There was a combination of relationship potential and intellectual compatibility, that made Heddy an irresistible choice.

Anthony suspected that her independent and assertive nature would cause a few sparks to fly amongst the other girls. Still, they had all survived the dynamism of girls like Deborah and Alison, and he felt that energy was currently lacking from the group.

Leticia returned to the deliberation room and interrupted the Charity Eligible in his musings. "Are you ready?" the hostess asked.

Anthony jumped. "I guess so," he said. "It doesn't feel like a quarter-of-an-hour since you led me in here."

"It has been roughly that," Leticia assured him. "We have to keep the show moving, some of the Charity Eligibles wish to ponder their choices forever, and it doesn't seem to help them any in the long run."

"You may be right," Anthony said. "Tonight was a surprise. I haven't had any unknown qualities in the equation for a few rounds."

"Ah yes," Leticia said. "You had become very comfortable, but this should make interesting viewing."

Anthony and Leticia arrived at the small reception room and entered the door. Anthony dutifully crossed the room and took up his position behind the carnation table. He picked up the first flower. "Betty, may I talk to you?" he asked.

Betty came forward with a huge smile: "Hello again Anthony," she said.

"I am so thrilled that you were able to come back and spend some more time with me Betty," Anthony said. "I have enjoyed talking to you again, and it has eased me of the guilt I felt at sending you off crying."

Betty nodded understandingly, "Me too – but not guilt."

"You told me that you have been dating other men since then, and I think that is something you should continue doing," Anthony concluded.

Betty gave the Charity Eligible a warm kiss on the cheek. "I agree," she said. "It has helped me to find out that you really did like me, and were not just flattering me to get rid of me. I can move on quite happily."

Betty walked to the door and left the room with a sunny expression that was a positive improvement on her previous exit.

Leticia hurried after the beautiful woman and caught up with her in the corridor. "Here is a gift for returning," she said.

"Ooh thanks," Betty gushed, opening the envelope to find movie and dinner vouchers. "I did not really expect anything."

"We like to look after our guests," Leticia said happily.

Meanwhile, back in the small reception room, Anthony called out to Kendra. "Kinny, would you come here please?

Kendra approached and gave the Charity Eligible a discrete hug. Anthony gave her a socially acceptable kiss in return.

"This is a special moment for me," the Charity Eligible said. "I get to tell you that I really do enjoy spending time with you, and would like you to stay on the show with me."

"Certainly Anthony," Kendra said. "And thank you for making such a positive thing out of this ceremony." The pair exchanged a secret hand-squeeze, and Anthony handed Kendra a carnation. She returned to her place amongst the girls.

"Janny," Anthony said picking up another carnation. "I need to speak with you."

Janny bounced forward, an encouraging smile plastered on her face. "What is it Anthony?" she asked.

"I want to be sure you are happy here," the Charity Eligible said. "I was afraid last night with your dance performance that you were trying too hard to impress me. A relationship should be fun!"

"Oh I absolutely agree Anthony," Janny said. "And I want to have fun on our dates."

"Will you accept this carnation then?" Anthony asked, handing the ballerina her carnation. Through the corner of his eye he seemed to see Vonda and Kendra exchange subtle glances, but he could not be sure.

"Yes I will," Janny replied. Trying to assure herself mentally that she really did respect Anthony and her romantic interest was genuine, Janny gave the Charity Eligible a kiss and returned to her place in the line-up.

Anthony picked up the next flower and called to Vonda. "Vonda, I would like to talk to you."

Vonda came forward with a quiet degree of confidence that had developed gradually over the past weeks. "I would like to talk to you too Anthony," she said.

"What did you want to talk to me about?" Anthony asked. He was slowly getting used to the girls taking the initiative whenever they felt the need.

"I am very grateful for the time you have spent talking to me, and the special effort you have put into designing outings that came within the range of my interests or fulfilled my needs," Vonda said.

"It was my pleasure," Anthony replied. "I hope you will accept this carnation and continue to go out with me."

"I believe I would like to accept the carnation," Vonda said, "Except that I occasionally wonder whether we might be too much alike for an actual relationship."

"I would definitely like to explore the meaning of our similarity in personality," Anthony assured the musician. "I believe it is a basis for something - even if it turns out to be friendship."

"In that case I am happy to stay," Vonda said. She accepted the proffered carnation and stepped serenely back to her position between Kendra and Janny.

"Ilese," Anthony called. He was not holding a carnation, and the pretty blonde looked disappointed. However, she stepped forward brightly and shook the Charity Eligible by the hand.

"I really appreciate your coming back onto the show," Anthony said. "And I am very sorry to have to send you home for a second time."

"As you know, I had decided to put as positive an interpretation upon it as possible," Ilese said.

"But it is easier said than done isn't it?" Anthony murmured sympathetically.

"Yes it is," Ilese agreed. "However much I tell myself it is not a personal matter, there is the rejection factor."

"I believe Leticia might come to our rescue with some sort of consolation prize," Anthony said.

Ilese tried valiantly to smile: "Give me a hug," she said. Anthony hugged her, and then she passed on by the female contestants, who all gave her a kiss on the cheek, pat on the back or other form of reassurance. "I feel like royalty," were her final words as she approached the door.

"It is you and me then Heddy," Anthony announced when the farewells were over. "I hope you won't feel too awkward joining the group in the Candidate House at this late date," he added considerately.

Heddy laughed. "I am happy to have this opportunity to begin dating you," she said. "I remember my way around, and will soon find my place amongst the others."

Heddy moved into her former room that night, and became part of the household once again.

Janny went through her exercise routine as usual the next morning, despite the twinging of stiff muscles. In her years of experience as a dancer, stretching out and moving were the best cures for chronic stiffness and lactic acid build-up. Her subsequent attempt to swim laps was brave but very fatiguing, as she had to work hard against the resistance of her own body, as well as move through the water.

After a while Kendra and Vonda, who were used to the ballerina's early morning routine, appeared on the patio. The two contestants were both moaning and flexing muscles sore from the unaccustomed martial arts moves from a couple of days ago, so Janny suggested that they join her for a luxurious soak in the spa.

The three were laughing and chatting together when Heddy appeared, her glorious dark hair loose from the bundle in which she had restrained it the night before.

"Oh there you are," the newcomer exclaimed. "I went to the dining room, but no one was there."

"We often breakfast late in the kitchen," Vonda said.

"I see," Heddy observed. "You have made yourselves really at home around here."

"It was the best thing to do," Kendra said. "No good being lost and lonely and waiting around all the time for the Charity Eligible.

How did you sleep?"

"I slept really well thank you," Heddy replied.

Vonda broke in diplomatically. "The girls' club attitude is to reduce the stress and drama involved in us all dating the same man."

"Does it work?" Heddy inquired sceptically.

Janny shrugged. "For most of us, most of the time," she said.

"Is there something I should know?" Heddy asked sharply, glancing from woman to woman.

The long term contestants all appeared to communicate with their expressions. "Probably hundreds of things," Kendra said thoughtfully, "But we can't possibly try to fill you in on it all. You will just have to take us as you find us."

"Lucky I have a fairly independent nature," Heddy said confidently. "Now if you don't mind, I will join you in the spa."

"Sure," Vonda said, carefully making a space between herself and Kendra for the African Beauty.

"I don't think we were ever told what you do for a job," Janny said.

"Ah," Heddy said. "I am a vet."

"What sort of animals do you treat?" Kendra asked. "Horses and cows?"

"Dogs and small pets mainly," Heddy said. "I run something of an animal hospital."

"Do you do much animal rescue?" Kendra queried.

"Not really, because I have to make a living," Heddy exclaimed. "Animal rescue is more like charity work."

"I am sure we all have our needs," Vonda said peaceably. She hauled herself out of the spa: "I am going in to breakfast."

Heddy looked at Janny. "Do you want to go in to breakfast as well?" the African Australia woman asked.

Janny pasted a thoughtful expression on her face. "I might take something back to my room," she said.

Heddy looked vaguely offended. "Suit yourself," she said. "I am going to try and catch up with the others."

"It's not what you think," Janny began to say, but she found she was talking to empty air.

CHAPTER ELEVEN: PLAYING FOR KEEPS

Anthony found that he was very much looking forward to his date with Heddy. It was a first date once again, which reduced the pressure and increased the possibilities. When Anthony was with the other contestants, he felt that he had to find something new and even more impressive for the date activity, but with Heddy who had not been on previous televised dates, he felt that he could simply take her out to a meal.

Anthony greeted Heddy on the front steps of the Candidate House and escorted her to the car, marvelling how much his confidence with women had risen over the last few weeks. He opened the back door of the limousine and Heddy slid smoothly inside. Anthony followed the beauty into the car and instructed the driver to convey them to a selected Mexican restaurant for lunch.

"I hope you like spicy food," Anthony said cautiously.

"Absolutely love it!" Heddy exclaimed. "And those create-your-own taco stacks are divine."

"I thought that I was reading you correctly," Anthony observed, feeling pleased with himself.

"I'm a fiery girl alright," Heddy remarked, putting a slim hand on Anthony's leg just above the knee.

Anthony jumped, but then he forced himself to relax. None of the other girls had been this pushy in the physical department, but Heddy was obviously from a more demonstrative background.

"I don't know exactly what your touch means at this stage in our acquaintance," Anthony observed carefully.

Heddy had noticed Anthony's brief moment of confusion and hastened to reassure him. "It means that Heddy is all right with you boy," the African-Australian beauty said. "Nothin' more and nothin' less!"

"So you are a very literal person as well," Anthony remarked.

"I am a lot of things," Heddy said. "Mostly always determined to be true to myself."

Anthony was impressed. "I like a woman who knows what she wants," he said.

They had arrived at the restaurant, which was built of a mellow gold brick, and lined with green painted wood panelling. Hand-woven rugs hung against the wall, giving the place an exotic atmosphere with their bright geometric patterns. More woven blankets were thrown down on the floor, softening the hard surface of the orange-brown terracotta tiles.

Cacti had been planted beside the front door, and smaller cactus plants were scatted against the interior wall in earthen pots. Carved ornaments were attached to the wall in several places, and the large sombrero hat, which was the trademark of all things Mexican was displayed in a position of prominence.

"I love it," Heddy said viewing the tapestry.

"Yes," Anthony agreed, "The place is sort of provincial and comfortable".

The duo joined the queue for service, as the food had to be ordered at the counter. A few minutes later, they were seated at a rustic wooden bench and two huge plates of corn-chips topped with a personalised selection of beans, meat, and cheese were placed before them, together with a bowl of potato wedges, sour cream and sweet chili sauce. Two side salads were also delivered promptly.

"This is the life," Anthony said, dipping a piece of potato skin into the sour cream.

"Why yes," Heddy agreed. "I just love being able to eat with my fingers in a restaurant."

"I guess we should use forks when we tackle our main course," Anthony said.

Heddy laughed: "If we must," she said.

Warming to his companion, Anthony told a series of comical stories and jokes. Heddy laughed heartily, making the normally serious doctor feel like an expert comedian. This was very good for his confidence.

Outside on the deck a band struck up a tune, sending the raw notes of flamenco in through the window. Anthony and Heddy served themselves some coffee and ordered pistachio ice-cream, moving out onto the terrace, which was paved and shaded.

The guitarist continued to play in a casual manner, and a couple of people got up to dance the rhythmic and enticing pattern of the flamenco. None of them had the manner of professional entertainers, so Anthony had to conclude that they had run into some ethic group on a regular day out.

Heddy stood up, and with a natural sense of rhythm, began to sway and stamp to the music as well. What she lacked in authentic Hispanic attitude, she made up for in enthusiasm and sexiness. Anthony sat enjoying the view for as long as Heddy would allow, and then submitted to persuasion to step and stamp alongside the beautiful woman.

Anthony managed to step around with the folk dancers for about a quarter of an hour, and then he admitted to being hot and exhausted. "I have to stop now," the Charity Eligible cried to Heddy, "Can I get you a drink?"

"Yes sure," Heddy called. "Whatever you are having."

Anthony frowned, for this was the awkward moment when he usually had to explain to his dates that he did not drink much alcohol. "Are you sure?" he asked, "I am getting lemon squash."

"That sounds fine," Heddy replied. She had been busy dancing and had worked up a thirst.

Anthony returned with the drinks, and the couple shared a 'moment' clinking their glasses together. Then Anthony found himself a seat and Heddy returned to the dance, the rhythm and style of which she was beginning to pick up quite naturally.

Making sure that he would not be in the way of any dancer, the Charity Eligible stretched out his legs, and sat back feeling very pleased with himself. Heddy was the dynamic sort of girl whom he would have been afraid to ask out in normal circumstances. However, she seemed to have enjoyed his company today, and did not even mind the fact that he was not drinking alcohol, or dancing full-time with her.

"What you doing?" Heddy queried, swinging past Anthony, and the young doctor pulled himself out of his reverie.

"Admiring you," Anthony replied honestly.

Heddy laughed a flattered note: "I am almost ready to head off back to the house if you are," she said.

"I thought you were having fun," Anthony remarked.

"I was - and I am," Heddy replied. "But I like to move on too."

"I will call the car," Anthony said. A thought struck him: "Would you like to join the group date tomorrow?" he asked. "It is not usual, but as you have missed so many weeks, it seems like a reasonable thing to do."

"I would be delighted!' Heddy exclaimed.

The other girls, however, were far from thrilled when they heard that Heddy would be joining the next afternoon. While none of them were mean by nature, this transgressed their sense of fair-play. The group understood why Heddy had been assigned an individual date, but by house tradition, anyone who had an exclusive date missed the following group date.

"We have all done our share of waiting around," Janny said. She was looking especially glum, as the villainous Sam had apparently picked up his back pack and left, but had not got to the point of contacting her with the apology she desperately desired.

"I know," Kendra retorted. "I am more troubled than I like to admit."

"I am upset too," Vonda said. "It is not really in my nature to be mean - however I can't help thinking that Heddy had Anthony to herself yesterday."

Then Janny fixed a steady gaze upon Vonda and Kendra: "We all like Anthony, and I feel that with the arrival of an intruder, if we don't fight for him, we could lose him to the intruder."

"What can we do?" Vonda cried, throwing her hands symbolically in the air. "It is Anthony's television show."

"It is our show too," Janny remarked. "You have to think of something to do."

"Leave it to me," Kendra said looking gently determined. "I will come up with something."

"Well it had better be good, and it had better be quick," Janny said.

Despite the heat of the day, the young women found they were looking forward to the trip to Centennial Park. Anthony was greeted with kisses as Heddy appeared determined to make a lasting impression, and despite their introverted personalities, Vonda and Kendra were determined not to be outdone.

Janny was also moderately cheerful, because unknown to the others, her agent Sam had sent a text message to her mobile phone. The tone was self-righteous, but an optimist could construe the wording into containing a vague form of apology.

Upon arrival at the park, everyone piled out of the car. The girls exclaimed in delight at the expanse of grass and shady trees. A wide track appeared to run in a rough oval shape around the heart of the park, while side gardens contained tennis courts, barbeque equipment, ponds and the occasional ornamental garden. One other area seemed to be quite densely forested.

"You wouldn't expect this in the middle of the city," cried Vonda, and Kendra nodded in agreement.

Heddy, who had travelled extensively, remarked that there were pockets of vegetation preserved in the heart of many of the large cities of the world. "It is a good thing too," she observed. "People need to be able to get out for a walk - although it is a good idea to take a large dog along with you some places."

"I've heard something like that," Anthony said. He offered his arm to the closest of the girls. "Come along, Janny. Normally this place closes a little before sun-down, but the television station has made special arrangements for us to stay late and have tea watching the sunset."

"It sounds exciting," Kendra said, subtlety making sure she had Anthony's full attention. "What do we do until then?"

"If we go across to the kiosk, we will find some bikes have been hired for us," Anthony said.

"I am glad I am wearing long pants then," Janny said. "The last thing a dancer needs is a scraped knee."

"You can share my bike if you like," Anthony offered.

"What?" Janny looked puzzled.

"You will see," Anthony said in amused anticipation.

"You don't mean that they have bicycles built for two do you?" Vonda asked in excitement. "I thought they went out in the early nineteen-hundreds."

"Tandems are a novelty item," Anthony replied.

Heddy snorted, "I'm having my own bike," she said.

"That might well be necessary," Kendra said. "Janny can share with me, but unless they have a bicycle built for three, there are five of us and that makes an odd number."

"They do have bicycles that pull a small cart, but that might be too heavy for you girls," Anthony said.

"I like the idea of a tandem much better," Vonda said. "I have never tried anything like it."

They collected their bikes, and as Anthony had suggested, he climbed on one tandem bicycle with Janny on the rear. Kendra and Vonda chose a second double bicycle, and Heddy chose a single racing cycle.

The pairs on the double cycles started off gingerly, wobbling as they learnt to co-ordinate their balance and pedalling action. Heddy was completely comfortable with her standard cycle and began to show off, riding off far ahead and then circling back to jeer good naturedly at the tandem riders.

"That girl can be annoying," Janny said, dropping a hint to the Charity Eligible.

Anthony, however, was merely amused by the outgoing woman's antics. "She is very independent," he said, "It is part of her charm. Once we learn how to manage this thing we will have twice the power she has, then we will give her a race."

"I can't wait," Janny exclaimed through her teeth.

Vonda and Kendra could be seen meandering quietly down the track. They were having steering complications and their front wheel led them a few inches to the right, and then across to the left as the girls over-compensated. The ragged edges of a pot-hole arose in front of them, and Kendra angled around it to make sure that they did not drop into the depression.

"We are getting better at this," Vonda observed from the rear.

"It is quite an accomplishment," Kendra agreed.

Anthony and Janny drew up beside the other girls. "You two are doing well," Anthony called.

"So are you," Kendra cried.

"Excuse us passing you now," Anthony said. "We are going to race with Heddy."

Holding the handle-bar tightly, Anthony steered the tandem bike after the tail of Heddy's bike. He was setting a blistering pace and Janny had to pedal to the top of her capacity to keep up. They gathered momentum and drew even with Heddy.

"What ho!" Anthony called.

Heddy looked surprised, and attempted to pedal her bike even faster. Anthony pushed the nose of the double bike just beyond that of the single racer and maintained that speed for several minutes. Having made his point, he then settled into an even pace, for which Janny was extremely grateful.

Heddy ceased pedalling and dropped back to a glide, while Janny and Anthony sped on past. They finished a circuit of the park and stopped to await the others.

"You know I let you win," Heddy remarked, jumping off her bike and sidling up to Anthony.

"I don't really believe you," Anthony remarked appreciably, "But thanks for the thought."

"We let you win too," Vonda remarked attempting to match Heddy's easy charm with her own more understated humour.

Anthony laughed. "That I do believe," he said. "You were very good sports to have a go on the bikes."

"Especially as it was just us two girls," Kendra observed. "Janny had the more experienced biking partner."

"Flattery will get you everywhere," Anthony replied. He stooped and kissed Kendra on the cheek. "Come and help me put the bikes away."

After the bikes had been returned to the kiosk, the counter closed for the evening, and the shop staff went home. Anthony asked the limousine driver to unpack the hampers of food from the car. It was then they discovered that the main hamper had been left back at the Eligible Residence. This was the first major miscalculation in the entire series of dates, and Kendra assured Anthony that they would be able to make do for the evening meal.

Vonda, Kendra and Heddy opened the cool-box and began to take stock of the food stuff. There were several packets of potato crisps, a stick of salami, a block of cheese, pickled onions, orange juice and a lemon cheese cake. The girls cut the food up, but the spread was not sufficient when divided amongst five hungry people and everyone admitted to remaining hungry.

Anthony finally suggested that they employ the limousine to take them back to the Eligible Residence and collect the rest of the food. The girls all agreed happily, with Heddy especially hinting that she was keen to see the accommodation Anthony had been provided.

When the party arrived back at the Eligible Residence, they all piled out of the car. Janny and Heddy asked Anthony to give them a guided tour; while Kendra and Vonda went into the kitchen in search of the missing baskets of food. The hampers were quite easy to locate, as they were sitting in state upon the bench beside the refrigerator.

Kendra laughed: "Let us get unpacking the food," she said.

"Sure," Vonda said. "I think I remember where Anthony keeps the plates."

"All kitchens are about the same anyway," Kendra said, diving into the drawer beside the sink for the cutlery.

It was a mere few minute's work to set out the meal. Vonda decided to microwave the small pasties, although she and Kendra agreed that the savouries would have been perfectly nice cold, if eaten outdoors.

"Go and get the others," Kendra suggested as the last item was placed upon the table, and Vonda headed back into the living area, finding that Janny was sitting in the lounge alone. The ballerina looked extremely pleased to see Vonda.

"Is tea ready?" the dancer asked.

"Yes it is," Vonda replied.

Janny gave Vonda a meaningful look. "Heddy insisted on seeing Anthony's bedroom," the dancer whispered. "I wasn't comfortable going with them."

Vonda looked mildly shocked. "Kendra and I did not even see the master bedroom when we spent the afternoon here," she said.

Janny shrugged: "Heddy clearly does not believe in getting embarrassed about such things," she said. "She just dives straight in."

The sound of muted voices attracted the musician's attention, and she knocked upon the door leading to the bedroom. The wood moved under her fingers and Vonda pushed the door open. The first thing Vonda noticed was the Charity Eligible and Heddy standing side by side, talking intensely and almost touching each other.

"The food is in the kitchen," Vonda called, looking firmly across the room at Anthony.

"Oh good," Anthony said, taking Heddy by the hand and drawing her out of the inner room.

Vonda noticed that Anthony adroitly let go of the veterinarian's palm as they approached the kitchen and hove into Kendra's line of sight. He had the somewhat guilty manner of a man who has been caught out two-timing a girlfriend.

Heddy however greeted Kendra confidently: "Thank you so much for preparing the meal. You did a great job, both here and back in the park."

Kendra threw Anthony and Heddy a shrewd glance. It was obvious that the Anthony was divided in his loyalty between the old and new contestants.

"I'm here when you need me," the Artist said mildly.

Janny clucked at Kendra in frustration: "You need to up the ante," she remarked.

"Err what?" Anthony asked in perplexity.

"Later," Kendra said cheerfully, helping herself to a nice serve of salad and savoury spinach roll. "All will be revealed in time."

The meal progressed smoothly, with everyone soon becoming comfortably satisfied by the additional food. The girls pitched in as a group and helped Anthony clear the table and wash the dishes. Then there was a mass migration into the lounge room.

Anthony looked uncertain at this point. "What do you ladies want to do now?" he asked. "Should I call the limousine to take you home, or what?"

Kendra brushed her arm against Anthony comfortably. "I seem to remember seeing a pack of cards," she murmured. "I thought we could have a little game."

"I think everything is here somewhere," Anthony said. He crossed to the wall and reached back into the main bookcase. "Ah yes, there are cards and whatever here."

Kendra shuffled the cards and dealt out four cards to each person, including herself. "Does everyone know how to play *Guts?*" she asked.

"I haven't heard of that one," Vonda said, "Someone will have to help me."

"I will do that," Anthony volunteered, returning his cards to the pack and squeezing his chair closer to that of the musician. "Which variation Kendra?"

"I was thinking four cards and a draw," Kendra suggested.

"I play like a professional gambler," Heddy announced confidently. The veterinarian faced Kendra challengingly: "Why don't we play for a kiss from Anthony?"

"Let's raise the stakes," Kendra suggested. "The winner gets to spend the night here in the Eligible Residence with Anthony, while the others go home in the limousine."

"Would you really be prepared to go through with that?" Anthony asked in surprise.

"Oh yes!" Kendra said firmly, and taking their cue from her, Vonda and Janny nodded seriously. After all, there was more than one way to interpret 'spending the night' at the Eligible Residence.

Not to be outdone, Heddy put out her hand: "Shake on it," she demanded.

"It is a deal then," Kendra declared. "For those of you who haven't played before, we look at our cards and they remain held in the air."

"Goodness," Vonda exclaimed. "Anthony, what should I do?"

"Look at your cards," Anthony said. "Check what values you have and decide whether you think they would win."

"Are the highest cards the best?" Vonda whispered.

"Generally," Anthony replied. "Here let me see."

"Now the dealer (that was me) calls out 'guts' and you either drop your cards, or continue to hold onto them if you think you have a winning combination," Kendra said.

"What happens next?" Janny asked. "I'm not like our old friends Gabby or Deborah who were good at all games!"

"Then we can choose to draw an even number of cards before revealing our hands," Kendra said.

Vonda made her decision and picked up two cards from the pile. The game then moved on to Janny, who also chose to draw two and viewed the new cards thoughtfully. Heddy completed her turn with a straight face, and then Kendra calmly declined to draw any cards because she was happy with her hand.

At the end of the round, because no one had dropped their cards, everyone was required to reveal their cards. Predictably enough, Vonda had the lowest score and dropped out of the competition. The musician announced that she would spectate comfortably from then on.

It was Janny's turn to deal the cards, and also shout "guts" next. Predictably none of the girls dropped their cards, but continued staring at each other defiantly. The veterinarian picked up another two cards, cheerfully keeping her face blank.

Kendra also picked up two more, then she surveyed her hand solemnly before settling back into her seat. Janny looked at her starting cards and gulped. The dancer then picked up four new cards. Her face brightened considerably.

The round finished, all three ladies placed their cards upon the table. Janny had an ace, a three, a pair of sixes, a seven, jack, ten and nine. This provided a moderately good score, but not sufficient to keep her in the game as Kendra had a four, two jacks, two tens and an ace; while Heddy had two aces, a pair of nines, a king, and a seven.

"Two doubles definitely beat one double," Heddy announced. "Janny is out."

"Who won out of Kendra and Heddy?' Vonda asked curiously.

"Heddy I think," Anthony said. "She had the aces."

"But aren't tens and jacks higher than nines?" Vonda asked.

"It doesn't matter," Anthony said. "I declare that the aces carry the day."

The game commenced again, with only Kendra and Heddy playing. Heddy was now the dealer and the person to call "guts." Kendra surveyed her cards carefully and decided to hold; Heddy also considered her cards and held. Then Kendra and Heddy both drew two more cards. The girls gazed sternly at each other across the top of the cards.

"Are you sure you don't want to just cancel the bet?" Heddy asked jubilantly.

"I am very sure," Kendra replied calmly.

"I am a very good player," Heddy pronounced.

"I believe you," Kendra agreed serenely.

"I sort of win either way," Anthony said, "But I must admit I am becoming curious regarding the outcome."

"Okay," Heddy said, laying her cards open upon the table. "Beat that if you can Kendra. Two queens!" Everyone gasped as Heddy had two queens, a five, two threes, and a jack.

"Oh no," Vonda murmured. "I think your plan might have backfired Kendra."

Kendra was now smiling. The artist laid her cards down upon the table top and there were three kings, two nines and an ace. "Three of a kind," she said, "Beats the other combination."

"Are you sure?" Janny was perplexed.

"I think she is right," Anthony said admiringly.

"Yeah she is right," Heddy conceded grudgingly. "But I don't know how she did it!"

"Easy," Kendra said, "I had two brothers and we played a lot at home."

"I give up," Heddy said. "You have outfoxed me." The veterinarian looked across at the artist with mild annoyance and growing respect. "Till our next encounter then!"

True to the terms of the bet, Anthony called for the limousine and Heddy, Vonda and Janny all piled inside. The car drove off and headed towards the Candidate House.

Anthony turned to Kendra: "Well you have got me," he said. "Do you want to see the master bedroom now?"

Kendra looked amused. "I would love to see the master bedroom," she said. "Although I did catch a glimpse of a very nice sofa in the private sitting room."

Anthony looked slightly disappointed: "I thought you might share the bed," he said.

"I might even for a little while," Kendra said, kissing the Charity Eligible affectionately, "But I mostly wanted the other girls to know I stayed overnight with you."

"So you plan to stake your territory and yet keep me longing for your body?" Anthony asked.

"That's right," Kendra whispered into his neck. "Heddy has been making a little too bold for my taste. I just want to make it clear."

"Aw, Kinny," Anthony whispered. "You know that if you really gave yourself to me, I would be unable to look at Heddy."

"I will be ready when I am ready," Kendra said. She leant against him and the heat spread between their bodies. The temptation was becoming difficult to resist, but a girl who gave in could be left broken hearted at the end. "And that is not likely to be while we are on the show. I cannot run that risk !"

"Because although I am the prize of this television show, you are determined to be the one that is difficult to capture?" Anthony laughed.

"Something like that," Kendra agreed. "I am so glad you understand...."

"Let us watch a movie then," Anthony said. "There is a big television screen mounted on the wall in the lounge."

The couple collected some nibbles from the basket in the kitchen and settled down to enjoy each other's company in a comfortable fashion. The rest we will leave to the imagination, suffice to say they exchanged a few passionate kisses, but Kendra allowed nothing to be caught on camera that might embarrass her when the show screened on television.

Moreover, when it came time for bed, Anthony informed Kendra that she deserved better than the sofa, and showed her into the lushly appointed spare bedroom.

CHAPTER TWELVE: THE FIRECRACKER

Normally after an escapade, the contestants were obliged to sneak back into the Candidate House. However, when Anthony dropped Kendra home about ten o'clock the next morning, she made a feature of their fond farewell. The point of the exercise after all had been to be known to have spent the night, thus setting minds working and tongues wagging.

Leticia, who had been watching the public display of affection, met Kendra just inside the front door. "I hope you are prepared for the consequences of what you have done," the hostess demanded earnestly.

Kendra laughed merrily. "Of course I am," she said. "But what exactly have I done? Other than kept one of your cameramen up all night trying to capture some indiscretion?"

"The show does not take any responsibility in the case of you having regrets," Leticia warned. "We protect the girls against rape, but we cannot protect them against their own choices."

"View the footage," Kendra ordered calmly. "You will see I slept safely in the spare room."

Leticia sighed. "Kendra you are usually the sensible one," she said. "Even if you did not sleep with Anthony, and somehow have the sympathy of the long-term contestants, you risked making an enemy of the new girl."

"I thought that was the general idea when you allowed the wildcard intruders back into the house," Kendra declared. "There was no way they would blend in the same as girls who have been here two months already."

"Well, so long as you are prepared for any fall-out," Leticia murmured retreating to her office. She had dealt with contestants who were determined to win their man on the show before, and who were prepared to do almost anything to make it happen, but never one with Kendra's quiet dignity and resolve.

Kendra continued on into the house and to her room, where she went straight to bed and slept throughout the remainder of the morning. Anthony and the Artist had talked late into the night, so she had gotten very little actual sleep. Moreover the second bedroom, to which she had retreated for discretions' sake, had not felt one hundred percent like home.

The remaining three women amused themselves the best they could until lunch. Janny and Vonda were curious and longing to gossip with their friend, while Heddy was silently fuming, knowing that she had been cleverly outplayed, and the other three were in alliance against her.

Anthony arrived at the Candidate House around noon looking somewhat self-conscious. While it was mildly amusing to pretend that he had scored with Kendra the previous evening, he was also concerned about the feelings of the others, especially the sensitive Vonda.

Seeking out each girl individually, the Charity Eligible attempted to assure them that although he did have warm feelings for Kendra, he was able to value each of them in their own special way. He was relieved to find that Janny and Vonda were still talking to him.

"Kendra was carrying the flag for all of us originals," Janny said with a shrug. "It is sweet of you to be concerned however, but we formed an alliance of sorts."

"I promise you, Kendra and I did not 'sleep' together," Anthony said. "Kendra wouldn't allow that on the show, and certainly not in front of the cameras."

"I am sure you could not resist making-out however," Vonda observed shrewdly.

Anthony blushed: "I don't know what to say."

"Don't try to deny it," Janny said. "And please stop apologising because you are beginning to sound just like a sheik arguing that he should be allowed to keep a harem."

"Do I really?" Anthony asked, somewhat perturbed. "It is not the way I see myself."

"I expect you think you are just doing your 'job' in terms of the television show Anthony," Vonda returned gently. "However I think every man has something of the philanderer in them, given enough opportunity."

"The opportunity to play the field without hurting anyone may be a universal dream," Anthony admitted. "But it is very far from reality in most cases. What will it take for you girls to forgive me?"

"I want to go to an exotic coffee shop and be shouted the most authentic Turkish coffee and gourmet pizza," Janny replied.

"Pizza?" Anthony was intrigued.

"I get really hungry when I am practicing dance," Janny admitted. "Nothing else fills me quickly enough."

"Pizza sounds good," Vonda agreed. "Let's do it soon."

Anthony crossed the lounge room to admire the Christmas tree, which had been set up in acknowledgement of the coming festive season. There was a selection of parcels under the tree, but no one could work out whether they were real presents, or merely ornamentally wrapped boxes.

Heddy, who had been avoiding the other two to some extent, entered the room and slid into position beside him: "I love summer," she said. "It is the season for the sun and endless parties."

"I am usually too busy with my work to enjoy it," Anthony said. "You would be surprised how many people fall ill over Christmas."

"That is a pity," Heddy said. "Anthony my man, I have been meaning to talk to you about something; I did appreciate your including me in the group date yesterday - but it seemed to stir some resentment with the other girls."

"How so?" Anthony inquired. He had a fair idea, but he wanted to know how the African Australian beauty saw things.

"On reflection, I would say the privilege back-fired on me," Heddy observed. "The other girls have ganged up against me."

"I am sorry about that," Anthony said.

"What I really want to know is whether I am still in the running," Heddy said. "If your mind is really made up about Kendra, there is no point my going on dates with you!"

"I AM interested in you Heddy," Anthony replied. "It is just different with Kendra because I have known her for longer."

"As long as you can honestly assure me that the final selection has not already been made," Heddy said. "I don't see why I should waste my effort if you have already chosen someone."

Anthony nodded. "I promise," he said, "The books are still open. I am getting to know everyone properly before making my choice."

"Well in that case, you should know that you are standing right underneath the mistletoe, boy," the Veterinarian observed.

"Am I?" Anthony exclaimed, trying to look completely innocent.

"You most certainly are," Heddy declared. She adopted a mischievous expression: "That means I have to kiss you."

"Oh do you really?" Anthony asked, flushing in embarrassment. He half expected the assertive girl to envelope him in a passionate embrace to publically incite jealousy amongst the other girls, but she contented herself with a brief peck on the cheek.

They were interrupted by Vonda. "Is this a private party," the musician asked. "Or can anyone join in?"

"You can join in by all means," Anthony said somewhat artlessly.

Heddy chortled, but Vonda looked only faintly amused. "Public affection isn't really my scene," the musician said.

"I can imagine," Heddy remarked sardonically.

"You have come out of your shell a lot so far," Anthony remarked pleasantly.

"Not to this extent," Vonda said firmly. "I overheard you two talking, and I have to say Heddy, that if it comes to an all-out competition for Anthony's affections, I will be out. I like my courtships peaceful."

"So do I," Anthony said. "Please be brave Vonda."

"This is me being brave," Vonda said. "I will not fight with the other girls over a man. I expect a man to show me he likes me."

The Charity Eligible leant forwards and kissed Vonda on the cheek: "Is that better?" he asked.

It was Vonda's turn to blush: "Much better," she stammered. "But I still mean what I said Anthony."

"I think we had better move away from under the mistletoe before Janny decides to join in as well," Heddy remarked in amusement. Privately Heddy thought that Vonda was embarrassed too easily, and if the musician was deterred by a little competition, that was all to Heddy's advantage.

Just then Kendra entered the room, and the tone of everything altered. Anthony pushed his way to Kendra's side and began the new and contradictory task of demonstrating himself to be still attentive after an intimate evening. Kendra accepted his protestations with good grace during the meal.

When desert was finished, Kendra turned to the Charity Eligible and invited him around to the pool for a swim. The party waited the regulation half an hour for their food to digest, and then began to frolic around in the water.

It was a warm afternoon, and the water was beautifully refreshing. The exercise released the majority of the tensions within the group, and Kendra found herself swimming around with Heddy as if they were good friends.

"This is nice, isn't it?" The Artist said, hauling herself up onto the side ledge of the pool.

"It certainly is pleasant," Heddy agreed. "So this is what you girls do when you are not actively chasing Anthony."

"Ah yes," Vonda said, "We have developed something of a team spirit."

"I still don't see myself fitting exactly," Heddy remarked. "Me and my friends, we have a very distinct style."

"So I have noticed," Kendra said. Heddy glanced at the Artist, but she apparently was not being sarcastic.

"Look at Janny," Vonda said, pointing across the pool to where Janny and the Charity Eligible were playing a sexy form of water tag. "She seems to be right back in the competition."

"Janny knows how to secure a guy's attention," Kendra observed. "But do you know whether she still hears from that Sam fellow?"

"I think so," Vonda said. "Her mobile phone keeps making little beeps. She says he is organising more work for her."

Heddy looked puzzled: "What is the deal with Janny and this Sam?" she asked.

"He is supposed to be her theatrical agent," Kendra replied, "But he does seem too controlling. I sent him away because he slapped her the night of the talent show."

"Did he really?" Vonda had not seen the slap, although she had been involved in the talent show.

"Sounds like a louse," Heddy observed. "I'm surprised she would speak to him again after that."

"It seems complicated," Kendra said. "We wonder whether Sam is interested in managing more than her career."

"We don't know for sure," Vonda said, "But we do not like the guy... now you know our biggest house secret. I trust you will keep it quiet."

"You got my word babes," Heddy said. "Just so long as it seems good for all concerned."

Leticia appeared just then with a box of interesting looking objects. Seeing the arrival of something unusual, Anthony and Janny swam across to the side of the pool to investigate.

"What are those?" Anthony exclaimed.

"Fireworks," the Hostess explained. "I thought you could have your own private showing this evening."

"Is that legal during a fire ban?" Vonda asked.

"I think so," Leticia said. "I have applied for special licenses and we have all the right extinguishing equipment."

"I am sure it is okay," Heddy said. "After all - the state government arranges a display on New Year's Eve."

"What are we celebrating?" Vonda asked. "It's a little late for Guy Fawkes."

"Diwali is sort of finished too," Kendra observed.

"What about Hanukkah – for Deborah?" Anthony suggested. "I think she was something like an eighth Jewish."

"Oh yes, Hanukkah for Deborah!" Janny exclaimed. "What a great idea."

Even Heddy, who had only briefly met the whirlwind that was Deborah, agreed that the house should celebrate Hanukkah in her honour.

"You will have to take some basic safety precautions," Leticia warned. "Step well away from the house, but do not go into the trees. Also make sure that spectators are all well clear."

"We will be good," Janny said. "Thank you so much Leticia."

"I am going to set the first one off," declared Heddy, but Kendra was already beside the box and reading the instructions on the wrapper.

"Let Kinny do it," Anthony said.

"It seems like Kendra gets to make all the fireworks around here!" the Veterinarian grumbled.

Janny and Vonda both laughed. "You do your bit too," Vonda said, archly.

"But I wouldn't be the first," Heddy complained.

"Are you sure you are still talking about the fireworks?" Janny inquired provocatively.

Kendra set a rocket up in a safe space out on the patio and ignited the fuse. Then she stepped back out of the way. A few seconds later, the cracker leapt into the air, showering the surrounding area with coloured sparks. It hovered for a few minutes before arcing across the garden.

"Cool," Anthony said.

"It is my turn now," Heddy announced, pushing her way forward. Kendra stepped aside and Heddy selected a mid-sized cartwheel from the box. The veterinarian set it up in a cleared area and it spun beautifully, sending sparks around in a coloured circle.

"This is fun," Janny said. "Can I set up a pair of rockets?"

"It should be okay, so long as you get well away from them," Anthony said. He selected a fine pair and handed them to Janny. The dancer put the two novelty crackers on their stands a few feet apart, and lit the fuse for the first one. A slight wind ruffled the second rocket and it tilted upon its stand.

"Get back out of there," Heddy called, for a spark from the first cracker had blown across to the second one.

Janny darted out to safety and the group admired the first rocket as it took off. The second rocket should have launched in close succession, but it toppled off its stand and hit the dirt.

"Don't go near it," Anthony said, laying a restraining hand upon Janny's arm.

A handful of dry leaves blew toward the grounded rocket and were in turn combusted. A mini-fire appeared in the yard as every twig and leaf in the vicinity appeared to catch alight.

Anthony was going to rush forward and smother the blaze with one of the pool-side blankets, but Vonda caught hold of the wall mounted extinguisher and pulled the implement off its hook. All would have been well, except that a final piece of rocket managed to launch itself, and a small shard embedded itself into the palm of her right hand.

Vonda began to scream in fright, and Kendra hauled her to safety.

The security staff appeared from their usual discrete positions to exhaust the flame, but they were a fraction too late as the damage had already been done. The guards then began to remove all sources of danger from the back yard and instructed the contestants to move inside.

Heddy ran inside to the phone and called for the ambulance, while Anthony turned to Vonda to attempt first aid. There was little the Charity Eligible could do for Vonda, other than cool the area under running water and protect her against shock, for a splinter of metal was embedded in her palm.

"I do not dare pull it out, until we get to the hospital," Anthony remarked, and Janny gave the surgeon a look that implied he was exceedingly cruel.

Kendra stepped into the breach: "He is right," she said. "That is exactly what I was taught last time I did first aid."

Vonda was accompanied in the ambulance by Kendra and Anthony, while the others waited around the Candidate House in a state of extreme anxiety. Leticia and the security staff checked the patio and garden for any other traces of fire and assessed the damage to the property.

The camera crew divided into two, with Simon Steeple following Vondra to the hospital. George and the rest of the crew remained in the mansion, and continued filming Heddy and Janny with ghoulish intensity, until Leticia told them to consider they had documented the event quite sufficiently.

Anthony and Kendra returned with the news that Vonda was being kept in the hospital for a few days, while the burns were healing and the need for surgery was being assessed. Everybody was very concerned, because as a musician Vonda required the full flexibility of her hand, and made daily use of her fine motor skills.

"I feel so awful," Anthony said. "This could be the end of her career."

"It is not your fault," Kendra said, putting her arm around the Charity Eligible.

"No it is mine!" a distraught Janny cried. "I set up the double rocket formation."

"It was just one of those things," Heddy said, attempting to comfort Janny. "Vonda was so brave, going forward with the fire extinguisher, but she was also fool-hardy. It would have been better to leave the fire to the security staff, they are trained for this sort of thing!"

"It doesn't help to blame anyone," Anthony said.

"I like to think Vonda will recover the full use of her hand," Kendra said. "The burns did not seem very deep and the shard of metal was very small."

"Kendra is right you know," Anthony said. "My physiotherapist friend told me much the same thing."

"Let us all go to bed now," Janny said. "We will be able to visit Vonda in the morning won't we?"

"I expect so," Anthony said. "I will arrange it with Leticia."

Anthony went home to the Eligible Residence, and Janny went to her bedroom. Kendra, who had maintained her cool for the sake of the others, collapsed in tears. It was up to Heddy, perhaps the most practical of the group and the least affected due to the shortness of her acquaintance with the victim; to comfort the artist and tuck her away in bed for the night.

Morning dawned and a black-eyed Kendra rose for an early attempt at eating breakfast. Janny had also slept lightly and dragged herself into the kitchen for coffee and company. The energetic Heddy appeared a few minutes later and joined the festival of anxiety.

"What time do you think the hospital will let us visit?" Janny demanded for the fourth time.

"Nine or ten at the earliest," Kendra replied.

"Are you sure we cannot get in earlier?" Janny inquired. "I did not get to see her last night."

"There wasn't much to see last night, except for the doctors and nurses wheeling Vonda away and admitting her," Kendra said.

"I am sure Anthony will be here to pick us up at the earliest possible moment," Heddy said.

"Are you coming too?" Kendra asked. "You don't know Vonda so well."

"Of course I am coming," Heddy said. "I don't like to see anyone injured, either human or animal."

"I really appreciated what you did last night," Kendra murmured.

"You are welcome," Heddy replied. "I am happy to be a friend in a crisis. This doesn't mean that the war is off in regard to winning Anthony though... girlfriend."

"Of course," Kendra remarked. "Everything has it's time and place. I had better go and have my shower now."

"Me too," Janny said, "In the other bathroom of course."
"I will be ready soon after you," Heddy assured them.

Anthony arrived in a more modest hire car than the usual limousine. "I thought this would be less conspicuous for a hospital visit," the Charity Eligible explained. "Besides, our numbers are down, so we fit all fit into one car now."
"I had not thought of that," Janny exclaimed.
Kendra began to look sad all over again. "I will miss Vonda so," she said.
"I am hoping she will agree to stay on the show," Anthony said. He was carrying a huge bouquet of flowers, with a prominent inclusion of pink carnations.
"I don't see how that would work exactly," Heddy said. "Vonda is surely going to need more treatment."
"Last night was going to be an elimination wasn't it?' Janny cried. "After the fireworks and everything, we would have gone to the small reception room."
"I think that was the plan," Anthony remarked.
"So one of us shouldn't be here," Janny observed. "If everything had gone to plan, someone would have gone home."
"I guess so," Heddy was thoughtful. "I wonder who it would have been. Probably me, because I am the newcomer."
"I actually had not made up my mind," Anthony said. "Half the time I do not know what I am going to say until I actually call you girls to receive your carnation."
The car arrived at the hospital and dropped the party at the front entrance, while the driver made his way around the back to find a parking space. The hospital had a cream brick facade, although some wards appeared to be of a different architectural generation than others. Utilitarian glass doors and single framed windows ran along the wall at relatively regular intervals.
"I wonder where Vonda is," Heddy said, and led the way to the reception desk to inquire as to the ward number. It was a good thing that they did check in with the nursing staff, because as it turned out, the musician had been relocated to a room on the second floor.
Kendra and Janny reached the entrance of Vonda's room together, and greeted the patient with effusions of affectionate sympathy. Vonda was propped up in bed with her hand swathed in a

large bandage.

"Thank you so much for coming," the Musician said. "The doctors are still not sure how much scar tissue will be left around the burn, but they are hoping for the best."

"I just hope you can play again," Janny exclaimed. "I would absolutely hate being unable to dance."

"Oh I am determined to play again," Vonda declared. "Even if it involves some rest, followed by physiotherapy."

"It is such a set-back," Kendra said. "I would be distraught to lose a few months of my painting time."

"I will miss the next concert series for sure," Vonda said. "Luckily I can still compose, in fact, I may concentrate upon that for a while."

Heddy and Anthony entered the room and Anthony handed Vonda the bouquet of flowers. Heddy presented her with a box of chocolates gathered hastily from the gift shop on the ground floor beside the cafeteria.

"Are these all for me?" Vonda exclaimed.

"Of course," Anthony said, stooping and giving the musician a discrete kiss on the cheek.

"A lot of these flowers are carnations," Vonda said coyly. She tilted her face towards Anthony: "Might you be trying to tell me something?"

"Yes certainly," Anthony said, dropping to one knee beside the bed. "I want you to find a way to stay on the show and continue dating me."

"That is so sweet," Vonda exclaimed. "Thank you so much Anthony... I just do not see how it would work!"

"We would have to allow you to have all your medical treatment of course," Anthony said. "As a doctor I know how important that would be."

Vonda looked very serious. "I have been doing some thinking," she said, "And I have come to the conclusion that you and I are just too alike for a romantic relationship. To be honest, I have been considering leaving ever since Heddy arrived. Nothing personal Heddy, but I am not up for another battle to win Anthony's heart."

Anthony looked disappointed. He had really liked Vonda, it was only her exclusive personality which had prevented him from pursuing their relationship further.

"I am sorry to hear that," he said, continuing to kneel down beside the bed. He took both of her hands in his and fixed her with his most appealing expression. "Vonda," he begged. "Is there any way I can change your mind?"

Vonda suddenly looked frightened. "Anthony," she said firmly: "I want you to stop right now. I like you, but I really want us to stay good friends, and that is that! Please don't make a fuss."

Anthony looked confused by her intensity. "This is not going the way it is meant to," he said.

"Why are you so surprised?" Vonda said. "This is the twenty-first century, and while most women are looking for love, they do have minds of their own. Now that I have learnt to come out of my shell, I am confident that I will find the love of my life eventually."

"I am sorry," Anthony said. "I feel like a fool here, trying so hard to persuade you in front of the others - and being turned down like an old boot."

"Here," Vonda said. "Take three carnations out of my bouquet and give to the other ladies. I would like to be present at my last carnation ceremony."

"Are you absolutely sure?" Anthony asked reluctantly.

Vonda leant forward and pulled a carnation out of the floral arrangement. "Heddy," she said, "I would like you to continue getting to know Anthony - with all my blessing!"

"Thank you Vonda," Heddy said. "With Anthony's co-operation, I will." The veterinarian threw a sideways glance at the Charity Eligible, who looked somewhat like a sulky child at that moment.

The camera crew had their equipment whirring at full power, as this simple hospital visit had turned into a most unusual form of drama.

Vonda picked up a second carnation. "Anthony," she said. "I want you to give this to Kendra."

Anthony reluctantly accepted the carnation. "Kendra," he said. "Vonda would like you to keep dating me."

"I am pleased to oblige Vonda," Kendra said with a laugh.

Vonda picked out a third carnation. "Now Anthony," she ordered. "I want you to give this to Janny, with all my best wishes."

"Vonda wants you to have good luck," Anthony said, passing the flower along. "She also hopes you will go out with me some more."

"Thank you Vonda," Janny said. She leant over the sick-bed and gave the other girl a huge hug. "I will do my best."

"That will have to be good enough for me," Vonda said. She leant back against the pillows. "Thank you all for coming. I am getting sleepy now from all the medications, and I would like to take a nap."

"We won't keep you awake any longer then," Kendra remarked affectionately. "I trust that the television station has notified your family?"

"Yes," Vonda replied. "I expect my father to fly in from Adelaide this afternoon."

"We will remove this television crew from your room then and let you have some peace," Anthony said. "I am sorry they insisted in coming along."

"Don't be," Vonda said sleepily. "I had fun - even at the end. I never in a million years expected to take control of a carnation ceremony like that! It might not have been quite worth a hurt hand, but I am glad I met you all." The musician laid her head back on the pillow and closed her eyes. The rest of the party exited the hospital room as quietly as they could.

"I am glad I met her too," Heddy whispered. "Even for such a short while."

Kendra and Janny were crying: "We will miss her so much," they sniffed.

"So will I," said Anthony. He still had three beautiful girls to date, but he would always have fond memories of Vonda. She would eternally be 'the one that got away'.

CHAPTER THIRTEEN: THREE'S A CROWD

Anthony parked the car in the driveway of the Candidate House and viewed the women sympathetically. They had all had a shock, and while it appeared Vonda would be alright, the previous evening had not been without cost.

"Janny," Anthony said carefully. "I am wondering whether you feel able to go on a date with me. There was a date scheduled for this afternoon."

"I don't know," Janny said cautiously. "It is the last thing on my mind at the moment."

"If I cannot take you," Anthony said, "I will have to take Heddy out again, and that would hardly be fair as she has had the most recent individual date."

Behind Anthony's back, Heddy pulled a face. "Fair" wasn't a word she would use regarding *The Charity Dating Show!* A scenario involving one man and a number of women pretty much ruled "fair" out. However, Anthony appeared to be applying his own form of integrity.

"I understand," Janny said. The dancer looked at Kendra: "Will you be alright if I go?" she asked. "I can miss Vonda anywhere, but Anthony would be with me, and you would be all alone."

"I will be okay," Kendra said bravely. "I will have Heddy for company and she was a great help last night."

"Are you sure?" Anthony inquired, for he too was genuinely concerned about Kendra.

"I really will look after Kendra for you boy," Heddy remarked. She gave Kendra a quick hug. "Kendra is the only girl I know who would choose my company over the company of a fellow."

Kendra laughed. "It is only one day Heddy!" she said, "I'm not exactly giving up the competition."

"That is settled then," Anthony said. "You girls go and have a quick lunch, then Janny and I will be off."

"You could eat with us too and save a bit of driving around," Kendra suggested, and Anthony looked pleased.

"Thanks," he said. "It would be easier than driving across to the Eligible Residence and then back here again to pick up Janny."

"And it will give us all those few more minutes to calm down," Heddy said. "I will go and tell the housekeeper you are here."

They had a simple but pleasant lunch, during which everyone regained their composure and began to talk more hopefully about Vonda making a full recovery. In the long run, it was likely that the musician's main loss would be a single season of concerts, and Anthony suggested that she might be compensated by the development of her composition skills.

At the end of the meal, Janny disappeared into the bedroom area to change into suitable casual clothes for a date, and Anthony amused himself by watching an afternoon soap opera with Heddy and Kendra. Not being a fan of day-time television, the surgeon soon expressed himself amazed at the characterisation and mystified by the convolutions of the plot. In fact, the way a bevy of frustrated women appeared to be fighting over one main male character made him squirm uncomfortably. It seemed just a little too reminiscent of *The Charity Dating Show*!

However, Anthony acknowledged that the drama was doing its job of keeping the girls' minds off their worries. He leaned back and closed his eyes for a few minutes, but opened them eagerly when a rustling sound told him Janny had emerged ready for their date.

Anthony drove Janny past the city and out south-west to Thirlmere, a regional centre situated in that direction. There the couple boarded a steam train which was run especially for the amusement of tourists. This was not a regular service, but a novelty trip which was staged on weekends and public holidays.

The passengers were shown the inside of the driver's compartment before the trip commenced. Climbing up the small ladder one by one, small groups were allowed to cluster around the engine as the engineer explained the controls and steam mechanism. Anthony listened with interest, as he did to anything scientific, but Janny climbed out of the driver's chamber after a perfunctory glance around.

A young woman with long red hair observed the dancer and smiled: "The men love anything mechanical don't they?" she remarked. "I am Tyna, by the way."

"Some do," Janny agreed. "I have actually known a few who don't. They were into the Arts and all that."

"Were they gay?" the Tyna inquired.

Janny shrugged. "No, not all of them," she replied non-committedly.

Tyna glanced around. "And who are all these other people?" she asked, "You appear to have quite an escort."

It was an awkward moment for someone required to maintain a certain amount of confidentiality until the Charity Eligible show had aired on television. "We are making a video," Janny hedged cautiously.

"Cool," Tyna cooed. She struck a pose and fluffed up her hair: "What sort of video is it?"

"Err... um... reality... documentary..." Janny desperately attempted to make eye contact with Anthony, who was climbing down out of the steam train engine.

The Charity Eligible observed Janny, and walked over to rescue her with a few well-chosen words. The gossipy Tyna was hard to discourage, however, and insisted on being introduced and hanging onto Anthony as if she believed he was a film star of some sort. Her young male companion joined the group and proved nearly as eager to talk. In the end, the conductor had to usher them all onto the train, and into different compartments.

"Phew!' Janny said. "That is our first real encounter with the public since coming on the show."

"Now that it has happened," Anthony remarked, "I can't help wondering why we weren't interrupted on our other dates."

"Some venues were booked especially," Janny observed.

"That must have helped immensely." Anthony said. "And other places had so many other activities that we were not so noticeable."

"Everyone is different," Janny said. "Some people will discretely get out of the line of a camera."

"Obviously not those two," Anthony commented. "They were determined to be on the show."

"They were young," Janny said comfortably.

"I wonder whether they will be edited out," Anthony mused.

"It might depend whether the camera crew found them amusing," Janny observed. "They must be on the lookout for bits of drama."

The train had been restored to some extent, but most of the historical features were intact and the seats were quite shabby. Janny frowned and dusted one chair off before sitting down. Anthony struggled with the ancient window sash in an attempt to secure it at a comfortable point for ventilation. Once the train was in motion, the passenger compartment became quite chilly, and the Charity Eligible had to adjust several nearby windows to control the air-flow.

Clanking and whistling, the train sped through the country-side and the pair admired the view. Trees and bushes seemed much more visible than they did from a modern electric train, with its tinted windows and multi-level compartments.

"This is real train travel," Anthony commented. "I can imagine people steaming across the countryside in the early days."

"We seem to be going very fast," Janny observed. "I would have expected an old train to go slow."

"Apparently steam is very powerful," Anthony replied. "The steam train that ran across from Adelaide to Perth could make some amazing speeds."

"Interesting," Janny said. "Is there a dining car at all? I wouldn't mind a cool drink."

"I think one might have been built in," Anthony said. He took Janny by the hand and they threaded their way through the carriages single file, being especially careful with the narrow platform forming the connection between carriages.

The dining car was a pleasant place where old fashioned fittings were mixed with modern refrigerated counters and cappuccino machines. Anthony ordered some sandwiches, while Janny selected a salad and fresh squeezed orange juice. The juice was thick and fleshy and almost blocked the straw, but it was clearly the genuine article. The sandwiches were soft bread with a delicate blend of fillings.

"This is pretty good for fast food," Anthony remarked, sipping the milk-shake he had ordered.

Janny laughed: "I guess they make something special for the tourists," she said.

"How are you going with your salad?" Anthony asked. "Would you like me to order some cake?"

"Err... no thanks," Janny said after a minute's hesitation. "It could affect my fitness to dance."

Anthony looked perturbed. The doctor in him did not like fad-dieting. "Surely you could manage a little sweet stuff," he objected. "How about some fruit? You had ice-cream when we were out before."

"That really was before," Janny said. "I am trying to get back into practice now."

"From what I saw the other day - you were never out of practice," Anthony said. He frowned: "Has something changed? Have you suddenly decided to leave the show?"

"No - nothing like that," Janny said firmly. "Everything is fine. Well to be honest - Sam reminded me I needed more practice."

"If you mean that stage technician fellow," Anthony said, "I actually thought he was a bit hard on you."

Janny sighed. "Sam is not just a technician," she said. "He is more like a manager."

"Well whatever," Anthony said. "I didn't really like him."

"The girls said that too," Janny admitted, "But Sam does know his business."

Janny was suddenly afraid she had said too much. Whatever had possessed her to bring Sam's name up in the middle of a date! The petite blonde slid out of her seat and walked around to Anthony's side of the booth, sliding into the seat beside him.

"I love being with you," the dancer breathed softly, holding her mouth up for a kiss.

Anthony accepted the invitation gently, reflecting that Janny seemed very sweet and submissive that day. "Love is a strong word," he breathed, "And not one I ever expected to hear from you."

"I didn't mean it in a complicated way," Janny whispered, looking into the eyes of the Charity Eligible. He appeared steadfast and comforting to a girl who had known recent rejection and exploitation. "I could say I enjoy being with you - if you prefer."

"Nevertheless, the romantic element was there," Anthony said, tightening his arm around the woman. "I don't understand you Janny. You can be a tease, but you are also a born flirt."

"Relax and enjoy the moment," Janny ordered. The dining car was relatively empty and the dancer figured few people could see the area under the table, so she slid a hand up her companion's leg. Anthony jumped, but he allowed the hand to progress.

Janny began to kiss Anthony, and he continued to return her kiss for some five minutes. It was one of the most sensual moments of romance that had occurred on this particular series of *The Charity Dating Show*, and the camera crew zoomed in as far as they could without being intrusive. Anthony found his head was reeling, and it was Janny who pulled herself out of his arms at last.

"I must go to the ladies' toilet," Janny said. She rose and made her way carefully through the dining car to the little built-in cubicle. Although it was cleaned regularly, the train toilet was unpleasant as such places are; and Janny stepped back into the main carriage with pleasure, and sat down in a nearby booth to recover her equilibrium.

The mobile phone tucked discretely at her side began to vibrate, and Janny unwrapped it to discover the message was from Sam.

"I have something great for you after *The Charity Dating Show*," the agent texted.

"What is it?" Janny messaged.

"Ballet company work - the best," Sam texted back quickly.

"I am glad to hear it," Janny messaged. "I never wanted my career to suffer because we disagreed."

"I wouldn't have let that happen babe," Sam messaged in reply. "You still want me to keep you on the books don't you?"

Janny thought guiltily of kissing Anthony a few minutes ago and then shrugged. Flirting with an agent was often a necessary evil in the dance industry. "I'm thinking about it," she texted. "If you behave yourself."

"Anything you say babe," Sam replied smoothly by text.

Janny squinted at the message and put aside any niggling doubts. She would have liked more assurance, but it obviously shamed the agent to admit he had lost his cool.

"I know you will look after me," she responded. "Take care."

"You too babe," Sam messaged, and then he was gone.

Janny put her mobile phone back on her belt and wended her way back to where she had left Anthony. He had risen and was walking down the carriage to meet her.

"You were back there for a while," the Charity Eligible said. "I began to think you might be ill."

"I had to rest," Janny jumped at the excuse. "The train was swaying a lot."

"It is a rickety old machine," Anthony agreed pleasantly.

The couple wended their way back through the carriages, Anthony assisting Janny with the doors at the narrow joins between the carriages once again. "Imagine this on a cold wet day," Anthony said.

"I should think one would stay home during winter in the olden days," Janny commented. "Light the kitchen fire, and tend to the farm animals."

"I guess people only travelled when they had to then," Anthony mused.

"Unless they were itinerant," Janny remarked. "I have heard it took a long time for some of the settlers to acquire their own land."

"The same applies nowadays," Anthony observed wryly. "I had to finish my internship before I could afford a mortgage, and some of my friends are still saving."

The television couple reached their assigned seats and settled down to continue their conversation in comfort. They were deep in dialogue when Janny's mobile telephone began to vibrate once again. Janny wriggled nervously and tried to ignore the disruption.

Anthony immediately noticed the dancer's gesture of discomfort. "What is wrong Janny?" he asked.

"Oh it's just my mobile phone," Janny admitted reluctantly.

"What are you doing bringing a mobile on a date?" Anthony asked incredulously. "I made sure that I left my pager at home. I would not want to encourage the hospital to chase me while I was on leave."

"Maybe I should do that," Janny agreed in an easy fashion. It was a reasonable point of view, and one with which the dancer wished she could coincide. In reality the girl could not bear to feel that she was out of range of contact with her trouble-some agent. "Please do not report me to Leticia."

"Check and see who it is," Anthony suggested.

Janny made a show of detaching her phone and checking her messages. "Just work," she said cautiously.

"Well, tell them that you won't be available for another couple of weeks," Anthony suggested. "Whoever it is should know better than to be contacting you while you are still on this show."

"I can't do that," Janny said awkwardly. "A good agent is quite hard to acquire, and once they begin to manage a career, the performer doesn't... er, dare offend them."

The dancer began to stammer and went bright red with guilt and embarrassment. Anthony observed Janny closely. "If I hadn't just been kissing you myself, I would suspect this was a boyfriend and not an agent," he concluded at last.

"Please don't go there," Janny whispered helplessly. "The past is the past."

"I agree absolutely," Anthony declared. "Well, so long as it really is in the past. I would be offended if I found you were playing a double game with me."

"When we were on the ranch I said I would have to tell you a few things," Janny whispered through frozen lips.

"I remember," Anthony agreed. "What did you want to tell me?"

"I said I had to work some things out," Janny said sullenly. "One of those things involved my agent. You have even met him once."

"Do you mean that Sam fellow?" Anthony demanded.
Janny nodded helplessly.

"He was introduced to me as your stage technician," Anthony said firmly. "Then today you said manager - now he is your agent? It seems you have both been lying to me by not telling me the full story."

"Truly, I had not spoken to him in many weeks," Janny cried. "Then when he found out where I was, he followed me back to the Candidate House without my permission."

"Why didn't you just tell him to get lost?" Anthony demanded.

"Like I said, an artist doesn't dare offend a good agent. The agents control the flow of work through the industry," Janny explained patiently. "Can we please forget about it and appreciate the rest of the outing?" she pleaded.

"There is not much else we can do," Anthony remarked shortly. "We are on camera and I have not had any time to consider matters. Besides, if I put pressure on you, I would be almost as bad as I saw Sam being towards you."

"Thank you," Janny said. "Thank you so much!"

The afternoon passed quickly enough, with a scenic hike at the end of the line, and a return train trip to the western edge of Sydney. Evening was approaching as Anthony drove Janny back to the Candidate House, and the atmosphere in the car was tense. Anthony was surprised at how affronted he felt regarding Janny's confession. He swung between feeling protective towards the dancer and jealous of his rival.

"I will call you later," Anthony said, and Janny nodded miserably. She understood that the Charity Eligible was not making her a promise, but demanding an eventual time of accounting.

Janny entered the Candidate House in a subdued fashion, hoping to retire to the solitude of her room. Not far into the hall however, the dancer found her way blocked by Heddy, who was looking casually inquisitive.

"Please get out of my way," Janny mumbled numbly.

Heddy jumped at the defensive tone. "What is wrong?" the self-possessed girl asked. "Your date not go so well?"

"That is none of your business," Janny returned shortly. The little blonde was in no mood for teasing, whether good natured or with a competitive edge. "Kindly let me pass."

"Not until you tell me how things went," Heddy retorted, somehow feeling puzzled and affronted. "I know what sort of rival Kendra is, but you are a puzzle. I am not sure what you are up to."

Janny laughed hysterically: "As a matter of fact, Anthony is extremely attracted to me," she cried. "However, you have no place asking me about anything I don't want to discuss. I don't care how much we are sharing a house and appearing on a television show together."

"Give Janny a break," ordered Kendra, rounding a corner and joining the cluster in the hallway. The graphic artist had turned pale at hearing mention of Anthony's attraction to Janny, but she was determined to be fair to her long-term companion. She turned to Janny: "Are you all right my dear?"

"Nothing really happened Kinny," Janny assured Kendra anxiously. "Anthony just found out that Sam has been messaging me about work. And he suspects Sam is more than an agent to me."

Heddy whistled. "How did he take that one?" she asked.

"He accused me of lying to him, and said he would be offended if it were still going on," Janny said. "So there!"

"I see," Kendra said thoughtfully. "You sorta walked into that one by introducing Anthony to Sam under false pretences."

"I know," Janny said. "I am absolutely miserable."

"It is up to you," Kendra said. "I think that you need to be honest if you are going to continue on the show."

"I don't know whether it is really worth it," Janny replied despondently. "I feel like going somewhere very quiet to sort my head out."

"Whatever you do - don't let Sam know where you are," Kendra advised sharply.

"I tried not to let him know I was here," Janny said unhappily. "It is very when hard someone controls your career like he has."

Kendra laid a hand upon the dancer's arm. "I understand how difficult it must be," she whispered. "What are you going to do?"

"I don't exactly know," Janny whispered unhappily. "I think I need to get a new agent, but I cannot organise that from in here." The petite blonde dodged around the area where Kendra and Heddy were standing, and made a run for her room.

"Poor girl," Kendra said soberly. The artist faced Heddy squarely: "It was mean of you to tease her."

"I didn't know that she couldn't take it," Heddy replied. "I haven't known any of you for very long, and I don't know all of your secrets. I am not a bad person you know."

"I know you are not a bad person," Kendra replied equitably. "It is just a competitive thing us females tend to do around men."

Heddy grinned with relief: "Talking about competition," she said "It looks like it is you and me now girlfriend! Starting from tomorrow, I'm going to do my best to charm the pants right off Anthony."

"I would prefer Anthony kept his pants on," Kendra replied firmly. "Around both you and me, and you had better not forget it."

"How boring," Heddy mocked. "No wonder Leticia felt I was needed back on the show!"

"I give you permission to do your worst then," Kendra announced. "That way if Anthony comes back to me in the end, I will know that he is truly mine!"

The Artist looked Heddy up and down, noting the long limbs and perfectly proportioned body. The long curly black hair was also very eye-catching. Heddy returned the gaze, assessing Kendra for her warm and comfortable demeanour, hourglass waist and slightly more curvaceous bosom. Both women were both very attractive in their own way.

"You have got yourself a deal, but you may not get the bloke," Heddy assured her rival.

"I'll live," Kendra said seriously.

The two women shook hands before heading into the dining room for their supper. The challenge had been thrown and accepted; with some serious emotional competition about to occur.

CHAPTER FOURTEEN: GIRL VERSUS GIRL

The next morning, Kendra and Heddy both dressed themselves in trendy casual gear, and eyed each other warily. It was one thing to throw out a challenge, and quite another to act upon it. The two girls could not be more different from each other in looks, motivation and temperament. Hence while they were in competition with each other for Anthony's attention, they were also both playing exceedingly different games.

Kendra was of medium height, with an hour-glass figure that bordered upon the voluptuous, her skin was moderately fair and her hair was that deep shade of honey-blonde that bordered upon light brown. The graphic artist was placid by nature, and had only recently become motivated into assertive action by the blossoming of her love for the Charity Eligible.

Heddy, on the other hand, was outgoing and confident. Her family and friends would tell you that she valued open speech to the point of bluntness, and she saw no reason to take anything but a direct approach to winning Anthony's heart. The veterinarian had dark skin and curly black hair, together with the height and willowy figure of a natural model, and she was motivated by a sense of entitlement to attention. She was also rendered somewhat anxious by a sense of the limited time she had available on the show.

"I don't understand why Janny puts up with that Sam guy," Heddy remarked by way of conversation at breakfast. It was the nearest thing the lively girl would make to an admission that she may have spoken a little too sharply the previous evening.

Kendra accepted the comment in the spirit in which it was offered. "It doesn't make a lot of sense to me either," she admitted. "I asked Sam to leave the Candidate House after he hit her. I sincerely wish that had been the end of him."

"I haven't met him," Heddy murmured, "But from what you said, I get the impression he was controlling in the extreme. No one should control a girl, either at home or work!"

"You obviously have a strong sense of your own worth," Kendra remarked.

"Doesn't everyone?" Heddy was genuinely surprised.

"It takes some people longer than others to build that level of confidence, and artistic careers instill some insecurity," Kendra observed diplomatically. "However, I do believe that everyone ultimately has the chance to realise their potential."

"You are an optimist girl!" Heddy observed. She didn't make it sound like a compliment.

"Aren't you?" Kendra asked in surprise. "You always seem very up-beat".

Heddy shrugged. "I don't think you could call me an optimist exactly, Kendra girl," she said. "I do not look for the positive in everything. If I see something I want - I go after it. I guess you could call me a pragmatist."

"I didn't understand you at first, but I am beginning to now," Kendra said. She laughed, "I thought today was going to be all about war, and here we are gossiping like old friends!"

"I am sure I will give you more than a few minutes worry throughout the day," Heddy remarked sunnily.

"I am sure you will too," Kendra replied practically. "And I am not so much an optimist as to stand back and merely hope for the best."

"I don't expect you to," Heddy said. "If I end up winning Anthony off you, I want it to have been a fair pitched battle. It shouldn't be too hard - Anthony still has a hungry sort of look despite all his dates with you girls."

Kendra shrugged. "I'm not even going to try to explain the psychology behind keeping Anthony hungry for one of us," she said with mock resignation.

Heddy merely scoffed. "Forget your psychology," she announced boldly. "People are basically animals ruled by biology!"

Anthony interrupted this charming conversation by the simple act of knocking at the front door of the Candidate House. Both women rushed to be the first to open the security screen and fixed their gazes intently upon the Charity Eligible; Kendra's look was soft and tender, while Heddy's expression was bright and alluring.

Anthony glanced from one to the other: "You both look lovely," he said. He had the uneasy feeling that something might be afoot.

"So do you boy," Heddy chortled. "Just delicious!"

"It is nice to see you again as always," Kendra said.

"Thank you girls," Anthony blushed. Heddy's flirtatious tone made him feel like he was something to eat; while Kendra's quiet confidence appeared to be designed claim long a long term connection.

"Are you two up to something?" he asked suspiciously.

"Just looking forward to a date with you boy," Heddy explained. She and Kendra exchanged meaningful glances. "Although..."

"We both feel we would like some alone time with you on this date," Kendra said. "To help you decide which of us you like best."

"Perhaps we could treat this as two mini-dates," Heddy purred enticingly.

"I'm sure something can be organised," Anthony said amiably. He opened the limousine door and they all three piled into the back seat, Kendra was on the right side, Heddy on the left, and Anthony was in the middle.

The fit in the back seat was relatively snug, and the ladies made the most of it by each allowing their leg to rest alongside that of their male companion. Heddy squirmed and made a feature of her physical proximity, while Kendra remained relaxed, emphasising her comfortable familiarity with the Charity Eligible.

Anthony began to blush at being the subject of their joint attentions. For a moment or two, the Charity Eligible wondered which way to look, and then he decided that the safest strategy would be absolute passivity.

"Aren't you ladies going to ask me where we are going?" he asked lazily.

"I am sure it will be somewhere really exciting," Heddy gushed, fluttering her eyelashes and playing the game for all she was worth. "Our other date was a hot Mexican one."

Kendra, who had the knack of seeing through any form of artifice, merely looked amused. "I assume you will tell us at some stage Anthony," she said.

"We are driving north at any rate," Heddy observed, looking through the car window.

"That is for sure," Kendra agreed. "Unless of course, the driver is disobeying his instructions."

Anthony laughed. "You are far too clever for me," he said. "I suppose I will have to tell you. We are going to visit the Gosford Reptile Reserve."

Heddy, who had been hoping for something more exotic, looked disappointed: "That could be something of a working holiday for me," she said. "I have ordered the odd bit of anti-venom from there. Cats and dogs get bitten by snakes too, you know."

"It was services like that made me think you would be interested," Anthony returned. "They have something of a tourist set-up as well as the laboratories.""

"I haven't been there actually," Heddy admitted. She did a quick turn-about in attitude and patted the Charity Eligible's knee encouragingly: "Thank you for thinking about me Antony."

Kendra however, shuddered. "I am sure it is a very nice set-up," the artist murmured, "But I am not fond of creepy crawly things."

Anthony looked surprised. "You didn't turn a hair when we went hiking and caving," he exclaimed.

"We didn't really see any snakes," Kendra explained.

"I am sure the snakes are securely housed at the Reptile Park," Anthony said. "I am keen to see it myself for reasons of medical curiosity. They have a lot of native animals as well as reptiles, you know! And then we will have our lunch somewhere nice, just for you Kinny."

Kendra sighed. "I will try to be interested because you are," she said.

"I am sure that Heddy and I will have a lot of questions for the ranger," Anthony said. "Then we will concentrate on having fun."

Heddy had frowned at the sense of cooperative understanding that existed between Anthony and Kendra; but a triumphant smirk appeared upon her face when Anthony bracketed their two names together. Kendra noticed, but wisely did not comment.

The car had been making excellent time. Once free of the city, it had to maneuver some backed up traffic on the free-way, but then the driver launched into the full legal speed and the wheels rapidly consumed the kilometres. The salon then eased out onto the exit track and drove up the approach to the Reptile Park, where the high walls and large front gate implied the presence of an impressive facility.

"This is where you get out," the driver announced, and the contestants climbed out of the car.

Heddy looped her arm securely through Anthony's arm, while Kendra gently placed her hand in his. Heddy pulled Anthony forward, while Kendra set a more sedate pace. Anthony hovered in the middle, an uneasy link in a human chain.

"Come on girls," Anthony exclaimed after a few steps. "We are all going in the same direction!"

Heddy tossed her head provocatively: "I am keen to explore," she said. "Aren't you Anthony?"

"Of course," Anthony said, "But what about you Kendra?"

"I'm all right," Kendra said. "Just taking things a little slower and enjoying the journey."

"Well you have had more time," Heddy remarked pointedly. "I need to work fast to make up for my disadvantage."

"Now you are talking at each other over me," Anthony remarked in mild exasperation, "And I don't think it is all about the Reptile Park – is it girls?"

Heddy looked innocent: "Why whatever do you mean Anthony?"

Anthony sighed. It was unrealistic to expect everything to go smoothly when he was dating several girls at the same time, but he could dream. And so far, he had been incredibly lucky.

"Welcome to the Reptile Reserve," the ranger who was to be their guide said, extending a hand in greeting. "My name is Oliver."

The party shook hands all around, while Oliver explained the purpose of the park. Like a zoo, it was designed to preserve the natural species, and educate the public. The Reptile Park served several other functions, including giving sanctuary to creatures that were on the endangered and protected list, and providing medical science with a source of anti-venom for potentially lethal bites. Moreover it functioned as a research facility.

Anthony and Heddy, who already knew most of these facts, still managed to look incredibly interested. Kendra, to whom the love of things reptilian was new, appeared reassured by the guide's obviously responsible approach to the management of the wild creatures.

Then Oliver led Anthony, Kendra and Heddy in the main gate, through the paved area and up to a large statue of a dinosaur.

The camera crew followed in close pursuit.

"Fantastic!" Anthony exclaimed as every scientific fibre in his mind began to glow. There was an immense satisfaction to be found in expanding his work-related biology and knowledge of pathology with comparative investigation.

"The figure is built to scale and filled out according to information gleaned from fossil remains," Oliver explained. "At one stage we had a whole host of these, but the rest of the display has moved on to other sites."

"I am glad you have one figure left," Kendra said. "It is quite impressive, standing all on its own." The artist whipped out her pad and began making some sketches.

Oliver then offered to show the party through the educational section of the facility. "We are lucky enough to have some bones on loan from the National Museum," he said.

"That would be great,' Anthony said, and was soon absorbed in talk of times and places millions of years distant, the area of history and evolution where science fact meets science fiction.

Kendra had kept her notebook out, and was making sketches mimicking the way in which a fragment of bone was translated into a water colour sketch by the artist commissioned to reconstruct an impression of the entire animal.

Heddy, sighed impatiently. Her interest as a veterinarian was in live animals, and she had less time for speculative creatures she would never have to treat in the surgery.

Oliver noticed her impatience and decided that it was time to move on with the planned tour. He called to Kendra, giving her a promise that there would be free time for her to continue sketching whatever she wished at the end of the afternoon.

Kendra somewhat reluctantly packed her notebook away, and followed the other two into the terrarium area. The first thing that met the artist's eye was a large red and black snake curled up in a glass case that appeared far too small for it.

The snake seemed perfectly comfortable, but Kendra shivered. The reptile would only need to be stirred into anger by an unwise tap on the glass, and it would thrash until it reached freedom. "That's what I don't like," the artist murmured to herself.

Oliver, who was obviously confident that the solid glass was adequate and that no unpleasant incident would occur, continued into the room.

"Come along my dear," he said. "Nothing in here will hurt you."

Kendra glanced at Anthony, who now surged ahead with Heddy. Sleek and snake-like herself, Heddy had moved in with grace and cunning. One hand rested lightly upon the sleeve of Anthony's casual jacket, and the other gestured casually towards the cases, as the dark beauty monopolised his attention.

The situation continued thus for some few minutes. No matter how hard Kendra tried to make general conversation and show an interest in the reptiles, she found herself out-classed by in-depth discussion of kingdom and phylum, and all the intricacies of taxonomy, of which she was largely ignorant. The guide moved onto explanations of poison, ante-venom and disease, to which both Heddy and Anthony listened with rapt attention.

Kendra shivered. While she appreciated the value of venom collection and the various treatment facilities, she was plagued by nightmarish visions of victims stranded far from telephones and help. A large spider moved its legs as the artist dutifully peered into the terrarium, and she drew back quickly.

Glancing through an open door, Kendra espied a courtyard surrounding a large stone walled enclosure. She burst out of the indoor area and into the blessed fresh air. While the central enclosure of snakes could be viewed by peering through a glass window, at least the creatures had a moderate amount of space to themselves, and some rocky areas interspersed with vegetation in which to hide. The black and brown snakes appeared quite peaceful sunning themselves on a rocky out-crop.

Kendra was pleased, and pointed this out to Oliver as the more ideal living situation for the animals. Oliver smiled and agreed, and there were a few welcome minutes respite as the party viewed the outdoor reptile areas.

Oliver then led the group into a laboratory, and while the area was clean and white, the conversation once again became purely scientific. Kendra could understand small snippets, and was mildly interested by the methodology by which these medical services were created and established for the good of man-kind, however the details were too complex for her.

Having observed Kendra's previous discomfort, Oliver attempted to couch his explanations in every-day language, which would have been a great help if Heddy had not kept deliberately steering the talk back into the area of terminology and acronym. The artist sighed and resigned herself to a few more minutes of polite boredom.

Despite his intention to remain sociable to both girls, Anthony barely noticed his lapses into technical debate with Heddy. In his mind, he was merely leaning over the displays and investigating the cages. In the process of doing this, he had somehow brushed up against Heddy, and completely lost contact with Kendra.

Heddy reacted coyly, making clear her enjoyment of both the conversation and the physical proximity of the Charity Eligible. Finally Kendra became disgusted with her companions and retreated into the visitor area in search of more relaxing surroundings.

Heddy eyed Anthony sultrily. She had never been one to bother about niceties such as good manners towards a rival.

"I think that Kendra went to the cafe," the beauty whispered.

Anthony looked around guiltily for Kendra.

"She will be all right, don't worry about her. We can take a walk down by the lake," Heddy said, glancing suggestively out of the window.

Anthony did not want the gentle and trusting Kendra to suffer because he had a special moment or two with the African-Australian beauty. Kendra however, was nowhere to be seen, and Anthony remembered what she had said about each girl wanting some alone time with him.

"We could too," Anthony said. "Just a little stroll."

"Come on then," Heddy said, taking Anthony by the hand. They walked hand in hand out of the laboratory, along the pebbled path and down to the edge of a large dam which had been landscaped to look like a lake. "Can't you just feel summer in the air?"

"It is beautiful," Anthony said, conscious that the day was sunny and peaceful, birds were singing in the trees and flowers had been planted at intervals along the path. There was even a fresh breeze which fanned their hair and prevented the day from being too hot.

Locating a warm patch of grass near the water's edge, and in the shade of a convenient tree, Heddy sat down and pulled Anthony to a reclining position beside her. The Charity Eligible found that the proximity of the beautiful woman, whose vivacious attitude reminded him vaguely of his ex-fiancé, went quickly to his head.

"Tell me about yourself boy," Heddy murmured. "Have you had many girlfriends?"

Anthony relaxed and allowed Heddy to touch him, barely noticing when her hands became possessive as they rested upon his back.

"I was engaged once," he murmured. "It didn't work out."

"Do I remind you of her?" Heddy inquired.

"Err yes," Anthony admitted, "Somewhat."

"In what way?" Heddy was not one to give up easily.

"You are both bright and out-going, stunningly beautiful and capable of demanding a man's full attention," Anthony replied.

"Interesting," Heddy mused. "It doesn't sound like a very strong similarity."

"You are not physically alike," Anthony said. "The similarities between you and Angelique are superficial. A mannerism here and there."

The doctor also knew that he was now fully qualified, the hero of a television show, and much more of an object of interest to women than he had been in his days of drudgery as a medical intern. The intoxicating thought ran through his mind that he did not have to settle for a temperate woman like Kendra, who was merely a comfortable fit.

"But the similarities are what have you thinking now," Heddy said. "Am I not right?" The veterinarian slid her hand down to his waist and began to unbuckle his belt.

"I go for what I want," Heddy whispered.

"I have no doubt of it," Anthony said. Her fingers tickled his stomach and he squirmed.

Heddy had finished with his belt buckle and her hand brushed against dangerous territory. Anthony jumped. They hadn't even started kissing yet.

"What are you doing?" he asked in confusion.

"Just checking whether you are interested," Heddy said. "I had a bet with Kendra that I could get you out of your pants!"

"Kendra's not like that," Anthony was mildly shocked.

"No, but I am," Heddy chuckled.

Anthony caught Heddy's hand in his and held it captive well away from his trousers.

"Of course I am interested," he whispered. "A man would have to be made of stone to resist you – especially with your bold – take what you want attitude."

"So kiss me then," Heddy whispered.

Anthony bent his head obediently and gave the African-Australian beauty an exploratory kiss. However, he was careful to keep hold of her hands. "How was that?"

"It was a start," Heddy said. "You might need some more practice boy!"

"Another time," Anthony said. He rose to his feet, buckling his belt and straightening his shirt. "I think we should go to the cafeteria, find Kendra and have our lunch."

"Good idea," Heddy said. She was supremely confident in her own attraction, and very little perturbed by the incident.

Anthony and Heddy walked back to the visitor area and approached the cafeteria. Kendra was not to be found inside, but they glimpsed her out in the garden petting a baby kangaroo, for the Gosford Reptile Reserve had a number of other Australian animals in residence.

"Look at that," Heddy said laughingly. "You bring Kendra to a reptile reserve and research facility, and what does she do? Ignore the main attraction and pat a furry creature!"

"Actually, I think it is rather sweet," Anthony said. He glanced at Heddy warily, suddenly noticing her strident tone. His ex-fiancé had a tough streak amongst her many attractions, and as the quieter partner, he had occasionally felt the rough side of her tongue. What if the similarities were not merely superficial? The Charity Eligible reflected that he could do without collecting another broken heart.

"Hey over here," Heddy yelled, and Kendra looked up.

However the artist refused to move, and the kangaroo continued to eat out of her hand.

"We had better go to her," Anthony remarked, "Tread gently".

Heddy snorted: "The 'roo will be all-right," she said. "They get pretty tame."

The young kangaroo did fidget as they approached, but the animal settled down when Kendra waved some more pellets in front of its nose. Anthony and Heddy both had a turn stroking along the creature's head and back.

"It's a male," Heddy said. "They develop very powerful hind legs - you wouldn't want to challenge it once it was grown."

"I am sure that it will always be treated well in here," Kendra murmured.

"I am sure it will too," Heddy said. She was obviously losing interest: "Let us wash our hands and get some lunch at the cafe."

"Okay," Kendra said, giving the kangaroo one last pellet of food in recognition of its generosity in lending her a few moments of bright company, and transforming an otherwise dull day into something more enjoyable.

The trio had a hearty meal of vegetable lasagna, curry puffs, chips and salad. They finished off with a selection of delectable cakes and fresh fruit juice. Heddy ordered a strong coffee, while Kendra was happy with soft drink.

After lunch, Kendra turned to Anthony and Heddy. "You two had your alone time earlier," she said. "How about my mini-date?"

"Would you like to go for a little stroll now," Anthony inquired.

On the way out of the cafeteria, they passed a souvenir shop, where Kendra exclaimed over some Aboriginal art and craft-works, finally selecting a woven bag to take home as a memento of the trip.

"I am sorry we are not more comfortable together as a group," Anthony said.

Kendra shrugged: "I am trying to think of it as a positive thing," she said. "When two women are interested in the same man, there is bound to be discomfort."

"And are you still interested?" Anthony asked with mild anxiety. He was aware that a budding relationship such as he had with Kendra required some maintenance. "I haven't been able to give you a lot of attention today. I wouldn't be surprised if you gave up on me."

"There are some limits..." Kendra said, "But yes, I am still interested."

"By the way, did you really make a bet with Heddy that she could take my pants off?" Anthony asked quietly.

Kendra laughed. "It wasn't meant literally!" the artist said. "Did she try anything?"

"She err – unbuckled my belt," Anthony said. "I thought I'd better let you know before she did."

"That was sort of cheating," Kendra said. "If there was any talk about that sort of thing... I had assumed you would disrobe voluntarily... or not at all!"

"Yeah," Anthony said. "It would have been nice to be consulted."

"Still, I'm a little upset Heddy found an opportunity," Kendra admitted.

"Heddy reminds me of my ex-fiancé Angelique," Anthony confessed. "You know - the lure of unfinished business and everything. We were talking about past relationships and I was vulnerable at that moment."

"That's dangerous," Kendra murmured.

"Angie always said she found me lacking," Anthony explained. "I was working and studying, so she was bored."

"It sounds as though you two were not meant to be," Kendra observed, and Anthony nodded. The pair lapsed into silence, for Kendra was naturally accepting by nature; and Anthony was happy to limit the degree of psychological analysis placed upon him in one day. Anthony also felt guilty for kissing Heddy, so he bought Kendra a plush dingo toy as compensation for his behaviour.

After Kendra and Anthony had finished looking through the gift shop, they returned to the cafeteria where they had left Heddy. The African-Australian beauty was sitting with Oliver talking animatedly and their laughter drifted across the room.

"Hey you two," Heddy called when she saw her companions. "Did you know that you can adopt an animal here?"

"No I didn't," Anthony said, looking intrigued.

"Does it have to be a reptile?" Kendra asked reluctantly.

"No, it can be a mammal," Oliver said. "Even sometimes a bird!"

"I rather fancy a snake," Heddy said.

Kendra shuddered. "No, please make it a mammal," she begged.

"I'm not sure that we get to choose," Anthony said. "The Reptile Park might assign the animal to us."

Oliver nodded. "You can indicate your preference, but the final decision will be based on animal availability."

Anthony, Heddy and Kendra filled out the papers and a quick call to Leticia secured approval to use funds for a basic level animal adoption. They put all three names on the one form, as parents of the assigned animal.

"Now all we have to do is wait till we hear about our allocated animal," Heddy said. She looked pleased, as she secretly hoped they would get a reptile, and then Kendra might lose interest. The veterinarian leant cheekily against Anthony in the car as the engine started and promptly fell asleep.

The Charity Eligible eyed Kendra wryly across the pile of curly dark hair he was supporting with his arm. "I'm glad that is over," he said. "I like to spend time with you girls, but there must be an easier way!"

CHAPTER FIFTEEN: THE TIMEOUT GAMES

If the Charity Eligible had been called directly to a carnation ceremony as he had half expected, he might have eliminated Janny. He now knew that the beautiful blonde had been carrying on behind his back with another man, her own theatrical agent no less, and the duplicity rankled. Moreover the ballerina had kissed Anthony, while all the time carrying a mobile telephone which could receive text messages from Sam.

However, the next morning Anthony arose to find a sports uniform laid out on the chair for him to wear. The stretchy green and yellow T-shirt reminded him of the Australian National Cricket team, and were complimented by the baggy green shorts which reached to just above his knees. The footwear provided were green football socks his own sneakers. The Charity Eligible donned the outfit and checked what he thought of the neat ensemble.

A message from Leticia accompanied the clothes. Anthony picked the envelope up and unfolded the contents with a mild sense of curiosity.

"*While this is primarily a dating show,*" the Hostess had written, "*It is also television entertainment for the viewers. I am taking over tomorrow and organising a series of challenges for the entire group. Be prepared to make the most of the opportunity to observe the remaining girls in a completely different situation. All the best of luck, Leticia Anderson.*"

Anthony read the note through several times, and then he began to see the bright side of the arrangement. As Leticia indicated, a games day would be something different, and might even function to take the pressure out of the situation in which he found himself.

As the Charity Eligible, he was spoilt for choice: Heddy, for example, was a fascinating woman whose vivacity drew Anthony as his former fiancé had once done. On the other hand, Kendra was loving and trusting, and Anthony could see himself establishing a home and raising children with her. His third option, Janny, was a mercurial star who both aroused and perplexed him.

Over time, his natural caution had eroded, and Anthony was suffering from an inability to resist temptation around all three girls. If he were completely honest, he was not very proud of himself.

Anthony was mildly surprised when he arrived at the Candidate House to find all the girls attired in outfits identical to his own, as he had half expected cute little basketball skirts. There also was no spare moment for him to pull any of the girls aside for a chat.

"The girls are not competing for your attention today," Leticia explained, "They are all part of the team."

Leticia led the group into the natural shrubbery around the side of the mansion. This area had been used very rarely on the show as the contestants preferred the pool or lawns. Indeed, it had only been used as the site of an impromptu picnic with Abraham.

The hostess held up two black silk scarves.

"We are going to play a trust game," Leticia announced. "One contestant will be blindfolded while the other will lead them around the garden." The hostess stepped up to Anthony and tied the scarf firmly around his eyes. "You will be working with Janny," she said, "And Heddy will be working with Kendra."

"So we don't even get to choose our partners," Kendra observed thoughtfully as she stood still to receive the blindfold across her eyes.

Heddy laughed. "Leticia has probably been reviewing the film footage from the last few days and concluded that you and I would be an amusing combination. We won't let no gameshow hostess trick us. Will we girlfriend?"

"I guess not," Kendra agreed. Her emotions had been somewhat more battered than those of the brunette beauty, but her firm belief in cosmic justice allowed her to continue with tranquillity.

Heddy was largely unconcerned. She knew she had many options, both on and off *The Charity Dating Show*. This new competition activated her competitive streak as thoroughly as the competition for Anthony's hand had done. "We are going to win this!" the beauty declared.

"Now here is the hard part," Leticia continued with a twinkle in her eye. The hostess led the teams towards an obstacle course which had been laid out using 'witches hats', hula-hoops and aerobic steps. The path to be circumnavigated was complex and convoluted, with steps to climb and ditches to jump, but was completely safe.

Anthony and Janny left the mark first, with Heddy and Kendra following three minutes later. Both pairs were being judged and timed.

Anthony found that he had to slow down his natural inclination to rush ahead. His habitually large steps caused him to stumble against the witches hats several times, losing valuable points. The steps were navigated without difficulty, and the ditch presented only a minor challenge, as Anthony jumped across according to instructions given by Janny. The very last obstacle was a fence, which the pair had to duck down and crawl under.

Heddy and Kendra may have had a slight advantage going second, because they could hear Anthony and Janny ahead of them. However, it was their decision to stay close together which gave them the competitive edge. They subsequently knocked down no witches hats and Heddy counted to three so the girls could jump in unison over the ditch. On Heddy's instructions, both ducked down low and slid under the fence.

"Congratulations, Kendra and Heddy," Leticia said. "Anthony and Janny made the better time, but you two stayed inside the lines." She presented the graphic artist and veterinarian with plastic medals strung on lanyards.

"Ooh thanks," Kendra and Heddy said, looking at their party favours.

"Now, for the next challenge," Leticia announced. "I am going to change the teams around. Janny you will join Kendra and Heddy you will work with Anthony."

The pairs dutifully swapped over. Kendra guessed that pairing her with Heddy had not produced enough drama, so the hostess was trying a different tactic. Janny and Anthony also had their issues, which they had been unable to talk through and resolve, and now they would be separated.

"Would you like to brave heights or hunt for treasure?" Leticia inquired.

They were pretty sure that someone among them was afraid of heights, so the contestants chose to hunt for treasure. Kendra and Janny frowned when they were handed a piece of paper containing a cryptic clue and an explorer's compass.

"Oh dear," Kendra said, reading their clue out loud. "Twenty paces to the east, I stand by myself".

"The sun shines on the brush side of the house in the morning," Janny suggested helpfully.

The girls experimented with the compass for a few moments and aligned the needle so they understood its tendency to swing towards the poles. The girls then marched towards the section of the yard indicated by the letter "E". After roughly twenty paces, they found twin rose bushes, and at the foot of the rose bushes was a jewellery box.

"Hang on," Kendra cried, "That can't be right. The clue says 'stand by myself.' We need a lone tree or bush."

"One rose bush stands by an identical rose bush - beside its twin," Janny observed. "I think we have the right spot after all!"

Kendra opened the jewellery box and took out the piece of paper containing the next clue. "Through the tunnel lies the way. Where would we find a tunnel around here?"

Janny pointed wordlessly to some brightly coloured play tubes that had been laid across the lawn. On closer inspection, the girls found the tunnel had been filled with a shallow pool of jell. "Oh no, they have been slimed," the dancer observed.

"It's detergent based," Kendra, who occasionally mixed custom and novelty paints for children's parties, observed. "It won't hurt us. All the same, I'm glad we are not wearing our good clothes!"

Janny giggled. "I can't say exactly why – but this makes me think of Deborah!"

"She would be complaining in her loudest voice, and yet loving everything," Kendra said.

"Do you think Heddy has been a good substitute for Deborah?" Janny asked.

Kendra shook her head. "No, I don't. Deborah was all bark and no bite, whereas Heddy definitely has a bite."

"Not to mention the fact that she is after Anthony too," Janny added with a giggle.

The girls dropped down onto the ground and wriggled through the tubes, sticky jell and all. Vanity was not even an issue by the time they had passed through. Janny crawled through first and leant back to give Kendra a hand.

"Thanks," Kendra said. "Where's the next box?"

"Just here beside the exit," Janny observed. "We nearly passed it!"

"Open it up quick", Kendra ordered.

Janny sprung the catch and tilted the lid. "Here we go again, the paper says, 'Around the corner lies the prize'."

"Around the corner?" Kendra queried. "The house has lots of corners."

"It must mean something in particular," Janny observed.

"What is that through the trees?" Asked Kendra. "It wasn't there before."

"A big gymnastic pad in the shape of a triangle," Janny said. "A triangle is the ultimate corner to me!"

Beyond the point of the triangle they found another box containing a clue. Kendra bent and picked it up.

"I'm afraid we have lost a lot of time," Kendra murmured.

"It all depends how quickly the other team found their clues..." Janny speculated. "Quick, what does it say?"

"Congratulations", Kendra read. "You have learnt to follow a compass, plunge the depths and think outside the square. Now you may go to the patio by the pool and claim whatever is in the ice-box."

The girls vacated the area and were directed to walk the long way around the house by Simon Steeple and camera crew number one, who were preventing the two teams from meeting in the middle of the challenge.

Heddy and Anthony had deciphered their set of clues in record time, as Anthony was used to working out puzzles and making deductions at work. They arrived at the ice-box slightly ahead of Kendra and Janny and were already enjoying cool drinks when the girls arrived.

"Heddy and Anthony were the winners of the treasure hunt," Leticia announced. She distributed two more party favour medals. "With Kendra and Heddy winning the obstacle course, the only contestant to have won two events is Heddy."

"That appears to make me the overall winner", Heddy observed. "Yay for me!"

"Exactly," Leticia confirmed. "So Heddy will get to choose the third challenge. Mini-golf or capture the flag?"

"Capture the flag is a glorified form of tag," Heddy said with a grin. "I have fun childhood memories of that game."

"I am glad you have chosen that," Leticia said, bringing out two coloured pendants mounted on light wands. "Come and see the forts we have set up on the tennis courts."

The Candidate House had its own well-groomed tennis lawns, and when the party arrived, they saw that a miniature fort had been set up at each end of the court.

"The only team combination that has not been used is Anthony and Kendra," Leticia said. "Playing against Janny and Heddy."

The contestants rotated allies once again. "Leticia is not letting us get comfortable with any partner," Kendra complained as she joined Anthony.

"Now you know a little of what I feel on dates," Anthony said.

Kendra flushed. "I think dates are a little more emotionally complicated," she said.

"Oh I agree," Anthony said, for the sake of peace, although he was more used to Kendra being indulgent of his point of view. The past few days had indeed been stressful for the artist, and he suspected the episode with Heddy and his trousers was not easily forgotten.

Each team was sent down one end to attach their flag to a fort. Janny and Heddy, who really had not socialised together a lot around the Candidate House, were forced to consult each other regarding stratagem.

"How do we sneak up on the other team?" Janny inquired in perplexity. "I'm used to playing this with bushes to hide behind."

"We will have to develop a strategy," Heddy replied. "You run out there and make a feint at their flag. Hopefully, they will chase you while I steal their flag."

Janny bravely ran across the field and attempted to snatch the flag in full view of Anthony and Kendra, who blocked her passage and began to chase the dancer back to her own end. Feeling silly, Janny ducked and weaved and concentrated upon reaching her own flag before Anthony and Kendra, who could also snatch at it. She reached her base just before the others and turned to assume the guard position.

Meanwhile, Heddy flew across the field and snatched up the red flag. Fleet of foot, Heddy almost made it back to her own fort, but she was intercepted by Anthony. Dodging around the Charity Eligible, she threw herself into the base area, where Leticia declared her "safe". Heddy hung the captured flag up beside her own team flag, where they both swayed merrily in the light breeze.

"Well, I will be a laughing stock at home," Anthony declared when he realised what had happened. "Fooled by an old footy trick - I should have known better."

"You didn't expect that of Heddy did you?" Heddy chortled. "Heddy likes to win!"

"Yeah I can see that," Anthony observed. His tone was indulgent, but his expression was thoughtful. Suppose Heddy liked to win too much – occasionally even at the expense of others?

Leticia presented Heddy with a paper crown as she was the overall winner of *The Charity Dating Show* games. The contestants were required to pose for one hot, sweaty and embarrassing poster shot; and then the camera crew released them to shower and change. The girls returned to their respective rooms, and Anthony was directed to use the shower in the pool changing rooms.

Leticia left the contestants to their ablutions and bustled to the kitchen to make sure a celebratory lunch was being prepared. The hostess had a satisfied gleam in her eye. It was obvious that the games had served their purpose in breaking down the rigid divisions that had developed over the last few days, and *The Charity Dating Show* was everybody's competition once again.

Anthony found himself sent into the deliberation room immediately after lunch. The Charity Eligible had not been able to speak to any of the girls without the cameras rolling, and this rendered his decision making process more difficult.

Anthony settled himself down on the settee in the deliberation room. A range of photographs of the girls had been placed in a photograph album before him. Heddy peered out of the pages in a number of vivacious and glamourous poses. Janny purred and pouted out of her photographs, displaying a cat-like grace that only the ballerina could. Kendra had been portrayed against a number of backgrounds, the very last one had a hint of naughtiness as she was clad in a leather jacket and short-shorts.

The Charity Eligible reviewed his feelings for the girls over the last few days. Heddy represented the novel and the unknown. Janny had intrigued Anthony from the beginning. Spurred on by advice from his friend Abraham, he had sought to get past her barriers and just when he succeeded, he found that things were not all they seemed. Kendra, on the other hand had always been honest with him. He looked forward to spending another day in her company and that guaranteed the artist a rose.

"I am not ready," Anthony muttered, and Leticia, who had arrived to collect him, looked stern.

"You must hurry," Leticia said. "The girls are waiting".

Anthony sighed and rose to follow the hostess. He entered the small reception room and exchanged greetings with all three girls. Each greeted him warmly and eyed him expectantly.

Anthony turned to Leticia. "I really need to speak to Janny for a few minutes alone," he said. Anthony had been able to think things over during the preceding day and had developed the belief that he owed it to himself to have one last conversation with Janny before she left; in order to find out how much of her behaviour on the show had been truth, and how much had been deception.

Leticia frowned. It was in her power to grant a private interview, but it was not part of the plan. While *The Charity Dating Show* raised money for charity, it was not itself a charity, and as part of a community television station it had to stimulate as much interest as possible from viewers and advertisers.

This particular series had a few secrets to leak later in after-interviews; however, the on-screen emotional dramatics had occasionally been lacking with the female contestants being so supportive towards each other. Allowing Anthony to speak to Janny off-camera would further reduce the drama.

"Try to say whatever you need to say in front of the camera please, Anthony," the Hostess requested.

Anthony considered throwing a scene, but it seemed inappropriate. He led Janny toward a seat in the corner of the room. "Janny," he said earnestly. "At a previous carnation ceremony I asked you whether you truly wanted to date me. Do you remember?"

"Yes, I remember," Janny replied nervously. "Please Anthony, do believe me - I have developed genuine feelings for you. I danced to show you my feelings too. I get to perform at concerts all the time and don't need this show to make my career a success."

"Do you mind my asking again, what were your motives for coming on this show?" Anthony inquired.

"I answered this before," Janny said, showing some slight signs of distress. "I had been through a series of unsuccessful relationships – not even relationships really – just encounters and I hoped to meet someone nice."

"Have I lived up to your expectations?" he asked.

"Yes, Anthony," Janny said. "I am so pleased to have met you, and you must believe I have told you the truth. A little late sometimes, but it takes me a while to share things."

Anthony nodded. "I know," he said.

Janny desperately hoped that Anthony would understand she also meant she wanted a break from the particular personalities who inhabited the dance world, including her agent Sam. "I also wanted time away from my training routine and performing in the more traditional sense."

Anthony hoped he was reading between the lines correctly.

Kendra, who had never heard Janny speak so clearly and strongly about her priorities, made a clapping gesture in the background. Heddy also gave the ballerina a thumbs-up signal. She had not known the ballerina for very long, but in her opinion, if the ballerina had a problem, it was centred in her malleability and changeability.

Anthony noticed the pantomime in the background and went red. "You said, you were single," he continued, "But it has come to my attention you do still hear from someone you were involved with in recent times. Lying to me, either directly or by omission is the easiest way to lose me... Please remember that for the future, Janny."

"I understand that now," Janny said. "Please don't make me say anymore on television." A desperate note had crept into her voice.

"It's alright," Anthony said. "Let us get on with the carnation ceremony now."

In truth, Anthony knew he had been angry because he had been mildly jealous. He did not know the full story, but he suspected the agent was a controlling type of fellow, one who might keep his female clients half-in-love to ensure their continued business.

The Charity Eligible crossed the room and selected a carnation from the little table.

"Kendra," he called. "Please come here."

Kendra stepped forward. "Yes Anthony," she breathed.

Anthony looked into her eyes, intending to share his joy at their having progressed through another round, but he noticed the artist's eyes were misty. "What is wrong?"

"I think perhaps you have begun to take me for granted," the Artist responded. "It is amazing how much of your attention the other girls have commanded over the past few days."

Anthony felt a sense of loss as his safe haven with the undemanding Kendra was threatened. "Cheer up Kinny," he said, taking both her hands in his. "I promise we will spend some time together in the near future."

"Thank you Anthony," Kendra said. She accepted the carnation and went to stand beside Janny and Heddy once again.

"Heddy," Anthony called.

Janny sighed and closed her eyes against the brimming tears. Kendra reached out and held her hand.

"Yes Anthony," Heddy said, stepping forward to stand in front of the Charity Eligible. She was looking especially beautiful that afternoon. Her spectacular black hair was loose down to her waist, and the red tint of her dress complimented her skin beautifully. She was tall and could wear a low backline with striking effect.

"You are a very beautiful woman," Anthony said. "And I feel very privileged you returned to spend some time with me."

"Thank you, Anthony," Heddy said.

"However, I am sorry to tell you that I have developed deeper feelings for Janny and Kendra, than I have for you. I don't think it is a mere matter of time - although that may have been a factor."

Heddy was blinking as if she could not understand what she was hearing. "But Anthony, you called me second," she said. "You still have a carnation."

"Yes, I called you out second," Anthony said. "I couldn't bear making you wait until the last moment. I'm sorry."

"Well, I wish you the best then," Heddy said and walked out of the room to the waiting limousine with her head held high to show she still valued herself.

"I am genuinely surprised to be leaving," Heddy told camera crew two who had followed her outside. "I honestly expected the volatile Janny to phase herself out of the competition with her irrational actions; or the mousy Kendra to prove unable to hold a man's attentions!"

Heddy leaned back in the seat and continued. "Don't get me wrong, they were my gals of course – but where I come from - there are plenty of other fish in the sea, and most of them are keen to get caught by me!"

Heddy continued to speak into the car microphone during her brief drive off the property, outlining her surprise and disappointment.

Inside the Candidate House, under the watchful eyes of camera crew one, the carnation ceremony continued.

"Janny," Anthony called.

Janny hardly heard him, so wrapped was she in feelings of rejection. Kendra gave the dancer a nudge, and she opened her eyes. It took a moment for her eyes to focus and see that Anthony was still holding a carnation!

"Please come here Janny," Anthony said. "I want you to stay at least another day."

"Oh thank you, Anthony!" Janny ran into the Charity Eligible's arms and gave him a kiss. She took the carnation and cradled it in her hand. "I thought it was all over."

"Many things may change, Janny," Anthony said with a smile, "But our friendship will never be all over!"

"Is that a promise?" Janny whispered, blinking the tears away.

"It is definitely a promise," Anthony repeated.

CHAPTER SIXTEEN: THE FAMILY VISITS

Janny and Kendra met on the patio early the next morning for a swim and a spa. After enjoying an hour of shared exercise, they went into the kitchen for breakfast. Leticia was already there, looking bright and busy.

"Guess what the plan is today girls?" the hostess said. "We are expecting some very important visitors, the Ellertons!"

"My parents," Janny exclaimed. "It has been so long since I have even spoken with them."

"They are keen to see you," Leticia said, "And of course, to meet Anthony."

"What do I do while this is going on?" Kendra asked, sounding amused. "I don't think I am required to meet Janny's parents, nice though they may be."

"I have arranged a pass to all the exhibitions at the Art Gallery of NSW and the Australian Museum for you," Leticia said.

"Oh goody," Kendra exclaimed. "A day spent in some of my favorite venues. Just so long as I'm not being filmed?"

"No," Leticia said, "Your time is completely your own."

The graphic artist finished her meal and left to collect her things for the day. She was humming to herself.

"The pressure is on me," Janny said to herself as she submitted to make-up and general neatening for the camera. Her family arrived around ten o'clock, and she greeted them at the mansion door. Janny's mother, Alicia, had red hair which she wore tied up in an elegant bun. The woman was thin and energetic with an indomitable will. She had always run her daughter's life, except when she delegated her authority to dance instructors and agents, most of whom had been hand-picked by Alicia.

Janny's father, Victor, was more easy-going. He had always wanted the best for his wife and daughter, and if he had a fault, it was his tendency to take the path of least resistance, especially where his wife was concerned. In this respect, Janny was like her father, but she had also inherited ambition from her mother.

The last member of Janny's family was a sharp little sister called Megan. Megan was something of a tom-boy and the father's firm favorite. She resisted her mother's manipulations and got away with it because she had no outstanding talent for dance, but got good academic grades. Young though she was, Megan tended to be scornful of Janny's theatrical acquaintances and the jealousy ridden world of dance.

Hugs and kisses were exchanged, and Alicia looked Janny over to determine whether she had kept herself in shape for dancing. Satisfied on that score, she asked for a tour of the mansion and its grounds.

Janny led the way through the Candidate House and her father took note of the dormitory-like set-up of the bedroom wing. "You must miss the other girls now that you are down to two," he said.

Janny nodded. "I am glad that the show has almost finished though," she said. "I would like to get back to the dance company."

"I am sure it is there waiting for you," Victor Ellerton agreed comfortingly.

"At first I thought you were a silly girl going off like that," Alicia Ellerton declared, "And then I began to understand."

Janny looked puzzled.

"The television experience will add to your artistic development," her mother explained.

"I just needed some time off, Mother," Janny said. "I don't know what you may have heard."

"Your agent Sam told me where you were," Alicia said. "He will be calling in later today."

Janny went stiff with shock, but she quickly pasted a smile on her face. The recently filmed episodes would not have gone to air, and her parents would have no idea Sam had already been on *The Charity Dating Show*, or that he had verbally abused her in front of the Charity Eligible and camera crew.

"This is meant to be a day for my family," the Ballerina stammered.

"Of course dear," Alicia gushed. "But Sam has done so much for your career in the last few years, he practically is family."

"I did the dancing and won the auditions," Janny began slowly, identifying a sense of injustice welling up from deep inside, but her mother waved her aside.

"You did very well dear," Alicia said. "But Sam has managed the business side of things beautifully."

"I don't want my career entirely dependent on Sam, Mother," Janny began.

Her little sister Megan laughed. "About time, sister," she remarked with all the wisdom of thirteen years.

"Well if it's not Sam that is going to manage your career, who will?" Alicia inquired.

"I'm thinking of listing with several agencies Mother," Janny said. "Increase my chances of getting work. Or Daddy could start negotiating my contracts. One of the other girls had her father as a manager – and he did very well for her. It must have saved a lot in commissions, or at least kept the commission within the family."

"What would your father know about dance?" Alicia began, but she was interrupted as Leticia indicated it was about time for Anthony to arrive. The Ellerton family moved into the large lounge to await the appearance of the Charity Eligible.

"What's this fellow like dear?" Victor asked as they were waiting. "I can't help wonder why a man would put himself up as a prize on a dating show."

"Anthony is gentle and serious," Janny began. "He really is a gentleman, and he went onto the show to raise money for a ward in the hospital he works for - that's the main reason."

"Or so he says!" laughed Alicia Ellerton. "I'm sure any young fellow would be pleased to meet a group of beautiful girls and be the centre of attention."

"That is what concerns me," Victor said. "I want my daughter to find someone nice and steady."

"I will be fine," Janny remarked. "Anthony is a nice man." Her relationship with her parents was complicated because her mother had functioned not only as a parent, but as a mentor and sometime slave-driver. Ambitious parents were well known in the sports and arts fields and her mother was a classic case.

There was a knock at the front door, and Anthony was ushered in by the housekeeper. He shook hands with Janny's father and turned to greet her mother. Alicia Ellerton gave the Charity Eligible a cool smile and a stiff hand to shake. Janny sighed. It appeared her mother was going to be difficult.

"I have been told you are a doctor," Victor Ellerton ventured politely.

"Oh yes," Anthony replied, glad to be on comfortable ground. "I am a surgeon. I normally work in emergency."

"That must be stressful work," Victor commented.

"I don't suppose you have much time for the appreciation of the Arts," Alicia observed stiffly. "You and Janny come from different worlds."

"I assure you I do enjoy the Arts, ma'am," Anthony replied politely.

He was determined not to take offence to anything for Janny's sake, however, the encounter was helping him understand Janny's edginess. The mother was not easy to be around. Everything from her well-groomed hair to her fashionable attire screamed tension. Alicia sniffed.

Victor and Anthony fell into a surface level conversation about each other's work. Victor was an engineer who had some understanding of hospital equipment. Although the men kept their conversation light, their inquisitive expressions suggested they wanted to explore deeper issues.

Finally, Anthony took the plunge. "I feel privileged to have met you daughter sir," he began. "I respect her greatly."

"I am pleased to hear that," Victor Ellerton said. "But – err - do you like her in any special way?"

"Yes, sir," Anthony replied. "I do find your daughter attractive. I am just not sure she will give me a chance to develop a serious relationship with her."

Victor Ellerton looked thoughtful. "The young men always seem keen to know young Jandice, but as soon as the going gets tough, they leave. Janny has been hurt a few times."

"I assure you, sir," Anthony said, "It is not my inclination to leave such a lovely young lady. Just sometimes – I feel pushed away."

"Have you two discussed these things?" Victor Ellerton inquired.

"Yes, we have," Anthony replied. "That was rather the point of my dating Janny."

Anthony turned to Alicia Ellerton. It was obvious she had very strong opinions and her approval would be important to Janny. However, he was struggling to make a connection.

The little sister Megan, regarded the Charity Eligible cheekily. "You are actually dating my sister on television", she said with a giggle.

"Yes, I am," Anthony replied.

"Do you get filmed kissing and everything?" Megan inquired cheekily.

"Unfortunately yes," Anthony replied. "It is very embarrassing. You should be too young to talk about these things."

"I'm not too young," Megan replied. "Although, I'm not interested in boys yet, I'm interested in sport."

"That's much safer," Anthony observed, remembering the perils of his teens. The girls got interested in boys, and the boys got shy. It took a few years for the two to be on the same page. "I used to like sport," he ventured.

"Really?" Megan was all goggle eyed. "What did you play?"

"Cricket in summer, and footy in winter," Anthony replied.

"I play hockey," Megan continued.

"That must keep you fit," Anthony observed.

"Oh it does," Megan agreed. The teenage girl glanced over Anthony's shoulder and frowned. "There is Janny's bossy agent. I hate him."

Anthony went rigid with shock, but resisted the impulse to turn.

"Sam is here?" he exclaimed.

"You know his name?" Megan observed. "He controls Janny's career something awful I think, but Mummy loves him. She would have invited him."

"I certainly did not," Anthony said with a frown. The Charity Eligible straightened his back and pasted a polite smile on his face before turning to shake hands with his rival. The smile did not quite reach his eyes.

Sam looked confident of his welcome. He kissed Alicia Ellerton on the cheek and thanked her for the invitation to join them. Then he playfully ruffled Megan's hair and ignored her teenage protests. He greeted Janny with words designed to imply he had not spoken to her for a few weeks and the hand he laid upon her arm was gentle but possessive.

Taking advantage of his position as the official suitor for Janny's hand, Anthony laid his arm around the dancer's shoulders.

"Shall we have that lovely lunch Leticia ordered?" he suggested.

"Yes, what a good idea," Janny said. She gave Anthony a grateful look and began to glide smoothly towards the dining room.

Anthony seated Janny and her parents at the table. Sam sat down with them and began talking to Alicia.

Anthony made an excuse to see Leticia privately. He was determined to fill the hostess in on the full situation, as far as he knew it.

"Leticia," Anthony said, approaching the hostess in her office. "Can I speak to you for a few minutes?"

"Yes, Anthony," Leticia replied. "What seems to be the problem?"

"That young man, Sam, who just turned up," Anthony began.

"Her stage manager," Leticia said. "I must admit that I was a bit surprised to see him in her family group."

"He's not family," Anthony said. "Among the other things we have been told, he is her agent."

"I see," Leticia murmured. "So what is he doing here?"

"He wants to interfere with Janny's involvement in *The Charity Dating Show* and keep control of her career," Anthony said. "He may even have been romantically involved with Janny at one time - I don't know the full story. But you have to get him out of there."

"Oh dear," Leticia murmured. "He is on camera now, so I can't create a scene. We want drama, but not that sort. I'll organize a tour of the studio or something flattering for him. It is more than he deserves, but we have to be diplomatic."

"Thank you for understanding," Anthony said.

He returned to the dining room and sat down next to Janny. "All organized!" he said.

"What is organized?" Inquired Alicia, who had sharp ears.

"A special dessert treat," Anthony hedged. "I am sure you will love it." He turned to Sam: "How is the business?"

Sam looked mildly surprised to be addressed by the Charity Eligible. "Fine," he replied.

"Do you have a lot of clients?" Anthony asked.

"Quite a few," Sam said. "I am in demand because I have good connections."

"Are the contracts always advantageous for the clients?" Anthony inquired.

Sam flushed. "I always try to do the best for the client," he replied. "However, sometimes in the Arts, it is necessary to work for the fame rather than the money."

"Ah, but it is exactly that sort of exploitation that an agent would be employed to protect their client against," Anthony observed.

Out of the corner of his eye, he saw that Alicia was beginning to look impressed. Score one for the Charity Eligible!

As the meal was drawing to a close and the promised dessert had been fully enjoyed, George the camera operator and several burly security guards approached Sam, and made him an offer of a tour of the studio area.

"Our set-up should be of great interest to a man who works in the Arts like yourself," George implied. Sam simply could not refuse and was led away on his 'VIP tour'. Score two for the Charity Eligible!

The agent was not seen again that afternoon, and Anthony was able to spend a few pleasant hours getting to know Janny's family after all. Score three for the Charity Eligible!

After Janny had finally waved farewell to her family, she heaved a sigh of relief. "That went better than I thought," she said. "My family are not easy on first acquaintance."

"Your father is a good fellow, and your sister is fun," Anthony observed. "It's just your mum is only interested in your dancing. She has to be related to on that level. I'm sure she means well."

"And Mother inviting Sam," Janny observed. "I could not believe it! He disappeared somewhere though, did you have anything to do with that?"

"I had a discrete word to Leticia," Anthony admitted somewhat shamefaced.

"Oh, I do love you," Janny bubbled and kissed him spontaneously on the lips. "I mean... how thoughtful of you."

"Janny," Anthony said seriously, "I think you ought to take steps to free yourself of that fellow. By his own admission, he hasn't always got you the best contracts – and I don't want you to feel your career is nothing without him. He's just a sleazy agent. I've seen more honourable pharmaceutical sales reps!"

"I know," Janny said. "I'm beginning to agree with you, but I can't do it alone."

"Let's speak to Leticia and see if she knows of any lawyers who specialize in entertainer's contracts," Anthony said. "I think it's time you had expert advice. And I swear – you won't be alone. I will stand by you and support you."

"Thank you Anthony," Janny said. "That means a lot to me."

The next morning, Kendra dressed herself with care. She was looking forward to seeing her beloved grandmother again. She was also nervous about seeing Anthony. Furthermore, the graphic artist had enjoyed having the previous day to herself and was looking forward to her return to the every-day world.

However, she had to admit her feelings for the Charity Eligible had grown quickly, despite all her efforts to protect her heart. If Anthony did not truly return those feelings, Kendra knew that she would be very badly hurt. At first, the artist had perceived his interest in the other women as one of the hazards of meeting on *The Charity Dating Show*, but over time, the stress had begun to wear her down.

Kendra was a stayer, but not necessarily a fighter. And now, towards the end, it was Janny, who had initially only appeared half-serious about the Charity Eligible, that was occupying his energy with her emotional commotions. Kendra had noticed the previous carnation ceremony had closed on a solemn promise to Janny.

Kendra had been promised more time together – but Janny had been promised eternal friendship. Kendra did not know if she had the energy for a final dramatic show-down, if that was what it would take to secure Anthony's love.

Kendra's thoughts were interrupted by Janny, who was bidding her a cheerful farewell. The ballerina had looked much happier since her visit with her parents the previous day, and Kendra suspected the change was due to Anthony, and not the parents themselves, who sounded like they brought mixed blessings.

"Have a good time," Kendra said absently.

Janny grinned. "Never fear, I will." She held up a City Explorer ticket and open pass to any show of her choice at the Sydney Opera House. "Look what Leticia gave me."

"I was provided with something similar yesterday," Kendra said.

"Nice of them, isn't it?" Janny said. "Have a good date while I am busy."

"I will try," Kendra said. "I'm getting tired of the game."

"It isn't a game anymore," Janny said. "Anthony is a very nice guy. He deserves the best!"

Kendra stared at the ballerina. If Janny was now serious about Anthony, that somehow made the artist feel even more discouraged.

Janny noticed Kendra's subdued expression. "Give him every chance," the ballerina said carefully. "You have always said, he would be suited to one of us, not all of us. We only have a very little while to wait to find out which one of us it is now."

Janny waved and left the room. A few minutes later, the door slammed and Kendra was the only contestant left in the Candidate House.

It was not long before Kendra's grandmother arrived. Mrs. Western was a round featured, slightly plump, motherly woman. Her presence was re-assuring and she was still sweet-faced and attractive at sixty. Kendra gave her a welcoming hug.

"I'm so glad you could make it," Kendra cried.

"I wouldn't have missed seeing you dear," Emmaline Western said. "Not for all the tea in the world."

"Oh I love you Grandma," Kendra exclaimed, enjoying the sensation of having family around at last.

"I love you too, Kinny," Emmaline said. "And your parents send their love too."

Kendra looked thrilled. "You have heard from Mother and Father?"

"Yes, I have," Emmaline said. "It is surprising how little telephone coverage there is still in the mountainous areas of the world, but Mark managed to make a call."

The main draw-back with having a father who was an international engineer was he was always accepting contracts to out-of-the-way places. Mark Western had been to many distant places, and ever since Kendra had been old enough to leave with her grandmother, his wife had accompanied him. Therefore, the mainstay of support through her school, university and working years had been her grandmother, Emmaline.

"They were surprised when I told them what you were off doing," Emmaline said.

"I'll bet," Kendra retorted. Her mother had been a romantic who expected Kendra to marry one of the first boys she met, just as her parents had met and married. Over the years, she had become increasingly puzzled by her daughter remaining single.

"Mark said *The Charity Dating Show* sounded like some sort of experiment psychologists are forbidden to conduct on people," Emmaline said.

"Father may be right," Kendra laughed somewhat ironically. "Psychologists cannot force people to date."

"Are you alright dear?" Emmaline asked with concern. "You do look a little dark under the eyes."

"Oh, Grandma," Kendra cried. "I really thought I had fallen in love with this Charity Eligible."

"Thought?" her Grandmother queried.

"I'm not so sure now," Kendra said. "For a while, Anthony seemed to return my feelings, then a new girl was brought in and he became distracted. Love is a two-way street, at least it is to me."

"Quite right, dear," Emmaline said. "But what you are describing could be any man in the early days of a relationship. It takes a while for commitment to grow, even when there is interest."

"It's not just the new girl," Kendra continued. "I know he has kissed some of the others, and recently he has become more involved with Janny, in-spite of or even because of, her problems."

"How do you think Janny feels?" Inquired Emmaline.

"I think she is beginning to care for Anthony too," Kendra admitted.

"So Anthony is going to have to make a very serious decision between now and the final ceremony," Emmaline said. "I won't hear of him messing you around after that! My grand-daughter has a heart of solid gold and must be treated as such."

"Thank you Grandma," Kendra said. "That's so nice to hear."

"That's what grandmothers are for," Emmaline returned cheerfully.

"So what should I do?" Kendra asked tearfully.

"By the time you get to my age," Emmaline said, "There is only one thing that matters and that is the truth. I think you should tell him exactly how you feel."

"I don't know whether I dare," Kendra exclaimed. "I do not like to be demanding."

"Sometimes it is necessary dear," Emmaline advised her granddaughter.

"Yet it is not easy," Kendra glanced nervously towards the door. "Anthony must be here by now surely," she said, looking mildly puzzled. "It's nice talking to you Grandma, but I want to get the introductions over."

Indeed, Anthony had already arrived and been surprised when Leticia had taken him around the house to the pool area.

"Kendra is having a private moment with her grandmother," the hostess explained, and made Anthony promise not to break up their dialogue.

The Charity Eligible had looked a little disappointed that his meeting with Kendra's family was being postponed, but amused himself by strolling through the shrubbery. Eventually, Kendra and her grandmother emerged through the double glass doors. They both looked apologetic.

"Hello Anthony," Kendra said, "I am sorry to have kept you waiting. I was talking to Grandma and Leticia did not announce your arrival."

"I understand perfectly," Anthony said. "It is nice that you had time to catch up."

"We did have a good talk," Kendra said. She blushed and it occurred to Anthony he might have been the topic of conversation. He flushed as well.

The grandmother stepped into the breach and introduced herself. "It is nice to meet you, Anthony," she said. "I am Kendra's grandmother, Emmaline Western. If you like, you may call me Emma."

Anthony surveyed the sweet face with its beaming lines of maturity. He decided that he liked Emmaline Western very much. She was like Kendra, only older, more confident and slightly more assertive. "How are you Emma?" he inquired.

"Very well thank you, Anthony," Emmaline said. "I enjoy good health and a quiet life. How about yourself?"

"I am well, thank you," Anthony replied. "I am curious, where are Kendra's parents?"

"They are overseas," Emmaline said. "Once Kendra was a toddler, her father went back to his work which involved much travel."

"I see," Anthony said. He glanced at Kendra, "You must miss them a lot."

"I do," Kendra replied. "But I have always had Grandma."

"The lunch looks lovely," Anthony suggested. "Shall we have some?"

"Oh yes," Emmaline exclaimed. "I quite envy you Kendra dear, all that delicious food laid on - and the beautiful house and garden."

"We have had some fun and interesting dates organized for us too," Anthony said.

He felt relaxed in Emmaline's presence, and found himself describing some of the activities of the past two months.

"I am glad I have met all the different girls," Anthony found himself confiding. "I used to be very shy with women who were not my patients."

"There would have been young nurses that liked you," Emmaline suggested.

Anthony shrugged: "I did not notice. I was too busy working."

"Now that you have met my Kinny," Emmaline said gently, "You must not hurt her."

"Believe me," Anthony said, "That is the last thing I want to do."

"Watching you with the other women does hurt her," Emmaline observed frankly.

"That is a part of *The Charity Dating Show*," Anthony was flushed. "I do not know what I can do about it."

"I understand both you and Kinny have chosen to participate in this *Charity Dating Show*," Emmaline concluded. "Luckily that is nearly over. My question is how you will treat the girl you choose out there in the real world?"

"I want a long term relationship," Anthony said. "Even marriage if it is right."

"I am glad to hear it," Emmaline murmured.

The meal finished, Emmaline requested a tour of the house and gardens. She admired the roses and was very much impressed by the recreation areas. It gave her immense satisfaction that her Kendra had been taken good care of, the grandmother declared. Then she said she was tired and needed to return to the hotel room the television station had booked for her accommodation.

Kendra hugged her grandmother goodbye, while Anthony shook her hand warmly. They both watched Emmaline's pleasantly plump back disappear down the front steps and into the car. When Emmaline had driven away, Kendra turned to Anthony.

"Don't go," she said. "Stay for tea. I don't know whether we will get to see each other again before the final carnation ceremony."

Anthony thanked Kendra for the invitation and they both went to sit down in the large lounge. Kendra turned the television on, but ignored the picture. She turned to face Anthony, took his hands in hers and looked him straight in the eye.

"My feelings for you are very deep," Kendra said. "I cannot take any more uncertainty. If you love me as I love you, choose me tomorrow. If you are not sure that you love me, tell me now and choose Janny tomorrow."

Anthony was stunned. He had known that the final carnation ceremony was close, but had fondly imagined he had a few more hours to process meeting the two families. He also needed to mull over his feelings for the girls and make sure he was comfortable with his decision.

"I cannot let you go Kendra," he cried. "But I cannot declare my intentions tonight either. It is very difficult and I really do need my thinking time. Trust me, I am not trying to string you along. I have broken my own rules and started to genuinely care for both of you girls."

The Charity Eligible hung his head in shame. "I thought you would lead me to a decision using hugs and kisses." The tiniest trace of a naughty smile played around his lips.

"I sincerely hope you are joking," Kendra declared. "Putting-out tonight would be the surest way to get my heart broken tomorrow."

"One little kiss then," Anthony insisted. He reached out and Kendra melted into his arms.

CHAPTER SEVENTEEN: THE LAST CARNATION

Janny and Kendra faced each other across a late breakfast the next morning. Kendra was dark eyed because she had been unable to fall asleep until the early hours of the morning.

"You were late last night," Kendra said to Janny.

Janny yawned and shrugged. "I saw a second show," she said. "Besides, I didn't want to interrupt you and Anthony deep in the throes of passion."

"Anthony left reasonably early," Kendra said. "You would have been welcome to join us once our official date was over."

Janny's expression brightened. "Really?" she said. "Any idea who he will pick?"

"Anthony wouldn't commit to anything," Kendra said. "Things aren't as comfortable between us as they once were. For all I know, he could even pick you!"

"We will have to wait until tonight and see," Janny said. The mobile phone at her belt began to ring. "I know it is against the rules," Janny said, "But I am going to answer that."

Kendra busied herself with a piece of toast as she listened curiously to Janny's half of the conversation.

"Really?" the Ballerina was saying, "You have proof the notice was delivered? So now I am free to negotiate my own contracts? Thank you that is very good news."

Janny hung the phone up and turned to Kendra with a glowing face. "I think this is going to be my lucky day!"

"Why?" Kendra inquired.

"Yesterday, Leticia gave me the number of a lawyer who was highly experienced with artists' contracts," Janny explained. "I asked him to go through my contract with Sam and find a way in which it could be nulled. Apparently he found the contract ought to have been renewed six months ago, but it wasn't. Under the circumstances, I only have to give Sam notice I want to cease using his services."

"How do you think Sam will take it?" Kendra inquired.

"I don't know," Janny said. "He has been ungracious enough about my coming on this show."

"I saw how ungracious if you need a witness," Kendra offered.

"Thanks," Janny said. "According to this lawyer, it should not get to that."

"I do hope not," Kendra said.

"I've always had heaps of talent," Janny declared. "People like agents just thrived on managing my career. It took coming on this show to teach me I didn't need to depend on anyone anymore."

"At least it has done that for you," Kendra observed.

Janny put her cup and plate in the sink, "I'm going to have a shower." She walked out of the room.

Not long after that, Leticia appeared in the kitchen. "Where is Janny?" she said.

"She went to the bathroom," Kendra replied.

"That agent, Sam is on the landline," Leticia said. "He sounds angry."

"Apparently he is not her agent anymore," Kendra said. "The lawyer you supplied found Janny a way out."

"I hope it was a good way out," Leticia said. "I meet a lot of agents. That one was inclined to be over-bearing, and not at all like a professional agent should."

"There was s loop-hole," Kendra replied. "Apparently Janny's contract lapsed six months ago. Sam was just presuming he would continue to manage her career."

"So if she gave him verbal notice before she came on *The Charity Dating Show*, she should be alright," Leticia said.

"I think she told him she was taking a break," Kendra said. "She definitely did not apply for this show through Sam."

"That should be good enough," Leticia said.

"Yeah, sure," Kendra said. Her own experience of agents and managers was more limited as she usually negotiated her own employment. "I had better have my shower too then."

"Be good girls," Leticia said. "Let me know if you need anything. And no last minute attempts to see Anthony!"

"Yes Leticia," Kendra was very meek.

The morning passed slowly and Kendra amused herself by packing the majority of her belongings. The only things she left out of her case were her cosmetics and a special dress for the final carnation ceremony. Whatever happened, regardless of who Anthony chose, both girls would be leaving the Candidate House that evening.

The artist found herself feeling grateful for the ban on contact with Anthony as it saved her from taking back the words she had uttered the day before. Her normally pacific soul was in revolt against having given Anthony an ultimatum, and she longed to re-establish an easy going friendship. She also half-regretted having declared her love. It seemed she had left herself little mystery and she felt very vulnerable.

Kendra had a strong belief in the just hand of fate, and on the rare occasions this had let her down, she had sought out a viable alternative for her desires. Something deep inside her heart told Kendra that the change in her habitual pattern was necessary. Some men, she knew preferred an easy going woman, while others preferred an assertive woman. Anthony was hard to read, it seemed he liked a little of both.

The history of their relationship flashed before her mind's eye. Anthony had nearly over-looked Kendra at first, bedazzled by all the glamourous women and spoilt for choice. Then for a while, he appeared drawn to her calm nature, until that had begun to pale again against the lure of the vivacious women who were able to challenge and excite him. Moreover, Vonda and perhaps to a certain extent, Janny had aroused protective impulses in the Charity Eligible that a sensible girl like Kendra rarely managed to inspire.

While the last carnation ceremony lay mere hours away, Kendra felt that she was long overdue knowing the mind of the young surgeon. Her heart desired security, monogamy and a future. If Anthony's inclinations lay elsewhere, or if he was not ready to settle down, it was better that she know straight away.

It was almost lunch time when Kendra decided to look in on Janny. The ballerina was lying on her back on the floral bedcover. Her mobile phone was cast to one side and a look of exasperation crossed her face.

"Are you alright?" Kendra asked.

"Yeah sure," Janny said. "It is just Sam. He keeps calling and texting me messages. I have been careful not to answer the phone when I suspected it was him, but it is getting me down."

"May I?" Kendra asked, picking up the phone and scrolling though the top messages. Her face assumed an instant expression of indignation, "I say Janz, these messages are seriously abusive!"

"He is just upset at having to let me go," Janny replied with remarkable resignation.

"I can see that," Kendra remarked. "However, he also includes a few swear words and tries to tell you that you were never worth his efforts."

"Oh, he was like that at times," Janny returned weakly.

"Always?" Kendra exclaimed. "And you put up with it?"

"Yes, my mistake," Janny said equitably. "However, now that is over. I must take care not to respond to any of his messages in a like manner."

"I would print the messages out and show to your new lawyer," Kendra suggested. "No artist wants an agent that talks like that to them. On a slightly different note, I was wondering whether you would like to come to lunch."

"Of course," Janny said. "It takes us one step closer to the main business of today!"

The beautician and stylist arrived around two o'clock in the afternoon and set to work to make each girl as attractive as possible. The effort was for the benefit of the Charity Eligible and in honour of their last official appearance before the cameras. Evening gowns had been especially designed for each girl and every effort was made to ensure the last episode would be memorable.

Janny was encased in a slinky sheath that outlined her athletic body perfectly. A long split up one side revealed her leg every time she moved, and her blonde hair was laced with costume jewellery. Black was an unusual colour for the ballerina, but it set off her fair skin perfectly.

Kendra, on the other hand, was dressed in an off-the-shoulder gown which was a froth of pale pink. The colour too was unusual, for the honey-blonde had a tendency to pick cool neutrals or autumn tones. The pink however, brought a flush to her cheeks which the make-up artist accentuated with powder and rouge. A temporary high-light had been rinsed through Kendra's hair, rendering it almost coppery just for the evening. Pale pink lipstick made her trembling lips appear vulnerable and inviting.

Once dressed, both girls sat side-by-side awaiting their respective limousines. Neither dared accept the proffered coffee and tea for fear of spoiling their make-up or staining their dresses.

"Almost time now, Kinny," Janny whispered and reached out to take Kendra by the hand. "No hard feelings, however this turns out."

"I promise you I will still be your friend," Kendra whispered. "And I will support you against Sam whatever happens!"

Janny's mobile phone had been left behind in the bedroom to clock up interminable messages from Sam all by itself. The ballerina was planning to pass them all onto her lawyer unread and get a new telephone with a different number.

The girls were surprised when the car arrived for Kendra first. The artist had become accustomed to bringing up the rear and she had come to find a sort of security in her position, because it seemed to indicate she might eventually be the last woman standing. Not tonight however.

"Good luck," Janny whispered.

Kendra returned the sentiment. "Good luck and goodbye if I don't see you again tonight."

Kendra walked to the car and climbed into the back seat. Simon Steeple approached with his camera and asked her a few embarrassing questions about her feelings for Anthony and then she was left alone. The vehicle began to move and Kendra clasped her hands together to stop them from trembling. She noted ironically that this meant all her fingers were crossed if one believed in such urban superstitions.

It was half an hour's drive to the secluded bay which had been chosen for the final carnation ceremony. The sun was getting low in the sky as Kendra alighted and followed the makeshift path down to the beach. The wind caught in her dress, making the folds billow out around her, and a few isolated strands of hair were whipped out of their pins and onto her face.

Anthony was waiting with a carnation in his hand and Kendra knew instantly that it was going to be alright. The Charity Eligible broke into a smile as the artist walked towards him, making awkward timing in her high-heels on the loose sand.

"This is for you," Anthony said, extending the carnation as soon as Kendra was within reach. "You are the one for me. Other women may look very pretty, but they don't make me feel as comfortable as you do. It is your soothing presence I will long for after a stressful day at work, and you I will want to come home to for the rest of my life. I don't know why you ever doubted that."

"It was the circumstances," Kendra cried. "I felt my personality was getting lost as you dated the other girls, and you did seriously like one or two of them."

"I am so glad you spoke your mind to me last night," Anthony said. "It was a real wake-up call. I was in danger of forming a habit of looking around for greener pastures and more demanding company. I had to sit down and sort out what true love was all about. Separate love, from sympathy and friendship and admiration and whatever brief attractions I had felt for every-one else."

"I will have to learn to inspire a few of those emotions in you myself," Kendra quipped jokingly.

Anthony nodded. "I don't want to ever hurt you again like that," he said. "I love you first and foremost because I can relax with you, but I don't want you to feel I take you for granted ever again. You have exciting depths to your personality and I want them to come out with me."

Anthony dropped onto one knee in the sand despite the well-cut black suit in which he had been dressed. "Kendra Western," he cried, "Will you marry me?"

"Maybe sometime in the future," Kendra replied laughingly. She reached out and tugged at the Anthony's hands, pulling him back onto his feet. "Please get up."

Anthony looked puzzled, "What's the problem?"

"Timing, my dear boy," Kendra said, having gained her confidence in the last few minutes. "I don't want you to propose on television. It will take us at least a month to see how our feelings survive our every-day lives, my work and your terribly important and demanding job at the hospital."

"True," Anthony said. He looked a little disappointed. "Can I ask you again then?"

"You surely can," Kendra said. "And you may kiss me now." She reached up and kissed the Charity Eligible without holding anything back, because the show was virtually over.

"There is only one problem," Anthony said, drawing back from the kiss at last. "One last thing I need to confess."

"What is it Anthony?" Kendra asked with a shadow of concern.

"Please, please don't be angry, Kinny, but I promised Janny I would support her as she was having a hard time getting free of that Sam fellow," Anthony admitted. "For a while there, last night I feared

I might have to choose her to support her - but then I thought - I could support her as a friend, especially if you agreed."

"Do you know what?" Kendra replied with relief. "I promised Janny something similar minutes before the car brought me down here. We can support her together!"

Anthony reached into his pocket and pulled out a jewellery box. "I want you to have this as a memento of our time together on the show."

Kendra took the box. "Thank you Anthony," she said. She balanced the box nervously in her fingers, half afraid to look inside.

"It is not a ring," Anthony said. "Open it and see."

Kendra eased open the box and looked inside. A sparking pendant in the shape of a horse shoe nestled at the end of a fine gold chain. The horse shoe was encrusted with very small diamonds set at strategic intervals.

"It is beautiful," Kendra gasped.

"Here, let me put it on you," Anthony said. He lifted the necklace out of the box and fumbled with the catch. Then he draped the chain around Kendra's neck, before fastening it at the back.

"It really suits you," he said. "I knew it would!"

"How did you get them to give you a necklace?" Kendra asked. "They only showed me rings."

"It was very difficult," Anthony said. "Very difficult indeed. I had to look at rings for the cameras sake, but I told them this would be a better surprise at the end."

"I think you are right," Kendra said. "I love it!" She angled the horse shoe at the closest camera. "What do you think audience?"

Simon Steeple, who was operating that camera, focused on the horse shoe, and an attractive hint of cleavage. He bet the audience would love that, especially compared to an engagement ring that might only stay on for five minutes after the show anyway. A few minutes later, the limousine took Kendra away to wait in secret at her grandmother's hotel. Her heart was singing and she was full of hope for the future.

Anthony stood alone on the beach facing the less pleasant task of bidding farewell to Janny. He had promised her friendship and support, and in the end, that is all he would have to offer the ballerina.

The Charity Eligible had spent much of the morning in tormented thought, wondering how he could resolve his desire to be of assistance to Janny in her time of need, with his commitment to Kendra. Now Kendra had granted him permission, he felt much better.

He also realized that placing himself between the ballerina and her former agent as a form of romantic barrier would have been foolish. He had been attracted to the ballerina on a physical level, but the emotional connection had been slower to grow, and was nothing compared to what he felt for Kendra.

As Janny approached, she looked sleek and sophisticated in her black sheath-dress, her calm appearance surely belying an anxious interior. Anthony saw her eyes drop to the small table upon which another carnation had been placed with deceitful art by the production crew, and his heart be smote him.

"Dear, dear Janny," the Charity Eligible commenced. "You are talented and attractive and I am so glad to have met you."

Janny searched his eyes with a glance and her expression became one of regret. "That sounds like an I-like-you-but statement," she said. "You have chosen Kendra."

"I am afraid so," Anthony said, sincerely glad that Janny had taken the burden of rejection off of his chest. "I know that I have promised you I would support you and be there for you, as you struggle to be free of Sam, but I have also promised Kendra that I would be faithful to her. I must ask you whether there is room for me to stay in your life as a friend."

"I am a little saddened," Janny admitted. "But I am also lucky to have you and Kendra both in my life as good friends. May I ask why you chose her?"

"A hundred little things," Anthony said. "She is kind and good, and when we are alone she is funny and sexy. She compliments my quiet side with her gentle nature, and broadens my horizons with her artistic interests. I can be myself with her, and I believe I can continue to grow in love with her all my life."

"I am glad to hear it," Janny said. "Your reasons sound so genuine. I am reassured."

"Thank you," Anthony said. He did not know what else to say. "Will you be alright?"

Janny nodded. "I will be fine given time," she said, "I understand that you give me the last carnation now, and a hug goodbye would be appropriate."

Anthony leant forward and drew the ballerina to him, whereupon she leant on the sleeve of his coat. The gesture was chivalrous and platonic.

"Once again, I am sorry," Anthony said.

"I understand, really I do," Janny said. She turned away from the Charity Eligible and stumbled towards the waiting limousine. Tears began streaming down the ballerina's face. The sun was setting behind her as she left, streaking the sky with orange and black.

"Just let me cry for a minute," she said to George, who was following her with a camera. The tears were streaming down her face, and continued all the way back to the Candidate House, where she picked up her luggage.

"I believe that I have done enough crying now," Janny said to the camera lens at last. She had dried her eyes and was standing on the lighted front steps. "I did not win the man and I should be sad. However, I am not. I came on a show designed to find love and instead I found my self-confidence. It is a beautiful gift, and I cannot thank the Charity Eligible, Anthony, his new girlfriend, Kendra, and all the good folks at the television station enough!"

There was a tap on her shoulder and Leticia appeared. "I must tell you, Sam visited the Candidate House while you were away filming," the hostess said. "He threatened to sue you for wrongful dismissal and claim a percentage of your earnings from us. I told him that you only received expenses and there was nothing to claim. I also checked our paperwork, you were definitely on a break from him when you signed with us. He cannot touch your money or prevent us from airing the show."

"That's good to know," Janny said. "The lawyer is taking care of the rest, and as my mother first approached my current ballet company, I might even be able to keep my contract with them!"

"Glad to hear it," Leticia said. "I like to see performers stand on their own feet, beyond that I will not interfere."

"I understand," Janny said. "You have done a lot for me really!"

"There is one more thing," Leticia commented. "*The Charity Dating Show* occasionally receives sponsorship from travel companies. We had a Queensland holiday to give to this year's winning couple. However, Anthony has to go straight back to work, so they suggested that I give the holiday to you!"

"Thank you," Janny said, accepting the ticket. A tropical holiday was exactly what she needed right now. She would take her father or sister with her for some undemanding company. Things were looking more positive by the moment!

EPILOGUE: THE WEDDING

Six months later, a small group gathered in the Sydney Botanic Gardens for a wedding ceremony. Private security guards patrolled the perimeter as the event was not open to the public or the media.

Indeed, the only representatives of the media were Simon Steeple, who was holding hands with his beloved brunette girlfriend; and George, who had opened his own photographic studio in addition to his employment at the television station. George had been hired as the official photographer for the wedding, and his fiancé was also present, doing duty as the maid of honour.

Abraham was the best man, while his new girlfriend was sitting with George's son, Parker keeping him amused and well behaved. The chief bridesmaid was showing some recent signs of stress, but had a radiant smile and healthy presence for all that. Rumour had it that she had recently been named principal artist with her company. The other bridesmaid had lately made a comeback as a creative artist after a period of rehabilitation from injury.

The groom, Dr. Anthony Jones, stood nervously awaiting his bride. There was some twittering amongst the gathering of family and friends because the carnation in his button-hole was not the traditional white, but pink, like the one he had presented to his chosen lady on the final episode of *The Charity Dating Show*, which had recently finished airing on television.

Anthony had almost proposed on television that day, but the sensible girl had turned him down, pleading the need for some time and normal courtship, pursued in the arena of real life. The young surgeon had returned home after the show, determined to pursue his career and continue his courtship of the lady with dedication and determination.

The donations proceeding from *The Charity Dating Show* had purchased much needed equipment for the emergency and children's wards at his hospital, and he had found himself a minor celebrity amongst his workmates. The young woman of his dreams had agreed to accept his proposal just one month after filming *The Charity Dating Show* had concluded.

The bride entered from behind a screen of ornamental hedge. She wore a strapless silk dress with a fitted bodice and filmy skirt.

The fabric had been lovingly hand-painted in the palest of greens and blues. It shone in the sun, reflecting whiter than white, and yet it was not white. It was quite unique, just like the beautiful girl who wore it. She wore no veil, but had a wreath of flowers in her hair.

The bride was accompanied by her grandmother, who had agreed to give her away. The rest of her family were travelling overseas, but they were very overjoyed to hear of their daughter's happiness and looked forward to meeting her husband in the future.

The bridesmaids wore long dresses in a pastel-blue colour. The georgette fabric was soft and flowing, dropping straight towards the ground from an empire waistline, draped just below the bust line. The maid of honour, wore the same style in light blue georgette.

The bride looked radiant and the groom had eyes for no one else. The couple held hands as they exchanged their vows, and the selected group of family, friends and business colleagues invited to the wedding clapped as Anthony and his chosen lady kissed for the first time as man and wife.

They were planning to live in Anthony's apartment, close to the hospital. Much of the bride's professional work could be done from home, and she had some lucrative contracts lined up for the near future. Then who knows - maybe a larger house and some children?

ABOUT THE AUTHOR

Cecelia grew up in the Barossa Valley, an area of South Australia predominantly settled by German immigrants.
She remembers the struggle to learn to read and how reading was a slow process until one birthday, when she sat down with a new book she had been given as a present.
The mystery story was so exciting, she finished it in one session. She has wanted to write her own stories ever since!

Cecelia writes from the perspective of a Bachelor of Education and Master of Arts, and experience as an Accredited Counsellor for four years. She is also a huge reality television fan and cannot get enough of gossip and media spin-offs, so she felt obliged to create her very own television dating story!

Cecelia is also the author of:

Special Pictures to Talk About (ISBN: 978-0-646-97235-0) which developed out of her work on language delay and speech development in Kindergartens.

Silver Springtime (ISBN-13: 978-0-6481160-1-1), the first of a series of Christian period romances following the developmental struggles of a group of teenagers attending university in the 1980s.

Mystic Evermore (ISBN: 978-0-6481160-0-4), the first of the vampire series "Nevermore Parables".

Saints and Sinners (ISBN: 978-0-6481160-4-2), the second of the vampire series "Nevermore Parables".

Faith and Love (ISBN: 978-0-6481160-3-5), the second "Silver Springs University" Christian college romance story.

www.ingramcontent.com/pod-product-compliance
Lightning Source LLC
Chambersburg PA
CBHW071738110726
47908CB00006B/1628